A LETHAL BATTLE IN THE COLD WAR HAS BEGUN

—AND THE WEST DOESN'T EVEN KNOW!

From Washington to London to New York, in every money center in the world, the bankers are slowly becoming aware of the fact that something is very wrong. Thomas Pike, Jr. is the first to put the pieces together, to see the pattern in the loans Moscow is making to the satellite and unaligned nations, and the money the Soviet Union is borrowing from the West.

His observations make him a superstar, but his personal life is in a tailspin—there's Janet; there's Jane; and most dangerously, there's the beautiful, dark-haired woman in whose hands the financial security of the world may rest.

From bed to board room, from poolside parties to the Oval Office, Tom Pike traces the web of financial machinations. One wrong turn, and the good times will come to an end . . .

Recent Titles by Brian Freemantle from Severn House

BETRAYALS
DIRTY WHITE
O'FARRELL'S LAW

THE KREMLIN CONSPIRACY

Brian Freemantle

SEVERN SH HOUSE

This title first published in Great Britain 1997 by
SEVERN HOUSE PUBLISHERS LTD of
9–15 High Street, Sutton, Surrey SM1 1DF.
Originally published in 1984 under the title *Monopoly*
and under the pseudonym of *Jonathan Evans.*
This title first published in the USA 1997 by
SEVERN HOUSE PUBLISHERS INC., of
595 Madison Avenue, New York, NY 10022.

British Library Cataloguing in Publication Data

Freemantle, Brian, 1936-
The Kremlin Conspiracy
1. International finance – Corrupt practices - Fiction
2. Default (Finance) - Soviet Union - Fiction
3. Thrillers
1. Title
823.9'14 [F]

ISBN 0-7278-5249-3

Typeset by Palimpsest Book Production Limited,
Polmont, Stirlingshire, Scotland.
Printed and bound in Great Britain by
Hartnolls Ltd, Bodmin, Cornwall.

For Bill and Caroline, with love.

Author's Note

It is the wisdom of the innocent to regard bankers as shrewdly calculating men who rarely—if ever—make mistakes.

In 1982, twenty countries were unable to pay their debts to Western banks and came to a postponement arrangement technically called rescheduling. By the end of that year, the Paris-based Organization of Economic Development assessed the total of medium- and long-term debts incurred by developing countries to be $626,000,000,000. In December, in an official report, the OECD said world finance was facing "the most serious economic difficulty experienced since the 1930's."

Brazil was the biggest debtor. It owed $89,000,000,000. Mexico owed $80,000,000,000. Venezuela owed $27,000,000,000. Chile owed $11,000,000,000. Costa Rica owed $600,000,000. Argentina owed $40,000,000,000, and to prevent a world banking crisis, Prime Minister Margaret Thatcher had to defend in the House of Commons the apparent illogicality of British banks participating in a loan rescue package for the country it had defeated in the Falklands war.

Most of the countries in Africa had repayment difficulties on loans; Zaire's debt was $3,500,000,000.

In Europe, Yugoslavia owed $20,000,000,000. Turkey owed $16,000,000,000.

In the Communist bloc, Poland owed $29,000,000,000, and under the terms of guaranteed financing of grain exports, the government of President Ronald Reagan paid $71,000,000 of Polish-owed interest to U.S. banks. Rumania owed $13,000,000,000 and declared, without consultation or agreement with its creditors, a moratorium—a suspension of debt payments. The banks did nothing positive to protest the Bucharest decision because they would have collapsed under the size of the accumulated debts; instead, the International Monetary Fund arranged further loans to pay back those already existing.

In the belief that some countries will—eventually—repay, the loans continue.

Some debts will be settled. Others never will.

"Countries don't go bust."

Walter Wriston, U.S. Citibank, at the
September, 1982, meeting in Toronto,
of the International Monetary Fund.

"In a serious struggle there is no worse cruelty than to be magnanimous at an inopportune time."

Leon Trotsky, *The History of the Russian Revolution*

Book One

1

Poland was one of the final tests, the occasion when so much detailed planning and preparation could have been destroyed, but everything went exactly as Lydia Kirov predicted. Her satisfaction at being proved right was a brief, passing emotion; after all, she hadn't expected to fail. Poland was further proof for the few who still doubted, not for herself. It was still difficult to avoid the personal impression that it was a triumphant homecoming.

The warning sign went on, and Lydia obediently fastened her safety belt as she gazed down at the approaching lights of Sheremetyevo airport. They created a squared pattern of unexpected brightness in the gray Russian landscape. The faraway glow would be from Moscow. It seemed dull, compared to the Western capitals into which she had flown over the past few years. And to which she'd fly again, before it was all over.

Washington would be interesting. She would have liked to be there for the International Monetary Fund meeting. The embassy had been briefed to monitor and report as much as possible, but, of course, because of the need for secrecy, they hadn't been told the reason for the demand, and Lydia knew there would be gaps in the information.

She wanted more than gossip and rumor. She wanted the conclusions. She was sure she could anticipate what they would be, but it would still have been useful to know, positively. Lydia frowned—she was unaccustomed to uncertainty—as the wheels snatched at the moment of landing and the engines went into reverse thrust.

They'd reach the right conclusion, she decided: what else could they do?

The desk was a mess, but Tom Pike knew the place of everything he wanted in the apparent chaos; he plucked the earlier analyses and graphs out of the confusion, completely engrossed in his own assessment. It would have been easier, had he been in London where he could actually sit in on the rescheduling meetings; all the information was available, but he didn't have the feel of the negotiations and the discussions. Having the feel of things was an affectation of his father's, and Pike had dutifully studied his father's success.

During his two years with the Federal Reserve Board, Pike had come to know the habits of the chairman—and one was that Richard Volger didn't like lengthy opinions. Pike's first draft had run to six pages, and it had taken two rewrites to bring it down to the two pages that were required. He carefully compared the original to the final report, to ensure that he had omitted nothing of importance, and decided to reinsert the potential of Poland's foreign earnings from its coal exports.

Its brevity meant it took his personal assistant, Loraine Becker, only half an hour to prepare and Xerox finished copies, so Volger had the analysis of Poland's debt rescheduling by midafternoon. Pike guessed there would be others, because Volger spread his options and got as many views as possible, but Pike knew his would be the first. He was a man who liked working against self-imposed deadlines, always proving himself. The need was carefully concealed, of course; Tom Pike was a man whom many thought they knew, but few did.

The call came on his private line, just before Pike was thinking of leaving the office.

"Coming down for the meeting?" asked his father.

"I'm part of the official delegation."

"Look forward to seeing you then," said the older man, who had a year of his five-year managing directorship of the International Monetary Fund still to run.

"Yes." It had to be four months since they had last met.

"What do you think of the Polish rescheduling?"

Pike looked down at the finished report that was already in the office of his own chairman. "Pretty satisfactory," he said generally.

"Agreement's too loose," insisted the other man. "The money should have been specifically assigned. Too loose by half."

He had left that opinion from the already submitted report. "It was rescheduling for existing loans and interest," Pike pointed out. "It wasn't for anything new."

"That was the problem in the first place: insufficient control."

"Maybe so. The problem now is getting out of trouble, not examining how it happened in the first place. It's too late for that."

"Your mother would like to see you, when you come down to Washington."

"Of course."

There was a hesitation from the other end of the line, and then his father said, "So would I."

Pike remained looking at the receiver for several minutes after replacing it, wondering, as he frequently did, whether he had been wise in breaking away from his father's influence. His personal assistant broke the reverie, entering from her outside office.

"Coming by tonight?" asked Loraine. "I've got some good stuff: guaranteed Colombian."

Pike looked at the woman. She was slimmer than he usually preferred, boyish almost, but it was a new affair and he was still enjoying it. "Sure."

"Want company?"

"No." It was safer by themselves. And he'd gone through the group scene anyway.

"Don't be late."

"I won't be."

"I thought you'd be pleased," said Paul Burnham.

"I am pleased."

"You don't show it."

"Am I going to Washington as Jane Rose, Bank of England supervisor who has earned the trip by effort and merit? Or Jane Rose, mistress of a member of the Bank's Court?"

Burnham frowned, looking instinctively around the paneled office, even though they were alone. "What the hell's the matter with you?"

Jane shrugged, not knowing herself why she was fomenting another argument. That wasn't true. She knew damned well why she was doing it. And why it was ridiculous.

"We'll be a big party," said Burnham. "Nearly all the directors as well as the governor."

"Not going to be easy, then, is it?"

"Easy?"

"To be together."

"Don't worry about that," he said confidently.

Which was the trouble, thought Jane. She did worry about it, practically all the time. Why had she fallen in love with a married man! "What about tonight?"

He smiled apologetically. "Marion's giving a cocktail

party: Conservative women's group or something. I promised I'd be there. Tomorrow is all right, though.''

For him, she thought; it never occurred to him anymore to ask if it were convenient for her. She could always tell him she was doing something, she realized. ''Tomorrow, then.''

2

There was still a guide, and an escort as well, because the Praesidium building of the Supreme Soviet is the most closely guarded area within the Kremlin, but after so long Lydia Kirov knew the passageways and corridors as well as any of them. She strode slightly ahead, to show she didn't need them, and there was no attempt to interfere or correct her. There would have been, once—but not now. Even here, among underlings whose robot-like function was shepherding people from point A to point B, hearing nothing, seeing nothing and saying nothing, Lydia Kirov was known to be important, to be regarded with respect. After so long. Nine years, she realized: almost ten. A decade during which every major forecast she had made had been proven right, even allowing for their stupid policy mistakes. A decade during which she had ceased being the shy, hesitant economics graduate with a plan so revolutionary that, at only twenty, she had been allowed to enter this guarded, prohibited place—but walked nervously behind her escort then—and become what she was today, someone able to telephone the Finance Minister and speak to him personally to fix a meeting, within hours. It hadn't been necessary to get Vladimir Malik to rearrange his schedule that day, but Lydia liked exercising her power, just as she liked walking ahead of her escorts to prove they were unnecessary. There was another reason for seeking Malik's company, too, but she was beginning to despair of his realizing it.

She slowed at the approach to Malik's office, so they could move ahead to open the door for her, and then swept through, moving fast again. There were hesitant smiles from the secretaries she passed and abrupt anticipation from the assistants who preceded her, to open more doors. There had been the warning from the outer offices, and Malik was standing in the center of his huge room, with its view of the Saviour Tower and St. Basil's Cathedral beyond. He came forward as she entered, seizing her shoulders and kissing her on both cheeks.

It was an official, not overtly sexual greeting, Lydia thought, disappointed.

"Welcome back, Comrade Kirov; welcome back."

"It's good to be back," she said. Impersonal though it had been, she had enjoyed his touch.

There was an area away from the desk, arranged with leather buttonback sofas and easy chairs, and it was there that he led her. Tea was already arranged and there was drink, imported whisky as well as vodka.

"I would have suggested the meeting myself, but I thought you'd be tired, so soon after your return," said Malik. He was a precise, neat man whose gray suits mirrored his unobtrusiveness, a demeanor unusual for a Georgian. He was one of the youngest members of the Politburo, and Lydia knew he was determined against any problem that might prevent his attaining the ultimate office. It had been three years—a three-year test period to ensure her proposals could actually work—before she got beyond the assistants and committees to meet him personally.

Even now their contact was rigidly official. She was aware that he was married, but knew nothing beyond that about his family. She didn't know if he had any children, despite working with him in relatively close proximity for more than two years. She would have liked to know more—much more. She'd once thought it might be possible, but increasingly she wasn't so sure.

"I thought it best we talk at once," she said. It had been a month since she'd seen him.

"Of course." He gestured towards the table.

"Tea," chose Lydia.

Malik poured for himself as well as her. They were each as careful as the other, she thought.

"So it went well?" Malik asked.

"I think so."

"What are the terms?"

"The immediate repayments for which Poland is responsible came out at something like $52,000,000," said Lydia. "We agreed on the overall rescheduling and an emergency loan allocation to refinance the interest."

"With the Narodny participating?"

Lydia, who had gone to London in her official position as a Moscow-based director of the Russian central bank, nodded. "And the remainder really the same consortia as the original debtors: Barclays and National Westminster in England, Citibank and Chase Manhattan in America, Societe Generale in France."

"How big is the concern in the West?"

Lydia made an uncertain motion with her hand. "Sufficient." Knowing the importance of apparent modesty, she added, "I never anticipated the overcommitment that would arise in Latin America, in my original proposal. That's become an advantage to us."

Malik smiled. "I was reading your original paper before you arrived. It's practically an historic document; it'll probably become one."

Lydia smiled at the exaggeration, pleased at praise from the man. "It was comparatively easy to predict the banks' eagerness to offer the Eurodollars and the Petrodollars after the OPEC oil increases of the '70s," she said.

"But not how to use that eagerness to our advantage," said Malik. "No one anticipated the financial brilliance of that."

Not even you, who held back for three years and was still distant, thought Lydia. "There's still a long way to go, before it's completely successful," she said, modest still.

"I've no doubt. No one has." He smiled again. "Those who matter in the Politburo have been convened for tomorrow. Do you consider we could move?"

Instead of answering directly, Lydia said, "Who's to be purged?"

"Anatoli Karelin, the man responsible for overall economic planning; he was the obvious one to go. Boris Medvedev, because it was necessary to include someone within agriculture. Arkady Chebotarev, within the ministry here. And Nikhail Paramov, of course."

"Well-known names."

"They need to be."

"Karelin is one of the originals—a true Bolshevik."

"Who'd realize the necessity for the sacrifice," said Malik. From an apparently old, gun-metal case Malik produced a Russian cigarette, loosely packed and half its length made up of a cardboard tube. "Do you mind?" he asked.

"No," said Lydia. In theory, her plan had been perfect. She hadn't properly realized the reality of it being put into practice, of people being destroyed. It was too late for any sentimentality. She added, "With these sort of people we can't fail to get the right assessments in the West."

"We don't intend to fail: I've told you that already."

"How many silos?"

"Four hundred completed, all concentrated around the major cities: Moscow, Leningrad, Kiev, Minsk, Kaunas, Gorki, Volvograd, Kazan, Sverdlovsk, Chita, Khabarovsk."

"The locations are not as important as the concealment," she pointed out.

Malik nodded. "All underground."

"What about constructional work? The Americans have satellites in geostationary as well as orbital patterns."

"Every installation was constructed in such a way as to conceal from any orbital system its true purpose," he insisted. "In Gorki and Chita, for instance, we know from intelligence reports from America that the work has been analyzed as being for railroad assembly yards; in Sverdlovsk, a chemical plant."

"Certainly, we're ready with the financial planning," she said finally.

"So we can move?" he said, repeating his original question.

Lydia hesitated, suddenly conscious that upon her reply depended an event practically as momentous as the revolution itself. She paused further, wondering at her own hyperbole. It *wasn't* an exaggeration, she decided; what was about to begin *was* momentous.

She spoke at last. "Yes," she said simply. "We can move." It was the moment of positive commitment; there had been checks and balances in everything that preceded this, avenues along which they could have escaped without censure or suspicion. But not any longer.

"It's going to mean a lot of work for you."

"It's meant a lot of work for several years now."

"Which all of us are very aware of," assured Malik. "There'll be proper gratitude, believe me."

She wanted something different from gratitude, thought Lydia. Sustaining the supposed modesty, she said, "It's still got to succeed."

"Nothing can go wrong," insisted Malik. He laughed suddenly, an unexpected eruption of noise in the echoing room.

"Isn't it going to be the most marvelous irony! We're going to teach capitalism to capitalists!"

"Marvelous," she agreed. She hadn't known he smoked until today. There was so much to learn.

*   *   *

The ordinary people weren't included within her comparisons—all of them entirely calculated against the favored, indulged hierachy in which she had existed for most of the past ten years—so, realistically, Lydia Fedorovna Kirov accepted that few Russians would consider she had made sacrifices.

The hierachy itself would have found it difficult.

Her three bedroomed apartment—unnecessarily spacious for only one—was in Kutuzovsky Prospekt, the enclosed, guarded Moscow compound in which they themselves lived. Its furnishings had been allowed to come, unimpeded, not only from Finland—the traditional source for the privileged— but also from Italy and America and France.

In the basement garage there was a Zil limousine, with its rota of chauffeurs on press-button readiness. Her salary of 6,000 rubles a month was irrelevant, because her purchases at the concessionary stores were always charged, never paid for. Nor was the rent. Nor the limousine. Nor the other charge accounts, the carefully concealed and rerouted billings from American Express and Diner's International and Visa which enabled her to have a wardrobe essential to match that of any $300,000-career executive—male or female—in the West. And necessary for exactly that reason: Lydia Fedorovna Kirov had not just to match, but to exceed.

Unusual among Russians who travelled to the West, to London and Washington and Paris and Tokyo and Frankfurt, she knew that the traditional surveillance, either from the local embassy or from someone in the accompanying subservient financial group, was now practically non-existent.

Not just unusual: unique. Because she—like her concept—was unique.

But there *had* still been sacrifices. It hadn't been a consideration at first, not even a thought. She'd evolved a financial plan and been lucky enough to have it accepted. Which had meant a twenty-four-hour, awakening-until-sleep control. The awareness of that commitment evolved slowly, unconsciously. One moment there had been nothing, the next minute. . . . The next minute, what? The only word that offered itself was resentment. Which was as ridiculous as expecting anyone to believe she had made sacrifices. Ridiculous or not, that was what she felt. Resentment. Illogical, unreasoned, immature, stupid resentment at a consuming involvement in an enterprise which had occupied her utterly for years—an enterprise which was about to conclude and confirm her power and leave her with . . . . again, what?

Lydia stared around her pristine, maid-maintained, plant-decorated, concealed-lighted apartment. And then, like a prospective purchaser, she embarked upon a tour. There were plants in the bedrooms, too. And ornaments. All positioned and placed, like essential parts of some elaborate pattern, a pattern that had been arranged by a computer, not by clumsy human hands. The bathroom was a reverberating reflection of images, from the surrounding glass and glimmering, polished chrome, and there was more chrome in the kitchen, computer-regimented again—mixers and blenders and utensils and freezers.

Lydia, one of whose few hobbies was literature, consciously twisted the quotation and said aloud, "Those whom we would destroy, we first copy."

Once, she would have impressed herself with the pretentious effort; tonight, that was what it seemed to be—an effort. Pretentious, too.

So much, she thought. But so little.

Within the Finance Ministry and the bank she had acquaintances, but no friends. Her social life was not of her choosing—although she had the choice of the Bolshoi or the ballet that bore her name—but of official requirement. Which, despite the unmonitored freedom, was what it was in the West. They'd never believe it—or even understand it—but she considered herself as much a robot as those escorts she had despised that afternoon in the Praesidium.

Depression, like uncertainty, was an unusual feeling for Lydia, and she tried to move herself from it. At the age of thirty years, five months, two weeks and three days, she was one of the luckiest and most favored women within the Soviet Union.

She had everything. She paused at the thought. Everything, she told herself again; even her virginity. That was the greatest problem of all.

Burnham arranged the seating to be next to her on the Concorde flight to Washington but, having done so, appeared embarrassed and treated Jane almost with ridiculous reserve during the journey.

At the Jefferson Hotel their rooms were on different floors, and the corridors and elevators seemed always to be crowded with members of the British delegation. He managed to make love to her on the second night, hurriedly, as if he were looking at the watch he hadn't bothered to take off, finishing way ahead of her and then immediately saying that he'd have to go back to his own room, in case the governor or any of the other directors tried to contact him and wondered at his absence.

"Bastard!"

He seemed surprised at the outburst. "What's the matter?"

"If you don't know what's the matter, then you're stupid!" Jane decided her sexual frustration was about evenly matched with her anger.

"I don't want to argue about nothing."

"I know what you want to do," she said. "You might as well have masturbated."

"That's obscene."

"That's true."

"I love you."

"Bullshit!" She was lying rigidly beside him, ready for him at last. God, how much she wished he'd take her. She was privately embarrassed at her sexuality.

"What do you want?"

"What you promised."

"When the children are able to take it," he said. "I told you I'd divorce Marion when I thought the children would be able to take it."

"When will that be?"

"I don't know. They're still young."

"So I'm expected to wait around for years, until you decide the time is right?"

"We've been through all this."

"I want to go through it again."

He moved in the bed and she was sure he'd looked at his watch again. "I won't hurt the children," he said.

"Children are convenient, aren't they?"

"That's a filthy thing to say."

"Or true."

"I'm going."

"I'm surprised you managed to stay so long."

"You're being stupid."

Was she? What the hell did she expect him to do? "I don't want to be your whore," she said.

He swung his legs out of bed, sitting hunched on the edge. She hadn't realized before how much hair was matted on his back. "I don't think of you as a whore."

"What do you think of me as?"

There was a long silence, and then he said, "I love you." And she hated him for not managing something better.

"I said I loved you," he repeated.

"I heard."

"So?"

"You'd better get back to your room," she said. "The governor might be trying to get hold of you."

3

Tom Pike arrived intentionally late at the Chase Manhattan reception to avoid the official receiving line. His father, who had gone to the IMF from the chairmanship of the Chase, was at the far side of the room, with the usual coterie of IMF officials, making a gradual, triumphal tour among his former colleagues. Pike waited to see the direction in which it was moving, then went the opposite way, not wanting immediately to encounter it.

It was the biggest reception during the International Monetary Fund's annual meeting, this time in Washington, and the Chase Manhattan had taken over one of the larger banquet suites at the Mayflower; it was already crowded and difficult to move.

Pike decided he'd stay just long enough to be recognized by some of his father's entourage and for his presence to be officially recorded. George Shearing was appearing at Blues Alley, and he was looking forward to an evening in Georgetown. But not alone. Perhaps he should have brought Loraine along, as she had suggested. Then again, perhaps not. It would have been obvious and therefore a political mistake, within the bank. Pike didn't make mistakes, not of any sort.

He looked around at the crush of people. There were a lot of women, so it wouldn't be difficult. It rarely was. Another way of proving himself, he knew—and that he was very good at proving himself that way.

He took a drink from a passing tray, sniffed and realized it was scotch. The ice had melted. Maybe that was why it seemed weak. He nodded and smiled to several bankers he knew and located the Federal Reserve group on the far side of the room, awaiting the arrival of his father. Richard Volger, the chairman, saw him and gave a beckoning wave, which Pike intentionally misunderstood, and he waved back, as if merely responding to a greeting, then looked away. If he were going to get company for the evening, he couldn't waste time with people he saw every day. To avoid it appearing rude, he supposed he'd have to get into some sort of conversation.

He saw her at the edge of the British delegation, nearer than he had at the opening ceremony two days earlier, and decided that his initial impression had been the right one; the standard of the British contingent was improving.

Why not? he thought. Conscious of his chairman's continued attention, he maneuvered himself close enough to read the name-tag directly below the green badge signifying that she was part of an official delegation, then went up and said, "Hello, Jane Rose."

She turned fully to him, smiling in an uncertain attempt at recollection. He said at once, "I confess: I read the name-tag." Pike was practiced at self-mockery.

She remained smiling and he was glad. She was a good reason for not fighting his way across the room to go through the dutiful son-greets-father routine. She wore very little make-up, just lipstick and a small amount of eye shadow, and her blonde hair was cut short, in a cowl around her face. Despite the severe tailoring of the suit, there was still sufficient movement beneath it for him to have enjoyed the second look at the identification pinned on her left breast.

"Hello, Tom Pike," she said, reading the name from his tag. At once she frowned and looked beyond him, to the procession. "Are you . . . ?" she began, but Pike talked over her.

"Yes," he said. "He's my father."

"I met him when we arrived."

"And he held your hand between each of his, looked directly at you as if there wasn't anyone else in the room, and said what a pleasure it was to meet you."

She put her head slightly to one side and smiled, "Yes, that's exactly what happened. I thought he was a nice man."

"People do," said Pike.

"Don't you?"

The directness off-balanced him. He stopped with the drink halfway to his mouth and said, "Of course."

"It didn't seem like it."

"He's a man of mannerisms," said Pike. And ambition, he thought; they both were.

"I thought he seemed sincere."

"That's the best mannerism of all."

"Do you practice it?"

This wasn't how it was supposed to go; he had to get back on course. "Are you always like this?" he asked.

"Like what?"

Seizing the chance to escape from discussing his father, Pike lowered his voice in a parody of a sonorous television commercial and intoned, "Jane Rose is a forceful, dynamic woman of today, someone who speaks her mind."

She laughed and Pike relaxed. Humor was always important, in the beginning. And later, too, to avoid it becoming serious; he didn't like serious morning scenes. Or evening scenes.

"Not really." Jane was conscious of Burnham's undivided attention upon her from the other side of their assembled group, but intentionally didn't respond. There wasn't any harm in momentarily using this American; he'd made the first approach, after all. And she was flattered, she admitted to herself. Pike was too sure of himself by half, but that was supposed to be a national characteristic. He certainly didn't appear a characteristic banker: It was expensive—mohair, she guessed—but he *was* wearing a sports jacket among a sartorial sea of suits, and even during this brief encounter, he seemed more irreverent than anyone else she'd met since she'd been in Washington. She didn't like the heavy, drooped mustache, which hardly seemed part of the banker's image, either, or the way—an affectation, almost—he had of staring directly into her eyes, as if he were positively trying to embarrass.

"Why, now then?" This was going to be fun, he thought.

She shrugged, slightly uncomfortable under the gaze, and said, "I don't know." Despite her determination not to, she looked towards the British group. Paul had put his back very positively to her. She thought it was childish.

"Am I keeping you?" Pike asked, seeing the look.

"Sorry," she said, turning to him. "It's my first time and I don't want to make any mistakes: I might have been wanted." Hypocrite, she thought: hopeful hypocrite.

"Enjoying it?"

A waiter intruded before she could reply. Pike exchanged glasses, but Jane shook her head. She gestured as the man walked away. "I didn't expect all this. A reception or two, certainly. And a couple of dinners. But this has been like the longest party in the world. When does the business start?"

"It started on the opening day, in upstairs suites and lobbies," said Pike. "That's where the loans are agreed and the deals done. You're supposed to be filmed and photographed at the public sessions and agree with the speeches that are made to assure Mr. and Mrs. Public that the world's financial structure remains sound and that everything is glued together."

She tried to match his mockery, lowering her voice and saying, "Mr. Thomas Pike, Jr. is a world-weary, cynical banker, suspicious of a collapsing system,'' but halfway through she couldn't sustain it and ended giggling.

''Isn't it?'' She had a crooked front tooth and he wondered why she hadn't had it fixed.

''I don't know,'' she said. ''I'm just a lowly supervisor being allowed out of a cell in Threadneedle Street as a reward for good works.'' And to be laid, when my lover can manage it, sometimes not very well.

''Lowly regarded people aren't brought to IMF meetings.'' Across the room Pike saw that his father had passed the Federal Reserve group; he supposed he would have to go across soon. There was always a carefully balanced time to stop making points.

''I'd still like to be learning and doing more,'' she said.

Remembering the purpose of the approach in the first place, he turned his attention back to her. ''How much of Washington have you seen?''

''The pretty drive in from the airport, the top of the Washington Monument and the Capitol building from inside the same car, and so many crowded rooms in so many hotels that I've lost count.''

''I'm getting out of here in a moment,'' he said. ''I'm going to eat in a part of the city called Georgetown, which is terrific. Why not come along?''

The surprising invitation confused her. Burnham was still ignoring her, pointedly. ''Oh . . . I don't know,'' she said. There was no reason why she shouldn't go. At once came the contradiction. There was every reason why she shouldn't go, and she knew it.

If he didn't speak to his father soon, Pike realized the rudeness would appear obvious; he wished he hadn't had to rush it with her. ''I'll tell you what, I'll wait for you in the lobby until nine.''

Jane recognized her escape, if Burnham stopped being stupid and ignoring her. ''O.K.'' she said.

''Promise,'' he pressed, recognizing the possibility of avoidance from long experience.

"Providing it's all right." She nodded towards the British group.

"Don't ask them."

"We'll see."

Worried that he had wasted his time, Pike eased his way through the crush, aware of one of the IMF aides alerting the older man to his approach, so that his father had time to turn to greet him.

"Tom!" Anyone who didn't know better would assume that they hadn't encountered each other for years. "Tom!" There was the encompassing, retained handshake, and Pike wondered if the woman were watching from behind. He hoped not.

"Hello, Father."

"Missed you at the beginning of the evening."

Pike knew that only he among the group would properly recognize the rebuke: His father showed a banker's discretion in everything. "I was delayed," he said, avoiding a direct apology.

His father stared at him for several seconds, then turned to the waiting men. "Gentlemen, I'd like you to meet my son, Tom."

Pike went through the ritual handshaking, glad it enabled him to separate physically from his father, recognizing most of the men before the formal introductions. "Going to be one of the world's great bankers," said the older man. "Isn't that what Volger said? One of the great bankers!"

There were nods and smiles of agreement from the men, and Pike felt like he had as a child, forced to stand in front of a crowd, engulfed by cigar smoke, at the family's annual Christmas party and recite the deliberately unlearned Civil War poetry that the old man tried to inculcate into him, to perpetuate a passing hobby. "Meeting going well?"

"No reason why it shouldn't," said his father. "No reason at all."

Pike wondered if his father's tendency to repeat himself

was a new mannerism; he hadn't been aware of it before. "There certainly seem to be a lot of people with money to sell."

"Grease to the wheels," said the older man. "Haven't I always told you that: grease to the wheels."

"Yes," Pike patiently agreed. "That's what you've always told me."

His father turned to his assembled officials and said, "Taught him all he knows, all he knows. Now he's leaving me behind."

You'd better believe it, thought Pike. He was going to be the best—always—at the Fed, and no one was going to say he'd done it clutching the coattails of this overindulgent, constantly hand-holding old man. "I've still got some way to go." He practiced deference like everything else.

"There's an official dinner after the reception," said his father. "There is a place kept for you."

"I replied saying I couldn't make it: prior engagement," said Pike, missing the offer in his father's voice.

"Thought your plans might have changed."

"Afraid not."

"Coming to the house at the week-end? Your mother's expecting you."

"I said I would."

"Wanted to be sure."

"I'll call."

"Make sure you do now."

One of the aides, whose name Pike couldn't recall, began moving at his father's elbow, indicating the Bank of England delegation, and the group moved to circulate again.

"I'll tell your mother you're coming then," said his father, insistently.

"I'll be there."

Pike looked after the IMF people, in the direction of the British, but couldn't see the girl. It had been a rushed encounter, he thought again: too rushed. There was no guarantee that she would show up in the lobby. The sensible thing to do would be to abandon her and try someone else, but Pike suddenly wanted to get away from the jostling, thronged room. He made a brief courtesy stop among his own Federal Reserve contingent, grateful that Volger was heavily involved with some German central bankers, and then edged towards the door.

It was the most popular party in the capital that night and the crowds continued in the corridors outside and downstairs in the lobby. Pike looked hopefully around when he finally reached it, but he couldn't see her. Shit, he thought. He didn't like empty evenings. He could go back to the reception, try again. He looked at the packed stairways and elevators. What the hell! There was a clock near the elevators, and he saw it was still not yet nine o'clock. It was worth a gamble. Wasn't that what bankers and financiers did all the time?

As it was impossible to sit, he wandered round the foyer, staring at the people. Collectively, he supposed, these men controlled all the money available in the free world. Upon their yea or nay to a multibillion loan depended the future of countries and, through those countries, of businesses and, through those businesses, the livelihoods of men and women who couldn't conceive what a billion was. Pike wondered if the people swirling around him could, either. They were supposed to, of course, but sometimes Pike doubted it; sometimes he got the impression that these expensively dressed and expensively perfumed and expensively chauffeured bankers had forgotten the enormity of what they were supposed to be doing and had come, instead, to treat the whole thing like some exclusive global Monopoly game without realizing that, like the game, the money they ended up with was worthless paper. He was suddenly seized with the desire—just as quickly controlled, because Pike was a controlled man—to stop any one of them and demand to know how many noughts there were in a billion.

He smiled when he saw her pushing her way enquiringly through the crowd—a satisfied expression. Some you win; some you lose, he thought. He usually won. She didn't see him at once, and he didn't go forward, wanting to watch her. She was extremely beautiful but appeared unaware of it, unlike a lot of other women around her, and it added to her attractiveness. He decided she wore the tailored suit because she felt she had to, and he wondered what she looked like in something less formal. It was going to be enjoyable finding out. He moved at last, so that she saw him, and at once there was the easy smile. The odd tooth didn't detract from her beauty.

"I wasn't sure you'd wait," she said.

"I said nine."

"It's gone nine."

"I'm glad I waited."

"So am I," she said. She'd seen Burnham move away from the British group, when he'd been aware of her leaving the reception, and used the stairs to avoid a confrontation in any of the elevators. The nervousness was making her feel physically sick.

He took her arm to lead her from the hotel, enjoying the physical contact. "What did you tell them you were going to do?"

"Meet someone from the Federal Reserve Board." She had told a man called Daniels, another supervisor. Would Burnham have found out by now?

They had reached Connecticut Avenue. He pulled away from her and said, "How did you know I worked for the Federal Reserve?"

"I asked around," she said, forcing her attitude. "Shouldn't a girl know about her escort?"

"Yes," he said, enjoying her lightness. "A girl should." He'd chosen well, he decided.

The pavement was jammed with people waiting to be funneled into their limousines. Pike took her arm again and propelled her up towards M Street. "I've got a car."

It was a hired Mercury compact, and when she saw it, she said, "Thank goodness for a sensibly sized vehicle at last."

"We're in the age of conservation," he said.

Although it was an indirect route to Georgetown, Pike drove her down Connecticut Avenue to show her the White House. As they passed the hotel they had just left, she indicated the crocodile of waiting limousines. "Our banking masters don't seem to have reformed. Odd, isn't it, that they should use vehicles like that when they, more than anybody else, were so affected in the oil crisis?"

"I thought I was supposed to be the cynic," he said. "Anyway, there's an oil glut now."

"That's not cynicism," protested the girl. "That's an objective observation. And the glut is only temporary."

Pike looped Lafayette Park and drove directly in front of the White House.

"I don't want to go on about the size of things," she said. "But *that*'s smaller than I thought it would be: I'd expected something more like a palace."

"We decided against a royalty, remember?"

She turned in her seat, keeping the residence in view. "I still think it should be something grander."

"So have quite a few presidents."

"*That's* cynical," said Jane. She was looking constantly around her and Pike misunderstood her uncertainty for little-girl-on-an-outing excitement. With one thought came another. Surely she couldn't be a virgin! No, he thought. No one was.

He asked her what sort of food she preferred and she told him to choose, so he decided upon French, managing to park almost directly outside the Chaumier restaurant at the very beginning of Georgetown. As they had no reservation, they had to wait. Pike arranged the time and took her back out onto the street. They walked up towards the Constitution junction, stopping to watch the street musicians playing through amplified equipment and then, at her insistence, going into the kite shop to buy a present to take back for a nephew. He reached for her hand and she let him take it, trying to make herself enjoy the evening. It wasn't proving easy. She hoped he wasn't going to prove tiresome. She supposed he could be forgiven for misunderstanding.

"I'm told it's like Chelsea, in London," he said, on their way back to the restaurant.

"Not really. I think this is more fun."

She ordered through him but in French better than Pike's, and after the waiter left, he asked, "French education?"

"Sorbonne after Cambridge. My family force-fed me education like a Strasbourg goose."

"I think I'm intimidated," said Pike mockingly.

"Don't be."

"Why the Bank of England?"

"I read economics at both universities. The Sorbonne gave the impression that it was on an international level, and the Bank seemed to believe it."

"Enjoy it?"

"Sometimes I get the impression that my real function is a female figurehead, like those semi-naked carvings they used to have on the front of sailing ships."

"Now who's being cynical!" The thought of her being strapped back naked was interesting. He and Janet had tried bondage, like they had experimented with everything during their marriage.

"I've been passed over in favor of a man three times in a year."

"Perhaps they were better qualified than you."

"They weren't," she insisted, without conceit. She and Paul had been extraordinarily careful to keep their relationship from being discovered by anyone at the bank. Would he have blocked her promotion, just in case anyone might have suspected favoritism? She grew angry at the doubt, and stiffened. He wouldn't have done a thing like that; she knew he wouldn't.

"I didn't expect it to be this sort of an evening," said Pike, misunderstanding her reaction. He wondered what she was going to be like in bed.

At once the stiffness went from her. Impulsively she reached across the table, touching his hand apologetically.

"I'm sorry," she said. "Really sorry. I didn't intend to go on like this; it's those damned receptions."

Pike frowned. "What have the receptions got to do with it?"

Stuck with her excuse, she said, "With everyone at the same place at the same time it's easy to look around and realize how male-dominated everything is."

"That's straight from a women's liberation manual if ever I heard it!"

She took her hand from his, holding it up in front of her to make a tiny barrier. "All right!" she said. "I'll stop! Not another word, I promise."

During their hand-holding walk Pike had already detected the ring. With her finger visible between them he nodded toward it. "Is there a Mr. Rose?"

Her face clouded in momentary misunderstanding. She began, "My father. . . ." and then stopped, shaking her head at him. "It's a family ring," she said, offering it for inspection "The motto over the crest says something like 'valour forever,' whatever that means."

"Why wear it on that finger?"

It had become a habit, when she was with Paul. Not a habit: her own private make-believe. The excuse ready, she said, "It was originally my grandmother's, and it's the only finger it fits."

"I've never met anyone with a family crest and a motto to match," said Pike. "I'm impressed, as well as intimidated."

She laughed. "It's a fading ancestry. Dead, in fact. My father never had a son, so the name can't be carried on. And there wasn't much to carry on anyway. He committed himself to a regiment in India and spent all his money educating my sister and me. Had to spend the last years of his life selling off family trinkets to survive. I feel guilty about it."

"Guilty?"

"I didn't really want to go to Cambridge. Or the Sorbonne. I wish he'd saved the money. He went broke for my sister and me."

"What do you want?"

To be a wife, thought Jane. "A career, I suppose," she said instead. "What about you?"

To prove myself always better than my father, thought Pike, in familiar secret admission. "Just to get the assessments right. That's what I do, for the Federal Reserve: Eastern European political analysis." He smiled and said "It sounds more dramatic than it is."

"Did you read politics?"

He nodded. "Studied is the word we use, or majored. But, yes, and business, too, at Harvard. And then there was Chase Manhattan, where my father was before the IMF."

"I know about your father."

"Everyone knows about my father," said Pike. "Most successful chairman Chase Manhattan ever had, outstanding managing director of the IMF, philanthropist, art collector, financial guru of the television channels. . . ."

"Know what I think?" she said, cutting him off.

"What?"

"You're jealous."

"Don't be ridiculous," he said, irritated both by a repetition of her directness and the nearness of the accusation.

"What then?" she persisted. "There's an attitude. I know there is."

How could he explain it to her without it sounding like an inferiority? Which it wasn't; he was sure it wasn't. *Why* need he explain it, anyway, to someone he intended to sleep with and probably never see again?

"There is," she said, pressing him.

"Maybe it's something like the way you feel," he said, running for cover. "A figurehead."

"I don't see the comparison," she said.

Why the hell did everything become a debate with her! "There isn't one, not absolutely," he admitted. He realized he was wallowing deeper and deeper, like someone trying to cross soft sand. It didn't usually happen this way—never, in fact. "I'm thirty-two years old. The guy I succeeded didn't get his appointment until he was forty-five; the guy before him was fifty. Would I have got it if my name hadn't been Thomas Hamilton Pike, Jr., scion of Thomas Hamilton Pike, Sr., whose whispers can be heard the length and breadth of Wall Street? Or got where I did at Chase, before that?"

"Probably not," she said realistically. "Why get a complex about it? The name and influence might have got you the job. But it won't keep it for you, if you make a mistake."

Which was the real fear, Pike admitted to himself. Of fouling up and everyone knowing it. Which *was* an inferiority complex. "I guess you're right."

"You know I'm right."

Neither wanted dessert, so Pike ordered coffee. Jane refused a liqueur.

"I've enjoyed the evening," she said. "Thank you."

"It hasn't finished yet," he said, regretting at once that it sounded like a cliché. He'd been right in what he said earlier; it wasn't the sort of evening he'd expected at all. Altogether too heavy.

She wouldn't be unfaithful to Paul, Jane had decided. It was unthinkable that she would go to bed with a man after a two-hour acquaintanceship and a casual dinner. But even if they'd known each other longer, she knew she wouldn't have slept with him. There was something convoluted about maintaining fidelity to a married man and making love to somebody else. She'd always supposed Paul still made love to his wife. Hoping to avoid any difficulty before it arose, she waved the crested ring in front of him. "What about Mrs. Pike?"

"There isn't a Mrs. Pike anymore," he said.

"I'm sorry," she blurted awkwardly. "I didn't mean. . . ."

"It's not a problem," assured Pike. "Her name was Janet Ambersom. Her father was chairman of Citibank when my father was at Chase. Now Ambersom is chairman of the World Bank. They don't lunch twice a week, like they used to in New York, but they still come to the country house here in Farquier County, and in the summer my family goes up to South Hampton for the sailing. The marriage was supposed to be the linking of dynasties."

"Supposed to be?"

"No one took love into consideration," said Pike, the explanation well-rehearsed by now. "Not even us. Her parents founded the Ambersom Gallery for Modern Art and Janet occupied herself being its director. One day at an exhibition she met a physics professor from UCLA and fell in love with him. . . ." He smiled down into his coffee cup. "It was all rather like one of those stories in a woman's magazine." And made him sound entirely innocent of guilt, he thought.

"It must have been unpleasant."

He shook his head. "Bankers don't allow unpleasantness. I haven't seen her for some time because she lives in California now. But the divorce was quite amicable and the families remained friends; there wasn't any reason why they shouldn't."

"I wasn't thinking of the families," she said. "I was thinking of you. And your wife. I've always thought it must be awful, to fall out of love with someone for whom you've cared—with whom you've known all the secrets."

"You've got to fall *in* love first," he said. "I told you we didn't."

I have, she thought, and I'm as miserable as hell now,

whatever might follow. "Is that why you resent your father? Because he forced you into a marriage?"

He smiled at her, refusing to get annoyed. "You certainly know how to keep a burr under a saddle blanket, don't you? I don't have any feeling against my father for what happened, or against any of the parents. We could have said no."

"Why didn't you?"

"Maybe I imagined I was in love at the time." Not true, he thought. Maybe Janet had, but he hadn't, ever. Which made the woman's question more important. Why *had* he gone through with it? Because there might have been some advantage, he supposed; her father was already being spoken of as the nominee for the World Bank.

"I wish love was like a cold or flu. If you catch a cold or flu, your nose runs and gets red and you ache all over. The symptoms are there and you realize what you've got. Why aren't there symptoms to show you when you've got love?"

Was she encouraging him to make a move? He was unsure, but decided it was worth pursuing. "Shall we go?" he asked.

When they emerged from the restaurant, there was a moment of embarrassment.

"Thank you," repeated Jane. "I've enjoyed the evening. It's been very nice."

"Surely it's not over yet." Pike gestured in the direction in which they had walked while they waited for their table to be prepared, and said, "There's a jazz club, Blues Alley; George Shearing is there. I thought we'd go."

"Thank you," she said. "But I'm not really a jazz fan."

"I don't suppose George Shearing could be strictly regarded as jazz."

"I should be getting back; we normally have an end-of-the-day meeting at the Jefferson." It sounded like the sort of thing that might happen, she thought, content with the lie.

Pike pointed across the road to the Four Seasons Hotel. "I'm staying there," he persisted. "How about a nightcap?"

"I really would like to go back to the Jefferson." It was said with quiet insistence.

"Sure," said Pike, conceding defeat. "I'll run you back."

"That's silly with your hotel directly opposite. I'll take a cab. Look; there's dozens about."

Before he could move, Jane was hailing a taxi, gesturing it into the curb and indicating the direction in which she wanted to go.

"Thank you," she said, offering her hand. "It was a lovely evening."

"I enjoyed it, too," said Pike mechanically. He kept the door open, watching her settle in the back of the vehicle. "Hope you get that promotion," he said.

He stood watching the car make its way back into the capital and decided against going to the club by himself. He'd fucked it up, decided Pike, a man to whom failure as unimportant as a casual seduction mattered: fucked it up completely.

Lydia Kirov was expecting the call and ordered her car ready at curbside, so she was en route to the Kremlin within minutes of the brief telephone conversation with the Finance Minister. She made her usual impatient progress through the government offices. Vladimir Malik, as always, was standing ready to greet her.

"Unanimous," he announced.

Lydia allowed herself the brief smile of satisfaction. "When?"

"As soon as you decide the time is right."

At this moment she had limitless power, Lydia realized.

More than any other woman in the Soviet Union—probably more than most men, as well. "Now!"

"You can call upon whatever assistance you require," said Malik. "Anything at all."

"Thank you."

"If you let me have a list, showing how you intend to move, I'll warn them in advance of your arrival. . . ." He smiled. "They must know you have the full authority of the Soviet government. We'll make it delegate strength, in fact."

"Yes, that's important," Lydia agreed. Even within the supposed equality of Communist societies there were disadvantages in being a woman. "And make an enquiry about their deferred loan, to worry them."

"You must feel elated."

"Yes," she said. "Elated." There was another far more important elation she wanted from this man. Why couldn't he see it!

The telephone sounded within minutes after Jane entered her room at the Jefferson. Burnham didn't speak, only wanting to confirm that she was back; he was at her door almost immediately, and as he entered, Jane saw he was flushed with anger.

"Where the hell have you been!"

"Out."

"Out! What do you mean—out? I'd planned for us to be together this evening."

"Why didn't you say?"

"Did I need to?"

"It might have been an idea."

"Where?"

"Where what?"

"Where have you been out to?"

"Dinner."

"Who with?" He was pacing the room, too annoyed to sit.

Jane lowered herself with a casualness she didn't feel into the only easy chair. So Daniels hadn't told him. She was glad. She said, "Someone I met at the reception tonight."

He stopped pacing. "Who?" he repeated.

Damn him! "Just someone I met."

"Are you going to tell me who?"

"Why is it important?"

"Because it is." He was being petulant in his anger.

"No," she said. "I'm not going to tell you."

"Why not? What's there to hide?"

"There's nothing to hide," she said. "I just don't choose to."

"You might have told me you were going."

"And you might have told me what you had in mind this evening."

"There was a meeting after the reception," said Burnham. "I wasn't sure until the last minute."

"About what? The meeting, I mean."

"The World debt: what else?"

"I would have thought there'd been enough meetings about that."

"There have been," he said. "It was a waste of time, like they usually are. And I don't want to talk about banking now." Burnham had started pacing again. Now he stopped in front of the chair and looked down at her. "It worked."

"What are you talking about?"

"Your little demonstration of independence. I was jealous—bloody jealous." He held out both his hands towards her, invitingly. Jane hesitated momentarily, then stretched up towards him, letting herself be pulled up by him, wanting it to happen. He started kissing her—small, pecking kisses—and at last the fragile reserve went, and she started kissing him back, eager for him. The love was good this time, better than it had been for weeks, and afterwards they stayed wetly together.

"What was the dinner like?" he said after a long time.

"All right."

"Just all right?"

She pulled slightly away. "Yes," she said. "What else could it have been?"

"Do you like him?"

"It was just an evening out; that's all."

"Do you like him?" he repeated.

She wondered if she had she won a victory.

4

Lydia Kirov was conscious of the confusion as soon as she disembarked from the Aeroflöt flight at Warsaw and saw the disarray among the waiting Poles; she hoped the careful preparations would continue to unsettle them. The Soviet Finance Ministry officials within her party were purposely too minor to demand the protocol, but she immediately recognized Florian Moczar, the deputy Polish finance minister, and guessed he was leading the reception party. He was a florid, roly-poly man whom she had encountered in London during the rescheduling of the Polish debt commitment. She'd been aware of his nervousness then and recognized it again now, as he stared among the arriving Russians, trying to determine the priority. Like skirmishers in some medieval encounter, the aides from the respective groups scurried out for the initial contact, and Lydia saw Moczar turn curiously towards her as she was identified as the leader of the Russian group. Further confusion, she decided.

The Pole approached, smiling, and said, "It is a great pleasure to meet you yet again, Comrade Kirov."

"And you, Comrade Moczar." Moczar spoke good Russian and she wondered how much interpretation the rest of his group would need. It was important there was no misunderstanding.

"An unexpected pleasure," Moczar went on immediately, trying to discover the reason for the visit.

Lydia decided the man was a bad negotiator to let his concern be so easily visible. Instead of replying to the implied question, she said, "All the bank representatives are here?"

Moczar gestured to the group standing behind him. "Permit me to introduce you."

"Later." Lydia was curt. "Let's keep the formalities to a minimum and begin the discussion as soon as possible."

The rudeness was intentional, to feed Moczar's nervousness, but when he hesitated, she felt a momentary uncertainty of her own at having forced the pace. Then the man nodded and said, "Of course," and she knew she was all right.

Moczar began to lead the way from the terminal building. "You'll want to refresh yourself first at the hotel?"

Sure of her control now, Lydia said, "No. I'd like to begin the conference at once."

"Of course." Moczar was obviously flustered.

Lydia deliberately retreated into the Soviet delegation during the delay over the car allocation, wanting to give the uncertain Pole the opportunity to return to his own people and convey to them her attitude, which, she guessed, he would presume to reflect that of the whole Russian party. The apprehension had to be stoked so that the gratitude would be that much greater, to overwhelm any doubt. She had climbed a high mountain and now she was confronting the sheer face to the ultimate peak.

At last she accepted his invitation into the lead car, with their respective, but unnecessary interpreters sitting on the jump seats facing them. There was an army as well as police escort, so the traffic control was operated in their favor.

"I didn't imagine that we would meet again so soon after London," said Moczar, trying again.

"I thought it possible." Every remark the man made seemed to make it easier for her. There was a grease of perspiration on Moczar's upper lip.

"I thought the resolve in London was very satisfactory."

Lydia turned fully in the car, to face the man. "It's because of London," she said, "that I have come here from Moscow today."

"What does that mean?"

"I think it best that we wait until the conference proper, don't you?"

She turned pointedly away, staring out at the approach to Warsaw. Few other capitals in Europe could have suffered worse destruction in the Second World War, and Lydia didn't think she liked the redevelopment. The planners had taken every opportunity to provide open park lands. The multilane highways were assembled on an easily understandable grid. And the public buildings appeared properly spacious. Lydia decided that it was precisely because everything in the new part of the city *was* so planned that the attempt failed. To her, Warsaw seemed like a practical place to put people into—a cage or a pen—not somewhere in which they could be expected to live and make homes. They crossed the Vistula from Praga into Warsaw on the Dganski bridge, then turned parallel to the river. They went briefly along Krakowskie Przedmiescie with its surviving palaces and churches, and Lydia thought briefly how much better the ancient was to the modern, and then, as if in contrast, they connected with Nowy Swiat and she was back among the regimented boxes.

They stopped at one of the largest, the headquarters of the National Bank of Poland. A message had obviously been relayed from the airport or from one of the escort cars, but the preparation was still being made in the conference room when they entered. Clerks and secretaries were hurriedly arranging seats and identification plaques, while engineers tried to make the wires to the translation headsets and microphones as inconspicuous as possible.

It was a formalized assembly—two long tables arranged facing each other, with smaller, linking benches at either end for minor members of each party. Behind each of the main tables, secondary seating and individual desks were positioned for immediate advisors and secretaries.

Moczar was directly opposite Lydia. To his right sat Zofia Opalko, acknowledging his position as chairman of the National Bank, the central financial authority for the country. Next to him was Stanislaw Madej, chairman of the Rolny Bank, responsible for financing all agricultural development. His neighbor was Jerzy Siwicki, representing the Powszechna Kasa Oszczednosci, the general savings bank whose authority included the activities of the workers' co-operative banks. To Moczar's left sat the representatives for the three banks with authority for foreign exchange dealings—the Bank for National Economy, the Polish Welfare Bank and the Commercial Bank of Warsaw.

Moscow's instructions had been dutifully obeyed, Lydia realized. Everyone whom she had wanted to attend was here.

There was a moment of immediate embarrassment, the Polish side uncertain whether they were conducting the meeting or attending it. Lydia let it stretch out, and finally Moczar said, "I would like to repeat what I said privately to Comrade Kirov at the airport, that we welcome the Soviet delegation here today."

"And for our part," responded Lydia, "I would like to say how useful I think it will be for me to talk to you all at one conference session." She paused, and then added, "I would like to say, also, that I bring fraternal greetings from my country."

The smiles from across the table were as perfunctory as the empty message. Lydia wondered how much of the traditional open hostility she would encounter, not that their attitude mattered.

Moczar said, "A difficulty of making any preparation for this meeting was our uncertainty as to its purpose. . . ." Now he paused, emboldened in the process by having others around him. "A most unusual and difficult procedure," he finished.

Lydia made much of spreading papers and graphs on the table in front of her, wanting to choose her moment. When she looked up, it was directly at Moczar. "I was a member of a delegation from socialist countries which had to negotiate standby credit and reloan financing in London to the extent of $52,000,000, against failed interest payments and a total foreign debt figure of practically $29,000,000,000."

Her abrupt halt surprised them. Opalko, chairman of the National Bank, broke the silence. "We are all of us completely aware of the terms. And the reason for them," he said. He had a thick, phlegmy voice.

"No discussion was conducted, during that London meeting, as to the scheduled repayments of credits allowed by the USSR to Poland between 1976 and 1980 under the Council for Mutual Economic Aid."

"Because any such discussion would have been completely inapplicable and because agreement has already been concluded between our two countries for a deferment of those payments until 1985," said Moczar.

"Which is less than two years away and which represents a further indebtedness of $120,000,000,000," said Lydia. Her suggested Moscow query had clearly worried the Poles.

"A further repetition of history," said Opalko forcefully.

He was a stronger man than Moczar, Lydia recognized. Opalko wouldn't have accepted the charade at the airport or in the car on the way into the capital.

"It was said about the bourgeois kings of France that they had forgotten nothing of their history, yet learned nothing from it either,'' said Lydia, enjoying the chance to use a quotation. She paused, letting the words hang. ''They lost the throne.''

''The rescheduling and additional loan facilities have given us a breathing space,'' said Moczar.

''For a race from which you're already panting and can't possibly win,'' insisted Lydia, picking up the cliché. ''It hasn't stopped with rescheduling and borrowing more money to pay interest on money borrowed earlier. The U.S. government has had to pay almost $100,000,000 on guaranteed agricultural and farm imports; France, too. You're running a trade deficit of $3,100,000,000 with collapsing world demand, collapsing exports and a hostile work force.''

''The Solidarity movement was the problem,'' insisted Madej, the spokesman for the farmers' bank. ''That's over now.''

''It was not *the* problem.'' Lydia's voice was hard. ''The problem is that previous governments used unassigned foreign loans to boost a consumer society to achieve popularity, like some spoiled child squandering an inheritance. Poland attempted to industrialize without spending sufficient funds on the necessary infrastructure; there was inefficient planning, and agriculture was neglected.''

''What are you saying?'' demanded Opalko.

''That your country is absolutely bankrupt, without any hope or possibility of meeting its commitments.'' They were sufficiently bruised from the sledgehammer. Soon it would be time to start tending the wounds.

''That is an extreme view,'' protested Moczar.

''It is the proper, objective view, unclouded by polite gatherings where bankers and financiers from both the East and the West refuse to admit the mistakes they have made and agree instead to postponements and deferments and reschedules, all of which mean nothing more nor nothing less than putting off the inevitable day of reckoning.''

''Which you have come here today to announce?'' anticipated Opalko.

Lydia recognized the perfect opening. "Yes, I suppose I have." For the first time since the meeting began, she went to her graphs and figures, more for effect than necessity. "Because of the lack of demand, your coal mines and coke-producing facilities are showing, against 1979, an underproduction of something like twelve per cent. Steel, both crude and rolled, shows the figures of fifteen per cent, and rising, over the same period. . . ." She glanced up, looking at Madej, the man who was supposed to know the problems of the farmers. "And your agricultural production is in chaos."

"Aren't you repeating yourself?" Opalko asked.

"Emphasizing points," qualified Lydia. "Without exception, every export facility this country possesses is underutilized and underproductive. The purpose of my coming here today, with a delegation capable of subsequent discussion with your relevant ministries, is to offer your government a program to expand every one of those capacities—not simply to 1979 level, but beyond it."

Lydia sat back, knowing there would need to be a period for them to assimilate what she had said. For several moments there was hardly any movement from the men facing her. Then there were curious sideways glances and, finally, snatched, head-together conversations as the background advisors huddled forward in consultation.

"*Increased* trade, between us?" queried Moczar, determined against any misunderstanding.

"Predominantly in exports, from this country into the Soviet Union," said Lydia. Producing the carrot she wanted them all blindly to pursue, she went on, "Paid for in foreign currency, which will enable you first to service and then, when the volume of trade is sufficient, reduce your presently impossible debts. And to make that possible, I am empowered today to make it clear that providing strict guarantees are agreed upon between us, there will be a further extension, beyond 1985, of the credits owed to my country."

"Extended for how long?" Moczar was more flushed than usual, and Lydia decided it was excitement.

"Until 1990," she said. "And even here a scale will be agreed, rather than an insistence upon single payment."

"Why?" demanded Opalko, predictably the most suspicious of the group.

The beginning was going to be easy, thought Lydia. "For several years we have been studying and monitoring the financial structure of the West," she said. "It is a study in which I have been exclusively involved. The conclusion is almost inescapable. Capitalism, however hard the effort may be to disguise the fact, is collapsing. It is collapsing through greed and overcommitment." She went needlessly again to her figures. "In Latin America alone, the current Western bank involvement is more than $250,000,000,000."

"How does this affect us in the Eastern bloc?" persisted Opalko.

"That is precisely why we are offering this to you," said Lydia. "To *avoid* it affecting the Eastern bloc. At the moment you are hopelessly, desperately in debt, with no possible way of extricating yourselves. The financial future of Poland will be a series of crises, each one lurching on to the other, always with more borrowing to pay for money already borrowed. Our proposal is to offer you a chance of getting out of that indebtedness, a chance to restore your factories and farms and mines to proper capacity and gradually create the structure demanded by your work force—a high-wage, consumer-orientated society."

"That sounds too simple," said Siwicki, the man into whose banks the workers made their deposits.

It had, conceded Lydia worriedly. It had even sounded, at the end, like an argument contrary to Communist doctrine. "We're not making you any gifts," she insisted. "We're not even offering you an *easy* way out. Rather, it's the only one which is practical. From the London meeting, I know that at the moment the majority of your debts are funded at one-half per cent above the London Inter-Bank Offered Rate. We would require 1½% over LIBOR on all the purchase credits allowed you."

"That's usury . . . ludicrous," protested Moczar. "You're suggesting we borrow at a high rate to expunge a debt obtained at a lower one!"

"*That's* ludicrous," said Lydia. "Sixty-five per cent of your debts are short-term, which is what makes the interest payments and the maturity impossible for you to meet. Under the proposals which the people with me will detail to your government, the *minimum* loan period will be ten years."

Behind the Polish contingent Lydia could see the advisors jabbing at calculators and scribbling notations on their pads.

"It's still not feasible," said Opalko quietly. "Attractive though the suggestion might appear upon surface examination, it's still not feasible."

"Why not?" Lydia fought to keep control; after so long there couldn't be anything she had overlooked . . . certainly nothing that this man could have realized after such a short period!

"The money already borrowed *wasn't* correctly channeled," conceded the central bank chairman. "We have insufficient ore smelters. Our farm equipment is obsolete. So is our mine equipment. For the scheme that you suggest to work properly, there would have to be massive reinvestment. Which would mean further borrowing. I don't imagine Western banks would advance us the capital required, even if we could afford to pay for it. Which we can't."

Imperceptibly, Lydia relaxed. Opalko was making it as easy for her as Moczar had earlier. "That's been taken into account," she said. "We're prepared to enter aid agreements for all capital and machinery investments you might need, to re-equip and retool."

"At what per cent?" demanded Moczar.

"One over LIBOR." They'd have to borrow to finance and that would require a margin of at least half a per cent.

Some of the people behind the Polish group were leaning forward, offering calculations, and there were further head-bent conversations between Moczar, Opalko and Siwicki.

"Your interest terms are too high," protested Moczar.

"No, they're practical. Apart from Chase Manhattan Bank, who linked their loan to an ore-smelting plant, Poland was allowed to borrow without specification. I've already said that we would require strict controls. Money advanced would be for definite projects, and because of the risk that my country would be undertaking, we would insist upon proper, profitable returns. We wouldn't permit a ruble to be wasted. Further, to make this scheme work, we are offering import credits, from the Soviet Union. With your exports high and import commitments low to the West, you could be in balance-of-payment surplus within a five-year period. Our interest might appear high at the moment, but that is because of the size of your external debt. With that indebtedness vastly reduced and moving on to the point of being settled, your terms with us would be well within your finance capability."

"You make it sound remarkably simple," repeated Siwicki.

"Because it really is simple." They were moving towards agreement, she decided: reluctantly, perhaps, but nevertheless moving in the right direction. It was time to impose more pressure. "You've applied to rejoin the International Monetary Fund," she said.

"It seemed prudent," said Moczar.

"Every country in the last ten years that has found itself on the brink of financial collapse has gone to the IMF to bail them out, and always the cure has been the same. Control and deflation. You've removed the figurehead of Lech Walesa and hopefully capped the Solidarity movement for the moment, but just how long do you think the people of this country would accept deflation beyond that which already exists?"

"It would be difficult for us to impose severe restrictions," Moczar admitted.

"The limitations we are proposing are financial ones, not those upon people," said Lydia, aware once more that she was advancing an alien capitalistic argument. "Our proposals are geared to create more jobs and higher earnings, not the opposite."

"These are very wide-ranging proposals," said Moczar. "There would need to be detailed study. And higher consultation."

"Of course." Lydia decided it had gone extremely well.

"When do you intend returning to Moscow?"

"Personally, almost at once," she said. "With me I have brought people from every applicable ministry who are prepared to remain here in Warsaw long enough to satisfy any query."

"On behalf of my government, I would like to thank you for the consideration and the breadth of all you have proposed," said the junior finance minister formally.

"Our ideology is one of comradeship and friendship," recited Lydia in return.

The weekend exodus into Virginia and Maryland combined with the rush hour, and Tom Pike moved slowly along the George Washington Parkway with the Potomac to his right, wondering why he hadn't tried a more direct route to the beltway around the city. The answer came at once. Because he wasn't in any hurry, that's why. He guessed there would be a full house party of guests after the IMF meeting, but he still wasn't looking forward to the visit. If Jane Rose had accepted the invitation to let him show her New York, he'd have canceled out altogether.

He should have hardly been surprised at her refusal. It was a presumptuous suggestion, more to assuage his rejected pride than anything else. Still a pity, though. She'd been an attractive girl. He didn't like even one getting away.

5

When he was young, before he'd been sent away for proper schooling and been able to spend most of his time on the Virginia estate, Pike thought of the house as his stockade. He'd created elaborate games and battles, repelling the attacks of marauding Indians he was sure the stern-faced, bewigged ancestors who stared down from their frozen pictures in the hallway had confronted two hundred years before. There'd been flintlocks and muzzle-loaders as well as the portraits, and what would they have been used for, if not to fight off Indians? There had been other preserved memorabilia, chain-liked metal anklets and a register where people only seemed to have one name and separate quarters, a line of tiny houses set away from the mansion, long ago converted into grain storage and tackle sheds for the horses. It had been during one of the later school holidays before he realized the connection between the ownership register and the quarters. He'd asked his father about it, still not quite believing that in a period as recent as two hundred years his family had owned slaves. It was the first time he'd heard the expression "demands of a market economy."

The gate was much bigger than it had been when he was

young, matching in size the electronically guarded surrounding wall, which was new, too. Pike identified himself into the mouth-grill set into a side pillar, and almost at once the ribbed metal barriers clicked apart to admit him. He drove the car forward, wondering how the Indians would have managed.

Elms stood rigidly to attention on the other side of the looping driveway, sentries to the paddocks that rolled away on either side; polished-haired thoroughbreds grazed unconcerned at his progress past them. It was a gradual incline, leading up to a proper hill, at the top of which the house was proudly displayed—a monument both to the durability of colonial architects and the historic Pike family. When he got nearer, to where the drive expanded at the immediate entrance, Pike saw the official cars with their pennants and diplomatic insignia; they were uniformly black and Pike thought they looked like some insect swarm, settling to forage. Who would be feeding from whom at this weekend?

Carlton was as efficient as always, opening the front door in greeting before Pike had time to switch off the ignition. Pike took his own bag from the vehicle and, when the butler reached him, stretched out to shake the man's hand.

"Good to see you again, sir," said the butler. The man appeared embarrassed at the greeting.

"And you," said Pike. He indicated the other cars. "Looks like quite a party."

"Biggest we've had for a long time. Every bedroom occupied."

"Am I in the outhouse?" There was a guest annex beyond the old slave quarters.

"Of course not," said Carlton. "You've got your usual room."

Conscious that he was indulging in inverted snobbery, Pike let the man take his grip and followed him into the house. The rigid portraits lined the hall, like a receiving line. Even though Carlton was white and English, Pike supposed the man was still a slave. At least he wasn't shackled with an anklet. Still a single name, though.

"Your father has gone riding with some of the other guests," said the butler. "Your mother is in the arbor room."

It was at the rear of the house, named after the flowered, hedged walkway that had been laid a hundred years earlier. The verandah windows were open on to it, and as Pike entered, he saw there were a lot of people, predominantly women, around the pool at the far end. Further on, both tennis courts appeared to be occupied. His mother rose to meet him. Pike kissed her on both cheeks and then allowed himself to be held at arms-length to be examined.

"Stranger," she said.

"How are you?" Pike responded, avoiding the accusation.

"Fine, just fine. We've a wonderful house party, but I've escaped for five minutes to see you by myself." She giggled girlishly. "I said there were dinner arrangements to make."

Escape was probably an apposite word, thought Pike, who didn't believe his mother would regard this many people in the house at one time as wonderful. His parents' marriage had been an understood affair, like they tried to make his, but the Burcote family had then been a minor and were now an extinct banking lineage. Pike always suspected that his mother was slightly in awe of encountering financiers with the reputation and the prestige of the Rockefellers or the Morgans or the Stillmans. It was an attitude she succeeded in concealing from everyone behind a publicly haughty, almost chilling, exterior: she'd even been described as matriarchal in the social columns of the *Washington Post* and the *Daily News*, and although she feigned annoyance—in keeping with the public demeanor—Pike knew her to be secretly pleased. It proved the protection was working.

"From the numbers of cars outside, I thought the IMF swapped meeting places."

"That's practically true." His mother paused and then said, "I wanted to see you by myself. To warn you."

"Warn me?"

"Janet's here."

"Janet!" Pike looked out towards the pool, but he couldn't locate his ex-wife. The tennis courts were too far away, if she were there.

"Do you mind?"

"It's your house," said Pike.

"I don't want you to be embarrassed."

"There's no need for us to be. We're still friends."

"She came back East to visit her parents. Your father invited the family down for the weekend and she came as well. Her father asked yours at the conference, apparently, and he said it would be all right."

He could have used it as an excuse not to come, Pike realized. Perhaps that was why his father hadn't mentioned it; there'd been enough opportunity. "What is her husband like?"

"She's by herself."

It would have been two years, Pike calculated. His mother didn't seem as embarrassed as he would have expected.

"How is she?"

"Seems wonderful."

"It'll be good to see her again." How would it be, after so long?

"You're by yourself?" said his mother.

"Yes."

"Would you mind being her escort, then? For dinner and things like that?"

He looked at her quizzically. "Isn't that a bit gauche?"

"I'll rearrange it, if you'd like."

"That would be even more ridiculous."

"You're annoyed."

"Surprised," Pike conceded. "Did she know I'd be coming?"

"I told her when she arrived, of course. She said she assumed you'd be here, that she was looking forward to seeing you again."

"I'm only staying tonight."

"Oh." She was obviously pained.

"I always intended to go back to New York tomorrow; I've been away almost two weeks."

"I'm sorry," she said, not believing him. "Your father should have discussed it with me. Or you."

"It's nothing to do with Janet."

"Why don't you come more often?"

"The Fed keeps me busy," Tom said uncomfortably.

"Not at weekends; it's only an hour, on the shuttle."

"Things to do," he said.

"I still don't see why you had to leave Chase."

"For experience," he said easily. "We discussed all this before."

"I felt comfortable, knowing you were at your father's bank."

It was like the poetry he had been forced to recite, thought Pike, lines repeated by rote. To break the stanza, he said, "Still enjoying the IMF?"

She gave a shy smile. "All the traveling gets boring. Which sounds an awful thing to say. I like Paris; there's a lovely apartment there."

"What about father?"

"He adores it," confided the woman. "I think he'll be sad when his term ends." She looked out into the grounds and said, "I suppose we should be getting back."

"I suppose so." If he were going to be the cabaret, shouldn't he be wearing a baggy suit and a false nose?

Pike followed his mother along the flowered walkway, entering the ritual of polite introductions to as many people as his mother could remember. There had to be at least thirty people around the pool, and his initial impression that the majority were women was confirmed. Not all were in costumes, and Pike recognized the demarcation between old and young. The men who were there didn't seem so concerned about the sag of age, and Pike thought they should have been: bankers didn't look like bankers with varicose veins cording their legs and indulged bellies bulging their boxer shorts—kings needed uniforms, if they didn't qualify for crowns. He moved slowly and politely through the group, pausing at the mobile bar and staring around while the waiter mixed the martini. Janet was further down the pool, reclining on a lounger, and he knew she had been looking at him before he saw her. She waved and he waved back, and when the drink was made, he walked down towards her.

"Hello, Thomas Hamilton Pike," she said, brightly.

"Hello, Janet."

"How's my ex-husband?"

"Pretty good. You?"

She tried to make a rocking motion with her hand and spilled some of her drink. She dipped her finger against the spill on her thigh and licked what she collected. "Surprised I came?"

"Yes," he said.

"Not sure now why I did. Angry?"

"Of course not." There was a lot of difference from what he remembered. The brown hair was still shoulder-length and the teeth brace-straight and the freckles she'd once worried about and used too much make-up to conceal patterned her nose, as they always would. But there wasn't the roundness he associated with her. And that wasn't just the physical appearance, although in the bikini her body had an edged sharpness that had also changed since the shorts-and-halter-top trips on her father's yacht.

"You look good," he said.

"You've got too many clothes on for me to judge how you look."

He'd forgotten her tendency to strive for *doubles entendre*;

the sex had always been good for them, ever since high school. "It's too late to change."

"Sit down at least. I'm getting a headache staring at you through the sun."

Pike pulled another lounger nearer and said "How's things?"

She gave a breast-wobbling shrug. "O.K., I guess."

"California?"

"America's crucible state for the future is like it always is," she said. "Sometimes hot, sometimes smoggy, but always anxious to initiate another trend."

Was this how he'd sounded to Jane Rose, all stand-up hip on Sunset Strip? He hoped not. "How long are you back for?"

She shrugged again, and Pike realized he hadn't remembered how full her breasts were, either. "Open ticket."

"Is your husband joining you?"

The gesture this time was dismissive. "Term doesn't end for some time yet." She looked pointedly at her empty glass and Pike gestured to the waiter. When he came, she indicated the measure with her thumb and forefinger. As he left to fill the order, she said, "Even that won't hit the spot."

"Something wrong?"

"Of course not. Should there be?"

"You seem to have changed," he said openly. "Changed a lot."

"How about you, Thomas Hamilton Pike?" she said, avoiding the question. "Word on the rarefied grapevine is that the Federal Reserve still can't believe their luck in getting you."

Pike wished there were a way for him to discover if the enthusiasm were genuine or generated by his father's influence. "It's an extension from the sort of banking I was used to," he said. "I'm enjoying it."

"The act's still good, darling."

"Act?"

"Apparent modesty beneath the apparent confidence—always was a winner." She accepted the drink from the returning waiter, lifted it towards him. "Cheers, bastard."

"Yours has improved," he said. "More Hollywood gloss. Cheers."

"With anyone?"

"Not for very long."

"That's still the same as well, then?"

"You're the one who fell in love."

"Maybe I got fed up competing."

"We'd never get fed up with that, Janet. We're brought up to it, remember?"

"How is your father?"

"Running half the world," Tom said. "How's yours?"

"Running the other half. There aren't any more races for them to run, are there?"

When Tom didn't respond, Janet went on with her thought. "They'll find one, though. Anyway, I gather we're being paired for dinner."

"To make the numbers balance," he qualified at once. "I'm sorry about that."

She gave a bouncy shrug. "Why? No problem."

There were some shouts from behind and then a general movement to the edge of the rise upon which the pool was constructed as everyone shifted to look down, to see the galloping return of Pike's father and the rest of the bankers who had gone riding. The old man was leading as they burst finally from the straggled trees on the far side of the valley, with Henry Ambersom only a head behind. Knowing the land better than his guests, Pike didn't try to ascend up the main path; instead, he cut sideways along a parallel gully to gain on his rival, and won by a length.

"I told you they'd find a race," said Janet, who had got up to stand by his side.

"I wonder if that's how the Indians would have done it?" said Pike.

"What?"

"Nothing," he said.

* * *

With so many house guests, any private meeting was impossible between Pike and his father. There was a brief, almost formal greeting, when the perspiring men got from their perspiring horses, and then introductions to people whom the older man thought Pike might not have met. Pike actually spent longer with Henry Ambersom than with his own father. That evening, when they assembled for drinks before dinner, they were only alone together for two or three minutes, during a break in the arrivals.

"I'd like to talk to you, before you go back," said the man.

"Whenever you like," said Pike.

"Something important." His father was a tall, burly man, able to dominate by size as well as attitude; Pike was shorter by a good two inches. They both saw Janet enter the room and his father said, "Not a problem for you, is it, Janet being here?"

"No."

"Hear things aren't good with her and her husband."

"We only met for a few moments by the pool," said Pike. "I wouldn't know."

"I was very sorry you two broke up, you know—very sorry."

"Yes, I know." Surely his father hadn't set this up deliberately!

"She's very pretty."

"She always was."

Janet saw them and walked across the room. She had a smooth, flowing stride, almost model-like. She was wearing a dramatic flame-colored dress, full-skirted, but with a tight bodice. Her breasts were very full and tanned. "Bet you were talking business," she accused. "You always do."

"As a matter of fact, we were talking about you," said the older man.

"In admiration," added Pike.

Janet made an elaborate curtsy. "I enjoy being talked about."

"I must mix," said Pike's father at once. "I'll leave you two alone."

He watched his father move further into the room and said, "I can hardly believe it!"

"Neither can I."

"Hope you're not embarrassed."

"When did you know me to be embarrassed?"

He nodded, accepting the correction. "Rarely," he agreed. "If ever." It was a bizarre situation, but he wasn't unhappy about it. Despite what their parents might think, he knew there was no danger of it becoming tacky; she'd enliven an otherwise boring week-end. Janet was never boring.

"What were you saying about me?"

"Dirty talk," he said.

She looked interested rather than offended, and Pike added, "Joke. We agreed you were pretty."

"I'm flattered."

"You'd be mad if we didn't think it."

"You flirting with me, Tom Pike?"

"Ex-husbands aren't permitted to."

"Who said?" she asked, taking a drink from a passing tray.

"Divorcee Book of Rules," he said. "That's your third cocktail."

"Who's counting?"

"I am. You had one when you entered, another crossing the room, and now that one."

"What's the book of rules say about nagging?"

"Permitted as an act of kindness."

"And about being patronizing?"

"What's the matter?" he said.

"Nothing. Don't get heavy."

That had been the problem with the English girl, Pike remembered. ''Sorry.''

''Congratulations, incidentally,'' she said.

''What for?''

''Getting under the wire and making it to the Fed.''

He smiled at her, realizing she'd have more reason to know than most people. ''Seemed a good idea.''

''Didn't your father try to stop you?''

''Proper timing is the basis for all good escapes,'' said Pike. ''I waited until he'd been at the IMF for a long time; it was a *fait accompli* before he knew anything about it.''

''Was he mad?''

''As hell, I guess. Never showed it, of course.''

Dinner was announced from the other side of the room. She looped her arm lightly through his, pinching the inside of his arm as she did so, and said, ''Might as well act out the scene they want to see.''

''That pinch hurt,'' he protested.

''Wanted to see your face move,'' she said. ''Stiff son-of-a-bitch.''

As they entered the dining room, they were both aware of their parents looking at them.

''Should I curtsy again?'' she whispered.

''Since when have I been a stiff son-of-a-bitch?''

''You've never relaxed for as long as I've known you.''

The house party was too large to have made a single setting practicable. Instead, the seating was arranged around individual tables, ten seats to a table. With Pike was Hal Prince, whom he knew from Citibank, and his wife, a Frenchman called something like Bouchiere and Louchiere, from the Credit Lyonnais, with a girl clearly too young to be his wife, and someone whom Pike didn't recognize from the IMF meeting, a German who introduced himself as Flieder, from the Deutsche Bank. Flieder had a jowly wife named Frieda, who couldn't speak English but who laughed a lot to compensate and said ''Ja'' every so often, appearing to think she was contributing to a conversation she couldn't comprehend. They talked about the financial meeting they had just attended and compared Washington to Paris and Bonn, the conversation moving slowly because of the German's constant need to translate to his acquiescent wife. Gradually the talk became less general, the Frenchman wanting to concentrate upon his companion and the German feeling the strain of bilingual effort. Towards the end of the meal, Janet leaned close to Pike, so that only he would hear. "How do you think they would react if I offered them a line?"

"They'd probably think you sailed a lot," he said.

"You still do it?"

"Doesn't everybody?" His personal assistant had a hell of a contact, thought Pike. Pity Loraine was such a rotten lay.

"I've got some good quality stuff in my room," she said.

Pike sipped his wine. Just like before, he remembered: one always pushing the other, always a challenge between them. She'd used cocaine more than him; booze, too. He'd been nervous he might lose control through too much of either. Perhaps she was right; perhaps he was a stiff son-of-a-bitch.

"You're blushing," she said happily.

Pike didn't know whether he was or wasn't; he thought it unlikely. "Have you any idea what would happen if coke were discovered among a group of people like this?"

"Don't be an asshole," she said. "A raid here is about as likely as a bust at the White House." She nodded across to the Frenchman. "And from the sort of action over there, I bet there's enough around the place to stock the medics for an average-sized war."

She was probably right, Pike conceded. He wished he hadn't reacted without thinking. "Game to you," he conceded.

She giggled. "Want to play some more?"

He smiled back at her. "It's good seeing you again."

"You, too."

"Why didn't you keep in touch?"

"Why didn't you?"

"Thought maybe your new husband wouldn't like it."

"Liar," she said. "You wanted me to be the first."

She was right again, thought Pike: more arm-wrestling.

The men remained where they were after dinner, for port and cigars. Several wanted to get into a deep discussion about the events of the previous week, but Pike was impressed at the way his father refused to let the talk develop, never preventing the conversation but always keeping it at a calm surface level. They changed seating, of course; Janet's father positioned himself beside Pike.

"Long time, Tom."

"Good to see you again, sir," said Pike.

"Getting your name known around Wall Street, I hear."

"It's a small village."

"Which can be good or bad for reputations," said Ambersom.

"I've been lucky," said Pike easily. Luck had nothing to do with it, he thought. He'd worked his ass off, the first to arrive and the last to leave.

"Happy at the Fed?"

"Very much so," said Pike.

"Always room for talent at the World Bank. Remember that, if you ever consider a change."

"Thank you." Pike's father had regarded as incomprehensible his transferring from Chase Manhattan to the Federal Reserve; the man would consider it outright betrayal if he moved to the World Bank.

"Good to see you and Janet together again."

"Yes," said Pike. Thank God he'd decided to go back to New York tomorrow.

"You must come out to the Island again soon; got myself a new yacht."

"I'd like that," lied Pike.

"Let's make a date, before the weekend is over."

"Sure."

Pike decided that his father was a good host as they emerged to join the women. The floodlights had been turned on around the pool, for anyone who wanted to swim, and a patio area between it and the house had been cleared for dancing to the accompaniment of a small orchestra. Backgammon sets were laid out in the larger of the lounges and two poker tables assembled in a card room. In the room next to it, pool was already racked up on the table, and for the benefit of the European guests, billiards were available as well. Pike played backgammon with Janet, carelessly, and lost $30, which seemed to excite her. She wanted to play another game, but he backed off, so she challenged Hal Prince and won $25 from the Citibank official. Only two or three people were swimming, so they wandered to the almost deserted bar and got drinks there. They walked further on into the garden and sat, staring back towards the light-flared mansion.

"Quite your night for winning."

"That's the name of the game," she said. "The Frenchman and his girl disappeared the moment you all came out of the dining room."

"It's the national pastime," he said. "It's in all the books."

"I made a count," she said. "I'd say five per cent of the women are wives, the rest mistresses."

"I guess that's about par. Wonder what the public would think if they knew their bankers were just like they are."

"They wouldn't believe it," said Janet. As if offering a truism, she intoned, "Idols must be infallible."

"Do people idolize bankers?"

"Lesser gods, perhaps: There's got to be someone to pray to for salvation, even financial salvation."

"I'd rather rely on a rabbit's foot."

Far away, in the darkness, there was a delighted scream and then a splash. Janet gestured out towards the glittering house. "I miss all this. It seemed a great adventure, campus life and academe, but Christ, I miss this!"

Pike was startled by her sudden change of mood, uncertain how to respond. "So there is something wrong?"

"Discreetly put, just like a banker."

"What are you going to do about it?"

"I don't know."

"Have you told your parents?"

Janet laughed bitterly. "That's a good question from someone who knows the dislike of scandal among the chosen few!" she said. "I told Mummy and she told Daddy and we all sat around and had one of those adult conversations."

"How do they feel about it?"

"They're not upset. They were very angry about *our* breaking up. Blamed me, like everyone did. They still can't understand how easy we find it to stay friends."

"I guess it is unusual."

"I'm glad we're not enemies."

"Will you come back East?" he said, wanting to move the conversation on.

She made another of her breast-moving shrugs. "I don't know."

"I'm sorry it didn't work out," he repeated, at a loss again.

"Maybe I don't win as often as people think."

Pike was discomforted by the seriousness, preferring her earlier mood. "We should be getting back," he said.

"Really think anyone will have missed us?"

"Probably, from the attention we were getting earlier."

They took another drink from the pool bar and carried it with them back into the mansion. A few more were dancing, but otherwise the same people appeared to be occupying the same rooms as before.

"Want to play some more backgammon?"

She shook her head. "Always quit while you're ahead."

"Dance?"

"No." She stood looking steadily at him. "I want to go to bed," she said. "Walk me to my room."

Pike was conscious of his father looking at them from the entrance to the billiard room as he mounted the wide, curving staircase around the vestibule to the upper floors. Janet's room was on the third level.

"I'm planning to go back to New York sometime tomorrow," said Pike.

"Oh," she said, seemingly disappointed.

"We could go riding in the morning."

"I'd like that."

"I'll fix it with the stables," Pike said as they reached her door.

"I wasn't joking at dinner," she said. "It's good quality stuff."

Competition time again, Pike thought, and then accepted the offer with a smile.

He locked the door behind them, and she grinned and said, "I guess there *could* be a raid."

The maid had already turned down the bed. Janet went to a make-up box on the dressing table. She pulled the top tier up on its cantilevered supports and brought a small, ornate box from the bottom. Also from the bottom she took a small-bowled spoon, and Pike saw that it was one that jewelers made specially.

"Got your own?" she asked.

Pike looked down at his evening dress and said, "I left it behind with my Magnum, medical kit, gun-dog and maps."

"Borrow mine," she offered.

"After you."

She went to the bed, hitched up her flowing skirts and sat cross-legged, with the tiny container directly in front of her. She patted the bed immediately beyond and said, "You sit there."

He did as he was told, folding his legs with difficulty. He was glad there was a bed support behind him. Janet prodded into the white powder, tapping the spoon gently against the edge of the box to displace the excess, blocked one nostril by pressing her finger against it, then inhaled deeply, her eyes closed in expectation. She repeated the process and then offered him the spoon. "Now you." She sat with her hands against her knees, tensed forward, waiting for the effect.

Pike did what she had done, feeling an immediate irritation in his nose and swallowing several times against the temptation to sneeze. She felt out for his hand and took it, squeezing his fingers. The irritation in his nose didn't go; it changed into another sensation—a numbness, but at the same time a tingling sensitivity. It extended to the surface of his skin, in his face and hands and arms, became a strange tightness, as if his body were growing too big to be contained, and then he felt the strangest emotion of all, the feeling that his mind was lifting free from his skull. None of it was unpleasant or frightening, and at no time did Pike feel he was losing control. He answered Janet's finger pressure and saw that her skirt had ridden higher around her legs. He felt out with his free hand, and she stretched towards him to make it easier. Her skin felt very smooth to his touch. She reached between them, carefully closing the tiny box. "We don't want to spill the stardust, do we?"

"No," he said.

"You're too far away."

He stretched beside her. She extended her tongue and he extended his, and they met, tip to tip. His hand was higher on her thigh. She was naked beneath the dress. She shifted, opening for him. She was very wet.

"Fuck me," she said. "Fuck me hard."

Every touch and sensation was heightened, tiny shocks bursting against his skin. It felt better than he'd ever known it, and he knew he wasn't going to climax, felt he could go on forever.

"Harder, I said. Really hard. Hurt me. Look at me when you're fucking me!"

He drove into her and she thrust up to take him, her back arched and her head thrown back, so he could see the veins roped along her throat. Her mouth was parted and she made little grunting sounds in time to him. She burst slightly ahead of him, pulling hurriedly at him at the last moment so that he would match her, and he did, just. They were too excited to stop, but slowed gradually, and when they halted, he still didn't pull away from her. She put out her tongue for his, and said, "I won again."

"A draw," he said.

Lydia was initially surprised, because the intended purges were still some way off, but by the time she returned from Poland her office and personal staff had been moved into the Praesidium building and onto the same floor as the Finance Minister. It was he who visited her the morning after her arrival.

"Like it?" he said.

"It's very nice." It was more spacious than her previous office and further along from Malik's, so that her view was of the Little Tsar's Tower and the Ulitza Razina.

"Well?" he said.

"I think it worked," the woman said cautiously. "We won't know definitely until we hear from the negotiating teams, but I think it worked!"

"Did you threaten to cancel the 1985 deferment if they didn't agree?"

Lydia shook her head. "I didn't consider it necessary, not during the first discussion. Nor wise," she said. "It'll be better if they do it because they want to, rather than under pressure."

"There was no awkward questioning?"

"Opalko was the most suspicious. He kept asking why."

Malik laughed. "He'll learn why, when the time comes; they all will."

"Everything ready here?" she said.

"Everything," assured Malik. "Two months from now, the Soviet Union will, over the preceding five years, have repaid something like $750,000,000 of its foreign debts."

"What about the gold?" she said.

"What were the last figures you had?"

"The special stockpile of four hundred and fifty tons, accumulated over six years."

"It now stands at five hundred and ten," said Malik. "In addition to the declared reserve of three fifty."

"When do we make the disclosure that there has been a miscalculation and that our production has been higher than previously thought?"

"Whenever you judge the time right," said the Finance Minister.

"It's got to be absolutely precise. Our borrowings are going to be astronomical, so they've got to be completely confident about our credit worthiness. Not yet, but soon."

"We're extending our loans throughout Africa, of course," said Malik. "It won't appear unusual, if it's spotted; there's a tradition of our lending to the Third World."

"It'll be interesting to see the Western reaction when we make our application," said Lydia.

"There'll be a rush to lend to us," predicted Malik.

"Lemmings rush," said Lydia. Why the hell couldn't he see how much she wanted him!

6

The message from his father was waiting when they returned to the stables from their morning ride. Janet said, "A summons from on high!"

They handed their mounts over to the grooms, and Pike said, "We planned a meeting sometime."

Janet took off her hat, shaking her hair free. She smiled at him and Pike smiled back, thinking that she looked beautiful. He'd enjoyed the morning with her.

"You still going back today?" she asked as they began walking towards the main house.

"I think so. I've been away from New York for a while. I've got things to do." He hoped she hadn't regarded the previous night as anything more than it had been.

"Are we going to see more of each other?"

"Of course," he said.

"That was too quick," she protested. She smiled again, unoffended.

"I'd like to," said Pike.

"Sure?"

No, he thought. If their families discovered they were seeing each other, all that damned-fool stupidity would start all over again. "Sure I'm sure," he said.

"When?"

"I'll call you."

"That's one of the world's three great lies," she said. "The other two are dirty. Have you heard the one about herpes?"

The brittle barrier was coming up again, Pike recognized. "Yes," he said. "I promise I'll call."

Just before they reached the house, she halted, so he had to stop with her. "Sorry," she said

"What for?"

"Coming on strong: I didn't mean to."

"You haven't," he lied. "Sometime during the week," he said. "Honestly."

"Well, you always were polite."

From Carlton's immediate approach when they entered the house, Pike realized the butler had been purposefully waiting for his return, so he decided against changing, going instead to the study to which the man directed him. When Pike entered, his father was standing at the window, watching the preparations by the pool for a buffet lunch.

"I've kept you from your guests," Pike apologized at once. "I'm sorry."

The older man turned back into the room. "That's all right. A lot of people are leaving early, to make plane connections back to Europe. I've some early good-byes to say."

He indicated the drinks table, but Pike shook his head.

"I'm glad you came down," said his father. "So's your mother."

"We had breakfast together this morning."

"She told me. Good to see you with Janet Ambersom again."

Pike walked to the window at which his father had been standing when he entered the room. By the pool he saw his mother talking to Janet's parents; they seemed to be laughing a lot.

"Satisfied with the way everything went?" he asked, still looking from the window.

"Everyone's worried to hell about Latin America—about Eastern Europe, too. All it needs is some itty-bitty bank that no one has ever heard of to declare a default and the money system is going to come tumbling down, like a pack of cards."

Pike turned back into the room. "It shouldn't have been built like a pack of cards in the first place."

"Don't I know it! At least I've tried to impose some control while I've been at the Fund."

"I've heard criticism on Wall Street that you've been too deflationary," said Pike.

"Purposefully," insisted his father. "How the hell else are we going to get some sort of stable sanity! It'll work in Brazil—in Mexico, too, although they don't like it. Argentina is the problem, like it's always been." He seemed suddenly to make up his mind, going to the drinks table and pouring himself bourbon. Momentarily he stood with his back to his son, and then he turned abruptly. "Judge my time with the IMF," he demanded.

Pike frowned at the request. "Very good," he said, awkwardly.

"Just *very good*?"

"No," conceded Pike, unsure why his father wanted the praise. "You've read the commentaries as much as I have. It's pretty unanimous that it's been a brilliant directorship."

The older man smiled wolfishly. "Which is how it's been meant to look."

"What do you mean?"

"What do you think I intend doing, when I leave the Fund?"

Pike made an uncertain gesture. "Go back to Chase, I suppose." Which is why I got away, he thought.

The older man shook his head. "That would be going backwards, not forwards."

"What's left, after the IMF?"

"Think!" demanded his father.

This was how it had always been, question-and-answer, for some goddamned prize. A prize he'd always been expected to win. So what the hell was the right answer? There was only one that came immediately to mind, but Pike found it difficult to accept. His father was a heavy contributor; twice he'd attended inauguration ceremonies by personal invitation, but Pike had never imagined the man wanting to get personally involved. "Politics?" he asked.

His father smiled. "You're good, Tom—damned good."

Pike wished there hadn't been the physical feeling of relief, to show it still mattered. "How?"

"What's the U.S. economy like now?"

One day, thought Pike, he'd get a response instead of a query. Surer now, he said, "High rates; tight money. Inflation coming down, but at the expense of employment."

His father nodded. "And there are presidential elections within six months of my leaving the IMF."

"So?" demanded Pike, determined to get his father to answer a question.

"The policy is good finance but bad politics: Nelson Jordan is in his first term and determined to get the second, but he won't at the moment. He's looking around for a better financial policy—and I'm going to give it to him, rather than somebody else."

"Somebody else?"

"Harry Ambersom is due to leave the World Bank around the same time as I leave the IMF. He wants the Treasury, too."

"So it's a competition?" Like it always was, with all of them, thought Pike.

"Something like that," said his father. "Jordan is an astute man. At the moment my track record is about the same as Ambersom's—maybe a point or two better."

"I wish you luck," said Pike.

"I want more than your good wishes."

Pike felt a stir of unease. "What else?"

"I spoke to Volger several times about you last week, got behind the platitudes that I knew he'd come up with when I asked about you. He's genuinely impressed."

"That's good to hear," said Pike cautiously.

"He says you're one of the best analysts in the Federal: one of the best bankers, too. That's a pretty good combination, for what I want."

Pike shook his head. "There are dozens just as good."

"Who aren't my sons. I want someone I can trust, someone with whom I can talk problems through. I want you to come with me to the IMF, Tom. I only generalized with Volger, of course, until I'd spoken to you, but I know he'd let you go if I asked him."

Back into the cage, thought Pike. Back into the father-dominated environment where people sneered because of the implied favoritism and perched like vultures waiting for the mistakes they could peck at.

"I'm very happy where I am," he said.

"The opportunities are greater at the IMF," said his father, unthinkingly choosing the right lure.

"What happens at the end of your term?" demanded Pike.

"Whatever you want to happen. Back to the Federal. Or Chase. Or stay with me here in Washington. In politics."

All so simple. "I don't know," he said uncomfortably. The proposition sounded attractive.

"I'm not expecting a decision today," said his father genially. "No hurry, not for weeks yet. Take all the time you want to think about it."

A difficult choice, Pike decided. The charge of nepotism was a logical one; it was to prove himself that he'd moved. But the opportunities *were* greater at the IMF, because of what was happening. "I'll think about it," he said.

"We'd make a fine combination, Tom. Establish the

name of Pike right up there among the great ones,'' said his father enthusiastically. ''Wouldn't that be great!''

''Great,'' agreed his son dutifully. He decided against telling his father of Ambersom's offer; that would only increase the pressure.

''I'm proud of the name,'' declared the man. ''Aren't you?''

Pike looked at his father across the desk, unable to discern the new direction in the conversation. ''Of course,'' he said. ''Why say something like that?''

''We've got a heritage,'' continued the older man, gesturing around the family house. ''Traditions that go back. A dynasty, if you like; something that should be preserved.''

''I would have thought you were doing a pretty good job of preserving it.''

''I was always sorry you and Janet didn't have a son.''

''I would have thought it fortunate we didn't, in view of the way the marriage turned out.''

''You still make a fine couple.''

Jesus Christ, thought Pike; the goddamned man wanted to manipulate him from bedroom to board room and back again. ''It's over!'' he said. ''Properly and legally over.''

''Knocked at your door last night,'' said his father. ''Thought we might have had our talk then.''

Pike swallowed, trying to stop himself coloring. ''I went for a walk,'' he said; it was the first thing that occurred to him.

''The grounds are nice at night.''

''Yes.''

''No trouble with security patrols?''

''No,'' said Pike. Sneaky old bastard, he thought.

''Good. They get jumpy sometimes.''

''They didn't last night.''

''You'll think seriously about what I said? About joining me?''

''Yes.''

"And let's see more of each other; we've grown too far apart in the last few months."

"I'd like that," said Pike, emptily.

"I'm very proud of you, Tom. You know that, don't you?"

No, decided Pike. He didn't know it, because his father had never told him before. "I hadn't thought about it," he said. Another lie.

"Well, I am," said his father. "Very proud indeed."

Pike packed after showering, so by the time he got to the garden, the buffet was crowded. He was glad.

"You can't go now!" protested his mother, when he started to say good-bye.

"The shuttle gets busy later in the afternoon."

"Our plane is taking people back. There'll be room for you, I'm sure."

"The shuttle will be all right," said Pike. On an estate of God-knows-how-many acres he felt claustrophobic.

"I thought we'd have lunch with the Ambersoms; we've waited."

"I'll apologize."

"Nothing wrong, is there?" demanded his mother alertly.

"Of course not," said Pike. "Everything's fine."

Despite his earlier warning, he was conscious of the disappointment on Janet's face when he announced he was leaving.

"Expected you to lunch with us," said her father.

"Sorry, sir," said Pike. "Plane to catch."

"There's plenty of planes."

"I've a lot to do in New York."

"You won't forget our little conversation, will you?" said Ambersom.

Pike saw the looks pass between Janet and her mother. "No, I won't forget."

"Harry says he's invited you up to sail sometime," said Mrs. Ambersom. She was a well-preserved woman, with blue-rinsed hair in rigid grooves.

"I'd like that," said Pike.

"So would we."

He shook hands with Janet's father, kissed her mother and then his own, and when he broke away to go to the front of the house to his car, Janet got up from her chair to walk with him.

"They're practically fixing dates!" she said.

"I got it, too."

"It's my fault, or at least it's because of me. I'm sorry."

"It's not important."

"No," she said. "I suppose it's not."

"That didn't sound like I meant it to."

"Forget it," she said. "What was the little conversation you had with my father?"

"Nothing," said Pike.

"About us?"

"No."

He tossed his grip into the back of the car and said, "I don't envy you the rest of the day."

"I'll manage."

"Take care," he said, uncertain how to leave her.

"Call?"

"I said I would."

"I'm being pushy again."

"Seems to have been part of the weekend."

"Bye," she said.

"Good-bye," he said.

7

Burnham maneuvered himself next to her on the homeward flight, but Jane wished he hadn't, because they were surrounded by bank people and intimacy was impossible. During the flight she became aware of his nervousness. He kept getting up from his seat, making excuses to speak to the governor and other members of the Court or the delegation, and then he took some papers from his briefcase and made the pretense of reading, as if he were practically unaware of her presence. The meal gave them the excuse to talk. Under the cover of the tray and the flap upon which it was placed he moved his leg, pressing it against hers, but she didn't answer the pressure.

"What's the matter?"

"It seems bloody stupid, that's all."

"I thought we'd made up."

Jane didn't bother to reply. The food seemed tasteless, so she stopped bothering to eat.

"Parker's preparing the delegation assessment," said Burnham, nodding to another director ahead of them on the Concorde flight. "Everyone's very impressed with you."

"That's good."

"You're not making yourself much fun to be with."

She wasn't, Jane realized miserably—which was stupid. She'd known what she was doing, when it started. He'd never lied to her about being married; he'd always talked openly about Marion, in fact. So why couldn't she do what other mistresses did, accept the situation as it was and grab at whatever was possible between them? "We weren't together as much as I'd hoped," she said. "Now you're going back home."

"I don't suppose I'll be able to get away at all next week."

"No, I suppose not," she said.

"I'll try."

Their luggage came up separately onto the carousel, for which she was grateful, because it meant they were not together when the bank party emerged into the public section of the arrival building. Marion was waiting for him, with the children. She didn't want to, but Jane couldn't avoid seeing how the children clustered around his legs and the way Marion eagerly kissed him and then clutched his arm, as if frightened to let him go. Jane hurried by and got into one of the arranged cars, not aware, until she was inside, with whom she would be sharing it. The other two were both supervisors, both men; she managed to sustain a monosyllabic conversation along the motorway and was glad her apartment was in Kensington, as it meant she was the first to get out.

She put her cases down immediately inside the door, momentarily remaining in the small vestibule, slump-shouldered and miserable, teeth clamped tight against the need to cry. The sensation went, gradually, although, when she tried to take a deep breath there was a tiny sob in it.

She lifted her case at last, carrying it into the bedroom:

Everything smelt musty and unused. She was a neat, almost obsessively tidy person. Tissue paper was interleafed throughout her clothing to prevent creasing, and as she unpacked, she carefully folded each sheet and stored it in the bottom drawer of her closet for the next time she traveled. She put her sweaters in the sweater drawer, her shirts in the shirt drawer and her underclothing in the underclothes drawer, and then hung her skirts in their allocated section of the wardrobe, followed by her dresses and finally her suits.

The kite she'd bought in Georgetown for her sister's son was in the last case. She stared at it, remembering the American and his invitation to New York. If she'd accepted it, she wouldn't be facing an empty Sunday, like all the other empty Sundays. He would have expected her to sleep with him, of course. Had he been with her right now, in the apartment, she would have gone to bed with him. Not for the sex. Just to have someone hold her and want her and not to feel so achingly lonely. Jane blushed at the thought, was embarrassed by it. Hurriedly she put the kite away and took the cases back out into the lobby to their storage cupboard.

She wandered about the empty apartment, opening windows in the lounge and the kitchen to get air into the place. In the kitchen she idly opened cupboards and then the refrigerator, aware that they were empty. Despite leaving the Concorde lunch, she wasn't hungry, but she would have liked a drink. There was a milk machine in Kensington High Street, but she decided not to bother.

There was a report to write. Jane went to the bureau and opened her briefcase, staring in at the documentation she had collected in Washington. Then she closed it again, positively. She didn't feel like writing reports, either.

She bathed leisurely, then put on a housecoat. There were films on two television channels. She'd seen one and the other was a Western; she didn't like Westerns. The Paul Scott novel she'd bought but forgotten to take to

Washington was lying on the table beside her chair. She got to page five before conceding that the words weren't registering and she put it down again.

"Shit!" she said, in sudden anger. "Shit! shit! shit!" And then, at last, she started crying.

It took eight days for the complete Polish agreement.

"It's a brilliant scenario," congratulated Malik. "There's practically an automatic impetus to it."

Lydia accepted the vodka he offered, feeling the liquor warm through her.

"There's no automatic impetus," she said. "There never will be. It will only work because we make it work. And there are still some tests to be made."

"You must be encouraged, at least," pressed the man.

"Encouraged," she agreed. "But not complacent."

"What about the Argentinians?"

"They arrived last night."

"You've no doubt the Americans will try to use wheat as a weapon?" asked Malik.

"They'll have to in the last resort," she said. "Although in actual fact it isn't much of a threat. At seventeen per cent of our overall consumption, it's a myth that we're so dependent upon American grain for our food."

"It's still wise to take precautions," said Malik.

"I'm taking all that are available," assured Lydia.

8

The requirement was Western awareness and reaction. Accordingly, there were three members of the Soviet Politburo among the military-band-accompanied welcoming party for the Argentinian delegation at Sheremetyevo airport, with the usually controlled Western media permitted every facility. Making allowances for the fatigue of the journey, the first evening was confined to a performance of *Swan Lake* at the Bolshoi, but to maintain the newspaper and television coverage, seven members of the Politburo were among the Soviet party and once again reporters were allowed every facility. The first working day was allocated to subsidiary meetings between the permanent officials of the Soviet and Argentinian finance ministries, which enabled continued reportage of the sightseeing of the Latin American Finance Minister, Manuel Lopez, and his immediate entourage, accompanied throughout by the deputy Soviet Finance Minister, Mikhail Paramov. In the evening there was a state banquet within the Kremlin, at which the First Secretary himself was the host. After the meal the Russian insisted on walking to every Argentinian place setting and toasting the finance delegation personally.

By choice and planning, Lydia occupied a subsidiary

position at the first proper negotiating session, with Paramov heading the Russian party. As with everything that had preceded it, the opening formalities were thrown open to newspaper and television coverage. There was a theatricality about the actual beginning of the conference; after the room had been cleared of journalists, a diplomatic minuet of hand-touching and bows and curtsies was performed, and the words were as formalized as the attitudes. Only at the very end, when Lopez ended a speech asserting continued friendships between the two countries, did Paramov appear to depart from the recognized ritual and disclose it was the hope of the Soviet government that such friendship could be increased and strengthened. He heightened the impression of indiscretion by retreating immediately into platitudes when Lopez seized upon the remark, breaking step himself by inviting the Russian to explain the hope more fully.

Because he had been instructed to, Paramov approached Lydia at the end of the session and said, resentfully: "Well?"

"Very good," said Lydia, who had rehearsed the man the previous day.

"I don't enjoy being a puppet."

"That isn't your function," said Lydia. He was the only one to be purged with whom she was likely to come into contact.

"It seems like it to me." Paramov was a fat, indulged man who, she suspected, took advantages of the favored life of the Soviet elite more than most. It didn't make what was going to happen to the man any easier for her to accept. She wondered if he were married, with children who would suffer too. She felt more for any family than for the man.

"Then you haven't properly understood the preparations in which you've been involved for the meeting," she said.

Paramov seemed startled by the response from someone who by rank and title was far his inferior. He recovered with the quickness of the Kremlin politician he'd always tried to be and said stiffly, "I am aware of your rather special relationship, Comrade Kirov, but I think you should also be conscious of my position."

"I am conscious of your position, Comrade Minister," she responded with matching stiffness. "I hope you are." Why was she behaving like other career women whom she knew within the Soviet system—soured, over-aggressive women needing to prove themselves at every opportunity in encounters with men whom they suspected considered them inferior? She should feel pity for this stupid, manipulated man, not arrogance.

Color suffused Paramov's face and a vein on his forehead throbbed with anger. "I will not tolerate insubordination!" he exclaimed pompously.

Lydia was conscious of the attention of other Russians who had remained with them in the conference chamber, too far away to hear the exchanges but knowing that an argument was erupting between them. "Then don't tolerate it, Comrade Paramov," she said, turning to leave the room on her own terms.

Lydia's anger remained, not at Paramov but at herself. It had all been so *pointless*! Insecure people were bullies, and she wasn't insecure. She had no reason to be. For sixty-six years the politicians of the Soviet Union had prattled and postured about world domination and failed in every attempt to achieve it. Now she, Lydia Fedorovna Kirov, was going to give it to them.

Could anyone about to do that feel—imagine, even—insecurity?

The waiting official car took her back to the waiting official apartment. She took the papers from her briefcase to prepare for the following day's meeting and very soon decided there was nothing upon which she needed refreshing, so she put them away again. She walked, without purpose or direction, around the apartment, halting finally at the expansive lounge window. It was completely dark now, the lights of Moscow yellowing the capital; to the left the color was tinged red, changed by the theatrical stars surmounting the towers of the Kremlin. Lydia had no religion, but she knew the Bible from her hobby of reading; she wondered if the designers of that bizarre decoration to Communism ever considered the parody against the signal that had guided the Three Wise Men to the birthplace of the supposed saviour of the World. Perhaps they had; perhaps that's why there was more than one star, indicating their uncertainty where in the fortress salvation lay.

Her book shelves dominated one entire wall of the apartment; books spilled over into other racks which she kept telling herself were temporary, but which she hadn't bothered to replace with other library compartments against the adjoining wall. She went to the existing shelves and took at random Griboyedov's *Woe from Wit*. She leafed casually through the satire play of a Moscow she couldn't imagine, finding the style leaden and the humor difficult. There were more Western than Russian novels and books, all in English, which Lydia spoke perfectly. She opened a Tom Sharpe novel at random, remembering the pleasure it had given her the first time. She wasn't attracted now; it seemed forced, unnatural.

She stared at the last line on the page at which she'd opened the book.

"Mr. Jipson slept easily," it said.

Lucky Mr. Jipson, Lydia thought.

The Argentinian curiosity was immediately obvious when they entered the conference room and saw the different composition of the Soviet side, with Lydia occupying the chief negotiator's chair and Paramov in a subsidiary role. Unlike the previous sessions, no photographers were permitted from either the Soviet or Argentinian media. The Argentinian delegation seated themselves amid hurried consultation, attempting to get from their back-up advisors the identity of the woman they were now facing.

"My name is Lydia Fedorovna Kirov," she said helpfully.

"We had hoped to continue discussion about expanding trade between our two countries," said Lopez.

The Latin American machismo was offended at having to talk with a woman, thought Lydia. Why were men so arrogant! "We hope that, too, on our side," said Lydia.

Lopez looked pointedly between the woman and Paramov. The obese Russian was hunched over the table, apparently engrossed in some document before him. Fools, thought Lydia: all of them.

"There is a great need for your trade expansion," said Lydia.

"Between all countries," said Lopez, lapsing into platitudes.

"Argentina's external debt is $40,000,000,000," pressed Lydia at once. "Since the Falklands war with the United Kingdom, your inflation has been practically uncontrollable. Within world banking there is a fear of a repetition of 1828."

Lopez's face blazed red in immediate annoyance. "I don't regard that remark within the spirit of friendship so far shown between our two countries." he said. "You're referring to history over one hundred years ago: Argentina does not intend to default as it did then. It would be unthinkable!"

"Quite so," agreed Lydia easily. "But it is a speculation considering the current economy of Argentina. From our studies we do not consider it possible for you to complete by 1985 the $10,000,000,000 plan to make your country self-sufficient in oil, which will therefore continue to impose a huge import burden. Your natural gas development can't be completed either. And your wheat exportation is half of what it was less than six years ago."

"Temporary difficulties," said Lopez. "World recession has affected every country, including your own."

"Which is why this meeting between us is so fortunate," said Lydia, moving from forcefulness into conciliation. "The Soviet Union has an oil surplus. But we need wheat; our harvests have consistently failed. There would seem to be room for an amicable arrangement."

There was a movement of interest among the Argentinian group: Lopez was leaning forward intently over the table. "What sort of an arrangement?" he demanded.

"Oil for wheat. Fixed prices for both, which would relieve our countries from the uncertainties of fluctuation." Wanting to show which side was getting the better bargain, Lydia added, "If you had a contractual guarantee over five years, at a fixed posted price for oil, that would represent a foreign currency saving to Argentina of $1,000,000,000. Currently you've 52,000,000 acres of land under cultivation; that's 22,000,000 short of what was under plough six years ago. With the pledged market we are offering, that land could be put back into production and reduce your unemployment through farming and the subsidiary industries by at least twelve per cent."

And if they entered that sort of expansion and became dependent upon it, then they would be dependent upon Russia to maintain it, thought Lydia. She didn't think that was a consideration in the minds of any of the people facing her. "It would be an extremely popular government that could achieve such a thing," she said, nudging them forward.

"It is an interesting proposal," said Lopez, trying to conceal his interest behind the diplomatic cliché.

"There would further be the need for transportation," said Lydia. "We would be prepared to contract with you for shipment."

"Argentinian shipment?" Lopez pounced at once.

"Either owned or leased." If Argentina acted as carriers, then payment would have to be made in foreign currency, predominantly dollars. It meant that as well as being freed of a $1,000,000,000 oil-purchase necessity, the country would be earning millions from their shipping.

"I'm not sure that our storage and conveyor capacity would be sufficient for the quantity this outline conversation indicates," said Lopez.

Greedy bastard, thought Lydia. It was unfortunate that the man would never know how the trap had clamped shut around his leg. "This trade agreement would be made public, of course. With the advantages to your economy obvious from it, I would anticipate your getting a favorable reaction to increasing your immediate loans."

"You yourself pointed out that our external debt is worsening." said Lopez.

Precisely for this moment, thought Lydia. "Yes," she said encouragingly.

"I don't think I would share your complete optimism if we sought to increase it, despite our trade agreement."

"I suppose there could be a balanced pledge," said Lydia, as if the idea had just occurred to her.

"How much of a balanced pledge?"

"I would imagine we could offer half of whatever expansion loan you sought. Surely you could get the remaining fifty per cent from Western banks?"

"Your commitment would act as a guarantee," said Lopez. "I'm sure they'd find that acceptable."

"Then we would seem to have a framework for negotiation." She decided that Lopez's color now was because of excitement at his belief in what he had achieved and no longer outraged machismo.

"Could there be a signing, in principle at least?" pressed the Argentinian.

"I would think it possible," said Lydia. "Could you extend your visit here, if the necessity arose?"

"Easily," said Lopez, showing his eagerness.

* * *

With the Soviet Union appearing to concede so much and the Argentinian anxiety to conclude, the negotiations only took another week, so there was no need for them to extend their stay. The Russians gave another reception to mark the official signing, which was televised and filmed as well as being photographed, because of the continued necessity for Western publicity. To guarantee it, this time five members of the Politburo attended.

Malik was with Lydia when the Argentinian trade minister approached, champagne glass in hand. "Our own private toast," proposed Lopez. "To a most successful negotiation."

The two Russians drank and Malik said, "It's been remarkably satisfactory."

"The final agreement shouldn't differ greatly from this draft document," said Lopez.

"The terms appear satisfactory upon our part," said Lydia.

"So we should be able to enter contractual commitment very quickly?"

"I don't see why not," said Malik.

Disclosing his impatience, Lopez said, "Weeks?"

"The Soviet delegation are assembling now," said Malik. "There's no reason why they shouldn't be in Buenos Aires within a few days."

"They'll be warmly welcomed," promised Lopez. Believing he'd earned another concession, he became anxious to return to his own party to pass on the news. There was a brief, superficial conversation for another few minutes, and then the Argentinian excused himself, leaving them alone again.

"He honestly believes he outwitted you at every stage," said Malik.

"Yes," said Lydia. "He'll never know otherwise."

"He's not the sort of victory you want, is he?"

"Of course not," she said.

"There's been some criticism."

"Official?"

He shook his head. "Rumors and innuendo."

"Paramov, then?"

"Obviously."

"The fool."

"The accusation is that you were unnecessarily aggressive and that the negotiations were put into jeopardy."

"How does that reconcile with what's happening here now?"

"With embarrassment, for him."

"So it doesn't matter."

Malik looked at her, almost sadly. "You're not being asked to defend yourself," he said patiently. "You're entering an echelon where it's important to know of everything possible that's happening."

She realized that at last he was going beyond the official barrier he always maintained. "I'm sorry," she said, too hurriedly in her surprise. "And thank you for telling me."

"I thought it important that you should know, although there was no personal danger."

"When will the political moves start?"

"Soon," said Malik. He hesitated and then said, "Can I ask you something?"

"What?"

"Why don't you behave more like a woman?"

"Why don't you give me the opportunity?"

9

There is a mythical hypnotism to gold, a metal as beguiling to bankers as it is to beneath-the-mattress hoarders, and it was with gold, of which it is the world's second largest producer, that the Soviet Union extended its first lure. The most detailed planning—and Soviet planning was exhaustively detailed—gains or loses by the unexpected, and it was Vladimir Malik who saw the advantage immediately when the announcement was made from Pretoria that the balance-of-payments deficit of South Africa—the world's biggest producer—necessitated the government to apply for a standby loan of $100,000,000 from the International Monetary Fund.

Now that their offices were so close, it took the Finance Minister only minutes to discuss it with Lydia and for them to agree the fortuitous South African application made the timing right.

The Moscow announcement that the Soviet stockpile of gold had been underestimated missed the European markets, but caught the last hour of Wall Street and the opening in Hong Kong. The American reaction was one of uncertainty. From $420 an ounce it automatically jerked upward to $430. There was some speculative profit-taking and then the sort of infectious worry, with which all exchanges can become infected, that the size of the amount might lead to some dumping; so it dipped to $400. Asia had the advantage of a Moscow announcement—purposefully delayed because it was precisely the sort of detailed planning that was being utilized—that the Russian government did not intend any abrupt disposals. The nervous overhang from New York only lasted an hour, and then the traditional confidence in metal established itself, so by the time London opened, in its pivotal position astride the time changes between East and West, prices on the Hong Kong market were hard at $450. Throughout the day London confirmed that confidence, closing at $453, with the Paris Bourse showing $450, because of the traditional French affection for gold, and the more conservative German exchange in Frankfurt registering $442.

New York opened on the second day with the sort of controlled excitement that follows enough bulls getting into the pen in the first day expectation of the prices rising to confront investors anxious to recover positions their faint-heartedness prevented their taking up when they first had the chance. By midday gold was being traded at $470. It was too high, fueled by auction fever, and by the close it had leveled at $450.

Because the trading stretched throughout the international metal exchanges, it meant that Malik and Lydia had to remain within the Kremlin complex until after midnight, Moscow time, in a telex room into which were relayed the fluctuations and reactions from around the world. By 2:00 a.m. they were sure, going to Malik's office because it was nearer. Their bone-aching weariness was as much from the suddenly relaxed tension as from the amount of time they had spent monitoring the global movements from machine to machine.

"The mystique of the stuff is amazing," said Malik.

"And now we appear rich in it," said Lydia. "Very rich indeed."

"I suppose this is really the beginning," said Malik grandiosely. "We've broken cover."

Lydia grimaced at the analogy, and when she realized Malik had seen the look, she expanded the expression because she did not want to offend him. "I wonder who'll be the first to pick up the scent?"

It was Tom Pike, with his always-win determination. By six o'clock in the evening, New York time, the majority of the offices around him were already dark, closed for the night; from further along the corridor, the whine and burr of the cleaners' machines intruded into the complete quiet of his room. That, too, was predominantly in darkness; only the desk was pooled in light.

Traditional philosophy was that the Russian economy was chaotic, inadequately governed by men constantly forced to change direction by unworkable agricultural collectivization and three- or five- or seven- or ten-year plans strong on Party rhetoric but impractical on application. Certainly the indicators Pike had assembled were confusing. Like trying to understand a picture by lifting the top patterned *matryoshkas* to find under the first wooden doll another just like it and another like that immediately beneath. The gold miscalculation indicated incompetence, although he had to consider fully the Russian announcement that the apparently large amount was an accumulative under estimate over an eight-year period. Averaged out, it meant miscounting by about sixty-nine tons a year. Still considerable, when the product was gold. Pike started doodling, drawing squares within squares, then stopped at a sudden thought. Could it have been intentional, to create the sort of heat that had been generated on the world exchanges and make a foreign currency killing out of their own speculation? Theoretically possible. Undetectable, too, because the buying and selling could have been concealed through nominees. But unlikely, he determined. There had been the announcement from Moscow that it was being committed to reserves. They wouldn't have said that if they were gambling; they'd have let the uncertainty continue. And there would have hardly been sufficient profit, for an exchequer of a country, to justify the exercise.

Simple, faulty accountancy still remained the likeliest explanation. Accountancy that had been improved, to make the discovery possible. Were there any other signs that there had been some economic improvement? Pike pulled the latest figures filed with the Federal Reserve from the American commercial banks, checking every sheet. He went through them, considering what he wanted, making his own calculations, smiling in satisfaction at the result. Every maturing loan and interest payment owed by the Soviet Union had been settled on every due date. Pike got up from his desk and went over to the stiff-backed dossiers which lined one wall, needing a comparison. It took him over an hour to compute it, and again there was a smile of satisfaction at the pattern he saw emerging. From being bad repayers—even to the point of arrogance—there seemed to have been a complete reverse. Debt settlements had been consistently met over the previous six-month period. In some cases, even earlier. Moscow had paid its United Nations contributions in full for the preceding five years, which it had never done before.

What about the Argentinian trade announcement? The file was fairly thick—official government communiques, opinions from financial commentators, and finally the assessment from the Reserve's own Latin American section. All were practically unanimous that the Argentinians had outmaneuvered the Russians, gaining surprising advantages—which went against the thought of there being fresh, more efficient guidances within the Soviet economic hierarchy. Pike once again sought a balance. It was obviously the wheat, the commodity for which the Soviet Union clamored year after year, following the wearying succession of harvest failures. To get wheat, Moscow would be prepared to make concessions. And even if their side of the negotiations seemed questionable, it made sound business sense to diversify the American source, even though the smallness of that supply surprised him.

Pike paused at the reasoning, his thoughts taking a necessary tangent. Wheat exportation to the Soviet Union was important, both politically in Washington and electorally in the overproductive wheat states of the Midwest. At the height of the Reagan administration's attempts to reverse the militarv control in Poland, pressuring Europe with pipeline embargoes and suspending Poland's Favored Nation trade agreement, the suspension of the wheat shipments was never considered. So, did the Argentinian deal represent any danger to America? From the wall of dossiers Pike got more statistics comparing American and Argentinian productions; he was almost immediately reassured. The possible Argentinian capacity represented useful additional supplies. But that's all they were—additional, for replacement was as impossible as it was inconceivable. No problem, then. In fact, decided Pike, for the West there could be positive advantages. If the debtor banks could impose sufficiently stringent controls, the foreign currency Argentina was going to earn under the Russian deal could go towards easing the country's enormous deficiency.

The financial analyst sat back, blinking, as he withdrew from the sudden concentration of light. Outside, the skyscraper lights and neon of Manhattan produced their nightly firework display, glittering rockets in readiness. Eight, Pike saw, from the desk clock. So what had he got from his late night dedication? Facsimile doll on top of facsimile doll, he thought again. There was a pattern, but he had insufficient data with which to recognize it—certainly insufficient data with which to consider any analysis. A memorandum then; an advisory note, going no further than to indicate the possibility of improved financial responsibility from the Soviet Union. Was that too strong, given the evidence available? Not if he stressed that it was only a possibility.

Pike put the material into the drawer for the following day, stretching the cramp from his shoulders. Energetic evening or a quiet one? Loraine had become boring, but the Japanese interpreter at the United Nations was a new novelty, and she'd been keen enough to give him her number at the UN reception a week ago. He tried it, but there was no reply, so he decided she was probably between First Avenue and home. Later, then. If not, then there was always Loraine. He made his way from the office, nodding good night to the cleaners, and with the evening rush hour over he easily got a cab uptown.

Pike had a telephone answering machine. He ran it back and put it on play. The first call was from his father, suggesting a convenient meeting, either lunch or dinner, and asking him to telephone. The other message was from Janet, timed an hour earlier. She was at the Plaza and lonely and would wait until nine for him to return the call. He wondered how many other answering machines the same message was waiting on. Did it matter? They were divorced, quite separate. More importantly, did he want to see her? Not a new question. He'd deliberately avoided calling her after the Washington meeting, unsure whether he wanted to resume the friendship. His mother had asked about Janet every time they spoke on the telephone, increasing his uncertainty. He could wait, long after nine, then leave a message at the hotel that he'd called back and so appear polite. But why? There was no reason why they shouldn't meet. She answered at once, her voice lifting when she realized it was him.

"You win," she said.

"What game?"

"The game of who calls first."

"Busy," he said.

"Liar."

"I intended to."

"Liar again."

"I have now."

"Only because I gave in."

"What's the prize?" The conversations had always been brittle, glass words that could break at any moment.

"Victor's choice."

Why not? Japan could wait until another day—or rather another night. "Dinner?"

"God, you're spontaneous!"

"How long will it take you to get ready?"

"I capitulated, remember? I'm ready now."

He took her to Elaine's, where he was known, and got a table immediately ahead of the patient bar-queuers who read society columns. Woody Allen was eating there and Janet said, "He looks just like he does in the movies."

"How would you expect him to look?"

"Maybe a little less lost."

"That's how he looks in movies."

"Maybe he doesn't like the spaghetti."

"How long are you staying in town?"

"Until Friday. I'm seeing lawyers."

"Oh," said Pike.

"The understanding 'Oh'," she said.

"I couldn't think of anything else."

"Hank wants a divorce. Seems he's been screwing a student for months and now she's pregnant. They all do it, you know—professors screwing students, I mean."

"I've heard," said Pike.

"Hank's fucked it up, of course: literally. But then he does. Usually they're more careful. Hank was always careless, dropping crockery and stuff like that. Maybe that's why I found him more attractive than you and the others. You don't drop things, make mistakes, do you?"

"Not if I can help it," he said.

"You weren't as pompous as that before."

"Sorry."

"Still collecting pubic scalps like a drunken Apache?"

"Did I ever?"

"The most worshipped totem pole in Manhattan, that was the word."

Their meal arrived and Pike ordered a second bottle of wine because Janet had drunk most of the first.

"I'm getting a lot of I-told-you-so's from my mother."

"Mine asks about you whenever I phone," he said.

"Why *don't* you phone?"

Pike shrugged. "I would have."

"Crap!" she said. "Did I make you nervous in Washington?"

"No."

"I don't believe you."

"So don't."

"I don't imagine us getting married again," she said. She looked across the restaurant at the actor. "That's for books and Ali MacGraw movies," she added.

"It's good to know," he said.

"Everyone else thinks it's possible: our parents, that is. I just don't want you to think I'm part of the D-Day assault."

"I didn't."

"Just so you know."

"What are you going to do?" he asked.

"There's always the gallery," she reminded him. "It was fun, before."

He felt suddenly very sorry for her and realized it was not an emotion he'd had about Janet, not even when they were married. She wasn't the sort of person to feel sorry for.

"Know something?" she asked.

"What?"

"My pride's hurt."

Pike frowned. "Your pride!"

"I don't know that I ever loved Hank or that I know what love is. I suppose doing what I did, shocking everyone by having an affair with a schoolteacher and making all those headlines when the divorce happened was me telling my parents—your parents, too, because they were just as involved—to go to hell. It couldn't possibly have worked, and I know that now and know that if it had been me who demanded the divorce and not him, I wouldn't have felt this way. . . ." She stopped, breathless from the rush of words. Recovering, she said, "Want to know something else?"

"What?"

"I wish I hadn't told you that because it makes it sound as if I couldn't have given a damn about you. And that's not true. I didn't think about it at the time, I'll admit, but I did afterwards. I know you didn't love me any more than I loved you, but I felt too much for you to have openly hurt you. . . ." There was another pause. Then she said, "Were you hurt?"

He shrugged, uncomfortable with the soul-baring and not wanting to join in. "I don't know," he said badly. Not wanting to hurt her, he said hurriedly, "Yes, sure I was hurt."

"Thanks . . . for trying to be kind."

"I wasn't."

"Shit."

"We don't like losing," he reminded her. "Neither of us."

"Sometimes it's difficult to play games all the time."

"Woody Allen's just left," he said, wanting to lift her mood.

"Told you he didn't like the spaghetti," she said. She reached across, pressing his hand. "Thanks for being a friend and not being put off by my upfront bullshit."

"That's in the Divorcee Book of Rules as well."

"You going to invite me back to your place?"

"All I've got is booze," he warned.

"I don't think I need even that."

"What would you have done if I hadn't called by nine?"

"Waited until ten."

Like everything else, the announcement of the trade agreement between Poland and the Soviet Union was carefully stage-managed. There were simultaneous declarations in Moscow and Warsaw and then, a week later, an official signing in the Russian capital by the Finance Ministers of both countries. Afterwards there was a banquet, with toasts to renewed friendships.

Vladimir Malik's speech was the most carefully stage-managed of all. The Soviet Union did not seek to dominate its partners but to work with them, one equally dependent upon the other, he declared. Mistakes of the past were recognized and would not be repeated. In a proper Socialist order, workers governed. It was right, therefore, that workers should be properly represented by trades unions with sufficient negotiating influence to rectify problems. The inability to recognize that was one of the mistakes of the past to which he was referring.

After the speech Malik said to Lydia, "Well?"

"Perfect," she said.

10

Tom Pike met his father at the Union Club, a quiet, mahogany-paneled oasis of soft-footed waiters and discreet conversation and more portraits of bewigged and frock-coated founding fathers. After lunch, at his father's suggestion, they took their coffee into the library and submerged themselves shoulder-level in high-backed, armed leather chairs. Pike looked across at his father and thought it was like seeing someone over the gunwhale of some clumsy boat. A canoe, maybe, like the ancients on the wall would have traveled in. He wondered how many had been slave-owners.

His father retained the brandy decanter between them. "We should do this more often," he said predictably.

"I spoke to Mother on the telephone yesterday," said Pike. "She told me you were soon off to Europe."

"Paris, mostly," said the older man. "I'll have to spend some time at the Fund's offices in Geneva, but I don't expect she'll come with me."

"How long will you be away?"

"A month."

The waiter returned with the humidor, but Pike shook his head against a cigar. His father took one, carefully wetting the leaf and then clipping the end. "Thought any more about our conversation in Washington?"

Frequently, thought Pike. He said, "I didn't think there was any hurry."

"There isn't, but I've just said I'm going to be away for a month."

"I'm very happy at the Fed."

"So Volger tells me. I gather you've got some interesting views about all this Russian activity."

Pike looked sharply at his father. The old man smiled and said, "We had lunch yesterday." Conscious of the suspicion, he added, "Long-standing arrangement: fixed up months ago."

"I'm not at all sure it would be a good idea if I did join you," said Pike. It would have had to come sooner or later.

"Why not?"

"Nepotism is the most obvious reason, I would have thought. What sort of respect do you imagine you're going to get from the permanent officials and the other directors if you start out filling spots with your immediate family?"

"I don't give a damn about their respect!" said his father. "I'm the one in control!"

"Whether you give a damn or not is immaterial. The IMF is like a government, a permanent bureaucracy on the top of which is grafted leaders who periodically change. The permanent officials can either work with you or against you. Latent opposition isn't going to help what you've got planned for later, is it?"

"It wouldn't be anything I couldn't handle."

"Why create the difficulty in the first place?"

"Because I want you."

"There are dozens of analysts."

"I explained in Washington why I didn't want anybody else. And Volger told me that your opinion was ahead of anybody else's on this Soviet thing. He's being submerged now, in matching opinions, but yours was the first."

Pike hadn't known that; there was a momentary stir of satisfaction. He put his hand over the bowl, against his father's offer of any more brandy, and said, "Being first isn't the major requirement. The major requirement was being right."

"Being first *and* right is the requirement."

"We don't know yet that I am—that any of us are."

"What about Poland?"

Pike raised and lowered his shoulders uncertainly. "I just don't know what to think about Poland."

"And the speech of Malik, the Finance Minister?"

"Or that, most of all," said Pike. "Admission of errors like that is unprecedented. And certainly on such an occasion."

"The *Wall Street Journal* and the *New York Times* are speculating at a change in Politburo leadership."

"There's always speculation about changes in Politburo leadership," said Pike. "But the *place* was wrong. There's a predictability about a lot of what Russia does. Purges usually begin with unattributed criticism, in *Pravda* or *Izvestia*. Then a name appears. And finally the open criticism. But *not* at a trade signing, where, whatever is conveyed to the contrary, Moscow *does* want to remain in the supremacy. The last thing they'd do is allow admissions of error."

"What if Malik is the one on the way out, already making his apologies?"

Pike shook his head. "Maybe at a Party Congress, and even then unlikely. And the days of Stalin and show trials are over, too."

"Whatever the reason, it's good news for us," said the older man. "It might be premature, but I've actually had bankers tell me they expect to get their money back now—some of them people who only a month or two back were talking of writing off their Polish debts as non-performing assets."

"The trade union promise was the most interesting," said Pike.

His father helped himself to more brandy. "The word in Washington is that the President is prepared to make a gesture if there's a positive indication of some proper type of trade unionism being allowed to operate in Poland again."

"I think it's a forlorn hope, but it would be a useful move, if it can be made politically," said Pike. "It would make it easier for the Poles to resume their suspended trading *and* to carry out the agreement with Moscow. Which will mean more capital and, in theory, greater likelihood of interest and loan repayments."

"Volger said you'd made an interesting point about Soviet loans."

"There was approximately $500,000,000 bunched up in short-term loans and interest payments on some more long-term—exactly the sort of situation in the past where Moscow has sought extensions or delays. This time they settled; to make sure, I checked every commercial bank and they all reported the same. Everything came in on time."

"Maybe the gold helped?" said his father.

Pike shook his head. "Last settlement was two weeks *before* the gold announcement. Certainly Moscow would have known of the underassessment by then, but there was no sudden selling to raise the foreign currency."

"So what's the answer?"

"I wish I knew," said Pike. "I've guessed at a policy change, reflecting more financial rectitude than they've shown in the past, but that really is all it is—a guess."

The older man stubbed out his cigar, repeatedly driving it into the ashtray until it was extinguished. "*I'm* impressed, guess or not."

"I still don't think so," said Pike, anticipating the fresh demands.

"Why not?"

"I've told you why not."

"I don't accept nepotism for anything more than it is—an excuse."

"I don't think it's right for us to work together so closely."

His father frowned across at him. "That isn't even logical."

"I want to be alone!"

"You'd be given every freedom, for God's sake!"

"By you?"

"Who else?"

"Then I wouldn't be alone."

"I don't understand you; you're not making sense. And for an analyst, that's ridiculous."

"Let's just leave things as they are."

"There's no hurry to make your mind up: take all the time you want," said his father, relentlessly.

Oh shit, thought Pike.

Jane Rose realized, objectively, that she was a fraud. She postured about equality—she was embarrassed at the recollection of the evening in Washington, with the American from the Federal Reserve—yet, in her private life, she endured an existence as demeaning as any Victorian housewife. Except that she wasn't even a housewife. Nor ever likely to be, she decided, trying to maintain the objectivity. So why go on? Why jump hopefully every time the telephone rang and accept the empty, boring weekends? Love—if that's what it was, and she wasn't sure—didn't seem enough. Perhaps it was something silly: Freudian. Perhaps, for all her posturing, she wanted to be dominated and humiliated. She felt a burn of anger at the amateur psychology.

Ridiculous, she thought. At once there was the balancing thought, as ridiculous as jumping at telephones and staying in bed alone until midday on Sundays.

"What's the matter?" asked Burnham.

"Nothing."

"You've been miles away all evening."

"Sorry."

"Sure nothing's wrong?"

"Positive."

They'd eaten in a restaurant in Kent because Burnham said it was about to get a golden rose designation in the Michelin guide. The food had certainly been excellent, but Jane knew that wasn't the main reason. A month before, in a restaurant in London, they'd met a couple who knew Marion. Jane had been embarrassed and felt cheapened at his stumbled, awkward attempt at an explanation, a rambling account of her employment at the Bank of England.

"Wish sometimes I was a commodity broker," he said.

"Why?"

"Some friends of mine made a lot of money in the gold scramble."

"Doesn't happen often."

"Enough," he said. "Strange mistake for the Russians to have made."

"There've been one or two strange things lately."

"Like what?" he said, glancing at her across the car.

"Moscow's been paying its debts," she said. "Every one of the Big Four banks have filed returns showing that they've been settling on time."

"What's that mean?"

"No one's sure at the moment." Ahead, Jane saw the lights of a bridge, the Albert she guessed, and realized they would be home soon. "Staying tonight?" Why was it always she who suggested it?

"Not tonight," he said.

"All right." In the beginning he'd averaged two nights out of the seven, sometimes three. It had only been once in the last fortnight.

"Maybe tomorrow."

"All right," she said again. Except that it wasn't. If she were prepared to be a whore, why didn't she do it properly and charge for it?

"And definitely Friday," he said, reaching across and squeezing her hand. "Marion's going down to Winchester, to get Rupert for an exeat; she's going to stay overnight with some friends."

"I'm going away on Friday." She spoke without thought or consideration, uttering the words as they came into her mind. Until that moment she hadn't the slightest intention of going anywhere.

"What!" He looked across the car at her—too long, so that he had to jerk the car away from its drift towards the curb when he looked back.

She hated him for the surprise in his voice that she should actually be thinking of doing something without consulting him. "I'm going to see my sister in Cambridge," she said. "I bought a present for her son, in Washington, and I haven't given it to him yet."

"Why not go on Saturday?"

"It's fixed now."

"Couldn't you unfix it?"

"No," she said. Her hands were tight together in her lap and she had to stare intently in front of her to maintain the determination.

"I see."

"I would have thought you'd go down to collect Rupert as well," she said.

"Now I will," he said tightly.

Damn! He'd made an arrangement to be with her and she'd ruined it! She could still back down, she realized.

"That is, if you're sure you can't rearrange Cambridge," he added, expecting her to.

She was squeezing so tight that her fingers were hurting, and ahead of her the bridge lights, nearer now, blurred as her eyes misted. "I can't," she said. "They've made plans. They're expecting me."

11

Of all the intended Soviet victims, Anatoli Karelin was the most well-known throughout the West, a contemporary of Stalin and for years deferred to as a hard-line Party theoretician, and so he was the first to be purged. It was a traditional attack, because it was important that it should be properly recognized, not only by the public commentators but also by the foreign ministries. There was the initial, unidentified criticism, and then Karelin was named. Predictably, media speculation began in the West about changes in Soviet leadership, leading articles in the *London* and *New York Times,* a commentary in *La Monde* and an actual anticipation in *Bild Zeitung* that Karelin was to be dismissed. He was, in a terse statement on the Tass news agency, where there was a departure from normal. At such an age—he was seventy-eight—it would have been the usual practice to say that Karelin was retiring because of declining health. The announcement made no mention of ill health, a nuance confirming the man's disgrace and continuing the comment in the West, as it was intended. Because Karelin's titular responsibility had been for the country's overall economic planning, his dismissal was tentatively linked with a change in Russia's economic policies.

Boris Medvedev was the next to go. The initial announcements of a poor grain harvest were immediately connected with the Argentinian trade deal, and then there were leading articles in both *Pravda* and *Izvestia* critical of the continued crop failures and of the men responsible for organizing agriculture within the Soviet Union. The replacement of Mikhail Paramov was announced without any preliminary indication, the statement issued on Tass again within an hour of the public naming and sacking of Medvedev. Western commentaries intensified, in magazines and on television and radio broadcasts, with all three men brought together in the conjecture about the reason for the apparent upheaval. The final sacking, that of Arkady Chebotarev from the post of deputy Finance Minister, provided the necessary confirmation that the cause was economic, a natural—and again, intended—conclusion from Karelin being the first to go.

Chebotarev's firing brought Lydia Kirov from the obscurity in which she had worked for ten years. She was named as his successor.

Lydia had known it was going to happen because it had always been part of the planning, but she did not enjoy it. Aware of the journalistic preferences in the West always to personalize coverage, particularly if a woman were involved, a week was set aside for photographs, sessions in which she had to sit under over-hot lights and twist and turn and pose and posture. The reassurance came with the knowledge that it was worthwhile, when the requests were made. Through the overseas embassies the pictures and biographical details were readily available, and the outcome surprising, even to those who knew every detail of the proposal. The West is accustomed to the known figures within the Russian government being aging, fixed-faced men. Here was not only someone of the unprecedented age of thirty-two, but a woman: a full-lipped, dark-eyed woman with auburn hair feathered Western-style around a perfectly oval face. Within days of being identified, she was remembered by

Western bankers with whom she had come into contact during the preceding years, and there were fresh stories of the quality of her clothes and the style of her dress. The *London Daily Mirror* published a full-length picture under the designation "Luscious Lydia." The *New York Post* christened her "Red's Ruble Reckoner."

"Preposterous!" protested Lydia, when she and Malik met to consider the full effect of the government dismissals and her appointment. "Preposterous and infantile!"

Malik was aware of how long she had remained looking at the photographs in some of the Western newspapers and wondered how outraged she really was. "Sometimes personality cults can be useful," he said. "I think everything has worked extremely well."

"They've made me out to be like some Western film starlet, all bosom and no brains . . . a joke."

Her breasts were really most attractive, thought Malik, round and full. "They'll learn about your brains soon enough. And the object wasn't to impress newspaper readers. What next?"

"Czechoslovakia," said Lydia. "Then Hungary. Finally Rumania."

"And the trap snaps shut," said the Finance Minister.

"And then the trap snaps shut," she agreed.

It was a conference specifically convened with one objective, and therefore limited strictly to the people intimately involved. Richard Volger sat at the head of the table as chairman of the Federal Reserve, with his two deputies, Archie Bellow and Raymond Funtle, on either side. Apart from Pike, who had been positioned to the left, James Strange and Peter Snape attended as analysts. Then came the bank's Eastern trade experts, Paul Byrne and Edward Reconzi. As the penthouse room—actually overlooking Wall Street—and the fittings were designed for larger meetings, there was an emptiness about the gathering. Pike thought that their arrangement around the table made them look like the occupants of a once-filled lifeboat gradually disappearing to provide a chance for the remainder, which he recognized as being as inappropriate as it was illogical. He wondered if Janet, with whom he was spending at least three nights a week now, was infecting him with her irreverence. He hadn't meant the relationship to develop as it had.

"Shall we start?" said Volger. He was a red-faced, beetle-browed man whose suits always appeared to be too tight. Around the table there was a gradual quieting, and Volger continued, "We've been asked to provide an opinion for the developments in the Soviet Union. Others have, too, of course: CIA, Treasury, State. I want you to know the spread to understand the importance that Washington is attaching to it. It's got to be right."

"Do we know sufficiently to respond to a request like that?" asked Bellow. He was a thin, crabbed man who, Pike suspected, found difficulty with global economics, preferring calculations he could accommodate on his nine figure pocket calculator.

"We're not required to furnish the definitive opinion, although I'd like ours to be the one that's right," said Volger. "The result of this meeting is to be considered with the views of every other agency."

"Who's going to collate it?" said Pike.

"Treasury, I suppose," said Volger.

"Who'll impose their own view before any others," predicted Funtle, the other deputy director.

"The conclusion is to be returned to us for consideration before being submitted to the White House," assured Volger. "If it is at variance with our opinion, we can dissent in footnotes."

"Can there be anything other than the opinion we've already formed?" asked Snape. The New Englander was the last of the analysts to propose the idea that the Soviet

Union was entering a period of responsible economic planning and felt left behind. He was eager to catch up.

"That's precisely the purpose of this meeting," said Volger unhelpfully.

Anxious to distance himself from the rebuke to the other analyst, Strange said, "I don't see how we can make any sort of intelligent assessment without considering the information and views of CIA, Treasury or State."

"Difficult though it is—and I don't argue that it is a difficulty—we've got to make the judgment upon what we know already," insisted Volger.

"The Argentinian deal could be interpreted to show some sort of increased responsibility," said Byrne, on behalf of the trade department.

"It could also be interpreted as immature negotiation," argued Pike immediately. "And Argentina isn't a new trading partner. Nor is it the first time that Moscow has advanced Argentina generous aid."

"I thought you were the initial proponent of financial responsibility?" demanded Bellow, anxious to get his figures into the right window.

"I advanced it as a *speculation*," qualified Pike. He looked to the other deputy. "I agree with what Strange said. We don't know enough."

"*Why* should the Soviet Union suddenly emerge as the world's lender?" said Funtle.

It was a careless question and Pike knew he wouldn't make himself a friend by the reply. "It isn't a sudden emergence," he said. "The Soviet Union is a creditor nation to a great many countries."

Funtle flushed at his mistake. "Developing countries," he said, making his own qualification.

"For obvious reason," said Snape. "To gain influence through money."

"Which could be the reasoning here."

"The scenario isn't quite right," argued Reconzi. "As Pike said, the association with Argentina isn't new, so there's no reason for attempting increased influence there. And with Poland I would have thought they had sufficient."

"Argentina is a particular case," said Pike. "Russia needs the wheat. I've made a calculation that in addition to the 23,000,000 tons they're getting from us, the Russians will still have a short-fall this year of something like 5,000,000 tons. And that doesn't take into account what they'll want for animal foodstuff."

"What recent information is there about their internal economy?" asked the chairman. It was a question for all the analysts, but he addressed it to Pike. The other two deferred to him, as much for the need to avoid error as to accede to Volger's choice.

'Theoretically, the Soviet Union should be the world's dominant industrial and financial power. They hold fifty-eight per cent of the world's coal deposits, nearly fifty-nine per cent of its oil, forty-one per cent of its iron ore, nearly seventy-seven per cent of the known reserves of apatite, twenty-five per cent of the timber, nearly nine per cent of the recognized deposits of manganese, fifty-four per cent of the potassium salts and one-third of the world's phosphates."

"Good God!" said Bellow.

"The irony is that under capitalist enterprise, it probably would be," continued Pike. "The reality is that mismanagement and improper capitalization has stultified the growth for years. Their agriculture is in a mess, and although they've got all that mineral capacity, the climate creates enormous problems for its development, even if it were properly managed."

"You're giving us traditional thinking and analysis," said Funtle.

Pike hadn't expected the man to respond so quickly to the earlier disagreement. "*Purposely*," he said. "I don't think we can properly assess what's happening now without considering the country's potential or its problems in the past."

The deputy flushed. "What else should be considered?" he demanded.

"Extensive nuclear power at Obnisk, Beloyarsk, Novo-Voronezh, Kursk and Chemobyl," recited Pike. "Oil at Samarska Luka, Tuimazy, Ishimbaev and Perm, as well as at Tyumen, in West Siberia. And the natural gas which has allowed the construction of the pipeline into Europe."

"What about *recent* information?" persisted Funtle, anxious to recover.

"There isn't any—or insufficient, anyway. The apparent gold production mistake gives them a higher reserve than anyone previously calculated, but as a single fact, it's difficult to draw any conclusion apart from its indicating the bad management I spoke about earlier. And we've no accurate, independent estimate of those reserves in any case. They could be lying."

"We haven't talked about the governmental changes," reminded Volger.

"Despite what I think is insufficient evidence for any sort of proper analysis, I've got to agree that indicates a change in their financial outlook," said Pike. "It's the most obvious explanation."

"I don't see that there's any other conclusion," said Snape in agreement.

"I was briefed about the need for this meeting in Washington, on Tuesday," Volger disclosed. "Heard an interesting snippet from Al Herridge, in State. They've spent a lot of time down in Argentina, trying to gauge what's happening. According to the delegation that negotiated the wheat deal in Moscow, Paramov was clearly on his way out, actually replaced as chairperson during negotiations by this woman that all the papers have been devoting so much attention to. They didn't realize then how important she was going to emerge."

"If she was the negotiator, then I don't think she made a very good deal," said Strange.

"Beggars can't be choosers," said Byrne, unembarrassed by the cliché. "If they don't get wheat, they've got famine. What else could she do but concede?"

"So far we're pretty short on conclusions," said Volger.

"I'd like to know the options first," said Funtle.

Pike responded quickly, "I don't think there are a lot. To me it seems a choice of two extremes. The government changes could be another shakeup like dozens that have occurred before—because of the continued failure of the Russian economy and the absolute leadership changes since Brezhnev's death—and all the other things could be coincidental, with no connection. The alternative is that there *is* a connection between it all—that the people have been fired because of proven incompetence and that at last there's some sort of guidance being attempted."

"So what's the majority opinion?" demanded Volger.

There was initially silence in the room. Then Pike said, "I'd like to repeat the remarks I made earlier: that I don't think we've sufficient evidence to make a judgment. But from what's available, I'd gamble on the financial control, after all these years. . . ." He paused, and before anyone else could speak, added, "But I'll stress the word I used. It's a guess."

"I agree," said Strange, at once.

"So do I," said Snape.

"Unanimity from the analysts," said Volger.

"With the understood provisos," insisted Pike.

Volger looked to the trade representatives. There was a hesitation, and then Byrne said, "There's a lot of coincidence, I agree—maybe too much. But things as apparently connected and yet, with the benefit of time, emerging as being quite separate have happened too many times in the Soviet Union for me to come out with any positive conclusion. And if you force me to make one, then I'll dissent. I think all we're seeing is the usual Soviet confusion, not sudden responsibility."

Everyone looked to Reconzi. There was matching hesitation from the second trade assessor, and then Reconzi said,

"As Paul pointed out, perhaps there's too much coincidence. I know there have been foul-ups in the past, in our guessing, but this time I'm going for financial control."

Volger went to Funtle. The deputy said cautiously, "We finally get a chance to consider the overall conclusion—the views of the other agencies?"

"Yes," said Volger shortly, irritated by the other man's reluctance.

"I don't think we've got enough," said Funtle.

"Everyone realizes that," said Volger, with strained patience.

"Responsibility," Funtle said quickly. Just as quickly, he added, "But with the right to reconsider, if more evidence becomes available."

Volger turned to his other deputy.

"I disagree," said Bellow. "I know all the indicators and take all the points, but I can't go along with such an abrupt change after so long and after so many failures. I don't think anything is going to change."

Volger looked down at the notes he had been making during the casual voting. "The majority is for responsible planning," he said. He looked around the table. "Anyone want to make any further points?"

From the assembled men there were vague movements and head-shaking. Talking again generally but looking once more directly at Pike, the chairman of the Federal Reserve said, "In which case I'll forward to Washington the initial view that financially within the Soviet Union we are being confronted with a dramatic change in their economic strategy."

"Let's hope it's not too dramatic, if it's happening at all," said Bellow, the doubter. "Those resource figures are terrifying; properly utilized, the Soviets could bring us to our knees."

"Tom made the point that they're not being properly utilized," reminded Volger.

"And we've just concluded, by majority vote, that there's been a dramatic change in the economic thinking of the Soviet Union," said Bellow.

The summons came an hour after the end of the formal meeting. When Pike entered the chairman's office directly above the conference room and with an even better view of Manhattan's skyscraper forest, he saw that Volger was alone.

"You weren't backtracking, at the meeting?" demanded Volger at once.

"No, sir. Trying to be objective."

The Federal Reserve chairman nodded. "Seen your father recently?"

"He's in Europe."

"We've had one or two conversations about you."

"I know."

"Feel like joining him?"

"I'm happy here."

"Your position would remain safe."

"I'm still trying to make up my mind." Pike supposed he should have anticipated the pressure extending from his father to include this other man.

"The Bank of International Settlements is meeting in Basel at the end of next week," said Volger. "I'd like you to go over, as an observer for us. I want to keep a tight rein on this Russian development; it'll be an ideal opportunity to check out what all the European central bankers are thinking."

"I'd like that," said Pike. It would be good to get away from the newly established regime of weekends at either South Hampton or Washington, with New York in the middle during the week—and from the settled involvement with Janet.

"Not just Switzerland," said Volger. "Make a proper

trip out of it. I'll fix introductions for you in Paris, Bonn and London. I want to run this thing down properly."

Volger saw the Washington request as some sort of challenge and wanted to win the prize, Pike realized. He wondered if he'd get the chance in London to see the girl he'd met in Washington. Momentarily he frowned, unable to remember her name. Rose, yes: Jane Rose.

Misunderstanding the doubtful expression on Pike's face, Volger said, "No reason why you can't go, is there?"

"No, none at all."

"When could you leave?"

Pike hesitated briefly. "Virtually right away," he said.

"I'll start setting up the meetings today."

"Thank you for the opportunity."

"You've earned it, Tom."

He *had*, decided Pike. He'd been the first within the bank to recognize the possibility of something unusual emerging from the Russian system, so the Swiss trip was rightfully his. The other analysts would see it as the benefit of influence and the right name. And not just the analysts.

"It's a frightening thought, isn't it?" said Pike, remembering Bellow's remark. "That if the Soviets were properly managed and capitalized, they could sink us."

"Frightening," agreed Volger. "Long live Soviet inefficiency."

At first Jane had been cautious against any accidental encounter, ensuring that their contact had only been official, with other people around, but as the time passed, she stopped bothering. She was practically up to the pink-uniformed attendants at the exit from the bank before she saw him and knew that he'd used the pillars for concealment.

"Hello," said Burnham.

"Hello, Paul."

"How are you?"

"Fine. You?"

"Fine."

She was aware other people were looking at them, standing there, and was surprised Burnham had made the meeting so public. Before, he had been the person who had worried.

"How's Marion?" she said.

He frowned. "Very well, thank you."

"And Rupert?"

"You don't have to, you know."

"I wasn't trying to be awkward."

"I'd like to see you again," he said.

"Why?"

"I'd have thought that was obvious."

"Maybe it is."

"Can't we have a drink, to talk about it? A meal, maybe?"

Jane paused, fighting the temptation. "I don't think so, Paul." Fool, she thought: stupid, bloody fool.

12

After the morning service there was coffee in the vicarage. Jane took the offered cup, refused a biscuit from a woman she knew to be the president of the Women's Institute but whose name she had forgotten, and stood at the edge of the room, looking around her. Comfortable, settled people with comfortable, settled lives, she thought. Lucky people.

"You seem to be becoming a regular visitor."

Jane turned, to see the nervous curate who'd been introduced into the parish at the service three weeks earlier. She'd forgotten his name, too. He looked extremely young.

"Yes," she said. "I do, don't I?" This would have been her fifth weekend with Ann since the break-up. The weeks were all right because she could immerse herself in work, but she couldn't stand Saturdays and Sundays—particularly Sundays. But she was going to have to, she knew: Ann and Henry had been very understanding, but it couldn't go on forever.

"Your sister tells me you're something terribly important in London."

The curate had a curious way of talking, mouthing each word as if he were tasting it. She supposed it probably had something to do with teaching Sunday school, ensuring that everything he said was understood. "I work in the City," she agreed. "The Bank of England."

"All that money!"

Jane laughed. "I don't actually see it. It's just numbers on paper."

"Fascinating," he said. "You must think us all very dull and parochial here in the country."

"Actually, I was thinking how nice it must be."

The man looked at her doubtfully as if he suspected her of mocking him. Apparently deciding she was not, he said: "Nice, but still rather dull. Highlight of this week is the election of officers for the Mother's Union. Not quite the same as keeping the country financially safe."

She laughed with him, appreciating the effort he was making. "I'll do what I can for you." If I get the chance, she thought. It was almost a month since she'd appeared before the review board; she should be hearing soon. She didn't think she'd made a good impression—not as good as she had wanted to, anyway. A bad performance shouldn't matter overly much. Review boards were a formality. The decision should be based upon her record, and she knew that upon her record she should get the promotion. Unless Paul interceded and stopped it. She'd had the doubt before, although she couldn't remember when. She remembered the conclusion, though: that he wouldn't.

"Are we going to see you in church next week?"

Jane hesitated uncertainly and then said, "I don't know." Maybe next week she'd stay in London. She'd thought the same thing about this weekend, she remembered.

"I hope so," he said. He looked across the room and said, "Excuse me, the vicar's making help-me gestures."

Her sister passed the curate as he crossed the room. "Seducing Mr. Privett?" asked Ann.

"What?"

"Our new curate."

Jane smiled after the man. "I don't think so," she said. "He was being very sweet, trying to make me feel at home."

"We enjoy having you here."

Jane looked directly at her sister but didn't respond. Instead, she said, "Where's Harry?"

"He and Edward have gone to fly your kite. Edward reckons you're the best auntie anyone can have; no one in the school has got a kite as elaborate as his." She looked around the emptying room. "Let's go and see about lunch."

Autumn tinged the countryside with reds and yellows and browns, and the wind, always seeming colder across the flatness of Cambridgeshire than it did in London, plucked at them as they went out into the lane. Jane shivered, pulling her jacket around her. Ann was far more sensibly dressed than she was, in boots and a sheepskin coat. Without looking at her sister, she said, "Thank you."

"What for?"

"Letting me hide here with you every weekend."

"Is that what you're doing—hiding?"

Jane shrugged. "I don't know."

"Do you want to talk about it?"

Ann had been very patient, never asking. "Nothing much to talk about," said Jane. "Soap opera, really. Supposedly hard-headed career girl becomes infatuated with married man; makes an idiot of herself; romance ends; utter misery."

A flock of birds, frightened by something, suddenly burst into the air from the bordering field, whirling about in panic. Only Jane jumped.

Ann said, "Sounds like too much bitterness for it to be just infatuation."

"I was crazy about him," conceded Jane.

"*Was*?"

"He's tried to start it again. I've said no."

"Why?"

"That's the silly part: I don't know." She hesitated and then said, "Yes, I do. I don't want it to be like it was before."

"What was that?"

"Just bed, as far as he was concerned." Jane felt herself blushing at the confession. Even bed hadn't been that good towards the end.

"Sure?"

Jane nodded, going first through the sidegate that her sister held open for her, a short cut from the main drive into the rambling Tudor farmhouse. Inside, Ann said, with attempted lightness, "A drink, to deaden the pain? Harry's got a new shipper since he's become master of the hunt—wants to impress people, I suppose. Sherry's excellent: Jerez."

Jane nodded, accepting the glass.

"What are you going to do?"

"Stop bothering you every weekend, to start with."

"You're not a bother."

"It's got to stop though, hasn't it?"

"Not as far as we're concerned; we like having you, really."

"Thank you," said Jane.

"And now I'll just go and check with cook," Ann said.

Glass in hand, Jane wandered to the diamond-leaded windows, staring out over the rolling lawns and the acreage beyond. Ann was lucky. She might complain of the burden of being the squire's wife, dinners and cocktail parties to give and to attend, but Jane didn't think she minded, not really. The most settled, comfortable life of all: riding to hounds twice a week, personally shot pheasant for Sunday lunch and deference from the vicar after church. She heard her sister return but didn't bother to turn back into the room.

"Hope the pheasant's haven't hung too long."

"I'm sure they'll be fine," said Jane.

Ann came alongside, gazing out into the garden.

"It's very pretty," Jane said softly.

"Takes a fortune to keep up," said Ann. "Church fête

next week; it'll take the gardeners weeks to get the heel marks out of the lawns. We expect you to be here.''

''You're making it very easy for me,'' said Jane gratefully.

They were quiet for a long time, and then Ann said, ''Want to know something?''

''What?''

''Sometimes I'm jealous of you.'' She frowned at her own remark. ''Not sometimes. A lot of times. A lot of times I think of what life must be like for you in London and I'm jealous of you.''

Jane laughed, genuinely. ''*You* want to know something?''

''What?''

''I was standing here, feeling sorry for myself, envying you!''

They both laughed.

''I'd swap with you any time,'' said Jane.

''I don't believe you. You might think so, but if you actually had to make the decision, I don't believe you would.''

''I'm not so sure.''

''Is it important to you, the work you do?'' asked Ann. She gestured towards the sherry, but her sister shook her head.

''It's become so, lately,'' said Jane. ''It's the lifeboat.''

''I always thought it was,'' said her sister. She stopped for a moment and said, ''Daddy was always so very proud of you. He was proud of me, too, I suppose. Done well by myself, he said: never seen a farmer on a bicycle. But you were the one that made it all worthwhile for him—all the sacrifices.''

Jane turned away from the view. ''Poor Daddy,'' she said. ''Mummy, too. I wish they hadn't done it.'' She sipped her drink and said, ''And yes, work has always been important to me. The break with Paul hasn't really altered anything.''

"Don't let it become too important, will you?" said Ann.

"What's that mean?"

"Career girls are envied when they're thirty and glamorous. And pitied when they're fifty-five and soured spinsters." Ann laughed nervously, at once apologetic. "Sorry," she said. "That was Agatha's Agony column philosophy."

"Appropriate, though." Jane moved the glass between her fingers and said, "I don't want to end up a soured spinster."

"He must have been a hell of a man, to leave you as depressed as this."

"That's the stupid part," said Jane. "He really wasn't. Really, he was a shit."

"They're usually the ones it happens with." She smiled again. "I *should* be writing a column, shouldn't I?"

"And I should start growing up."

Jane regarded Edward Parker as a traditionalist upon the Court—the governing board—of the bank, one of the directors who saw no place for women above a secretarial level. As a senior director, he had an office overlooking the Mansion House and the statue of a horse-borne Duke of Wellington. Double glazing cut out any sound, so that the traffic swarmed noiselessly outside in unreal, silent procession. He stood to greet her as she entered the room—a dried-out, aloof man; there was a residue of white powder on the lapels of his regulation black jacket, from where he talcumed his face after shaving. He remained standing until she seated herself in the chair he indicated, then lowered himself behind the desk. It was dark wood and large and intricately carved and there was a smell of polish. She thought it was better than Paul's office, to which she no longer went.

"I have to offer you congratulations," said the man at once. "Your appearance before the review panel was successful. They were particularly impressed with your exposition of the Soviet situation. . . ." He paused, smiling mechanically, just drawing his lips back from his teeth. "It goes against the general feeling in the bank and they were impressed with the strength of your argument, even though you realized it was a minority opinion."

Despite her conviction that she deserved the promotion, Jane had prepared herself for rejection again and the announcement momentarily surprised her. Recovering, she said "Thank you, sir."

"You're entering a level of very great responsibility."

"I appreciate that," she said.

"But one for which we feel you've adequately proved yourself capable of occupying."

"Thank you," she said again, because there wasn't anything else.

"I would like to offer you my personal congratulations. I think you are a valuable asset to the bank."

"You're very kind."

"It will involve a commitment that might intrude into your personal life."

"I recognize that," she said. Without a personal life, there wouldn't be much to commit.

"And are prepared for it to happen?"

"Quite prepared," assured Jane.

"I'm delighted to hear it," Parker said.

Soured spinster, she thought.

It wasn't until she returned to her own office and sat, head bent at her desk, that Jane fully appreciated what the promotion meant. She'd have staff now, practically a division of her own. The euphoria spread through her, a physical feeling of warmth. She wanted to tell somebody, to boast. But there wasn't anybody, she realized. Only Ann. And Ann did parochial committee work most afternoons; she'd call her tonight, from the apartment.

Jane wished there were somebody else. She supposed she *could* telephone Paul. The promotion was reason enough. And there was no reason why he should imagine she'd changed her mind since last time. If he asked, she'd refuse again. Or would she? She was reaching out towards the telephone when it rang, actually startling her.

"Sorry to call you during office time, but I didn't have any other number," said a voice.

"Who is this?"

"Tom Pike."

"I'm sorry?"

"Washington, remember? I bought dinner and you lectured on equality."

"Hello," she said, recalling him now.

"I'm on a trip," he said. "Thought I'd say hello."

"London?" she said, frowning at the echoing line.

"Paris at the moment, then Germany. I get to England at the end of the week." He paused and said, "I wondered if there was a chance of my seeing you again."

"The end of the week?" she said.

"I'm due in on Friday," he said.

And after Friday came Saturday and after Saturday came Sunday, she thought.

When she didn't respond at once, Pike said, "Can I call, when I get in?"

"Yes," she said. "Why don't you call?"

13

The immediate period after her confirmation within the Soviet Finance Ministry was the busiest Lydia could remember. In the first month she spent only two nights in her Moscow apartment; the remainder of the time she traveled. She headed a delegation first to Prague, for the trade and finance talks, leaving behind a negotiating group when the outline agreement was reached and going directly from Czechoslovakia to Hungary. The conferences in Budapest took longer because of the stronger Hungarian financial position, but after a week she got almost all the provisional terms she wanted. She left a second team of officials in the Hungarian capital and flew to Bucharest. The Rumanian discussions were the easiest of the three because of their financial desperation. She stressed the advantages of strengthening their financial dependence upon the Soviet Union, citing the action of the International Monetary Fund in putting them into suspension over their $13,000,000,000 international debt and, as she had with Argentina, offered oil and, in addition, directly cabled electricity to ease the country's energy demands without any drain upon foreign reserves. From Bucharest she began the cycle all over again, returning to Prague to check and confirm the final details. It proved to be a wise precaution when she returned to Budapest because she discovered the Hungarians had attempted to include some of their existing debts into the sum they were negotiating for additional uncommitted aid, which necessitated another week's renegotiations to return to the original Soviet proposals. The Rumanians, she found, had complied with every term with which she had left them after the initial sessions, so there was only need to remain in Bucharest for two days.

Lydia traveled in an Aeroflöt aircraft, assigned specifically for her convenience, with officials responsible for making all arrangements and appointments for her, but she still ached with fatigue when she arrived back in Moscow. The chauffeured Zil was at the aircraft steps when she landed at Sheremetyevo, and as she drove into the Soviet capital, Lydia idly pushed back the rear curtains to look out at the straggled pines lining the roadway. There was a scattering of early snow, the first dust of winter; the landscape was flat and gray and the sky leaden, threatening more. She shivered, despite the warmth of the car. She had never been to Siberia or to that part of Russia beyond the Arctic Circle, the places of permanent snow and subzero temperatures. Nor did she want to. Yet, in those regions, were most of the minerals and the deposits with which she had been bargaining across comfortable conference tables in warm, centrally heated rooms. She thought how terrible it must be to have to work where the tundra was permanently frozen, rock-hard, where metal was so cold that the flesh stuck to it and tore off and the oil froze so that machinery had to be lubricated with graphite.

The reflection made her angry at herself. What right had she to feel as resentful and as unsettled as she did, at something she couldn't even identify to her own complete satisfaction? She had as many concessions and approved comforts as any Western financier or capitalist—more, in some cases. And prestige now, since her official appointment. Was the lack of someone to share it with the cause of her uncertainty? If it was, then it was an immature attitude. She had known the commitment she was making, how total her involvement would have to be, from the first weeks of making her proposal and of the reaction to it all those years ago. To get precisely what she had now, a luxury apartment and chauffeured cars and personal aircraft and secretaries and officials to react to every request, she had knowingly and consciously abandoned any thoughts of private life. She was an elite in the country in which there was supposed to be no elitism. So she had achieved her ambition. Perhaps, when it was over and she had fully succeeded, she would be able to fill in the social gaps and become completely happy.

The apartment of which recently she had seen so little was as pristine and orderly as always. She dumped her cases in the bedroom, for the maid to unpack the following day, then brewed some tea and sat bent at the kitchen table, drinking it. The tiredness surprised her, because she hadn't anticipated it. How much was real fatigue, and how much tension, the nervousness that one link in her carefully fashioned chain might slip from the position in which she wanted it to be? Quite a lot, she conceded. And so far unjustified. So far the pieces had fitted into shape like the simplest of children's puzzles. Maybe she could afford to relax a little. She hoped so. The hardest part was yet to come. It was too early to become exhausted.

She bathed in order to try to ease the physical ache from her body, got gratefully into bed and, after an hour, decided that overtiredness was keeping proper sleep from her. A lie, she thought. Not overtiredness. She slipped her hand down, a practised movement, luxuriating in her own familiar touch, but wishing it were someone else's. Why hadn't he responded to her invitation? She'd been clear enough, surely! She made it last, unhurriedly prolonging the final warmth of relief. Afterwards she drifted into a half-consciousness, neither fully awake nor fully asleep, recognizing the dreams as dreams, knowing she could wake up when she wanted to. They came to her as disjointed pictures, like rippling rapidly through a selection of photographs in a book. There were a lot of rooms, all crowded with men who were not dressed like Russians. They were shouting at her and then began to chase her, and she could feel the breath tightening in her chest, even though she knew it was a dream and there wasn't any need to run. She kept looking behind her and she saw that one of the pursuers was Paramov and he wasn't dressed like the rest; he was quilted in protective clothing, with a fur-lined hood, the sort of dress she imagined people wore in the frigid north.

There were hands snatching at her, at her dress, and she felt her clothes being pulled from her as she ran. She shouted for help and saw Malik in one of the rooms. Then she realized it was the last, which meant she couldn't run any more.

She was pleading with Malik to help, but he just stood against the wall, smiling at what was happening to her. They were stripping her, lots of men whose faces she couldn't see, plucking her clothing away. She tried to cover her nakedness, clutching a hand between her legs again and putting her arm across her breasts, but she recognized that she wasn't in any sexual danger. They were laughing at her, not molesting her, and one by one they turned and walked away, leaving her untouched but feeling violated. The last to go was Malik, still smiling.

Lydia forced herself awake at last, conscious as she did so that her hand was actually between her legs. She got out of bed and put on a robe and went to the window, staring out over the sleeping capital.

"We should show life neither as it is nor as it ought to be, but as we see it in our dreams," she quoted to herself.

It was easy to understand Chekhov's play and what he meant by those words. But what did her dreams mean? Nothing, she decided irritably: certainly nothing about which she ought to feel ashamed. She was sure other women felt like she did and as often as she did.

She went back to bed finally, willing sleep to come. When it did, it was as fitful as before, so she finally awoke unrested and the tiredness remained with her when she reached the Kremlin complex.

The meeting was arranged for ten, but Malik entered her office fifteen minutes early. She rose to meet him, accepting the customary impersonal embrace. But was it impersonal? Fleetingly, she imagined he had held her slightly longer than usual. She hurried the thought away, as a mother might jostle aside an awkward child. She had presented the opportunity and he had ignored it.

"Welcome back, Comrade Kirov."

"It's good to be back."

"You look tired."

"It's been a strenuous tour."

"But successful," said the Finance Minister. "I've studied the progress reports; you've achieved everything, as always."

"The Hungarians were difficult."

"But you got what you wanted—what we all wanted."

"Yes," she agreed.

Malik sat easily in the chair opposite her desk, crossing his legs and carefully lighting the tubed Russian cigarette he seemed to enjoy. "There were developments here, while you were traveling."

"Like what?"

"A special subcommittee has been formed, by the Politburo, to consider every aspect of what's happening." Seeing the look upon her face, Malik said, "That is no reflection upon you. Or me, for that matter. You must accept their feeling about control for something as important as this."

"I suppose so," said Lydia reluctantly. "What does it mean?"

Malik shrugged, smiling. "Bureaucracy, like these things

always mean,'' he said. ''Meetings, at which we'll both have to report.''

''What about this trip?''

''Convened for two o'clock this afternoon.''

''That doesn't give me time to prepare a report!''

''I assured them you didn't need time, that you could make a verbal presentation and that they would be fully briefed.''

''That was confident of you!''

''You don't need any proof of the confidence I have in you, Comrade Kirov.''

Lydia thought there was almost a mockery in the way he insisted upon the formal address to her. But a friendly, almost intimate mockery. ''What else has happened?''

''All our international loans were met on the due date,'' said Malik. ''In addition, we advanced payment on $35,000,000, not due until three months to European consortia. I decided it would be good cosmetics for the Bank of International Settlement meeting that's starting in Basel. We're obviously going to be the prime subject of discussion.''

''That was clever,'' agreed Lydia. ''What about the wheat?''

''We asked for and got 8,000,000 tons from America in addition to the existing agreements. And 2,000,000 from Argentina. We picked up small amounts from Australia and Canada.''

''So what's our storage figure at the moment?''

''A total of 35,000,000 tons: only eight silos still empty.''

''The American satellite reconnaissance worries me,'' conceded Lydia. ''The photographs will show that our harvest isn't as bad as we've complained it was.''

''I've anticipated that,'' said Malik.

''How?''

''Medvedev is going to be officially charged with falsifying agricultural returns. It will serve two purposes. It will satisfy any doubt in the American minds about the disparity in the figures, and it will provide the reason for his being purged. It makes the need for a lot of the additional grain unnecessary, of course. But we're going to prove ourselves responsible businessmen and honor a signed agreement."

"That's good," said Lydia, genuinely impressed. "That's *very* good."

Malik smiled, pleased at the praise. "With our sharing agreement, the Western banks are falling over themselves to advance more money to Argentina to tool up and construct warehouses for our wheat deal."

"How much?"

"The latest figures for the additional loans were $350,000,000."

"Short or long-term?" asked Lydia at once.

Malik smiled. "Very short!" he said. "A third three months, the remainder six."

"What about Poland?"

"Almost a mirror image. With our declared backing, Poland is suddenly acceptable again. There are three European consortia and two from the United States. Total amount runs to $450,000,000 and there have been further rescheduling agreements on $150,000,000."

"I'd estimated more," admitted Lydia.

"It's enough," said the Soviet Finance Minister. "What will the figures be for the rest?"

"They're estimates, you understand?" said Lydia cautiously.

"Naturally."

"I would expect that with the expansion necessary because of the trade agreements with Czechoslovakia they'll get $500,000,000 from the West—maybe a little higher, as much as $700,000,000. Hungary has a good financial record anyway, even before our support. I calculate $1,500,000,000. Rumania is classic chicken-and-egg. With the need to recover what they've already got invested, I'd say the advance there could be as high as $1,000,000,000."

"Which leaves us," said Malik.

"With the agreed pledges to the Bloc, with the wheat and with the trade deals we've negotiated with the West since this whole operation properly began eight years ago, I would calculate the need to raise through Western banks loans of $600,000,000,000."

"Wouldn't it be wonderful to make the bait short-term?"

"Wonderful but impractical," said Lydia, business-like. "I think we should seek $200,000,000,000 short-term, which should be bait enough. The rest long."

"I was joking," emphasized Malik. "Don't you think $200,000,000,000 is too high short-term? I don't want to choke the fish."

It was time to defer, Lydia recognized, politically. "What figure would you consider right?"

"One hundred and fifty billion," suggested Malik. "And allow ourselves to be negotiated into $200,000,000,000. It must always appear to be going their way."

It was a good economic argument, Lydia realized. "I agree," she said at once.

"What's the computation?" asked Malik.

"Slightly short of $604,000,000,000," said Lydia, the figure already prepared.

"In addition to the $29,000,000,000 owed by Poland and the $13,000,000,000 by Rumania?"

"Argentina's $40,000,000,000 will be linked as well," reminded Lydia. "With some minor debts held by the Czechs and ourselves."

"So what's the overall figure?"

"Something only a computer could accept," said the woman. "With existing world debt it would be over $1,000,000,000,000."

Malik let his breath out with a whistle, a threatrical gesture. "This afternoon's committee won't be able to comprehend it," he forecast. "They'll ask for a written report and pass an interim vote of confidence in your outstanding ability."

Which was exactly what happened. Afterwards Malik said, "I thought we might celebrate."

"Celebrate what?" said Lydia, momentarily careless.

"The success so far."

"That would be nice," she said hesitantly. *At last!*

Dining out in Moscow is a frustrating experience, a three or four hour agony of unregistered table reservations and wrongly recorded orders that take an interminable time to be served—and are cold when they should be hot—by truculent, unwilling waiters. Except for the elite. It was a privilege that Lydia had not properly explored and she was impressed, as Malik hoped she would be.

He took her to the Russkiy Zal restaurant, at the National Hotel, but not to the main, crowded chamber. They ate instead in a tiny room furnished, despite its smallness, with heavily flocked, crimson wallpaper and heavy furniture. In space sufficient for just two voluminous chairs, they sat in awkward, unfamiliar familiarity for aperitifs at a miniscule table with two place settings, a fresh flower centerpiece and crisp, rigidly starched napkins. There had been Russian champagne in the easy chairs and pale red Georgian wine at the table.

Just as he ordered the wine without reference to her, Malik selected the meal as well. He avoided caviar, even Beluga, for which she was grateful because she didn't like it. Instead they started with fillets of some white fish she couldn't identify, with dill pickle and beet and afterwards wild boar, for which there was a heavier red wine. They were attended by three waiters, who came immediately when Malik summoned them by bell and left the room the moment their function was over.

"There's a name for places like this," he said. "*Salon particulaire*."

"I know," said Lydia. She added hurriedly, "From books: I didn't know they existed here."

He laughed. "In Paris every year the Prix Goncourt, the literary prize, is presented at a restaurant at which the mirror of the *salon particulaire* above the main restaurant is decorated around its edge with the initials of the lady visitors, inscribed into the reflected glass with the diamonds they were given for their favors."

Lydia knew that, too, but didn't want to spoil his attempt at worldliness. Instead, she said, "I think that's beautiful."

"I'm glad," he said.

"About what?"

"That you think it's beautiful. And were brave enough to say so, without imagining this place full of listening devices and cameras."

"Is it!" said Lydia, at once concerned.

Again he laughed at her. "No" he said. "Of course not: that's from books, too."

"Can you be sure?"

"No."

"You're mocking me," she protested. "Why are you mocking me?"

"I'm not mocking you," he said. "I'm just trying to make you less serious."

"How can I be less serious!"

"Just by being less serious," he said unhelpfully.

"You're making me uncomfortable, instead."

"Why?"

"Because you are." Lydia was enjoying the flirtation, hoping it wasn't going to end as just that. Away from the official surroundings, Malik was relaxed and easy. What was his body like under that discreet gray suit? she wondered.

"I don't mock you," he insisted.

"It seems you do, sometimes."

"I'm surprised."

"About what?"

"Inferiority, in someone like you."

She flared at the accusation. "I am *not* inferior!"

"I didn't say you were."

"Of course you did."

"I said you felt an inferiority and that I was surprised at it."

She thought of running through an endless procession of rooms and of Malik laughing at her, and she wished she were better able to defend herself in situations like this. It was a bizarre irony—almost an obscene one—that she could confront international financiers across a negotiating table and match their every argument, and yet, in the very social situation she had wanted so desperately, she had no awareness of the words to use or the attitudes to adopt. "I don't have an inferiority complex."

"Good," he said, pleased at the affect he was having upon her.

"Why good?"

"It would be a disaster for all that we've planned if you did have one, wouldn't it?"

"Damn you, Vladimir Malik! Damn you in hell!"

"I hope there *aren't* recording devices," he said. "Hell opposes Heaven and we don't believe in either; we just believe in the man."

"There aren't . . .?" she started again, stopping herself abruptly, knowing that she had run into another blocked room.

He reached across for her hand. "Don't be frightened," he said. "Of anyone I know, you've least cause to be frightened. Or to feel inferior. Or to be uncertain. Believe in yourself."

"I'm confused. I don't know how to feel."

"Why not be yourself?"

There was a part of herself that Lydia was frightened to recognize—frightened, even, to admit. She'd subjugated the need, as she had her social life, for her financial scheme, but increasingly the financial scheme wasn't enough. God, how she hated her financial scheme! The check came at once; she couldn't invoke God because, as he'd just said, she didn't believe in Him. Any more than she could hate her financial scheme. It had given her everything she had ever craved and wanted. Except what she craved and wanted more than anything and which ambition couldn't dominate anymore.

"I didn't think it was going to be like this," she said.

"Like what?"

"I feel like you're chasing me, and every time I find a place to hide, you discover it." Fuck the dream, she thought. Fuck it, fuck it, fuck it!

"Don't hide from me," said the man.

"That's another corner."

"I know."

"Stop being such a shit."

"What do you think of the boar?"

"Shit!"

"Good," he said.

"What the hell's good?"

"Good is you saying shit and actually getting angry and not behaving like one of those stupid computers."

"I'm not a computer! I'm a woman!"

"You disguise it well."

She felt the accusation like a knife going deep into her, so sharp she could feel the pain. "You *are* mocking me," she said. She stopped and then said, "All right, mocking isn't the right word. Taking advantage of me; playing with me. Everything I say is wrong, so you can turn it against me."

"Inferiority!"

"Stop it!"

"Why?"

"It isn't fair!"

"I don't want to be fair."

"You're doing it again."

"I'll do it as long as I think it's necessary."

"That's patronizing!"

"Be a woman, Lydia Fedorovna."

She started to cry then, helplessly at first, like a child suddenly lost. And then like she *was* lost hopelessly and sobbing. "Bastard!" she said. "Bastard!"

Malik lived, as Lydia did, in the Kutuzovsky complex, so there was no embarrassment about entry. He looked in frank admiration at her apartment and said, "I have never seen anything like it!" And she was pleased, wanting to impress him, as he had wanted to impress her at the restaurant.

She undressed in the bathroom, nervous now that it was finally about to happen. Malik kept the side lamps on and she was glad he did because she'd explored her own body so many times and knew it was good.

"You're beautiful," he said thickly.

"Let me see you," she said.

"Why?"

"It's going to be part of me: I want to see."

He pulled the bedclothes away and she felt the excitement blaze through her. Instinctively she bent to kiss him and he moaned at the movement.

"Now me," he said.

"Not yet."

"When?"

"Not yet." How would he react, when he discovered?

"This is wonderful," he said.

It was for her, too: more wonderful than she'd imagined, in all the fantasies.

"Let me," he said.

"Yes," she said.

His mouth was soft yet properly hard, and she held him, wanting to feel him there, to keep him there, too, because she didn't want any of this to end.

He stayed obedient for a long time, and then he said, "I want to make love to you."

"Don't hurt me," she said.

"I won't, I promise I won't."

14

The uncertainties remained instead of being resolved—indeed, about the government changes, they'd worsened—and Pike felt frustrated. Which he recognized to be a wrong and even ridiculous attitude—certainly not one fitting for a supposedly objective analyst. But still one he couldn't avoid. A lot of the feeling was personal annoyance at what he now recognized to have been the totally unfounded optimism with which he'd arrived in France. It hadn't taken long for the optimism to falter, during the two days of talks with French Finance Ministry officials. It was Pike's first experience of Gallic insularity and he was bemused by it. And worried, too. From the discussions it was quite clear that the French had attempted no detailed analysis to link all the factors that appeared important in Washington and New York. In fact, towards the end of the second day, when he tried to argue the possible connection between the ministerial replacements in Moscow and the Argentinian and Polish agreements, balanced by the Soviet debt repayments, Pike had found himself being listened to with patronizing tolerance and almost complete disinterest.

That hadn't been the attitude in Bonn, but there still hadn't been the answers Pike wanted. The Bundesbank officials with whom he talked offered the additional information that the German clearing banks reported prompt—and in some cases, premature—settlement of debts and interest, both from the Soviet Union and Poland, but they refused to agree with him that it was further confirmation of improved financial thinking in Moscow. Nor would they accept the government changes with the other indicators which Pike considered important. They argued that periodic shake-ups were not uncommon and that the apparent financial responsibility was one of necessity, to impress the West—and particularly America—from whom they wanted wheat and grain.

There was a headwind against the flight from Germany and then congestion over Heathrow, so Pike was later than he expected landing in England. Remembering it was Friday and suspecting that the City might start its weekend as early as most of the people he knew in Wall Street, Pike telephoned Jane from the airport, glad when she answered the telephone on the second ring.

"I was late getting in," he said. "I thought you might be getting ready to leave."

"No," said Jane. She tried to keep the relief from her voice.

"I said I'd call."

"I know," she said. "How are you?"

"All right. And you?"

"Fine. Trip working out well?"

"So-so," he said. "I wondered if we might meet sometime while I'm here. Dinner or something?"

For God's sake, don't be so casual about it. "Why not?" she said, trying to match his attitude—and why shouldn't she? They'd been out once and she'd found him reasonably pleasant, that was all. It wasn't fair to consider him a surrogate for Paul. How could he be?

"What about tonight?"

"I'm not doing anything tonight." She was maintaining the lightness, she decided.

"It'll take me a while to get into town, I guess."

"Where are you staying?"

"The Churchill."

She gave him her home number. "Why not call me, when you get in?"

Jane was still experimenting with her promotion, adjusting to her own secretary and support staff and the right to come and go as she pleased. She hadn't taken advantage of the freedom, until this afternoon. She was in Kensington by four, standing undecided in front of the regimented wardrobe—as she'd stood undecided before it the previous night, hoping that he would telephone. Paul had been very generous to her when their affair began, and he had bought her a lot of clothes. She chose a gray dress she had purchased herself, after the break-up, a gesture for her own benefit but one which was important to her. After her bath she remained in her dressing gown, not wanting to crease it by sitting.

It was past seven when he telephoned. "Took longer than I thought," he said.

"I've only just got in."

"Where do you want to go?"

"I don't mind."

"It's your town, Jane Rose," he said.

And she knew it not at all, she realized. The restaurants were the ones Paul had taken her to. In the first weeks, when he was impressing her, he'd taken her to Annabel's and to a club that had since closed down in the King's Road, but he'd been the member, able to get in; it had never seemed important to get membership for herself.

"Soho's the name in all the guidebooks," he said, breaking the silence.

"Covent Garden is better," she said. It had been a remark of Paul's.

"Let's go there then."

"It's not the same as Georgetown."

"I don't want it to be," he said. "Shall I pick you up?"

"Yes."

"Half an hour?"

"Forty-five minutes," she insisted, maintaining the pretense.

He arrived in forty, carrying a single chrysanthemum, which he confessed to having stolen from an arrangement in the hotel foyer. He didn't try to kiss her, as if they were more friendly than they were, or shake her hand, which would have been too formal—and she was glad, on both counts. There was a slight embarrassment when he let her give the cab driver the address and she said Covent Garden and the man asked where, which she covered by choosing the opera house so they could walk through the redevelopment behind. He seemed to enjoy the explanation of it having been the vegetable market of the city, and there was an added advantage in that it allowed her to examine the restaurants and choose one as if she knew it well, which she didn't. It was fortunate there was a table available.

"Better than Georgetown," he declared, when they sat down.

"That's not true, but thank you for being gallant."

"Here's to resumed friendships," he toasted, raising his wineglass. Would she sleep with him? he wondered.

"I was surprised to get your call," she said, drinking with him.

"I'm surprised to be here."

"Why are you?"

"It's shop," he warned.

"I enjoy shop."

He told her of his Russian analysis and of his briefing by Volger, but not about the composite study requested by Washington as that was government information that he regarded as classified. He looked at her curiously when she began shaking her head and smiling at him. "What is it?"

"I made the same assessment," she said. "I started

when I saw our clearing bank returns and realized the Russians were settling on time.''

Pike put aside his knife and fork, no longer interested in the meal. ''What's the verdict?'' he demanded. ''Financial control or coincidence?''

''Control,'' she said at once.

''Thank Christ for that! I've a meeting with your people on Monday: It'll be good to get the same opinion as I've got and talk it through.''

''It isn't the same opinion,'' she said shortly.

''But you said. . . .''

''My verdict,'' she qualified. ''I suppose I'm breaching convention by telling you in advance, but the bank's view is that it's unconnected.''

''It can't be!''

''Yes, it can,'' she said. ''I went right back, to the immediate postwar period. There are examples of things occurring just like this and of financial experts making just the sort of analysis that you've done and I've done, and then suddenly it falls apart.''

He had made a mistake in not going back as far as she had, Pike realized, disconcerted; he guessed someone in the Treasury or the CIA would have done so and would argue against the Federal opinion—which was his opinion—when it was presented in Washington. He'd have to warn Volger to prevent embarrassment. Which would seem to be tempering his own conviction. *Shit.*

''I know I'm right,'' he insisted.

''You can't be,'' said Jane, with even stronger insistence. ''You don't know enough; none of us do. Which is the problem. We can assemble everything we know so far and make from it whatever we want.''

''That's not the view in America,'' said Pike. An exaggeration, he realized. He didn't know anyone's view in America, apart from the Federal Reserve. His own, he thought again.

''Then it should be,'' said Jane. ''Personally, I believe

you're right—and believe, too, that in weeks or months or whatever time we're going to be vindicated. But objectively, which is surely what we've got to be, I can see the stronger counterargument."

"Certainly it's what Germany seems to be accepting," said Pike. "And France doesn't seem to believe anything is happening at all."

"The French traditionally distrust banks and keep their gold under the bed," reminded Jane. "Sometimes I think they're right, too."

"It's not people I'm talking about. It's financiers and bankers, who should know better."

"That's the biggest problem," she said reflectively.

"I don't understand."

"Have you studied the history of banking?"

"Of course."

"Hasn't something ever occurred to you?"

"What?"

"That bankers should know better. I accept the argument that money is a commodity, to be sold, like every other commodity is sold. But traders in marketplaces don't hand over their goods without getting their value back, in return. . . ." She waved her arms around the now crowded restaurant. "We've eaten their food, and if we don't pay for it, they'll call the police; they certainly wouldn't serve us the same meal tomorrow night if we didn't pay for this one. But that's what banks do. Too often."

"Thank you, for 'Banking Made Easy!' " he said.

She blushed, embarrassed. "I didn't mean to lecture."

"I enjoyed the lesson," said Pike. As he was enjoying her. He felt relaxed, free again. Janet was the problem, he decided. Everything was becoming regular and established and he felt hemmed in. If only the sex hadn't been so good! She had taken to insisting upon putting a few grains of numbing cocaine beneath his foreskin, so that it seemed to last forever, and she'd experimented upon herself, too, when he'd asked her, but it was beginning to pall.

"Don't you ever worry?" she asked.

"About what?"

"Everything collapsing."

"Financially, you mean?"

"Yes."

"Sometimes," he said. "Not often."

"Always a resolve?"

"There always seems to be."

"I was wrong," she said. "In Washington."

"About what?"

"Being a feminist figure head. I got my promotion."

"Congratulations."

"You sound surprised."

"You sound like an offended feminist."

"I deserved it."

"Would you have got it, if you hadn't deserved it?"

"No."

"So why the need to justify yourself?"

"Now *you*'re lecturing."

He extended his finger and said, "Touché," and she met his touch and said, "I don't know the fencing term for an even score."

"I don't either," he said. "Settle for even?"

"Yes."

"How old are you?"

"That's a rude question," she said, unoffended.

"Thirty?"

"That's even ruder. I'm twenty-eight."

"Why?"

"Why what?"

"What aren't you locked up in some tower by some loving husband, with guards outside to keep the other guys out?"

"He was somebody else's husband." She hadn't meant to make the admission. She was actually enjoying the flirtation, recognizing it as harmless, and now she knew she'd ruined it, making the whole thing serious.

"Bet he regretted it," he said.

She appreciated that he was trying to help her and liked him for it. "Actually, he didn't."

"Jerk," said Pike.

"Wonder how long it'll take me to think that?"

"I've introduced a sombre note," said Pike. "I wanted it to be fun."

"I've had fun: really."

"So have I."

"Honestly?"

"Honestly."

She expected him to suggest going on to a club and became nervous when he didn't. She'd made herself sound easy, confessing the affair. The nervousness increased when he insisted on walking her beyond the entrance, actually to her apartment door.

"Thank you," she said, stopping outside. "I've enjoyed the evening."

"I enjoyed it, too."

Knowing she had to, Jane said, "Would you like to come in: a coffee or a drink or something?"

"No, thank you," he said, the ploy already decided.

The answer surprised her, and it showed. "Oh."

"Not unless. . . ." he said intentionally.

"Unless what?"

"Unless you agree to see me tomorrow. If you say no, I'll accept the invitation to a drink and make a nuisance of myself."

She laughed with him. "You were cynical last time," she said.

"First impressions."

"This one's better."

"You haven't agreed about tomorrow."

"Eleven?"

"Ten."

"Ten-thirty."

"That's a good banking compromise," he said.

"What do you want to do?"

"Nothing. For as long as I can remember, my weekends have been full of people that were trying to do lots of things and pretending it was nothing, that they were relaxing. I don't want us to make any plans or think of anything until I arrive, and we'll work it out from there."

The possibility of disorder occurred to her orderly mind. "What happens if we can't think of anything?" The naivete of the question came to her the moment she spoke, and she waited for his reply with the apprehension with which she'd expected him to come into her apartment.

He shrugged and said, "We'll send out for Chinese," he said, and she loved him for it.

Which is what they did, from a Peking restaurant where he made the selection, which was good. He stayed the Saturday night and they made love, badly, at first, because of her nervousness, and then better because he was very patient and very expert.

"You're amazing," she said.

"So are you."

"No" she said. "Will you teach me?"

"Yes."

"Everything?"

"Yes."

"I want everything you want."

They walked through Hyde Park on Sunday, and in Piccadilly he bought her a painting from one of the pavement displays and they made a ceremony of hanging it when they got back to her flat.

"When are you going to Basel?" she asked.

"Wednesday."

"And then New York?"

"I could probably swing another weekend. Would you like that?"

"I'd like that very much indeed." She was still using this amusing, friendly American, Jane realized. But she'd told him about Paul, so there wasn't any deceit. He probably had a million mistresses in New York.

Pike realized that he would like it, too.

"I hurt you," apologized Malik.

"No."

"I know I did."

"It doesn't matter."

"Of course it matters."

She didn't realize at once what he was doing, not until she felt his face against her stomach, kissing her. "Don't!"

"I'm saying sorry."

"I've told you that you don't have to apologize." The soreness burned her, like a fire deep inside her body, but it had been as wonderful as she'd always expected it to be and she wanted to do it again and for it never to stop.

"There's a terrible mess," he said.

"Come up here, to me."

"I didn't mean to hurt you," he repeated. "I didn't know . . . expect. . . ."

"I told you that you didn't hurt me." His face was stained with her stain. She wiped it away, holding his face to kiss him. "There isn't any glass," she said.

"Glass?"

"For me to engrave my initials, like they do in the *salon particulaire*."

"You'd identify yourself then," he said.

"So?"

"I want you for myself," said Malik.

"You've got me for yourself," she said, knowing that was what he wanted her to say.

"I want to make love to you again," he said. "Can I make love to you again?"

"I want you to." Lydia managed to control the wince as he entered her and to sustain the pain, which actually became exciting.

"I love you," he said.

"Don't stop," she said.

15

To create the maximum impact, details of the new Soviet trade and finance arrangements with Czechoslovakia, Hungary and Rumania were released on the eve of the Basel meeting. There was no agenda space and, therefore, no official discussion—but the announcement was the sole topic among the bank supervisors from the eleven member countries as they talked in the corridors and cocktail party enclaves that Pike found reminiscent of the IMF gathering in Washington. He was helped by the way things worked out. With only observer status, he was excluded from many of the scheduled discussions but needed no official accreditation for the corridor talk. There were still dissenters, predominantly the French and the Japanese, but the consensus thinking was that it indicated control. Pike didn't rush to inform New York, wanting to be absolutely sure before he did. It was three days before he made the telephone call.

"So we were right!"

Pike was aware of the satisfaction in Volger's voice. "That's the majority feeling," he said.

"We were the only ones prepared to put our heads on the block!" said Volger. "State, CIA and Treasury all went for options. Which was how the report was written. Now they'll have to change it."

"There are still some doubters," Pike warned.

"There won't be here, believe me," said Volger. "There's only one way this can be read."

He'd *really* proved himself, Pike realized: and to others, too. He'd been ahead of everyone all the way—not just people in his own Board, but experienced financiers in other parts of the government and in treasuries here, in Europe.

"Thought I'd stop off in London on my way back," said Pike. He deserved a reward.

"I'm afraid you can't."

"*What?*"

"I told you this was important."

"I know, but. . . ."

"There's a conference this weekend in Washington. . . ." Volger stopped, but Pike knew he hadn't finished. "With the President."

"The President!" Pike was surprised. "Why so high? What's wrong with the Treasury Secretary?" As he asked the question, Pike remembered the conversation with his father and Nelson Jordan's determination to correct the economy before the next election.

"It's the President's idea," said Volger. "Don't want to miss out on your proper recognition, do you?"

No, thought Pike, he certainly didn't want to miss out on that in front of whoever else would be present. "I'll check the direct flights," he said.

"Tonight, if possible," said Volger. "I'd like to go through everything with you myself, before we go down."

"Sure."

"And Tom."

"Sir?"

"Congratulations."

"Thank you," said Pike.

Jane picked up the telephone on the first ring and, when she heard his voice, said, "I was waiting."

"Bad news," he said.

"What?"

"I can't get back to London."

"Oh." In the London apartment, Jane closed her eyes, knuckles of her free hand against her mouth.

"I'm sorry—really sorry," he said. Why? he wondered. He'd already decided it was only another affair, like all the rest.

"I understand."

"You don't," he said. "There's a weekend conference in Washington: important. I've got to be there."

"Of course."

He wasn't sure that she believed him, and he wanted her to. "You all right?"

"Fine."

"I thought your voice sounded strange."

"It's nothing, really," she said.

"I really am very sorry."

"Me, too."

"I enjoyed it."

"Yes."

"No chance of your getting to America soon?" Why was he prolonging the conversation?

"I don't think so."

"Pity."

"How about your coming back to Europe?"

"I don't know."

"Keep safe," she said.

"And you. I'll write." Would he? He never did.

"Do that," she said. She didn't want a pen-friend, she thought, suddenly angry in her disappointment. She wanted him.

"I'm sure I'll get back, sometime."

"That would be nice."

He couldn't think of anything else to say, but he didn't want to break the contact.

"How was the meeting?" she said, trying to extend the conversation from her end.

"Like they all are; lots of eating and drinking."

"Little wonder thin bankers are so rare."

"I'm glad it happened," he said.

"So am I."

"Sure?"

"Of course."

"Keep safe."

"We've said that," she reminded him.

"Can I call you, as well as write?" This was getting ridiculous.

"Of course."

"Maybe I could come across one weekend."

She laughed, despite the way she felt. "You trying to impress me?"

"No," he said.

"You would, if you flew the Atlantic just for the weekend." Please do it, she thought.

"I should go; I've got a plane reservation to make."

"Of course."

"Thanks again."

"It was fun," she said, not wanting him to know her seriousness.

"Good-bye," he said.

"Good-bye."

He really didn't want to go back to Washington, even for proper recognition and a conference with the President, Pike realized. In London Jane was wondering why, if love was supposed to be so wonderful, she was always crying over it.

* * *

"We're respectable," said Malik. "Respectable and responsible."

"Yes," said Lydia.

The reports from the Russian embassies from every European capital and from Washington and Ottowa as well were piled on the desk between them. The opinion was unanimous.

"Where do you think we should start?" Malik asked.

"London," replied Lydia at once. "London has the influence in world finance. That's where the first loans should be raised."

"I agree. And I think, initially, we should stay in Europe."

"Yes," said Lydia. "American banks should feel they're being left out. It'll make them all the more eager."

"I think you're very beautiful," said Malik.

She smiled at him. "We're supposed to be working."

"There's not going to be a lot for us to do, while the loans are being arranged."

"There's a cliché in English: something about the lull before the storm."

"Looking forward to the storm?"

"I think so," she said.

"You're going to be famous." Remembering the Western press coverage, he added, "More famous than you already are."

"Infamous," she corrected.

"Depends which side you're on," he said.

"The winning side."

16

Pike felt gritty-eyed from tiredness, his mind fogged by crossing time zones and by the concentration with which he worked on his report on the homeward flight, writing through the night in the darkened aircraft, squinting in the beam of the miniscule overhead light. Volger had a car waiting for him at Kennedy, to take him directly to the bank. The chairman offered breakfast while the account of the Basel meeting was being typed, but Pike felt overfed on unremembered aircraft food and took only coffee. The Federal Reserve chairman had pedantically listed his queries and went carefully through them with Pike after reading the written account, for he was determined to make a good showing in Washington.

"We came out ahead on this one," said Volger. "I'm very pleased."

"I'm glad," said Pike.

"I was right about the combined assessment; it's being redrafted for this afternoon."

"What time are we due?"

"Three."

"I'd like to go to the apartment to change and shower."

"Keep the car."

"Thanks."

"But don't risk the flight. Need you with me."

Pike's mailbox was overflowing. He went quickly through the correspondence, isolating the bills from the advertising brochures, which he discarded unread. There were two letters he recognized to be in Janet's handwriting, which he put into his briefcase for later. There were three messages from her on his machine, the first a week earlier. There was a call-back message from his father, too. Pike decided he didn't have time to return them. He booked an alarm call and fell immediately to sleep, wishing he hadn't when the telephone rang after just two hours and he didn't feel any better. The shower and fresh clothes helped. Volger was standing impatiently in the departure lounge of the private section in LaGuardia, between Funtle and Bellows. The chairman's face cleared when he saw Pike's car pull in.

"I was getting worried," said Volger.

"See it was a successful trip," said Funtle, indicating that morning's report which he had in his hand.

"Things seem to happen at the right time," said Pike modestly. He wondered why the two men hadn't been summoned to the bank that morning. He filed politely last from the room to board the bank plane. It was a Learjet, the same as his father's. Pike thought the internal fittings of his father's aircraft were more elaborate. Bellow went immediately to the small self-service bar. Pike shook his head, still aware of his tiredness, and Funtle didn't have one, either. Bellow and Volger drank scotch.

"Been to the White House before?" asked Volgar, as the plane climbed out over the water, circled and then set down for a flight path along the coast.

"Couple of times," said Pike. "Not in this administration, though. "How big a conference is this going to be?"

"Big," assured Volger.

It was, bigger than Pike had imagined even from Volger's

warning. There was a jam of official cars outside the entrance to the East Wing, limousines actually up on the pavement in front of the Treasury building as the police tried to clear the obstruction. It was easier to walk down along Pennsylvannia Avenue, but they still had to wait while their accreditation was checked by the Secret Service officials. There were nods and smiles of recognition between the assembling bankers and politicians as they filed slowly through the outer rooms towards the meeting.

It was one of the larger conference rooms, overlooking the lawns and the monuments beyond. As he entered, Pike detected the black line of tourists waiting their turn to enter the Washington obelisk. Jane had said she would take him to the Tower of London today. He checked his watch, calculating the time difference; in London it would be seven-thirty in the evening. He wondered what she would be doing. He'd forgotten to read Janet's letters on the plane. There was no hurry.

The room was dominated by the huge rectangular table. The President's position was marked by a small lectern in the middle, so he would be sitting with his back to the gardens. On either side were settings for cabinet officers, and behind their seats were smaller tables and chairs for their support officials. The arrangement continued around the table, so that only the heads of the various agencies and their immediate deputies would actually sit at the President's table, with the advisory staff in second tiers. The Central Intelligence Agency contingent separated the Federal Reserve position from that of State. Next came Treasury, and then in line were the chairmen of the big banks. Further down the line he identified the chairmen of Morgan Guaranty Trust, Chase Manhattan, Citibank, the Bank of America, Manufacturers Hanover Bank, the Marine Midland . . . and then he stopped bothering.

Some signal of which Pike wasn't aware must have been given that they were assembled, because almost at once a side door opened and the President strode briskly in, nodding and smiling to the standing assembly. Nelson Jordan was followed by the Secretaries of State, Treasury and Commerce. Jordan made a series of pressing-down gestures with his hands, for them to be seated, while he himself remained standing at the lectern. He was a tall, heavily featured man who knew how to use his size to dominate any gathering. Before his election to the Presidency he'd been a legend in the Senate, with a reputation as one of the best caucus politicians since Lyndon Johnson, whom he physically resembled. The impression was heightened by the Texas accent.

"Sorry to cut into your weekends, gentlemen," he said. "Decided this was an interesting one that needed immediate attention. I want to get this right, from the outset."

He hesitated, looking around the table. "If this thing shakes down the way it seems to be, then we're looking at a change of policy within the Soviet Union more dramatic than anything we've seen for years . . . many years. Which is why I want to get it *right*. . . ." He drove the fist of one hand theatrically into the palm of his other. "Because I've got to respond to it. And respond correctly. The right reaction could be vital to the relationship between our two countries."

And to you achieving a second term of office, thought Pike.

Jordon looked to his immediate left, to where the Secretary of State was sitting. "Secretary Bowen has some views," he announced, seating himself.

Henry Bowen was a bespectacled, rotund man given to the tweeds of the academic he had been until Jordan plucked him from Harvard to put into practical effect a theory of global politics already expounded in three best-selling books. Pike had read them all and found them facile, an argument for being fast on the draw with the biggest gun possible, like some Wild West shoot-out. Collecting frontier memorabilia was Bowen's hobby; he was supposed to own a palm-size derringer that once belonged to Wild Bill Hickock.

"There seems to be . . . and I say 'seems' because I'm still holding back on positive judgment about this . . . a dramatic change in the financial attitude of the Soviet Union." He held out a cupped hand, as if he were holding something. "Money is the heart of it, but if the change is as it's being interpreted by our experts. . . ." He paused, nodding in the direction of the Federal Reserve delegation. Volger half turned, to include Pike in the praise. ". . . then it could be interpreted to show other changes, as well—changes as important, if not more so, than the new, apparent financial responsibility. The *most* important is the seeming willingness of the Soviet authorities to countenance some sort of trade unionism in Poland. That's a direct contradiction to every previous attitude—something that could spread to other Bloc countries and undermine the whole concept of the current Communism pushed out by Moscow.. . ."

He stopped, at a gesture from the President.

"Any comments, so far?" demanded Jordan.

He was seeing a master survivor politician at work, decided Pike: get every opinion before reaching a conclusion.

To Pike's left there was movement from the CIA delegation, and Jordan nodded permission to the Director, Richard Adam. He was a thin, erudite-looking man, and Pike realized Adam was the first spy he'd ever seen. He didn't look very different from other people. Rather ordinary, in fact.

"I think the snowball is running away down the hill," said Adam. "We've had our financial people look at it at Langley, and certainly the indications are that there's new control and a new attitude. But there's the possibility for other analyses. The Soviet Union has always been linked financially and with trade to their satellites through COMCON. We've had rebellions in Czechoslovakia and rebellions in Hungary and more recently rebellions against Moscow control in Poland.'' There was a slow, almost patronizing tone to his voice.

''So what's the point you're making?'' said Jordan.

''People can see military control on every street corner. It gives a focus for the resentment, for kids to tear up cobblestones and be shown on television throwing them at tanks. You can't see financial control; it's an invisible oppression. I'm suggesting that what Moscow is doing is locking their satellites into greater and far more effective financial dependence than any that could be achieved with a tank or a gun.''

Volger turned enquiringly towards Pike. Quickly on the yellow prompt-pad laid out in readiness, Pike scribbled, ''Good point. I concede the contrary argument as valid. Why Moscow repay Western loans?''

Volger advanced only the question when the President came to him for an opinion. Pike was surprised by the uncertainty in his chairman's voice. It was a fleeting reflection, because the CIA Director's reply was instantaneous and Pike realized Adam was a very competent conference bureaucrat.

''Because they've got to!'' seized Adam, at once. ''They can't hope to sustain the sort of financial support to which they've committed themselves without massive borrowing from the West.''

Pike was writing quickly now, ripping the sheets away a sentence at a time, to brief the chairman fully in front of him. ''Repayment foreign currency,'' he wrote first. Then ''Possible complete Soviet dependence upon West''.

Volger talked as the notes came to him, but it was not the CIA chief who reacted; rather, it was the Secretary of State. ''Precisely!'' Bowen said. ''Which is why I remarked at the beginning of this discussion how fundamental the change we're discussing could be.'' The Secretary of State extended his cupped hand again and Pike realized the symbolism of the gesture now. ''We'd have them!''

said the man who collected Western guns. "Here, in the palm of our hands."

"What's the Treasury feeling?" invited the President, turning to the man on the other side of him. The Treasury Secretary, William Bell, was personally a retiring, shy man with a contradictory attitude towards monetary control. He had an unshakable belief in monetarism. Under Bell, U.S. interest rates had peaked at twenty per cent.

"I'm thinking a little towards both views that have been put forward," said the man. He removed his spectacles and began moving them through his fingers, a reflective mannerism. "I agree it indicates a move towards stronger financial links between Moscow and its satellites, although I'm not sure I'd go as far as assessing it as oppression. But I can't avoid the conclusion, either, that there's some new, hard attitude being shown as well." He hesitated, looking towards the President. "An attitude I agree that we should respond to. The Argentinian deal hasn't solved that country's problems, but it's provided an indication of confidence and, with the trade arrangements now confirmed, it's given some Western banks, our own included, the confidence to increase their loan commitment and make the whole scheme work. . . ." Bell replaced his glasses and went to some notes in front of him. "Certainly it enabled Buenos Aires to meet $75,000,000 of repayments on interest and short-term loans in the last week." He turned a page. "Poland, too. Three American consortia got payments on their due dates of $100,000,000."

Pike scribbled another note on his yellow pad, passing it forward to Volger. Jordan saw the gesture and looked fully towards the Federal Reserve group. "A point to be made there?"

"You're aware that we had a representative at the Basel meeting," said the Federal chairman, nodding backwards towards Pike. "English, French and German banks all reported in committee discussions that Poland was meeting its debts now. The country's still a long way from the lifeboat, but it's swimming in the right direction at least."

Jordan went back to his side of the table and said, "Commerce, any views?" William Johnson, the Secretary of Commerce, moved as if to stand, then went back into his seat again because everyone else had talked sitting down. He started uncertainly, his voice high, and said, "Picking up the earlier point about ultimate Soviet financial dependence, I would point out that they are this year—as they have been in the past—purchasing grain supplies from us. Here again they've shown responsibility: When we agreed to the increased shipment three weeks ago, an eight-day payment time was stipulated. And met on the nail, every cent."

"There's an illogicality over that deal," broke in the CIA chief. He indicated a dossier on the table before him. "I've the actual photographs here for anyone who's interested in seeing them, but our satellite reconnaissance of the Soviet grain-growing areas doesn't show the failure that Moscow announced. According to the calculations made by our agronomists from these aerial surveys, Russia had one of the best harvests it's had for years, not the worst."

"There's surely an explanation for that?" said the Commerce chairman.

"I agree the man responsible within their ministry for assessing yield has been replaced," said Adam. "I'm surprised the crime was underassessment; our experience of the Soviet system is almost consistently to overestimate."

"They've held to the deal," said Johnson.

"Which is an even greater illogicality," said Adam. "Why, having concluded the Argentinian deal and done well by their own farmers, are they taking wheat from us they don't need?"

"We look to your Agency for answers to questions like that," said the President.

"I can't provide one," admitted the CIA Director at

once. "It's something we kept stubbing our toe against, on every analysis."

"What about stockpiling?" said Johnson. "That would make sense, wouldn't it, with an agricultural system as uncertain as theirs?"

"Yes," agreed Adam.

Jordan indicated the dossier in front of the man. "How definite is your aerial reconnaissance?"

"Very detailed," assured Adam.

"Any indication of storage facilities—the sort of facilities that would be necessary for this sort of quantity?"

Adam shook his head. "None," he said.

The President turned in the direction of the assembled bankers, nodding to Hector Belcher, who had replaced Pike's father at Chase Manhattan. "What's the banking feeling?" he said.

Belcher was a quiet-spoken, cautious man who weighed words before uttering them. "There have been strains imposed—almost intolerable strains—over the last few years on the Free World banking system. Strains that have led—falsely, I believe, but nevertheless to serious consideration among a large number of men whom I still respect—to the conjecture that the whole structure might collapse. The bank I represent, a bank with considerable commitment in the Eastern bloc, welcomes anything that reverses both the strain and the negative thinking. On the evidence available to us, the recent developments in Moscow seem to be doing just that. . . ." He stopped, looking towards the Secretary of State. "I don't go along with the thought of using money as some kind of weapon: I think that's unreal and irresponsible. I go along, however, with intermeshing the links between us. . . ."

"Gentlemen?" said the President, continuing the invitation.

There was a momentary uncertainty between the bankers, and then Alan Mewsom, of the Bank of America, said, "Six months ago we were involved in rescheduling discussions and giving serious thought to setting off some of our debts as non-recoverable. We are short just $20,000,000 on current repayments, and we've an undertaking—one we believe will be met—from Argentina that it'll be resolved in days rather than weeks. I couldn't be more encouraged."

"Anyone else?" asked Jordan.

"I'd like to know more," said William Jeynes, of Citibank. "But it's looking good to our analyst."

"I think the biggest fear of what's been happening in the past is that some small bank that couldn't really afford it but overstretched itself to get into a loan consortia might have declared a default," said Richard Railton, the chairman of Manufacturers Hanover. "In the last three or four months that fear has receded because of the repayments from the Soviets and those they control. Moscow might not realize it, but they're pulling us back from the brink."

"I agree," said Belcher. "For the first time since I can't remember when, my board feel things are working properly."

The President nodded, gazing momentarily down at the desk in front of him. Then he looked up and said, "O.K., what's the concensus?"

"Control, to our advantage," said Belcher. From alongside him came head-nodding and mutterings of "agreed," from the bankers.

"Control," echoed Volger.

"Control," said Johnson.

"Control," said Bowen.

"I'd like more information," said Bell, refusing to commit.

"Manipulation," said the CIA Director.

"Majority for control," said the President, unnecessarily. "So how do we respond?"

"Not directly with any comment about the financial arrangements," advised Bowen at once. "We're still guessing."

"What is there positive to comment upon?" asked Jordan.

"Trade unionism in Poland," said Adam. "There's the

additional advantage that we won't be making any direct reference to the Soviet Union.''

Looking across the room at the President, Pike got the impression of a man staring down at a hand of cards, wondering which one to pick up in the hope of it being the trump.

''I agree trade unionism and Poland,'' said Jordan. ''But not immediately.'' He turned to Bowen again. ''Call the Soviet ambassador in,'' he said. ''Make it an unpublicized meeting; we don't want to antagonize them because it could be interpreted that we're crowing over our sanctions. Let it be known that we welcome the relaxation. I'll go public with a remark sometime next week.'' Jordan came back to the others in the room. It was a general point, but he made it looking directly at the Federal Reserve contingent whose analysis had just been adopted. ''There's still a lot of grey areas. . . . too many, for my peace of mind. If anyone comes upon anything that appears to clarify the matter, I'd like immediate advice.''

There were nods and movements of agreement from around the room.

The President stood, positively, and said, ''Thank you, gentlemen, for your attendance and your help. Useful; very useful indeed. Enjoy the rest of your weekend.''

Everyone rose with the man and stood as he strode from the room.

''You staying down?'' asked Volger, turning to Pike.

The thought hadn't occurred to him until now, but it made better sense than returning to New York, tired as he was. He wondered if his father would be at the house. He was, when Pike called to say he was coming.

As a child, when perhaps it should have, the Virginia house had never seemed big to Pike. But it did now. The rooms seemed to echo with their voices and the corridors with their footsteps, and although they'd eaten around one of the smaller circular tables, it still seemed too large for the three of them. Perhaps the impression came from almost forty-eight hours without sleep.

The older man's curiosity was understandable, and initially Pike wondered about the integrity of talking about Basel and the White House meeting. Then he decided his father would learn everything from Volger anyway and that he might as well tell him. He gave a complete summary of the Swiss meeting and then of what had happened that afternoon during the conference with the President. He was aware of his mother smiling proudly as he talked.

"I think the CIA reservations have got a lot of validity," he said.

His father shook his head. "The Agency never likes to commit itself. They're up to their ears in analysts who only seem able to make assessments against the criteria of what's happened in the past. Anything new frightens the hell out of them."

"I still think the danger is momentum getting ahead of the facts."

"Don't go faint-hearted because of the level at which it's being considered," said his father. "No one's forcing the opinion. And there's been enough independent analysis from the time you first spotted it."

"What's the feeling in the Fund?" asked Pike, the questioner now.

"Not unanimous, of course," said the older man. "The majority seem to be going for responsibility. England isn't so sure."

"And they're the most experienced," pointed out Pike.

The other man pulled down the corners of his mouth theatrically. "Maybe they've been bitten too hard in the past. I think they're being too cautious, just like the CIA." He leaned across the table, to emphasize the question. "What did Treasury do at the meeting?"

Pike considered the query. "Sat on the fence," he said.

The IMF director nodded. ''Bell's frightened of his own shadow,'' he said, as if the assessment were confirmation. ''Jordan knows he needs a stronger man there.''

''The President was very determined to get the widest concensus, to get the response right.''

''Pity I couldn't have been officially involved,'' said his father. ''Damned pity.''

''What about unofficially?'' asked Pike.

There was one of the wolfish grins. ''Like you said, Jordan is going as far as he can to get a wide concensus.''

''Which means he'll be in contact with Ambersom as well.''

The smile faded, just slightly. ''But Ambersom doesn't have the advantage of knowing what's already been said,'' he reminded.

''Isn't it time we stopped talking business?''

Pike turned to his mother. ''Sorry.''

''How's Janet?'' she said at once.

''I've been away,'' Pike reminded her.

''Haven't you called her since you got back?''

''It's only been a few hours, Mother!''

''I thought you could have made time.''

It hadn't taken long, thought Pike, for the feeling of size to disappear and be replaced by an impression that the walls were closing in around him.

17

There was no longer the formality about the Politburo review committee that existed when Lydia first appeared before them. The reserve still existed, and she deferred to their authority, but gone was the suspicion she had come to recognize from people when they first began considering her proposals. Yakov Lenev controlled the meeting, a square-bodied, square-headed man with a Georgian rasp in his voice. The two other members were Viktor Korobov, a scholarly-looking man who had once been Deputy Director of the KGB and had been seconded to the committee because of the experience, and Ivan Pushkov, who had replaced Anatoli Karelin as economic expert on the governing Soviet body and who was a bespectacled, clerk-like looking man. Protocol decreed that Malik should be the spokesman, as Finance Minister, but the biggest indication of the easing formality was the way questions were frequently addressed directly to her; she wondered if Malik would have been irritated but for their personal relationship.

"Are you absolutely sure that nothing has been overlooked?" demanded Pushkov, with an accountant's dislike of any risk involving money. He was worried at incurring the same fate as Karelin if anything went wrong.

"Yes," said Malik. "You've considered all our reports."

"If something had been overlooked, it wouldn't be in the reports, would it?" said Pushkov testily.

"We are sure every preparation has been made," assured Malik. He glanced at Lydia, and she decided he was irritated at being pressured in her presence.

"How advanced are the loan applications?" said Lenev.

Malik looked more fully sideways, to Lydia. She saw it as an opportunity to convince Pushkov . . . and take the pressure from Malik.

"In the process of being established," she said. "We've moved into Europe, so London was the natural starting point, through their merchant banks. In England the consortia involves Lloyds, Barclays, National Westminster, Midland and Williams and Glyn's, and because of the close European interlinking that exists that naturally feeds into Europe. . . ."

"What is this interlinking?" demanded Korobov.

"Let me give you an example of one bank we want to involve—Algemene, in the Netherlands. Algemene is one of a number who refer to themselves collectively as Abecor, the associated banks of Europe. Which means a bank from every country. Abecor, for instance, is composed of Algemene, the Banca Nazionale de Lavoro, the Banque de Bruxelles Lambert, the Banque Nationale de Paris, Britain's Barclays that I've already referred to, Bayerische Hypothken-und-Wechsel Bank and the Dresdner Bank."

"So one becomes many?" said Korobov.

"For the maximum impact," agreed Lydia. "Continuing with Algemene, for instance. Whatever happens to that one bank, apart from its Abecor association, directly affects the twenty-eight financial subsidiaries it controls in the Netherlands and its thirty-five additional international subsidiaries."

"How widely are the loans being spread?" asked Pushkov.

This time it was Malik who answered. "Worldwide," he said. "Would you like some detailed indication?"

"Of course," said Pushkov.

"In addition to Algemene, other banks involved in the Netherlands are the Amsterdam and Rotterdam Bank and Nederlandsche Middenstrandsbank. There's a heavy concentration in Germany. They include Baden-Wurttembergische Bank Aktiengesellschaft, Badische Kommunale Landesbank, Bank Fur Gemeinwirtschaft, Bayerische Landesbank Girozentrale, Bayerische Vereinsbank, Berliner Bank, Berliner Handels und Frankfurter, Bremen Landesbank Girozentrale und Staatlische Kreditanstalt, Commerzbank, Deutsche Bank, the Deutsche Girozentrale and Deutsche Kommunelbank, Deutsche Genossenschaftsbank, the Desdner Bank, the Hamsburgische Landesbank Girozentrale and Hessische Landesbank Girozentrale. . . ."

Pushkov nodded at Malik's listing and said, "That seems comprehensive enough."

"The feeling was that the Germans retain a paranoid fear of hyperinflation, with their memory of the Weimar Republic, and that any financial difficulty will have a major and immediate effect. They'll panic," said Lydia.

"And as Comrade Kirov has already explained with the Algemene bank," endorsed Malik, "each of those listed has extensive domestic and international holdings and affiliates. For every one bank, you can calculate a ripple effect upon at least twenty more banks and financial institutions."

"What beyond Germany?" asked Korobov.

"Italy is another country with an oversensitive reaction to financial upheaval," said Lydia. "There's the Commerciale Italiana, the Nazionale Dell'Agricoltura, the Nazionale del Lavovo, the Popolaire di Novara, the Toscana, the Banco di Napoli, the Banco di Roma. . . ." She hesitated, looking up from the papers before her. "The Banco di Roma will cause the greatest repercussion here. Being ninety per cent state-owned, it controls at least twenty banks within the country, with forty international links.'' She went back to her records again. ''There are, in addition, the Banco di Santo Spirito, the Banco di Sicilia, the Cassa di Risparmio de Provincie Limbardie and their subsidiary banks in Firenze, Genova, Tirono and Verona and the Credito Italiano.''

She stopped, dry-throated, and drank from the water glass to her right. If the pendantic Pushkov wanted facts, then he could have them. Lydia felt irritated at the man's attitude towards Malik.

''France?'' persisted Pushkov.

''A similar approach to that of the Netherlands,'' said Lydia. ''In France the combination is, however, quite internal. It's called Gisofra and is composed of the Banque Nationale de Paris, Credit Lyonnais and Societe Generale. In addition, we are hoping to involve the Commerciale Pour L'Europe, the de L'Indochine et de Suez, the Francaise du Commerce Exterieur, the Worms, the Caise Centrale des Banque Populaires, the Compagnie Financiere de Paris et des Pays-Bus, the Credit Commercial de France, the Credit du Nord, and the Credit Industriel et Commerciale.''

Lydia reached for the water again, so Malik took up the listing. ''In Switzerland the grouping is intended to include Credit Suisse, Union Bank of Switzerland, the Swiss Banking Corporation, and the Swiss Volksbank.''

Recovering, Lydia said, ''Consortia are being established to include banks from Spain, Portugal, Luxemburg, Ireland, Belgium and all three of the Scandinavian countries. . . .'' She lifted her papers. ''I have the names, if you would like them.''

''I think we can accept them in a written report,'' said Lenev.

''Just Europe?'' said Pushkov.

''No,'' said Malik at once. ''The Far East, as well. In Japan, the combination involves the Bank of Tokyo, Dai-Ichi Kangyo, Daiwa, Fuji, Hokkaido Takushoka, the Industrial Bank of Japan, Kyowa, Long Term Credit Bank of

Japan, Mitsubishi, the Mitsubishi Trust and Banking Corporation and the Nippon Credit Bank. The Hong Kong and Shanghai Bank are linked in a funding group with the Overseas Chinese Banking Corporation of Singapore."

"Why the concentration on Japan?" asked Korobov.

"The Western opinion, despite the current reverses of its balance-of-payments difficulties, is that Japan is the economic miracle of the postwar years. And because of the close links with American finance," said Lydia. "In addition, we've also got an already agreed consortia involving the Australia and New Zealand Banking Group, the Bank of New South Wales, the Commercial Banking Company of Sydney and the Commercial Bank of Australia, the Commonwealth Banking Corporation and the National Bank of Australasia."

"I'm worried that it will be impossible to conceal the full extent of the loans with such an extensive involvement," said Pushkov.

Lydia conceded that he was a clever man to have isolated perhaps the greatest weakness of the whole proposal. "We think it will," she said. "The ceiling of every loan has been minutely calculated in the case of every country. Nowhere has a major bank been included where its subsidiary link with other major institutions can cause too much suspicion. The Bank of England has probably got the best central supervisory system for their clearing houses and here we've been particularly careful. There'll be an impression of great activity, but we don't think it will be possible for a sufficiently accurate count to cause any early apprehension."

"No American banks have been itemized?" said Pushkov.

"None are, not yet," said Malik.

The Politburo group waited, and when the Finance Minister did not continue, Pushkov said, "Why not?"

"We want them to come to us," said Lydia.

"Come to us!"

"A number of the European and Far Eastern banks

already involved in the funding have affiliation with American finance. They'll know what's happening, but not to what degree. They'll realize the potential and start clamoring to be let in."

"That's speculation," said Korobov, just ahead of Pushkov.

"Speculation," agreed Lydia. "But it's based upon the studied reaction over a twenty-year period of Western bankers. We speculated upon every Western reaction so far, with the anticipation of how they would react. And every time that speculation has proven us right."

Korobov looked down at the table, irritated at having been the one caught out by the question. Coming to his colleague's rescue, Pushkov said, "What happens if, for the first time, this particular assessment is wrong—that they don't come to us?"

Lydia smiled. "Then we go to them," she said simply. "There's no dictated order of preference as to whom one should go for sovereign loans. Indeed, to the West, the way our negotiations are progressing will show good business acumen, seeking the best interest rates and repayment periods possible. Which makes sound economic sense when American rates are still higher than those of Europe. It also provides us with a good bargaining base when we do get involved with the Americans."

Pushkov smiled; it was an expression which surprised Lydia. "We had to be sure," he said, and she realized he was making an apology for the persistence.

"We understand," said Malik, still the more accomplished Kremlin politician.

"I take your assurance," continued the economic expert. "Nothing appears to have been overlooked."

"How long will everything take?" said Lenev, who had been prepared to let the other two Politburo members dominate the questioning.

"It is an estimate, one which we will have to adjust practically from day to day when we see how fast the loan agreements are being reached, not just with us but with Poland and Hungary and Czechoslovakia and Rumania," said Lydia, "but I would think three months."

"It seems a long time," said Lenev.

"This concept has been evolving for ten years," reminded Malik.

"I admire your patience," said Korobov.

They went to the Russkiy Zal, to the same private room, for the first time since their affair began and then afterwards to her apartment, the usual conclusion to any evening they spent together. They were sure of each other now, enjoying the experimentation, neither one embarrassed or offended by the needs of the other.

"I can't imagine now how sore I was," she said.

"I didn't know you were a virgin."

"I didn't want you to."

"I love you very much," he said.

"Don't!"

"Why not?"

"You know why not."

"I want to ask Irena for a divorce."

"What!" She pulled away, staring across the bed at him, just able to discern his features in the darkness.

"A divorce," he repeated. "I want to divorce her and marry you."

She turned away from him, lying on her back and staring up at the ceiling.

"Well?" he said.

"I don't know what to say."

"Don't you want to marry me?"

"I don't know that, either," she replied honestly. Would he be enough, forever?

"I thought you'd be pleased."

"I am pleased . . . flattered. . . ." she stumbled. "It's just a surprise."

"You didn't think I just wanted you as a mistress, did you?"

"I hadn't thought about it," she lied. She *had* thought about it, on numerous occasions since the affair had started. She admired Vladimir Malik as an economist and she liked him as a man and he was kind and considerate. And the sex that she needed so badly had so far nearly always satisfied her. So she *had* wondered how it would end, or continue. And she'd wondered something else, too. Whether she loved him. She wished she knew the formulas and the codes of love as well as she knew those of economy.

"I have," he said. "I want you as a wife."

"How do you think Irena will react?"

"I don't think she'll be surprised. Or even upset. It's not been good for a long time. But Irena's reaction isn't the thing that's concerning me at the moment. It's your reaction."

"I'm sorry," she said.

"Are you saying you don't want to marry me?"

"Of course not!" She turned back to him, feeling out hurriedly for his hand.

"What then?"

"I told you: I'm surprised."

She felt him move towards her and then felt his lips, lightly against her cheek. "Please marry me," he said. "Please say yes."

"Yes," she said. She wasn't someone who made decisions like this, impulsively, without any consideration—without time to think and debate the arguments against the counterarguments and assemble everything in parallel equations and contrasting graphs.

"Happy?"

"Very," she said, knowing it was a lie.

*   *   *

"This is the seventh time you've called!" said Jane.

"Who's counting?" said Pike.

"I am."

"How are you, since the last time?"

"Missing you more than I was the last time."

"Me, too."

"How's New York?"

"Dirty and in a hurry."

"Remember Hyde Park, where we went walking?"

"Of course I do."

"I went there on Sunday. All the leaves are turning; everything's yellow and red and brown. I scuffed through them and made them crackle, like a kid."

"Wish I'd been with you."

"I wish you'd been with me, too." Illogically, the weekends weren't so bad now, even though she was still alone. She felt she had someone, even though he was thousands of miles away.

"That's why I called," he said.

"What do you mean?"

"What are you doing this weekend?"

"You're *joking*!" The words came out in a squeal, in her excitement.

"No."

"Oh, darling, please come!"

"I'm taking the Concorde flight, so I can be there by Friday evening."

"I *am* impressed."

"You're meant to be."

18

Even the prospect of seeing Jane Rose again couldn't completely lift the ennui from Tom Pike; indeed, he wasn't absolutely sure that the feeling of flatness wasn't the underlying reason he was considering a weekend in London at all, rather than the need to be with her again. For weeks—months—there had been the gradual developments in Russia to assemble and assess, compilations and assessments that had earned him the reputation he'd always sought. And wanted to keep. Like an athlete going through the qualifying rounds, he'd developed a pace and a rhythm, and suddenly, when he'd imagined the medal to go for, there weren't any more hurdles to cross. Nothing that could be recognized as a hurdle, anyway. The loan-raising was continuing, of course. And Soviet now. As soon as the rumours had started, he'd canvassed the banks, not just the Wall Street establishments but the smaller out-of-town and state institutions, and managed to confirm some minimal affiliate association—but he'd already forecast that development, and the trend wasn't solid enough for him to make any sort of intelligent gauge as to the amount. He supposed the Warsaw confirmation about a government-free union to replace Solidarity in Poland was a further indication of how right he'd been, but that now seemed a long time ago, just as the Washington conference that had anticipated its establishment and the Bank of International Settlement meeting in Basel seemed a long time ago. Everything was routine now. The Federal Reserve was a routine, and the daily, inconclusive discussions with Volger were routine, and the drifting relationship with Janet was a routine.

Pike knew he was being stupid about Janet, stupid in maintaining the affair because the sex was good and he enjoyed sex and because it was easier to let it go on than to end it. Weak, as well as stupid. So was he going to avoid the exhibition? That was the initial inclination, but almost immediately he rejected it. Weakness again, he thought. Stupidity, too. The exhibition was the first major occasion since Janet had been reestablished as the director of the Ambersom gallery, the hanging of work by some unknown artist she'd discovered and whom, through Ambersom influence, she'd been promoting for the past two months with radio and newspaper and television interviews and coverage. She'd noticed his absence, maybe, but it was *that* night's event for the names of Washington who were flying in, as well as those from Manhattan—a gathering of the glorious, so his non-appearance wouldn't appear the rejection he wanted it to be.

The Ambersom gallery was at 62nd and 2nd, and by the time Pike's cab got uptown, the traffic was already beginning to tail-back from the event. He waited ten minutes to travel to 61st from 60th, then paid the taxi off and walked the remaining block. Police had erected barriers to keep onlookers back. The building was whitened by the glare of an outside TV recording team, and as he slowly edged through to join the entry line, Pike saw that the majority of the men were wearing evening dress. He hadn't, and his invitation was scrutinized more closely than the people immediately preceding him at the door. Just inside, there was a long table and a group of secretaries, listing the names of the arrivals. Alongside were more press and television cameras.

Pike allowed himself to be carried further into the gallery by the automatic movement of the crowd; it thinned beyond the entrance bottleneck, but not much. He saw Janet in the middle of a group of people in the main salon; the only others he recognized were her mother and father. Ambersom saw him and waved, and Pike smiled back. When he got close, Ambersom detached himself, coming forward to meet him.

"Quite a crowd," said the World Bank chairman proudly.

"It's very good," agreed Pike.

Janet saw him at last and made a kissing motion with her lips. Pike smiled back, aware of the man close to her, frequently cupping her elbow in his hand. The man was slight and extremely slim, thin almost, with black hair tumbling around a sallow face. Like the majority of the crowd, he wore evening dress. He became aware of Pike's attention and held the eye contact. Pike looked away.

"How's things at the Fed?"

Pike shrugged at Ambersom's question. "Pretty good."

"You must be the man they all listen to now."

"That's not quite the way it works," said Pike.

"Still hearing good things about you."

"I do what I'm paid for." It was Janet who'd accused him of practicing modesty, he remembered. Like everything else, that seemed a long time ago.

"I'd still like you to come across to the World Bank with me," said Ambersom.

"I'm not sure that I'm ready for a move yet."

"Don't miss your chance, Tom. There's a lot of opportunity there; it's the place to get noticed."

Janet saved him, breaking away from the crowd and bringing the slim man with her. "Darling," she gushed. "Meet Leon; Leon Santez. It's his exhibition. Isn't it fantastic!"

"Fantastic," agreed Pike, shaking the offered hand. It

was a brief, limp contact. Pike was surprised to see the artist so formally dressed. Why had he expected the stereotype of jeans and sweat shirt? There was more eye contact.

"I'm very fortunate to have the opportunity," said the man politely.

"We've three television stations and the *New York Times* and *Washington Post* are giving us coverage." Janet stopped, pecking sideways to kiss the man on the cheek. "You're going to be famous, darling. Famous!"

Ambersom touched Pike briefly on the shoulder and said, "Why not call me soon? We'll talk further." Then he moved back to join his wife, who smiled over the man's approach towards Pike.

"What's that about?" asked Janet.

"Nothing important," said Pike. She was excited and happy at being the center of attention, he thought; but, then, she always had been.

One of the television crews she'd talked about approached the artist, leading him away to a side room for an interview. Janet hesitated, as if she were unsure whether to follow, and then turned back to her ex-husband. "He doesn't need any help," she said.

"He doesn't look as if he does."

"He's so promotable! Don't you think he's wonderful!"

"Wonderful. Quite a crowd."

"*The* crowd," said Janet. "I've checked the arrival sheets; the turn-out's marvelous." She looked around her, smiling and waving to people she recognized. "There's even talk of taking it on tour—Chicago, Washington, Philadelphia, Los Angeles." She looked back to him. "I've made it, all on my own."

"Congratulations," he said. For the first time, Pike began to look at the paintings displayed. They were futuristic and quite beyond his comprehension, kaleidescopes of color clots and arrow-like lines. "Would you go on the tour?"

"Probably," she said. "I don't want anything to go wrong."

"Be an interesting trip."

She came back to him, frowning. "What's the matter?"

"Nothing."

"You needn't be jealous, darling," she said. "He's gay."

"I'd guessed he was gay and I wasn't jealous," he said patiently. Damn her for misunderstanding.

"I've got to circulate."

"Go ahead."

"There's a table booked at the Four Seasons for afterwards: I've included you."

"I don't think so," he said. "Things to do."

She had moved away, but now she came back. "What things?"

"Work," he lied.

She felt out for his hand. "Please," she said, shedding the brittleness. "It's my night. Don't spoil my night."

"I really am busy." Weak, he thought: weak and stupid.

"*Please!*"

"Just for a while, then".

Still holding his hand she came forward and kissed him on the cheek, as she had the artist. "Have you tucked up in your own bed by ten," she promised.

It was her bed, not his, at two o'clock in the morning, and they were both coming down from the coke, and he was sore, from the sex.

"Perfect end to a perfect day," she said.

"Yes." Why the hell had he allowed it to happen again, like all the other times?

"Sorry about the work."

Momentarily, he forgot. Then he said, "I can do it tomorrow."

"There's a terrific party up at the house this weekend; the French and the Argentinian teams have arrived for America's Cup practice."

"I'm going away this weekend." He felt a brief satisfaction, which he decided was juvenile.

He felt her turn towards him in the darkness. "Where?"

"Europe," he said. "England." He hesitated and said "Business."

"On the weekend!"

"I'm going on Friday; there's a Saturday meeting."

"I'd included you in the plans for everything."

"Which was taking me for granted."

There was another movement, as she went onto her back again. "Sorry," she said tightly.

"We're not married anymore, Janet."

"I said sorry."

"We've both been letting it happen," he said, taking the opportunity. "Which was silly."

"I don't think so."

"I do."

"How long will you be away?"

"Back on Monday."

"Hope you have a good trip," she said, trying for lightness.

"So do I."

"It hasn't been a perfect day, after all," she said. "You ruined it."

The meeting was properly convened, so Jane knew it was official. Her confidence faltered, just slightly, when she entered Burnham's office to find it empty, apart from himself. He greeted her without any familiarity, remaining behind his desk and gesturing her to a chair facing him.

"There was the meeting of Court this morning," he said.

"Yes?"

"With a lot of discussion about the Russian and the East European loans."

"They're not excessive, against the reserves," she said.

"Not excessive," he agreed. "But we're getting close to the permitted percentage margin."

"Are we going to issue a warning to the clearing banks?"

Burnham shook his head. "We're going to establish a temporary monitoring unit, in addition to the normal supervisory system. I've been asked to head it."

Jane sat, waiting.

"I'd like you to be part of it," he said.

"Is that a good idea?"

"It's a professional request," said Burnham. "I want you to join me because of your proven ability; nothing more."

Jane paused, considering. "Professional," she insisted. "Absolutely nothing more."

"I've given you that assurance."

"I don't want there to be any misunderstanding."

"There won't be."

She gave a further hesitation. "It'll be an interesting exercise," she said.

Burnham smiled at her acceptance. "Let's hope that's all it is, an exercise."

19

His father again suggested the Union Club, and Pike accepted because it was as good a meeting place as any and he was more concerned at his father's reaction to the rejection he intended than with bothering to think of somewhere else. There wouldn't be any indication of anger, Pike knew—not outwardly, at least. But the man would be annoyed; he wasn't used to having any request turned down, and certainly not from his own family.

Pike arrived early, but the permanently reserved table was already occupied. The older man smiled up at his arrival, and said, "Clams are today's special. I ordered for you. Martini, too."

"Thank you," said Pike.

Indicating the immediately attentive *maitre de table,* he continued: "George says the best thing to follow is the beef."

Pike nodded his agreement to the head waiter, wondering if his father had the slightest suspicion how irritating it all was. Jane had been right. It wasn't surprising that thin bankers were rare.

"How's the IMF?" He might as well get it over with.

"Just about to set an example."

"Who?"

"France. Socialist programs costing billions, as usual without the proper degree of planning. And, as usual, the approach has come to bail them out."

"How much?"

"Ten billion. Sent the negotiating team to Paris last week."

"I saw it reported in the *Journal*," remembered Pike.

"They're already protesting, privately, at the terms. Unacceptable austerity measures, too fierce a deflation—all the predictable protests. But we're not going to shift our position. We'd be fools to consider it. They've already gone through the $4,000,000,000 standby loan they raised internationally at the end of 1982. Their trade gap could go as high as $8,000,000,000."

"You've a strong argument," conceded Pike. When would the demand come?

"Russia has gone quiet," said the older man.

Pike recognized the lure. "Lot of loans being raised," he said.

The man smiled at his son's awareness. "That's what I hear, too," he said. "But not here."

"No," agreed Pike. "Europe and Asia."

"Necessary, with the sort of expansion they've gone into. Why do you think America's being ignored?"

"Interest rates higher than anywhere else."

"No other reason than that? That's almost too obvious."

"I can't imagine any other," said Pike. He wished he could. He felt impotent.

"For the sort of funding the Eastern bloc requires now, I wouldn't have thought rates would have been an overwhelming barrier."

"They would be if there's the sort of control in Moscow that we've agreed upon," Pike pointed out. Suddenly realizing an advantage of his own from the meal, he added, "You've got a worldwide monitor, through the Fund. Any problems with payments on the new loans?"

"They're too diversified for us to get any full assessment," said the older man cautiously. "But I'd have expected to hear if there were difficulties. There's not been the slightest suggestion."

"So, world banking goes on its healthy way."

"Except that America isn't involved," reminded his father. "And it has to be, if the President is going to get the economy moving."

"Seems to be a simple enough resolve."

"How are the clams?"

"Fine."

"I ordered wine with the beef. Margaux."

"That'll be good."

"Volger's a damned fine man: Didn't try to hog the credit for himself on your early assessments."

"Lucky break," said Pike.

The wine arrived. The older man tasted it, nodded acceptance, then said across the table, "Luck wasn't involved. Your name's Pike."

Any moment now.

"Still like to keep ahead of this Russian change," said the IMF director.

"It'll become clearer in time."

"I don't want to be told! I want to do the telling. It's important to me, remember?"

Father and son looked directly at each other across the table, neither eating nor drinking.

"It's time I heard your answer."

"I know," said Pike. "I've thought a lot about it. . . ."

"I've changed my mind," stopped his father, holding up his hand in a halting gesture. "Not about wanting you, but about the function I'd want you to fulfill." He smiled and said with his unshakable confidence, "So, before you accept, I think I should tell you what it is. Russia is important and they've made Europe important, so I think that's the place to be."

"I don't understand," said Pike, who thought he did but wanted to hear it from the other man.

"I want you to go to Europe."

"Whereabouts in Europe?"

"Wherever the information is quickest and best," said the man. "Either London or Paris, I would think." He leaned across, patting his son's wrist. "Which I realize makes it difficult for you. So I'll understand if you say no."

"Difficult?" queried Pike, genuinely confused now.

"With you and Janet—you are getting back together again, aren't you?"

"That's not a difficulty," said Pike.

"It certainly wouldn't be, if you got married right away," agreed the older man, immediately enthusiastic. "Probably be the best thing, to make a fresh start, initially, somewhere away from America."

"I'm not thinking of remarrying Janet."

His father gazed again at him across the table, not responding at once. "But I understood. . . ."

"There was never anything to understand," said Pike, able for once to be more forceful with his father than he was with the woman. "She divorced me to marry someone else and that hasn't worked. For which I feel sorry for her. We met after the IMF meeting and we've seen each other a few times since. As friends. And that's all it is. There's no question of remarriage."

"I'm surprised," said the man, pushing his plate away disinterestedly. "Extremely surprised. Both families would have been very happy, you know."

"The most active participants wouldn't," insisted Pike. Janet would have accepted if he'd asked her, he supposed. Another experiment.

"Surprised and disappointed," said his father, lapsing into the habit of repetition.

"The job *has* changed," reminded Pike.

"But the obstacle I imagined isn't there anymore," said the older man, always quick to see an advantage.

"Give me a little more time."

"How long?"

"Until after the weekend."

Jane met him at the airport and said she wasn't hungry, so they went directly to her apartment. They stayed in bed until noon on Saturday, shopped briefly in Kensington High Street and went back to bed in the afternoon. They ate watching television, which they both found boring, so they went back to bed again. On the Sunday they drove in her car to Hampstead Heath and walked until her nose became red with the cold, and then they went to the Spaniard pub for sandwiches and beer.

"Hardly a jet-setting weekend, is it?" she said.

"Have I complained?"

"What would you have done if you hadn't come here?"

He laughed. "You won't believe me if I tell you."

"What?"

"Gone up to Rhode Island," he said. "The French and Argentinian America Cup teams are practicing. There were parties and stuff like that."

"Christ!" she said.

"I'd rather be here."

"I'm glad you are."

"I've been offered a new job."

"Where?"

"With the IMF."

"Your father?"

He nodded. "He wants me in Europe."

"Europe!"

"Paris, nominally. But in London a lot."

She looked away from him, staring into her glass, lower lip trapped between her teeth.

"Say something," he said.

"I'm not sure what to say."

"Would you like me to be here?"

She came up to him, serious-faced. "I can't imagine anything I'd like more."

"I think I'd like it, too," he said. What mattered more, he asked himself—the unquestionable opportunity at the IMF or Jane Rose? A ridiculous question, he thought.

Janet's apartment was on Riverside Drive. She stood at the window with her back to him, staring out over the water. He thought the stance was overly theatrical.

"When?" she said.

"As soon as I've cleared things up here—closed the apartment down, stuff like that."

"Am I being cleared up?" She turned to face him, and he was surprised at the sadness in her usually controlled face. Pike was suddenly angry at himself; it was an unaccustomed feeling. "No ties or commitments, remember?"

"There weren't, at first; you let it go on."

"I didn't make any promises."

"You did—by not making them."

"Maybe I was a bit of a bastard."

"*Maybe!*" She laughed bitterly. "A belated admission, for no one else to hear. You've always been a bastard, Tom. I said I didn't because I didn't want to frighten you away again, but I've always loved you. And you knew it. You fucked it up the first time, until I couldn't stand it anymore and I was labeled the whore. And now you've done it again. You let me believe and you let the families believe, but it's me who'll be laughed at and you'll go on being the golden boy, someone who can do no wrong. . . ." The laugh trembled, coming close to tears. "You've perfected it, haven't you?" she hurried on, determined to finish. "Never being wrong, I mean. You *are* a bastard,

Tom: a rotten bastard who uses whatever and whoever is available, but the only one who's important is Tom Pike, Junior."

Pike let the accusations wash over him, his self-anger evaporating. Overwrought and near hysterical, he thought. He stood abruptly, not wanting the farewell to degenerate any further. Another error, to have come to see her at all.

"Good-bye Janet."

"What are you going to do?" she demanded, shrill-voiced, as he walked away. "What are you going to do on that awful day when you make the mistake you've always been so frightened of?"

He turned, at the door. "Never make it."

Book Two

"I've never been so optimistic."

Beryl Sprinkel, U.S. Treasury Undersecretary, September, 1982, at the meeting in Toronto of the International Monetary Fund.

20

Through their individual European and Far East subsidiaries, all the major American banks knew within a month of loans being raised by the Eastern bloc, led by Moscow, although, because the affiliate links were individual, there was no facility through which they could gauge the extent or spread of the borrowing. Wall Street is, however, a small community. It took only a few more days of apparently casual inquiry between chairman and directors, in paneled luncheon clubs and discreet cocktail receptions, to reach the conclusion that they were substantial. With that decision came several others. Predominant was that, backed by the newly responsible Soviet Union with its reassessed and substantial gold reserves, the borrowings were sound. Of equal importance was the realization that it was the financial structures of the United States, and not their separate corporations, that were being excluded. The luncheon and cocktail party gatherings were unanimous in blaming the continued high interest rates within the United States as the reason.

The pressure began simultaneously upon Richard Volger, at the Federal Reserve, and William Bell, at the Treasury in Washington. During Jordan's presidency, the traditional independence of the Federal Reserve had been lessened, and from the conference at which his Board had been singled out for open praise, Volger knew the diplomatic importance the President attached to the Eastern bloc developments.

At his own suggestion, Volger flew to Washington for a private meeting with the Treasury Secretary. In the preceding six months there had been a three per cent drop in the country's inflation rate, and Bell assessed this as proof that his tight money policy was at last succeeding. He therefore argued against any reduction in the discount rates. Volger had heard the rumors of Bell's growing unpopularity within the White House and had no intention of going down in a sinking ship, in addition to which he considered the United States bankers' concern justified.

It had been unusual for the President to chair the earlier Washington conference, and Volger reminded Bell of it, not just to stress the President's feeling about what Moscow was doing but also to infer that it could have indicated the President's lack of confidence in his own Secretary. It was a thought that Bell had at the time, and after an hour he agreed to Volger's suggestion that another conference of bankers should be called, this time with himself as chairman.

It was smaller than the original meeting, in the main conference room of the Treasury Building across the street from the White House, limited, apart from Bell and Federal Reserve bankers, to representatives from every major United States bank and financial institution.

Bell knew very well just how much he was threatened, both personally and professionally, just as he knew that, but for the goddamned Russians and their sudden financial moves, his monetary planning would be proven right. Realistically, he doubted now that he would get his chance to be shown so: Presidents demanded panacea policies that worked overnight, and bankers were greedy bastards who'd climb international money mountains to pluck half a percentage point from beyond the snowline. But he set out starting to try, quoting from the reports he'd prepared since the earlier encounter with Volger on the value of money supply control and high discount rates to confront inflation—aware, as he talked, of the unresponsive faces confronting him across the table.

It was Chase Manhattan's Hector Belcher who spoke first, when Bell threw the meeting open to debate. "Do you think a three per cent inflation drop justifies its cost?" he demanded. "We've got the highest unemployment figures in years, with destitute families wandering the cities like something out of a Steinbeck novel. There's going to be a ripple effect from what's happening because of the Soviets. They're buying, and because they're buying, things have to be manufactured. While we're counting lay-offs in thousands and tens of thousands, the manufacturing industries in Europe and the Far East will be reemploying and reequipping to meet the demands."

They were being damned clever, Bell realized: rehearsed, almost. It was a political argument they were advancing—a home consumption political argument the President would seize with both hands—not an apparent demand to get into the lending scramble, which was what they wanted.

"We're out of step," came in the Manufacturers Hanover chairman, Richard Railton. He splayed his hands, collapsing a finger as he made each point. "England is involved, along with every other country in Europe; Japan is involved; Australia is involved; Canada is involved; New Zealand is involved. . . ." The hand closed tight, Blair concluded, "Everyone is involved—except us."

Bell turned for assistance to the Federal Reserve chairman, but Volger said unhelpfully, "I don't think we can have any doubt about the security. There hasn't been a repayment crisis for months now, not even a request for rescheduling. That's directly attributable to the new attitude of the Soviet Union."

"Look what's happening to commodities," demanded

Alan Mewsom, from the Bank of America. "There's not an underdeveloped Third World country not selling its products, and suddenly things are working again."

"I don't see the economic sense of maintaining high interest rates that deprive our manufacturers of too expensive investment capital on the one hand and of the opportunity to expand overseas markets on the other," said Belcher, returning to his original point. "To me, that seems a contradiction of the free enterprise economy America is supposed to epitomize. That's not just hobbling the horse; that's breaking its legs."

"Two years ago we talked, quite seriously, of the danger of our monetary system collapsing because of overextension," said Bell, advancing an argument he knew to be weak before he spoke.

It was Railton who seized it. "Which *was* two years ago!" he said. "Since then, the international financial system has worked more smoothly than it ever has before. Brazil is coming out of the hole; so's Mexico. Even Argentina, through its trade dealings with Russia, is paying on time now."

"Is the policy of this administration complete isolationism?" demanded Belcher.

Bell gazed around at the men before him, aware that every one of them in the conference room overlooking Lafayette Park had alternative and powerful access to the President. And that they'd use it, if they hadn't already. He'd tried, he decided; maybe it couldn't be reckoned as much more than a token effort, but at least he'd made it. To Volger, he said, "What do you think it would take?"

"A percentage point-and-a-half would bring us into line with most of the rates in Europe. That's what I want to make it."

"It's a lot," said Bell.

"No, it's not," protested William Jeynes, from Citibank. "It's good competitive adjustment."

"It would cause a run against the dollar," insisted the Treasury Secretary.

"A hiccup, nothing more," insisted Belcher. "It would settle in weeks."

"What if you don't get the business?" asked Bell.

"With the right rates, we'll get the business," said Mewsom positively. He nodded towards the Bank of America chairman. "Alan's right; at the moment, we're crippled by the rates."

Bell was a proud man who'd come to enjoy Washington, even if he despised some of the compromises of politics. He didn't want to leave it yet—certainly not as the result of a cabinet reshuffle that would reflect upon his ability. A lost battle didn't mean a lost war, merely a retreat and a regrouping. He needed someone with whom to discuss another strategy. He smiled around the table at the assembled bankers, with no intention of appearing to capitulate to the arguments of a single conference. "I take your points, gentlemen. There's a cabinet meeting scheduled for Monday. You've my undertaking that I'll raise it then."

In addition to the opinions and assessments provided by Volger, Bell was backed by a large structure of permanent financial officials, with analysis and advisory functions, but from experience he knew that a report would take weeks to prepare. He was aware of the bankers' impatience and that he didn't have weeks. And he didn't want a flat, reasoned exposition anyway. He wanted an unbiased, authoritative assessment from someone with the proper international perspective.

The managing director of the IMF was an American and a former Wall Street banker, thought Bell. So was the chairman of the World Bank. Unorthodox, perhaps, but not unheard of. He wrote the names on a desk jotter and stared down at them. He knew Ambersom marginally better than Pike, but he knew neither well enough to gauge their reactions to an approach—whether they'd be offended, considering it an indiscretion. Bell remained undecided for a long time, until he remembered the younger Pike, the Federal analyst who'd been the first to isolate the Soviet behavior. He was with his father now, at the IMF, and Pike, Sr. lived in Washington.

Pike was surprised to get the call from the man he intended to replace. From his end, Bell interpreted the hesitation as offense, hurrying an explanation to reassure the other man. Pike let Bell talk, considering advantage against disadvantage. Had Bell learned of the maneuvers against himself, initiating some counterattack with this direct approach? A possibility. But a vague one. Direct confrontation wasn't the way of Washington, even from someone as inept as Bell. And the uncertainty appeared genuine, despite the telephone. Certainly, he decided, a situation to be explored. Saturday was convenient, he agreed; the Army and Navy Club would be fine.

The Treasury Secretary reiterated the attempted reassurance the moment they met. "This is completely unofficial, of course," he said.

Until I choose to make it otherwise, thought Pike. "Of course."

"Just an exchange of views between bankers."

"Just an exchange of views." He'd let the other man make the running; that way he'd tire first.

On their way through the wood-paneled halls, past the glass-encased models of ships, Pike exchanged greetings with two senators and was recognized by a third in the first floor dining room. It was a lucky meeting place, he decided, for the stories he might want to circulate afterwards.

"I want to make some sort of recommendation by Monday," said Bell, after they had been seated, continuing his explanation. "Normal channels are too slow."

When the moment was opportune, the fact that Bell sat like a nervous virgin with his hands between his knees instead of reacting immediately to what was happening in the rest of the world would be an important accusation.

"I'll help all I can," promised Pike. *And help myself more*.

"You've monitors, worldwide?"

"Naturally," said Pike. Since he'd been in Europe, Tom had kept his finger on a lot of developments. It was a hell of a comfort, having a son as able as Tom.

"*Are* we being left out?" demanded Bell.

"Undoubtedly," said Pike. "The borrowing is worldwide, with the exception of America."

"Just because of the rates?"

"What else?" Pike shrugged. There was only one logical direction in which America could go. He'd have to make it quite clear that he was the man who pointed the way, not Bell.

"What's the assessment of total loans being raised?"

"Best estimate is something like $300,000,000,000," said Pike. "It's impossible to be precise, of course."

"It's a hell of a lot of money, even at $300,000,000,000."

"It's a hell of a lot of business."

"What about repayments?"

Pike decided that the other man was a clerk. Bankers—proper bankers—weren't clerks. Proper bankers and financiers were entrepreneurs. "You know that at the end of '82 we increased our Special Drawing Right quotas and our General Arrangement to Borrow fund," he said. "It stands now at $120,000,000,000. We did it because of the $500,000,000,000 Third World debt, particularly in Latin America and South Korea. Since the Soviet turn-around, we haven't needed it. Argentina is paying on every due date, and Brazil and Mexico have accepted our conditionality, despite the deflation that involves. There's a confidence now about world banking that hasn't been around for years, even from the time before I joined the IMF. We've removed Rumania from suspension, and they haven't gone ahead with a moratorium on 1983 debts. Hungary belongs to the IMF and so does Poland. We've access to their finances; they look pretty good to me." He was offering the man no information that wasn't available in any financial journal, so there was no problem with discretion. The problem was Bell's, in making the approach in the first place.

"Do you think the policy is wrong, keeping money dear?"

"I think it was a very successful policy, one that's worked. Now I think it's time to adjust. It's ludicrous for a country like America not to be involved." Pike paused, for effect. "It could even be argued that the Soviets are ridiculing us, by keeping us out." The last point occurred to Pike as he spoke, but he thought it was a good one—certainly something to be included in the stories he intended to initiate throughout the capital. Nelson Jordan wasn't a president to accept ridicule from Russia.

"Is there any indication that the Eastern bloc want any further funding?" asked Bell.

The Treasury Secretary was running scared now. "None," said Pike, wanting to increase the other man's unease. "It would be unfortunate, wouldn't it, if we missed out because of a policy not adjusted in sufficient time?" Another angle for the stories if the rates were dropped but no loans taken up. Pike decided he couldn't lose either way.

"I think there's got to be a reduction in the rate," said Bell, as if he were announcing an uninfluenced policy decision. "I think I should tell Volger to go ahead."

"I think it would be wise."

"I'm grateful for your thoughts," said Bell.

"We're on the same side, surely?"

"I didn't embarrass you, suggesting we should meet?"

"Not at all," assured Pike. The embarrassment certainly wouldn't be his.

The luncheon bill was placed between them, and instinctively Pike reached out to sign it. Bell snatched ahead of the other man. "It was me who invited you," he said. "I'm the one who's benefited from the meeting."

Pike smiled.

* * *

Unspeaking, Malik reached out, and Lydia moved closer to him, nestling herself in the crook of his arm with her head upon his naked chest.

"Shall I tell you something?" she said.

"What?"

"I didn't think you liked me."

She felt him pull away from her in the darkness. "Didn't like you!"

"You kept your distance for a long time."

He pulled her back against him. "I was nervous," he admitted.

Now it was her turn to be surprised. "Nervous? Of me!"

"Your ideas were so unusual: I couldn't understand how they'd ever been considered."

"That wasn't nervousness," she said, understanding. "That was politics. You didn't want to be associated with something that might fail."

He didn't speak for several moments. Then he said in confession, "Offended?"

"No. I guessed that was involved, as well as a dislike."

"It was never that," he said. "Certainly not now. You believe that, don't you?"

"Yes."

"I've been thinking," he said.

"About what?"

"The divorce. Our marrying."

Lydia lay unmoving beside him in the bed, eyes tightly closed, knowing he wouldn't be able to detect her expression in the darkness. "What about it?"

"It wouldn't be right. Not at this moment. The next few weeks and months are going to be busy, the busiest yet. It just wouldn't look right, introducing a personal relationship in the middle of everything."

He waited for her to speak, but when she didn't, he said, "You do understand, don't you?"

"Yes," she said quietly. Still politics, she thought. She hoped that was all it was. Or did she? She realized she welcomed the delay.

"It doesn't mean that I don't want to—that I don't love you. I do. I want us to be married. The timing has just got to be correct."

Her life seemed to revolve around the correct timing, thought Lydia. "I understand," she said.

"Just a few months, that's all."

"Yes."

"We're going to be very happy."

"Yes," she said again. She still wished she were surer about him. But more about herself.

The guidance for the lowering of the interest rates came, as it had to, from the Federal Reserve, and Chase Manhattan was the first to move, because of their previous loan arrangement with Poland. They headed a consortia of five United States banks, with the additional involvement of Barclays and National Westminster in England, in a $60,000,000 loan to Warsaw. The other American banks were immediately behind. Two months after the lowering of the American rates, the spread of loans throughout the Eastern bloc was $1,500,000,000, with $600,000,000 taken up by the Soviet Union. American banks were extremely happy: Moscow was happier.

21

Jane decided she was in love, and it frightened her. Because she didn't want to lose it, as she had with Paul. There could only be a surface comparison, of course. Her feelings for Tom were far greater than they had ever been for Paul Burnham. She was sure of it. It was just that she could find small, secret similarities. With Burnham, it had been a competition with a wife; with Tom, it was his job. Although she didn't regret it now—welcomed it, even—Jane recognized it was her possessiveness that had caused an end of things with Burnham, and she didn't want it to happen again. So she was very careful, never showing any resentment when something happened that prevented Tom leaving Paris, where he was nominally attached to the IMF offices, always letting him initiate. Which was how it had been with Paul, she supposed. Again only a surface comparison. Paul had always been selfish, never considering her. That never happened with Tom. He'd spent more weekends in London than in Paris; on two of the four occasions he hadn't managed to get away, he'd asked her to go to France and they'd spent the free time exploring the city she knew so well from her university days, able to show off and take him to bistros and clubs he wouldn't normally have visited. And during the week there were frequent telephone calls, either to the bank during the day or the apartment at night. He wouldn't have bothered with any of it if there were other women, if he didn't care. When she thought about them, which she did all the time, Jane never considered the word love, on Tom's part. She was careful about that, just as she was careful about overpossessiveness. A searcher for omens, she found other things to indicate that he considered it more than just a passing affair. He discussed everything with her about his unusual assignment in Europe, and he wouldn't have done that with a casual acquaintance. Often he told her things she wouldn't have heard about, or he expressed a more balanced view than she might have reached and she knew the additional knowledge had made her indispensable to Burnham and the special unit that had been formed at the Bank of England. In the beginning, when Tom had first arrived, she'd hesitated at matching his information with her own, because a lot of it was officially confidential, but she'd lost the reserve with time. She had no secrets from him now, knowing that he had none from her. And he was a wonderful lover, exceeding even her sexuality.

Jane had been uncertain about Ann's invitation to Cambridge, confused by a mixture of feelings. It meant, of course, a suggestion coming from her, something she normally avoided. And she was nervous that Tom might see the visit as some official family approval or disapproval. Against the hesitation was her desire for the family *to* approve, as she knew they would. She was still undecided when he arrived from Paris, uncustomarily early on Thursday night. She mentioned it, finally, and he said he'd like to go and she was glad because it turned out to be a perfect weekend.

They drove up on the Friday, Jane invoking her elevated status by leaving the bank early so they were able to get away from London before the weekend rush. Ann matter-of-factly showed them into a double bedroom, smiling at her sister's obvious embarrassment. While the women supervised the evening meal, Pike explained to Edward the intricacies of American football, which was being broadcast on the newest television channel. On Saturday they went to a point-to-point, where Pike was able to maintain an impressive conversation with Harry about the merits and demerits of the horses and ended the day with a betting profit of £30, which Jane vetoed his giving Edward as a parting present because it was too much. Harry and Ann invited people for drinks after Sunday morning church and there were six guests at the luncheon party. They left after lunch on Sunday, pleading the need to beat the returning traffic and promising to visit again.

"Well?" said Jane.

Pike, who was driving, looked quickly at her, and then back to the road. "Well what?"

"I thought they were a bit overwhelming."

"I thought they made us very welcome."

"Not quite Rhode Island and the America's Cup practice, was it?"

"I had a hell of a time," said Pike. "Stop being an inverted snob."

She was, Jane realized. "I think they liked you," she said. She wished there'd been more opportunity for her to have talked to Ann.

"I liked them."

She put her hand out, resting it lightly on his thigh. "I enjoy being with you."

"We've got an extra day."

"Why?"

"I'm taking up the formal introduction to the Bank of England tomorrow." He'd left it until last, with the benefit of learning everything from Jane; he was sure she wasn't holding anything back.

"I would have expected to have heard, if it's someone from the unit," she said.

"It is," said Pike. "Paul Burnham."

Jane pulled her hand away from his leg, too abruptly.

"What's wrong?" he said.

"Nothing," she said shortly. She'd never identified Burnham as the man with whom she'd had the affair she confessed during their first meeting in Washington; he'd never shown any curiosity.

Pike reached across for her withdrawn hand. "Don't imagine any embarrassment because of us, do you?" he said, misunderstanding.

"No," she said.

"What then?"

"I said nothing." She was being stupid and she knew it; they'd never argued and she didn't want to now.

He drove on in silence for several miles and then said, "What's he like?"

"Head of the unit, as you know. Senior director, a member of the Court," she said. "There was speculation a few months ago that he might get a deputy chairmanship, but it hasn't happened yet."

"Like him?"

When Jane didn't reply, Pike said again, "Like him?"

"I did, once," she said at last.

"Once?"

"It was Paul I had the affair with," she said. "The one I told you about." She was staring directly ahead, frightened of his reaction.

He laughed, surprising her. "Now I'll know what sort of guy you really fancy."

"That's a stupid thing to say." The words blurted from her. "I'm sorry, I didn't mean that."

"You seem very uptight about it."

"I'm not. I'm sorry. Really." What the hell was she doing!

"Still in love with him?"

"No!" Jane shouted the denial, snatching out for his arm. He wasn't expecting the sudden movement and the car twitched sideways before he managed to correct it.

“Hey!” he said. “Steady.”

“Stop the car.”

“What?”

“Stop the car. I want you to stop the car.”

Momentarily he appeared unsure, and then he moved to the side of the road. “This isn’t a very good place to park you know.”

“I’m not interested in good parking spots,” she said. “I’m interested in making you understand something. What I said was stupid and I could have bitten my tongue off the moment I said it. When I was having the affair with Paul, I thought I loved him. Maybe I did. I don’t know. But it’s over now—completely ended. . . .” She stopped, wishing it wasn’t so dark within the vehicle, so that she could see better the expression on his face. “There’s only one person I love now,” she began again. “I love you.” She was breaking the self-imposed rules, she thought desperately.

“O.K.”

“What’s O.K. mean?”

“It means that I understand and I’m not jealous and that everything is O.K.”

“You’re making it sound like a joke.”

“You’re making it sound like a tragedy.”

A car went by, flashing its lights, but the illumination was too brief for her to see his face in any detail. “Shit!” she said. “This is becoming ridiculous!”

“Remember I told you I’d been married?” said Pike suddenly.

“Yes.”

“We met again at the end of the IMF meeting in Washington. Her marriage has broken up; there’s going to be a divorce. We got together a few times.”

“*Slept* together?” she said.

“Yes.”

“After you came to England?” said Jane, thick-voiced. “After we’d . . . after we’d made love?”

“Yes.”

"I see."

"No, you don't." He felt out in the darkness, cupping her chin. "I'm balancing the scales, dummy. Absolute confession time. If I'd wanted to remarry Janet, I'd have said no to my father's offer—which I originally intended to, anyway—and stayed in New York. But I wanted to come to Europe. I wanted to come to Europe to be close to a very beautiful, very clever, very sexy lady that I'm mad about and who shouldn't doubt me. Any more than she should doubt herself."

There was a long silence in the car. He hadn't used the word love, Jane realized. "I don't doubt myself!"

He pulled her forward, to kiss her, and then he said, "Who's talking about you?"

"What?" she said, the nervousness bunched in her stomach.

"The very beautiful, very clever, very sexy lady I was talking about is named Agnes Cludd and is the attendant of a rest room in a little bar I know off the Champs Elysées."

"Bastard!" she said, snatching out to kiss him again.

"No more goofy scenes?"

"No more goofy scenes," she promised.

Pike restarted the car and edged back out into the traffic.

"Tell you something," he said.

"What?"

"You've got a better ass than Agnes Cludd."

Pike had expected an older banker—not as old as his father, naturally, because that would have reflected upon Jane, but certainly not the hard-bodied, athletic-looking man who came, his hand outstretched, across the room and took his fingers in an almost too tight squeeze. Burnham had tousled black hair and open face, and he wore a sports club tie of some sort.

"At last," said Burnham. "I was expecting you weeks ago."

"It hasn't been an easy job to settle into," lied Pike. The feeling towards the other man was curiosity, Pike decided: definitely not the jealousy he had so easily denied to Jane on the way back from Cambridge. What was there to be jealous about, after all? Could she still be having an affair with the man? It was possible, he supposed, except that she always appeared to be at the apartment when he called. And her weekends were always free. Hardly convincing indicators. And did it matter? There was no commitment, from either side. He hadn't bothered in Paris because he wanted to get the job under control first; in fact, there was a sexual convenience to the arrangement with Jane going beyond the Bank of England thinking that she gave him. But there was no restriction upon what she did when he was away.

"No," agreed Burnham. "It isn't easy, is it?"

Pike settled into the chair Burnham indicated, aware of the photograph of the man's family framed upon the desk.

"The involvement seems to be global, with the entry of American banks," said Pike.

"Being an international organization, you've more accurate facilities than us in making an overall assessment."

Unoffended by the blatant lure, Pike said, "There's no absolutely accurate way of assessment. Our estimate is in the region of $300,000,000,000."

"In new loans, additional to those already allocated?"

"Yes," said Pike. When, he wondered, was the other man going to contribute something?

"I think it's too high," said Burnham.

Knowing from Jane of Burnham's feeling, Pike said, "Is that a personal opinion or that of the Bank?"

"It began as a personal one. But it's gaining support."

Jane hadn't told him that, thought Pike. "There's a remarkable stability."

"Thank God," said Burnham.

"How much concern is there here?"

"I head a special unit," said Burnham, unaware of the American's knowledge. "They're not often formed."

"Are your commercial banks aware of it?"

Burnham hesitated. "No. Confidence is always a fragile thing; the impression might be conveyed that we're more worried than we are."

"Its very existence is a danger, if word were to get out."

"We're being extremely careful to ensure that it doesn't," said Burnham.

"What do you intend doing, beyond monitoring?" Although he'd been expecting it, the caution concerned Pike. He realized he had become infected with the unanimous enthusiasm of every other European bank and international financier with whom he'd had contact in the last few months, an enthusiasm he remembered warning against when the financial movements first began.

This time the hesitation from Burnham was longer as he became aware that Pike had taken over the dominant role. At last, he said, "The Bank of England has a clearly defined and established responsibility. Nearly all our major clearing banks are approaching what is considered the limit of their reserve ratio."

"You mean a public warning?"

"No," corrected Burnham at once. "An extremely discreet one."

"Let's be practical," argued Pike. "No matter how discreet you attempt to make it and no matter how confidential it's treated by the individual banks, word would inevitably leak out. And there would go the confidence you've already spoken about, like water down a drain."

"I know," said Burnham heavily.

This was the first cloud in an otherwise clear sky, thought Pike. And a big one. London was still the leader. A story that began as a ripple here in Threadneedle Street would be a tidal wave by the time it hit the banks of New

York and Melbourne and Tokyo. Things got washed away by tidal waves. Like reputations. It was something he was going to have to keep under tight control through Jane. How much, he wondered, was Burnham imposing his own hesitant attitude upon the special unit and the bank directors beyond that? Another thing to find out from Jane. He was damned lucky to have formed the relationship.

"Knowing the knock-on effect it would have, it'll be a big decision to make," said Pike. "Maybe even catastrophic."

"I know that, too," said Burnham.

They'd ended the exchange with the score about even, decided Pike. He wondered how Burnham compared in bed.

Janet's affair with the painter began on the tour, when neither had anyone else. She was excited by it because she'd never made love to a bisexual and she was always excited by something new. When they returned to New York, Santez introduced her to his male lovers and the intimacy with the homosexual scene was another new experience, and Janet was thrilled by that, too. Santez had one particular man, a former seaman named James who was a painter now. Janet hung his pictures in the gallery and that exhibition was a success, like the earlier exhibition of Santez. It was in James' apartment that Janet first took heroin: another experiment. She was nervous with the hypodermic and James helped her, and afterwards all three went to bed. She watched them make love, and then they made love to her—both of them. It became very regular and Janet enjoyed it every time, better than she'd enjoyed other drugs or other sex before.

James did the buying, because he knew the dealers. The gallery was crowded on the Saturday, because both Santez and James were displaying some new work. There were photographers there, too, which made it worse.

She realized later that it was James she heard shout, although she didn't hear what he said, and then there was a scream, from some woman. James' arms were already handcuffed behind his back when she reached them, and a second FBI man was on the point of arresting Santez.

"This is entrapment, motherfucker," shouted James.

"Kiss my ass, fag," said the Bureau man.

"What's happening?" demanded Janet.

"You Janet Ambersom?"

"Yes."

"You're being busted, lady. That's what's happening."

22

It was their final appearance in front of the economic subcommittee before it presented its report to the full Politburo, and Lydia and Malik prepared themselves carefully for it, conscious of its importance. Separately, they reviewed the scheme from the moment of its inception, in order to ensure that nothing had been overlooked or neglected, and then they held their own conference, their professionalism subjugating their personal relationship. They entered the Kremlin session confidently, nodding with accustomed familiarity to the assembled men. Yakov Lenev was chairman, as usual. Viktor Korobov and Ivan Pushkov flanked him on either side. The places for Lydia and Malik were no longer arranged away from the table, making them appear, by their isolation, witnesses at some enquiry, but directly against the table, so that they formed part of the committee.

"Everything is complete?" asked Lenev.

"We think so," said Malik.

"We've attained sufficient indebtedness?" asked Korobov.

"The total is $650,000,000,000," said Lydia. "Of that, $230,000,000,000 is against the Soviet Union, the remainder throughout the satellites."

"Western money?" qualified Pushkov.

Malik nodded. "The spread is fairly even, but Europe is the predominant lender."

"America sought involvement?" said Lenev.

Malik smiled briefly towards Lydia, recalling the earlier doubt of the committee that the American banks would come forward. "Their total is $1,500,000,000," he said. "They have to be less than anyone else at the moment, of course."

"What's the satellite dependence upon us?" asked Pushkov.

"Three hundred thousand million," said Malik. "Predominantly short-term. And then there's Third World. That's important, as we have already explained."

"The call-in will not arouse suspicion?"

"None," assured Malik. "That's been important throughout, but is particularly so at this stage. It'll only be from our own bloc, of course; we don't want to lose influence in the uncommitted nations."

"When does the gold sale commence?" said Pushkov.

"Immediately," said Malik. "There's no danger from calling in the loans, but the sale will provide an explanation if one is sought by any of the analysts."

"How much?"

"We've arranged complete cover through nominees," said Lydia. "They'll only be able to make the vaguest estimate. It will appear that a sudden shortage of foreign currency made the sale necessary, specifically for the purpose of meeting the debts."

"But that we're still being absolutely responsible, by making the sale," added Malik. "That's got to be the keynote throughout."

"So far we've only talked about financial debts," said Lenev. "What about export guarantees?"

"As widespread as the loans themselves," said Lydia. "To ourselves and the other six within the Bloc, Western governments are extended to guarantee pledges of $260,000,000,000. That's always been how it was to start."

Lenev looked to the men on either side of him and then back at Malik and Lydia. "This is an exciting moment," he said. "An historic one."

"We hope it will be shown to be," said Malik modestly. He remembered saying that to Lydia, months ago. He paused and said, "We need authority to proceed to the final stage."

Again Lenev looked to both committee men with him and then said, "We'll make a full presentment to the Politburo tomorrow. But I can assure you there will be no difficulty. From this moment you can take it that approval has been given."

Jane asked him not to wait for her at the bank, so Pike used the time to return to her apartment and to contact Paris for any weekend messages. It was his analyst's training to maintain records, so he made a careful resumé of his meeting with Burnham. He was checking it when Jane came home. It was difficult for Pike to hold back until he'd made her a drink. As he gave it to her, he said, "I hadn't appreciated the attitude I'd find." He tried to avoid it sounding accusatory, but he wasn't sure he succeeded.

"What attitude?"

"Your people are scared."

"I told you that."

She had, conceded Pike. "I hadn't anticipated how much. Or that it was becoming an attitude beyond Burnham and his immediate unit."

"I'm not sure it has," said Jane. "Last week's analysis pointed up the estimated commitment of the commercial banks, but I'm not aware of any response from the Court. Burnham's a member, so maybe he knows in advance."

It had been a mistake to be complacent about the advantage he had with Jane at the Bank of England, decided Pike. "Burnham said warnings might be sent out."

Jane frowned at his persistence. "Darling," she said patiently, "banks can only lend a percentage of their stated assets. If we see that they're nudging the limit or likely to exceed it, a warning is practically automatic."

She was right to be patronizing, admitted Pike. "That could cause uncertainty: panic, even. Burnham's worried about confidence. Every banker is."

"No one's reached the limit yet," Jane pointed out reasonably. "Paul was bound to be pessimistic; don't forget he's opposed the accepted assessment all along. He's arguing his case."

Right again, thought Pike. "Seemed strange, getting a contrary view."

Her frown deepened. "Don't say Paul's changed your mind!"

"Of course not," said Pike. "How could he have done!"

Jane looked away, into her glass. "What did you think of him?"

Pike paused. Had he been jealous at the meeting with Burnham? He pushed the thought aside, irritably. "Clever," he said. "Intelligent, too; clever people often aren't. On top of everything, very confident. . . ." There was another hesitation. "Also very attractive, I guess." He wondered again how he compared in bed.

"Yes," she said.

"What did you think of him?" demanded Pike. Surely that was a jealous question?

She looked at him curiously. "Something like that."

Neither spoke for several moments and then she said, "It's over. Finished. You know that, don't you?"

"We've never talked about it," he reminded her. "But I guess so, yes."

"It is," she insisted.

"Good," he said. "I don't want to share you."

She smiled, pleased with his attitude. "Going back tomorrow?"

"Yes," said Pike. "I called Paris before you came in; my father's making a visit."

23

It was the first time since Pike's European assignment that his father had visited Paris, and Pike felt a burn of embarrassment at the nervous preparation that preceded the older man's arrival. But the reaction was less than usual, he realized, surprised—certainly less than when they'd been together at Chase Manhattan, and even during their encounters afterwards, when he'd moved to the Federal Reserve. Pike was curious of his own attitude, conscious of it during the official greetings and the immediate meetings which followed, in all of which he was included. Before Pike had always felt imprisoned, which he recognised as a clumsy analogy but one that fitted his almost constant impression. But now he didn't. The jail gates had opened—he hadn't known when or how—and he felt free. Which was a contradiction, because he was as closely linked at the IMF as he had been at Chase, apart from a physical distance of 3,500 miles.

The meetings were formalities, staged performances for which he did not have to concentrate fully in order to follow the lines and he thought instead of the changed demeanor. *Was* he as closely linked? Superficially, perhaps. But there was a difference from everything that had happened before. Inherently there was the influence of the name, but Pike knew he'd proved himself to everyone in Paris and Geneva, independently of any sycophancy the officials might have felt necessary to show.

And not just here, in Europe. There was New York, before that. Proved himself and stayed ahead of the game, in every assessment. It had been an aberration to become affected by Burnham's pessimism. The English attitude shouldn't be ignored, but neither should it be made more than it was.

After the formal morning meetings there was the formal lunch, followed by formal afternoon sessions and a formal cocktail party before the formal official dinner, so it was nearly midnight before they returned together to the Seine-bordering apartment, with its view of the floodlit Notre Dame. Pike thought his father looked tired, which was hardly surprising, considering the activities of the day directly following the flight from America, but still something which registered with him. His father had always seemed indestructible, someone spared the frailties of others—another altered impression, Pike realized.

"Your mother almost came," said the older man. "She was keen to see you. I put her off when I realized the tightness of the schedule."

"Maybe I'll make a trip home soon," said Pike. "Still a lot to be done here first."

The IMF director unbuttoned his vest and eased off his shoes, sighing back into a chair with the best view of the French capital through the uncurtained windows. "Appreciate what you've done for me, Tom. It's been a first-class job."

"I've enjoyed it."

"Surprised by the reduction in the Federal rate?"

"Not really," said Pike. "It had to happen."

"Except that the damned fool Bell didn't realize the need. I made it happen."

"You!"

His father nodded, pleased with his son's surprise. "Running scared to make a decision after Volger and the others backed him into a corner, so he came to me." He smiled. "And guess what?"

"What?"

"He made it clear in the Cabinet meeting that I approved the lowering—that I thought it was a good idea."

Pike frowned. "Aren't the boundary lines getting a little crossed here?"

"Damned sure they are, but Bell's committing the indiscretions, not me. And he's too stupid to see the hole he's digging for himself. He promised me it was a private meeting, but he let the Cabinet know about it so that if it went wrong he wouldn't be carrying the can. So I'm going to get the credit and Bell is going to be the Treasury Secretary who tried to hedge his bet. I can't go wrong."

"What about Ambersom?"

His father looked at him surprised and then said, "Of course, you wouldn't know: I'm sorry."

"Know what?"

"Janet has been arrested: allowing the gallery to be used for heroin trafficking."

"What!"

"Involved with some homosexual painters, apparently. It hasn't come to trial yet, but the scandal is big enough. Won't affect Ambersom at the World Bank, of course. But he's out of the running as far as coming into the government is concerned. I've got a clear field."

Pike waited to feel some distaste at his father's attitude. Nothing came. "Poor Janet," he said.

"Always was a wayward girl," said the other man dismissively. "Easy to understand why things didn't work out between you—glad they didn't now."

Jesus! thought Pike. He said, "You wanted us to get back together!"

His father gazed up at him without any embarrassment. "Would have been a mistake, a great mistake."

"Wonder if I could help in any way?"

The elder Pike frowned. "You're out of it, Tom; best to stay that way."

It had been an instinctive response. Objectively, Pike couldn't think of anything he could do; maybe his father was right. "You got a promise about the Treasury?"

"Good enough indications."

"Congratulations."

His father smiled. "It hasn't happened yet. But a lot of it is due to you, Tom. You haven't put a foot wrong. Thank you."

"Not everyone seems to think as I do."

"Who?"

"I told you about the special monitor put on their clearing banks loans, beyond the normal supervisors check, by the Bank of England?"

The older man nodded.

"I met their director, man called Burnham. He says the Bank is getting increasingly concerned. Might even issue a warning."

"I don't like that," said the IMF director.

"Neither do I," said Pike. "We both agreed to the danger."

"What did he say?"

"That the Bank appreciated it, too."

"What do *you* think?"

Pike hesitated, conscious of the confidence shown by the question. "There's always been a residual doubt, from the very beginning," he said. "It's stronger in England than from anywhere else. Having said that, I'll agree that, set out on paper, the calculated figures are pretty frightening."

"We've always been able to roughly assess the commitment," reminded Pike's father. "Were there any positive facts to give grounds for the feeling?"

"None. Certainly none that Burnham offered." He paused, holding back from disclosing his association with

Jane. Instead, he said, "I think I would know them, if there were."

"There's no repayment difficulties?"

"That's always the indicator I look for first, in any analysis," disclosed Pike. "I've managed to establish a pretty efficient checking system, through our own resources and those I've made in individual central banks."

"And?"

"It's unprecedented," said Pike. "There hasn't been a repayment delay or a rescheduling request from anyone in the last eight months. And that figure is accurate up to last Friday."

The tenseness seemed to go from the older man and he smiled broadly. "So where's the problem?"

"There isn't one," admitted Pike.

The Russians spread the gold sale worldwide, and once again Malik and Lydia remained late every night in the telex room, linked to the metal exchanges, monitoring the movements. It registered first in Paris, then Hong Kong, and finally in America, over a period of a week.

"How much have we sold?" asked Lydia.

"Tons, not ounces!" said Malik.

"That's enormous."

"It has to be, to register," said the Finance Minister. "People are going to start asking where it's coming from."

"We'll tell them, in good time," said the woman.

24

Once the volume became obvious, Pike began monitoring the gold disposals, calling for daily reports from the world's metal markets to maintain an accurate check on the amounts and making a formal enquiry to Pretoria to establish if South Africa were the source. Being IMF debtors, South Africa was obliged to answer truthfully, and when their denial came, he went back to the markets again, attempting an answer from there and failing, because everywhere the vendors were nominees.

Until then he'd held back from the speculation, unwilling to sound the alarm at the suspicion of a fire, but the size of the sale made the Soviet Union the obvious answer.

Jane came to him on two successive weekends, and on the second she confirmed that the Bank of England had decided upon Moscow, too. Pike named Russia in a report to Washington a week before the speculation became public, appearing simultaneously in the *Wall Street Journal* in America and the *Financial Times* in England. Concerned there might have been something he'd missed, Pike reviewed everything that had happened since the Soviet financial development. He found it after three days. The telephone contact, beyond their normal telex communication, started between Pike and his father from the moment of his identifying Russia as the possible seller, calls always from Washington. The official confirmation from Moscow was timed at 5:00 p.m. Astride the time changes between East and West, Pike initiated the call to his father's Fauquier County home, catching the older man before he left for the IMF's Washington headquarters.

"What's your feeling?" demanded his father at once.

"They had repayments due of about $60,000,000," said Pike. "The gold sales were in tons, not ounces. The obvious answer is that they were raising foreign currency."

"Does the official announcement say that?"

"No," said Pike. "It's a confirmation of sale, nothing more. They don't give an amount, either."

"They're being responsible?"

Pike hesitated. "That's one interpretation."

From Washington the man discerned the doubt. "They had a debt and they met the payment," he insisted.

"They upset the metal markets doing it."

"Markets are markets, whether they're selling vegetables or gold," said the IMF chairman. "Prices rise and prices fall. The important thing is that the Soviets had assets and they realized them. You were the first to argue responsibility, and they're showing it."

"Yes," agreed Pike.

"So there's no problem?"

"There might be," cautioned Pike.

"What?"

"I've reviewed everything during the gold sale, gone back beyond the new loan agreements. And found something I'd overlooked."

From Washington there was a silence. Once, thought Pike, he would have been nervous with a reaction like that: frightened, even. He didn't think he was now.

"What mistake?" demanded his father, finally.

"I didn't say mistake," qualified Pike. "I said something I'd overlooked. All the immediate Soviet loans are bunched short-term."

"So?"

His father should have realized what that meant without having to ask the question.

"There's a maturity next month: $40,000,000 worldwide, as far as I can calculate. A similar sum a month later."

"I see," said his father heavily.

"The current gold sale might have covered their shortfall," said Pike. "There were pockets of disposals from other holders: France, I know for a fact. And I suspect some of the Gulf States. Because all the Soviet sales were under nominee, it's absolutely impossible to assess how much currency they raised. Or how much they sold."

"We know they've got a substantial stockpile, because of the error in calculation they admitted a few months back."

"They've hardly bitten into it, if the figures in that admission were correct," said Pike. "Price fluctuations make it extremely difficult, and, as I say, others joined in the selling, but working backwards from the disposal, I guess something like twenty tons was sold."

"I wish we'd isolated the short-term repayments sooner," said the IMF director.

"I'm sorry."

"It's not your fault," said his father at once. "The facts were there for others to see as well." There was a moment of silence, and then he said, "This could go badly for me, Tom."

"I know; that's why I called right away."

"Bell has me marked as the main challenger. And he mentioned me at the cabinet meeting that agreed to lower the discount rates. He'll use it, sure as hell, if a problem arises."

"Yes," said Pike.

"Do you think I should pass it on? A lot of my friends . . . people you know as well . . . are extended on this."

"You'd be exposing yourself if you did," warned Pike. "And maybe causing unnecessary concern. Panic, even. I don't think you should, not yet."

"No," agreed the older man at once. "No panic. But I don't want the accusation that I held back when I should have been sounding warnings."

His father was boxed in either way, thought Pike. He said, "That's not your function, not yet. They've all got analysts. They're capable of reading the signs, just like we are."

"They might not have balanced the sales against the short-term settlements," pointed out his father. "And if they have and I'm asked unofficially for an opinion, what do I say?"

Pike recognized the question as rhetorical but answered it anyway.

"Your initial reaction was that they are acting responsibly," he pointed out. "Which they are. And their publicly admitted gold reserves make another sale practicable. There's a positive as well as a negative way of looking at what's happening." Pike realized as he spoke that he was reluctant to abandon the position that had established his reputation. There was another realization, too. It could mean that Burnham was right. And he was wrong. He didn't want Burnham to win at anything.

"No need for undue concern?"

"Awareness of a possible difficulty," advised Pike. "But certainly no need for undue concern, not yet. And certainly no reaction on our part that might cause a misinterpretation." He hoped to God he wasn't being too sanguine.

"I hope you're right," said the older man.

As always, the timetable was strictly regimented. A Polish delegation was summoned to Moscow first, and once again Lydia confronted Florian Moczar and Zofia

Opalko, although it was Malik who formally headed the Russian negotiating team. After the Poles came the Rumanians, then the Hungarians, and finally the Czechs, to whom had been advanced loans. Because it was from Buenos Aires the Russians wanted everything to begin again, the negotiators who concluded the Argentinian trade agreement were invited to the Soviet capital. This time there were no Bolshoi performances or champagne receptions attended by Politburo members. It was a stiff, formal conference, summoned for only one reason—the announcement by Russia that they were suspending the support finance for the aid arrangements reached earlier.

The announcement from Buenos Aires of the Soviet suspension coincided with the request to the IMF from Poland to recycle short-term debts and interest payments on just under three billion dollars. Poland at least showed the necessary financial propriety.

The following day, Rumania—a country whose traditions of unilaterally refusing to pay without the formality of negotiations had already resulted in an earlier suspension from the IMF—announced it would neither meet interest nor capital repayments during the forthcoming six months. This time slightly more than three billion was involved.

His father caught Pike at the Paris apartment while he was packing for his normal weekend in London. "I've called a meeting of the executive directors," said the older man. "I don't like the way it looks."

"No," agreed Pike. "Neither do I."

"I think you'd better come home."

It sounded like the sort of rebuke that his father had made when he failed to get the Civil War poetry right during the childhood recitations.

*   *   *

Once the plea of entrapment was rejected, the two men pleaded guilty. To represent Janet, Ambersom employed a battery of counsel who called the two painters as defense witnesses. Both gave evidence that Janet was unaware of the transactions. It wasn't believed against prosecution evidence of the FBI surveillance of previous purchases, two from FBI agents who attested Janet was an aware and an involved party to what was going on. Both men had previous convictions and were jailed. Janet was placed on probation with the condition that she enter residence in a rehabilitation program.

Default is another word for bankruptcy, and declaring it gives a bank the right to seize whatever assets of the indebted country it can. One declaration would automatically have carried its consortium with it. Once one gave, the international bankers knew others would crumble and the financial system of the West would be carried away in the flood pouring over the breached barrier.

The need was for absolute secrecy.

In America, because of the ease of travel between New York and Washington, the Treasury Secretary had a personal meeting with the Federal Reserve chairman and the entire Federal board of governors. Before leaving New York, Volger had an hour-long telephone conversation with the chairman of the Bank of England in an effort to establish the size of any total rescheduling throughout Europe. The Bank of England chairman, Sir Herbert Course, said the figures were still being assessed by his special unit and confirmed that he was holding talks with the British Chancellor of the Exchequer, in common with meetings being held throughout Europe between central bank chairmen and finance ministers.

The necessity to discover the worldwide extent of the endangered debts made logical Volger's approach to the

IMF—to whom the Polish and Rumanian moves had, after all, been made—and the World Bank.

The gathering of the IMF executive directors summoned by Pike's father was the only proper conference, and that was inconclusive because, despite the particular efforts of Pike through the preceding months, the information available was inadequate due to some of the lenders not being members of the Fund and, therefore, with no duty to report the size or degree of the loans.

Apart from the IMF conference, all the other liaisons were discreet—usually by telephone to avoid gossip by telex operators—and on a personal level between respective directors trying to make a full discovery.

The IMF became the central collation agency for the information, which in cases continued to be divulged reluctantly, and sometimes incompletely, and the need for time was realized. To gain it and to defeat the possibility of speculation and rumor undermining the confidence they were working to maintain, the IMF publicly announced the Polish and Rumanian requests with a communique of agreement for the rescheduling, with the calming comment that, spread as it was between two countries and among so many different banking outlets, the amount in international terms was not large. The World Bank declared it would advance funds through its international development system to ease the Argentinian short-fall created by the Russian trade credit withdrawal.

Within a fortnight and still without a complete evaluation of the total debt, there was general agreement between the Bank of International Settlements, the IMF, the World Bank and the boards of the central banks of Europe, Asia and Australasia that potentially there existed the possibility of a disaster.

With one agreement came another—that there was cause for an international conference convened in such a way as to continue the secrecy that had so far, almost miraculously, been achieved. Once more the IMF made it possible.

Scheduled at the month's end was a meeting in Washington of the Monetary Fund's Interim Committee, its policy-forming body composed frequently by Finance Ministers, Chancellors of Exchequers and Treasury Secretaries of member countries. Those ministers, chancellors and secretaries had all been involved and knew the possible danger. It was decided that the Interim Committee should be the shield behind which they formed up in an attempt to confront it.

For Pike, the period leading up to the special meeting became an existence of snatched sleep in the closest hotel possible and near dawn to late night occupation of the IMF building in Washington in an effort to create an accurate compilation of the total indebtedness. Not once, since Pike's return from Europe, had there been an open accusation or criticism from his father. Or from anyone else. Not that there needed to be. Pike recognized it as an exaggeration—conceit, even—to imagine himself singularly responsible. Men with far more experience and influence had made assessments unaware of his views. So there were many originators. But Pike had come to regard himself as *the* originator. His early recognition of what was happening in Russia had been the banner he trailed from his lance at Washington meetings and Federal Reserve conferences and, later, confidently, with the IMF in France. So there were conflicting and interlocked reasons for his apparent dedication. Every enquiry he initiated or analysis he prepared *was* to create the debt assessment. But equally—perhaps predominantly—it was also to assure Thomas Hamilton Pike, Jr. that he had not begun the most catastrophic mistake in banking history. It was an assurance he had not been able to find. And the thought that he might have done it was a constant, unremitting fear, a fear that gnawed at the carefully created impression of confidence; he became irritable and over-demanding, shouting impatient orders instead of making moderate-voiced requests.

The attitude extended to his contact with Jane. Less and

less were the telephone calls personal, as he had managed to make them between Paris and London; more and more his blatant interest was to discover what was happening within the Bank of England's special unit. Jane was reluctant to have such conversations routed through the Bank's switchboard and even more reluctant to conduct them from the casual insecurity of her apartment telephone. Pike misinterpreted her reluctance as being influenced by Burnham, and when he hinted at it, she accused him in return of not being interested in her but in the work she was doing.

The distance between them was more than in miles by the time he called, a week before the special conference.

"I've been chosen as part of the British delegation," she said.

"Good."

"Is that all—good?"

Shit, he thought. "I'm very glad, really. Let's not pick a fight."

"I'm not trying to pick a fight."

"Is Burnham part of it, too?"

"Of course," she said. "He was chairman of the unit; he'd hardly be left behind, would he?"

"He must be feeling very pleased with himself."

"Why?"

"It looks as if he was right, doesn't it?" said Pike.

There was a pause from her end of the line. Then she said, "I don't believe he's thinking of it in personal terms."

Of course he was, thought Pike. "It'll be good to see you again," he said, trying to bridge the gap.

"Really?" The hope was obvious in the question.

"Really," he said. "I've taken a suite in a hotel near the IMF."

There was another brief silence. "You want me to stay with you?"

"Of course," he said.

"That wouldn't be very sensible, would it?"

"Why not?"

"I'm part of an official delegation."

"Wouldn't Burnham like it?"

"Stop it, Tom!"

"Why shouldn't you stay where you want to?"

"Be realistic, darling! Please!"

"I don't give a damn about appearances."

"It wouldn't be yours at risk, would it?" Was she being hypocritical, after the last Washington visit? She'd been anxious enough to occupy someone's bed then. Why was everything going sour like this? Tom's fault or hers?

"It's going to be ridiculous, living in the same city and not being together," Pike said.

"I didn't say we wouldn't be together. I said I'd have to appear at least to be living as part of the delegation."

"Where?"

"The Jefferson again." When he didn't respond she said, "We'll spend a lot of time together. I promise."

"Sure."

"That sounds as if you're not interested."

"You know that isn't true."

"Do I?"

"I said I didn't want to fight."

"I said I didn't want to, either."

"Think about staying with me?" he persisted.

"All right." It was easier than keeping up this brittle duel, though she knew she wouldn't.

"It isn't going to be an easy meeting."

Briefly she thought he was still talking about them, but then, sadly, she understood. "We're not sure of the extent of the problem yet, even if there is one," she said. "And if there is, there'll be a resolve; there always is."

Pike was immediately attentive, imagining a lead to the special unit's thinking. "What?" he said.

"That's what the meeting is being called to decide," said Jane.

* * *

The period for Lydia and Malik had been as nerve-stretching as it had been for Pike six thousand miles away. Although the IMF and the World Bank had publicly reacted as anticipated, it had always been a possibility that some bank would prematurely declare a default, spoiling everything. It was two months after the announcements before they began to relax.

"It could still happen," warned Malik. He sat in his office with his chin cupped in his hands, gazing in admiration across the desk at her.

"Unlikely now," she said.

"It would still be a catastrophe for them," said Malik. "Looking forward to our getting married?"

"It isn't the catastrophe towards which we've been working," she reminded.

"You haven't answered my question."

"Of course I'm looking forward to it," she said. She wished it were true. Why was she dissatisfied?

Henry Ambersom was waiting in the corridor, and Pike's immediate impression was of a nervousness he hadn't recognized before in the World Bank chairman. Surely the telephone call didn't mean the man still wanted to pursue the invitation to join him?

"How are you, Tom?"

"Fine, thank you, sir."

"Enjoying Europe?"

"Very much, thank you." Belatedly, Pike said, "I was very sorry to hear about Janet."

"That's what I wanted to talk to you about," said Ambersom.

Tom looked at the older man curiously.

"She's very unwell, Tom. Very unwell indeed."

"I'm very sorry," Pike repeated, not knowing what else to say.

"I've a favor to ask you."

"What?"

"I think she'd appreciate a visit; no one goes to see her anymore, only her mother and me."

Pike realized the cause of the man's apparent nervousness: Ambersom seemed not just old but physically smaller, he thought. "I don't have a lot of time," he said.

"It would mean a great deal to me, Tom. A great deal to Janet, too."

"I'll try," said Pike unsurely.

"That would be very kind of you, very kind indeed."

Why, wondered Pike, was the man repetitious, like his father?

25

Every government as well as every central bank was represented, so accommodation was difficult. For that reason, the advisory groups were strictly limited, but the conference chamber was still tightly packed, with insufficient room for the usual delineation between delegations. Pike, as part of the IMF, was practically opposite the British contingent. Jane and Burnham were side-by-side, directly behind the chairman of the Bank of England and the British chancellor, and close together because of the seating problem. He knew they couldn't have sat any differently, but Pike still felt a surge of irritation. Jane had pleaded a planning conference for not seeing him as soon as she arrived, the previous night, and he'd been angered by that, too. There had been a brief encounter outside the chamber and she'd agreed to lunch, but Pike had imagined her embarrassed. She saw him looking across at her now and she blushed, smiling hesitantly. Almost at once she was interrupted by Burnham, bending even closer towards her, and she looked away.

Although it was a meeting of the Interim Committee in name only, it retained the committee's operating procedure, so the control remained with the committee's chairman,

British chancellor Stephen Wilder. He was a pouch-eyed, mottle-faced man who wore a bow tie and affected an attitude of nothing-new weariness.

"I'd like to welcome you here today for a meeting that I hope will prove premature and unnecessary," Wilder began, with attempted lightness, and from various parts of the room there were polite smiles. "If it is," he took up, "then I shall be delighted. The alternative would be very unsettling. . . ." He allowed the pause. "Very unsettling indeed. For some months past, the international monetary system has operated in a manner better than ever before. It's given everyone renewed confidence: proper confidence. Which is why this meeting is important. It would be a gross exaggeration to make a comparison with any discussion we might have here today with the Bretton Woods conference after the Second World War that attempted to create a global financial system. But maybe there are slight similarities. The aim then was lasting stability. The aim now is lasting stability."

The conference had settled now, Pike realized. The adjustments had been made to the translation headsets and people had arranged themselves as comfortably as possible in such crowded conditions. An effort had been made to identify the groups by name plaques. Australia and New Zealand were together, with Japan alongside. The Far East continued with Hong Kong and Singapore, and the European countries were grouped together, too—Germany, France, Italy, Spain, the Netherlands, Belgium, then Denmark and Norway of the Scandinavian countries. South Africa separated the American contingent, to his right, beyond the World Bank, grouped with Canada. Pike looked again towards the British delegation. Jane was still in conversation with Burnham.

Wilder indicated the IMF grouping and said, "Can we have the most accurate assessment, please?"

It was as recent as the previous night, completed by

Pike a few moments before his unsuccessful contact with Jane. His father needlessly took up the folder and said, "From the information available to us, it would seem that capital indebtedness overall is $600,000,000,000. . . ."

Pike was looking around the room at the disclosure, intent upon the reaction from the assembled financiers. Almost unanimously it was one of consternation.

"This is, of course," continued his father, "in addition to the outstanding loans prior to the changes of which we are all familiar within the Soviet Union and the Eastern bloc. That figure is $630,000,000,000. . . ."

He hesitated at movement from the British assembly: Pike saw Burnham leaning forward, head close to the chairman of the Bank of England. Wilder became aware of it as well and turned inquiringly to Sir Herbert Course. The Bank of England chairman responded to the look as an invitation. Bending towards the microphone, he said, "Our own analysis put the new loan debts higher than $600,000,000,000. Our figure is closer to $650,000,000,000."

Son-of-a-bitch! thought Pike. He reached forward, thrusting the breakdown list of figures in front of his father. The older man hesitated and then began reciting it. Around the vast room every delegation was bent forward, taking notes of the itemized figures. The exception was the British, who appeared only to be comparing against their own lists. ". . . which comes to $600,000,000,000," concluded the IMF managing director.

Once again Burnham came forward, offering another list to his chairman. Course looked at it briefly, then turned back towards the crowded room. He said, "Our information indicates that to be incomplete. We've confirmed figures of four separate consortia, two involving our own Lloyds, National Westminster and Midland groups, which adds $30,000,000,000 to that figure. One of the other consortia is headed by Brazil; the fourth is spread throughout Asia, with the Japanese Mitsubishi heading the group."

Brazil was not represented at the conference. The attention automatically went to the Japanese delegation. The British document was handed to them for brief comparison, and then the Japanese finance minister, Ienari Tanaka, spoke sibilantly into his microphone. Pike adjusted his earphones in time to hear agreement of the British assessment.

He was being ridiculed, Pike accepted. The purpose of this conference was to challenge his original theory, and he was now shown to be lacking in assembling the very material it needed to make any sort of decision about the mistakes of that theory. Burnham would have withheld the British figures to prove himself superior. That was still no excuse for failing to include the Japanese and Brazilian loans. His father turned towards him and Pike gave a shrug of acceptance. The IMF managing director looked back to the room and said, tight-faced, "There would seem to be a miscalculation. We accept the higher figure of $650,000,000,000."

The American financiers were grouped to their right. Pike was aware of the United States Treasury Secretary in mouth-to-ear conversation with Volger and with Ambersom. He knew his father had also detected Bell's muttering.

"We're considering total indebtedness of $1,289,000,000,000?" demanded Wilder, determined upon clarity.

"That would seem to be the figure of old and new loans," agreed the IMF official. Pike saw that his father was white-faced and guessed at the anger. It was a justified reaction at being exposed to correction among people like this, he decided.

"Is there a breakdown of guaranteed export credits?" asked Wilder.

Pike's father hesitated, looking beyond the chairman to the British back-up. "At risk at the moment would only appear to be Poland, Rumania and Argentina," he said. "The total of their guarantees, over the coming six months, is in the region of $110,000,000."

"If the guarantor governments of the West have to meet those commitments for failed payments, then that increases the possible difficulty to $1,280,110,000,000?" said the pedantic Wilder.

Again the IMF controller looked to the British before saying, "That would seem to be the figure." He stopped, awaiting a reaction. The Bank of England chairman nodded agreement.

"I think it is important to realize, however," continued the elder Pike, gaining confidence, "that the export credits could go higher. Were there to be a default throughout the six Eastern bloc nations, then that $110,000,000 could go as high as $230,000,000. And it would, of course, be a recurring debt, in addition to both the capital sum and the interest on that sum."

"Any views?" invited Wilder, generally.

"There's also the accumulative problem," came in Sir Herbert Course at once. "Some of the lenders are also the borrowers. We've already itemized a commitment by Brazil, a country with debts of $89,000,000,000 in its own right. Mexican banks are also involved in three consortia, according to our evidence; Chile, too."

"Providing the difficulties don't escalate, that makes sound fiscal practice," pointed out Harry Ambersom, whose World Bank was heavily extended throughout South America. "The interest payments on their own lending can be set against their own loan premiums, giving them their export earnings to reduce the capital."

"Which brings us to the core of the problem," interrupted the American Treasury Secretary. Pike was conscious of his father's stiffening as Bell began to speak.

"For months now there's been an impression of security," continued Bell. "Commodity prices and markets worldwide have strengthened; countries have been earning, and in turn they have been paying. . . ." He nodded towards the chairman. "We've come nearer than ever before to reaching the sort of system that our chairman referred to earlier as being the ambition of the Bretton Woods conference.'' He paused again. ''But I think it has been a false impression of security.'' Now Bell was looking accusingly at the IMF managing director, and Pike, just behind his father, was conscious of other people realizing the direction of the Treasury Secretary's attention. ''Mistakes have been made,'' said Bell. ''Maybe disastrous mistakes. The exposure is too great and too widespread. We know from their own indebtedness that Brazil and Mexico and Chile couldn't withstand even the minimum period of a moratorium . . . May I invite, through you, Mr. Chairman, an indication of how other countries might be affected?''

Wilder looked pointedly at the American, as if imagining his own function being usurped, and then he said, generally again, ''Would anyone like to comment?''

''It is no secret that we would need assistance from the Bank for International Settlements,'' said Pierre Larouse, the French finance minister. ''We've already intimated as much.''

''Italy would also experience difficulty,'' said Luigi Cambino, its central bank chairman.

''We don't need a country-by-country analysis to recognize that the extent of the loans creates the sort of nightmare we've all been fearing for almost forty years,'' said the Bank of England chairman.

''But to which we are nearer, more than at any time during those last forty years,'' resumed Bell, still looking towards the IMF group. ''Brought nearer because of an ostrich-like refusal to learn the lessons of the immediate past. Each country indicating difficulties now is a country which has shown financial recklessness before, a recklessness that we have fostered and of which we may well be the ultimate victim.''

This conference might be secret at the moment, Pike

realized, but Bell didn't intend it to remain that way forever. In front of him he was aware of his father stirring, gesturing for the chairman's attention. Wilder nodded, and when he stood, the IMF managing director did so facing Bell, physically to confront the attack.

"Isn't this conference being led off on the wildest, most defeatist tangent!" he said. "There is nothing whatsoever to justify the sort of hyperbole and exaggeration we have heard in the last fifteen minutes. The rescheduling requests from Poland and Rumania have been agreed and imposed not the slightest difficulty upon the liquidity available to my Fund." He nodded towards Ambersom. "The World Bank has covered the Argentinian shortage just as easily. The Soviet Union has shown the responsibility for which they have been judged and assessed and continued to meet their obligations, by the sale of gold of which they are substantial producers and of which we have every reason to believe they have adequate reserves. . . ." He stopped again, gulping from a water glass; he had been made more fluent than usual by his anger. "The global indebtedness is certainly a cosmic figure. So it is right and proper that we should have this conference and formulate proposals against a possible—and I repeat, *possible*—difficulty hinted at by Poland, Rumania and Argentina. It is quite *wrong* to conclude that those difficulties have already arisen and we are confronted by a financial Armageddon."

Wilder appeared at last to realize the personal antipathy between the two men and moved to intervene. "I think," he said, "that it's a convenient time for a luncheon adjournment."

Pike tried to hurry from the room but couldn't because of the congestion. His father caught up with him by the door, seizing his arm.

"My office," he said.

"I've got a meeting."

"Postpone it."

His father's anger wasn't only at the Treasury Secretary, Pike realized. Jane was already outside in the corridor, looking around. Pike moved her into a window alcove and said, "My father wants a conference."

"I can catch up with my own party," she said.

"I'm sorry."

"Can't be helped."

"Thought you might have been more disappointed."

"Don't start all that again, Tom."

"What about tonight?"

She pulled her bottom lip between her teeth, so that her crooked tooth showed. "I'll try," she said.

"For Christ's sake!" he said, too loudly.

She looked around the crowded corridor, embarrassed. "What's the matter with you!"

Pike clamped his mouth together, against another outburst. "I want to *see* you," he said. "That's what's the matter."

"Tonight," she promised. "Sometime tonight."

Pike expected to find the rest of the delegation in his father's office suite, but when he entered, the man was alone. He was standing rigidly in front of his desk, and Pike knew the anger was still there.

"How the hell did we miss those loans?"

"I don't know," said Pike tightly. "I'm sorry."

"Made me look a goddamned idiot."

Me, too, thought Pike. "I think the British might have deliberately withheld from disclosing their own."

His father looked intently at him. "Why should they want to do a thing like that?"

"It made them look the definitive analysts."

The IMF director nodded agreement. "Bell's using the conference like some election platform. And he's arguing the sort of fiscal restriction that I used to advocate, until a few months ago! Would you believe that!"

"It's not an election audience that will do him much good."

"Can you think of anything else we might be surprised with?"

"No," said Pike, after some thought.

"I'll concede the short-term bunching this afternoon," said the older man. "I don't want that coming out like another discovery."

"You were right," said Pike, attempting encouragement. "There was very much a defeatist attitude in there."

"I need something positive," said the man, driving his fist into the palm of his other hand. "I don't like being on the defensive."

For all of them it had become a personal thing, thought Pike. "Maybe something will emerge this afternoon," he said.

It didn't.

Pike's father announced the short-term commitment immediately after the resumption, and Wilder at once insisted on a country-by-country review of the strain likely to be felt if the apparent Eastern bloc difficulty increased because of it. For the United States—less committed than any other country—Volger indicated they could withstand the pressure. Tanaka declared that Japan could, too. Which left overexposed the rest of the Far East, Europe, Scandinavia, Canada, Australia and four Latin American countries unrepresented but with known debts of their own.

"Confirmation of the stupidity of what's been allowed to happen," said Bell, determined upon the last word.

He didn't quite get it.

Wilder was on the point of adjourning until the following day when an aide came into the room and handed him a message. The British chancellor read the brief news agency slip and then looked slowly around the room before speaking. "There's been a statement issued in Warsaw," he said. "Hungary is seeking a deferment from France, Germany and England on loan repayments of $750,000,000."

26

The closing revelation sent every delegation into separate committee gatherings, with the exception of the Interim Committee itself, which completed the formal adjournment until the following day to allow the subsidiary discussions. There was another peremptory summons to the managing director's suite, and Pike was at once aware of his father's changed attitude. At lunch time it had been anger; now it was concern.

"It's serious," said the older man. "Really serious."

The tendency for repetition had returned, Pike realized. "There seems to be a chain reaction developing."

"France can't withstand it; it's said as much, without the need for any more talk."

"One-and-a-half billion isn't a large sum," said Pike. "The Bank for International Settlement has more than adequate reserves to cover that."

"It's a snowball, growing bigger as it rolls down the hill," said the IMF director. "First Argentina, then Poland, then Rumania—and now Hungary." He stared across his massive inlaid desk. "We've got to anticipate an approach from the Soviets. What's the full extent of their short-term bunching?"

Pike considered his files, determined against any further mistakes. "Interest in the region of $800,000,000: capital repayments of $2,000,000,000." He closed the file. "Those are the figures if everyone has been honest," he said. "If anything at all emerges from this, it's surely the need for some centralized method of accurately gauging worldwide loan spreading."

"I hoped we had something like it," said his father.

"This conference has proven we haven't," said Pike. "It's a gap that's got to be closed." Like a stable door after a horse has bolted.

"This could ruin everything, you know—ruin everything." His father made his fist-punching gesture and said, "Just when everything was sewn up, for God's sake! Ambersom out of the running and Bell shown as scared as chicken shit."

"He's not acting chicken-shit at the moment."

"Son-of-a-bitch!" said the other man. "I wanted it: I wanted it and I actually had it!" He stretched out, palm upwards. "Here, in my hand!"

"You haven't lost it, not yet."

"It'll need something pretty dramatic. I'm trailing badly. I need the corridor gossip, Tom. I don't want to be caught out anymore."

Neither do I, thought Pike. "I'll try."

As one of the named countries in the Hungarian announcement, the meeting of the British delegation was among the longest and it was nine before Jane telephoned him. Pike was sure he kept the anxiety from his voice.

"Sorry I'm late. Can we still meet?"

"Of course."

She was already in the foyer of the Jefferson when he arrived. Pike saw she hadn't changed from what she'd worn during the day.

"Hello, stranger," he said.

"Hello."

There was an attitude about her of which he was unsure

but which he guessed was apprehension; the foyer was crowded with people and Pike wondered if it were because of them or him. He couldn't see Burnham anywhere.

"Do I get a kiss?"

"Later," she said.

The people in the foyer, decided Pike. She seemed to hesitate responding to his embrace in the car and then to realize it, kissing him back belatedly.

"You all right?"

"Tired," she replied. "I'm fed up with conferences and with talking."

"That's what you wanted last time," he said. He wouldn't rush it; he didn't want to increase the apparent distance between them.

"Last time was different," she said. Some things weren't. She'd been nervous about a relationship then. And destroyed it. She wished she weren't so tired. She didn't want to destroy this one, uncertain though she was about it.

Pike turned immediately onto M Street, reaching out for her hand. There was the momentary reluctance there had been about the kiss.

"I've missed you," he said.

She hoped it was true. "Me, too," she said.

"Thought we'd go out to my father's house for the weekend."

"That would be nice."

"Not a problem?"

He was aware of her looking sharply at him. "No," she said. "Not a problem."

"Burnham caught me out today," he said.

"About five minutes," she said.

"What?"

"Five minutes before we managed to get around to Paul Burnham."

"Just a remark." *Careful,* he thought.

In a flat, resigned voice she said, "The British returns

only came in the day before we left London to come here. We learned of Brazil through affiliate checking; Lloyds are part of the consortium. Japan seemed available to everyone. I don't know how you missed it."

Neither do I, thought Pike. He said, "I didn't ask for an explanation."

"There it is, whether you wanted it or not!"

The arrival at the restaurant interrupted any further conversation. Pike had considered taking her to Georgetown, to remind her of the first time, but decided instead upon somewhere quieter, so he chose Dominiques. They were late for their reservation, so they had to wait in the small side-bar. He *had* missed her, Pike decided. Despite the obvious weariness, she was very beautiful. Impulsively, he leaned forward, kissing her lightly on the cheek, and for the first time since they met, she smiled and appeared to relax.

"Why did we start to fight?" he asked.

"I don't know."

"I don't want to."

"Neither do I."

"Then, let's not."

She smiled again. "All right."

"Should be a rough day tomorrow," he said, wanting to guide the conversation.

"It's been a rough one today," she said. "The talk goes around and around in circles, like a jammed record."

"That's how it's been with us," said Pike honestly. "The problem is what it's always been—insufficient information." As he spoke, the idea settled in the back of his mind, not yet properly formed.

"I don't like what we're getting now," she said.

They were called to their table. Pike carried the unfinished drinks and, when he sat down, said, "My father's not so sure now about Armageddon." It was an exaggeration, but he wanted to test her reaction. Instead of replying, she began studying the menu. Dominiques is a restaurant with a flamboyant menu that extends to rattlesnake appetizers. Unimpressed, Jane told him to choose. Impatiently, Pike ordered steak for them both.

"Is Hungary going to be a problem?" he pressed.

"It's been difficult at such short notice obtaining from London our precise commitment," said the woman. "The time change is the wrong way around. It seems in the region of $45,000,000. So, yes, it's a problem. But one which we could probably accommodate, separately. But it's not separate. Everything is intermeshed, our banks in arrangements with banks of Germany and France. And it doesn't stop there; it spread to other affiliates in Europe, too."

So his father had been right, Pike realized; it was serious. "And we know about France," he said.

Jane nodded. "Larouse and Sir Herbert had a meeting tonight; Paris would need massive support. And quickly. Larouse isn't sure they'd get it, in the short time they'd need. Neither's Sir Herbert."

Pike shook his head against her doubt. "They'd get it. Everyone's together, in one room: IMF, World Bank, International Settlements. Knowing the difficulty, the cover could be extended quickly enough."

"And last for how long?" she demanded, qualifying his confidence.

The idea was becoming clearer to Pike now; it had drawbacks, but the advantage was the positiveness. That's what his father had wanted. And what his father wanted, he wanted. Pike recognized that he *was* bound more tightly to the older man than he had ever been. Maybe the IMF hadn't been the opportunity he had envisioned.

"That's what we've got to find out," said Pike. Not *we*, he thought; that's what *I've* got to find out. He saw it as the way to recover and the excitement warmed through him.

"Paul's been assigned to it," she said.

Pike came back to her, concentrating. ''Assigned to what?''

''Sir Herbert agreed to the need for a full assessment, going as far ahead as a year, if possible. Capital repayments, interest spreads; everything. He sees the major outcome of this conference being an anticipation of any future crisis, so they can be contained before they arise.''

Pike's excitement turned to anger at the thought of his proposal being diminished by the British move. ''Whose idea?'' he said.

She hesitated at the tone of his voice. ''Paul's,'' she said quietly.

''Emerging as the star, isn't he?''

Jane looked sadly across the table at the American. ''He's very able,'' she said. Was the jealousy for what had once existed between her and Paul? Or for Paul's performance at the conference?

''Are you coming back with me?'' he said.

Paul was involved in that question, too, Jane realized. ''Yes,'' she said. She looked down at the clothes she had been wearing all day. ''But not to stay: I didn't bring anything.''

Was that why she hadn't bothered to change, to give herself an excuse? he wondered.

Their lovemaking was bad, both nervously stiff and trying too hard, each feigning the enjoyment and each knowing it about the other. As soon as he pretended to finish, she said, ''I must be going now.''

''I'll run you back.''

''I'll take a cab.''

''Don't be ridiculous.''

At the Jefferson she leaned across the car, kissing him on the cheek before he turned the ignition off. ''It's been a lovely evening,'' she lied. ''I enjoyed it.''

''What about tomorrow?'' he said.

She hesitated, halfway out of the vehicle. ''We'll see.''

Pike drove tight-faced back to the Mayflower, hands

gripped whitely around the wheel. That bastard Burnham was taking everything away from him, he thought—everything. But the man hadn't succeeded yet. And he wouldn't.

The bar of the Jefferson is very small, with a view of the elevators. Jane heard her name called as she pushed the summons button and turned to see Burnham at the entrance.

"It's late," he said.

"But you're still up." She felt embarrassed. She hoped she'd dressed properly in Tom's suite.

"I waited to make sure you're O.K."

"What on earth for!" The feeling now was annoyance at being spied upon; of course she'd dressed properly.

"Just to make sure you're O.K." he repeated. "Would you like a drink?"

"For God's sake, Paul, I'm old enough to go out by myself!" she said, ignoring the invitation.

"*Were* you by yourself?"

She opened her mouth to reply, then stopped. "Is there anything you want to talk to me about concerning the conference?" she asked formally.

"No," he said.

"I'll see you in the morning," she said, glad the lift arrived to make the exit possible. It had been a bloody awful evening: absolutely bloody awful.

27

Pike learned enough from Jane to brief his father completely in advance of the day's conference, and when he finished detailing the French and British contact, he put forward the idea that had occurred to him, intent upon the older man's response. The IMF managing director sat alertly behind his desk, moving his head in slow, nodding gestures. When he said it might work, they talked it through, to anticipate the objections, so by the time they entered the packed chamber, they were fully prepared. Wilder remained chairman, of course, which meant the British delegation had a procedural advantage of being able to speak first, but they were unaware of the IMF preparations, clearly intending a general discussion for the difficulties to be reexamined.

Pike's father moved for control immediately when the British chancellor suggested open debate upon the latest request. There was no purpose in a fuller debate, the IMF director declared at once, gaining the complete attention of the delegates by the forcefulness of the statement, which was what he intended. They already knew of the French difficulty and of the strains that would be imposed upon Britain and Germany by the Hungarian move. And there was nothing further that could objectively be discussed about Argentina, Poland and Rumania. The IMF and the World Bank had dampened the problems that might have already arisen, and although it would have to be agreed by the Interim Committee sitting in proper session, as managing director of the IMF, he felt that as members of the Fund, Britain, France and Germany could call upon their justifiable access to Special Drawing Rights and the General Agreement to Borrow to cushion themselves against any stress from the Warsaw application.

Sitting directly behind his father, Pike stared around the chamber, gauging the reaction from the delegation. At the announcement of IMF help, the relief was obvious from the French and the German delegates. There seemed uncertainty from the British, the group behind Wilder hunched together in whispered conversation. As he looked, Jane looked back. Her face was tight and quite expressionless.

The current difficulties were serious but not intolerable, his father continued. The need was for them to take concerted, positive action to prevent recurring crises which had threatened their financial structure in the past and would threaten it again. In his opening remarks the chairman had talked of the need for monetary stability, and the IMF had a proposal to achieve that stability. In the case of the long-term, he intended to establish a global monitoring system to go beyond the normal supervisory arrangements of central banks. Member countries of the Fund would be required to submit their borrowings and their loans, from which it would be possible to assess, on a monthly or even weekly basis, any overextension, and from that, in turn, a warning could be issued and corrective measures introduced.

Pike could see that Jane wasn't expressionless any longer. The whispering had intensified all around her, with Burnham in the center, but she was staring across the room at him, her face blazing with anger.

"Which leaves the uncertainty of the short-term," his father went on. "It is a logical inference that what has so far happened, the requests which have brought us here in conference, have their source in some difficulty within the Soviet Union, of which none of us has sufficient information. Until we have that fuller information, no proper forecast can be made nor provisions taken against it dribbling on, in a series of confidence-sapping applications and requests. I therefore propose that, on behalf of the world banking system assembled here today, the IMF make a direct approach to the Soviet Union. Their indebtedness makes them as dependent upon us as we are upon them. The invitation would be for them to discuss the problems with us, so that a mutually advantageous resolve can be made."

For several moments there was complete silence in the room after the man sat down. In just one hour, thought Pike, the IMF—which meant his father—had emerged the positive-thinking, practical organization that once again was going to pull everyone assembled in the room back from some disaster. His father's political ambitions couldn't be harmed now by any gossip that the Treasury Secretary tried to leak. The reverse, in fact. It would be difficult for Bell to oppose any of the suggestions without damaging his already shaky position.

It was Bell who spoke first. "The proposals are interesting and the intention to create a worldwide monitoring system a valid one," he said. "I am unsure of the diplomatic propriety of approaching the Soviet Union."

It was a good political point, admitted Pike, opening the door for other representatives at the conference to make stronger objections.

"Diplomatic propriety isn't a factor," his father said at once. "The IMF comes within the aegis of the United Nations. The Soviet Union is a member of the United Nations. The fact that the approach *will* come from the IMF frees anyone here of diplomatic difficulty."

Which was a better political point, thought Pike; the pre-conference planning was justifying itself.

"By coincidence," said Sir Herbert Course, from across the room, "the IMF suggestions are very much in line with those which the Bank of England had intended putting forward. . . ." He paused, then said, "The thinking was to create the monitor center through the Bank, in London, although I concede the sense of centralizing it through the Fund. . . ."

He'd beaten Burnham, Pike decided. The British group were quiet now, no one speaking: Jane was staring down at the table in front of her, appearing engrossed.

"The approach to Moscow has validity also, but shouldn't it come through one of the central banks involved in the existing rescheduling requests?"

Which meant the Bank of England, which meant Paul Burnham, thought Pike. He tensed against his father's response.

"Your bank, for instance?"

Course smiled at the IMF controller's question. "We are involved," he said. "And we do have considerable experience."

"Wouldn't that allow for the diplomatic uncertainty that Secretary Bell has already raised?"

"It would be a bank approach, absolutely nonpolitical," insisted Course.

Beneath the protection of the table, Pike wiped his hands against the edge of his trousers, conscious of the perspiration. His father was taking a softer line than he would have.

"It would be necessary, of course, to discuss it with your government?" said the IMF director.

"Involved as I am in this meeting, I would naturally raise it within the Cabinet," came in the British chancellor.

"Which would create delay?"

Perhaps his father wasn't being too soft, exposing the drawbacks one by one.

"Minimal," insisted Wilder.

"The IMF is an international organization, a composite through its committees and structure of 146 countries," reminded the elder Pike. "The Bank of England is one central bank, properly but primarily responsible to its own country. We gathered because the possible difficulties are international, not concentrated in one country. I think international difficulties should be resolved through international bodies. If we agree today to the Bank of England making its representations, then surely we should agree to the central bank of France making an approach. And that of Germany. Every country, in fact. And so we would lose the point of centralization which Sir Herbert has already agreed to be a necessary and overdue innovation."

Brilliant, decided Pike, losing any reservation at his father's handling; the prod to national rivalries had been superbly subtle.

Pierre Larouse, for the French contingent, responded to it. "I would like first to thank the IMF for the intimation of help in meeting the Hungarian problem," said the man. "On behalf of French bankers here today, I would like to congratulate the Fund and its managing director on the forethought and validity of the proposals that have been put forward. Again on behalf of those bankers, I would like to say that we would have every confidence in the Fund making the approach to Moscow. . . ." He turned slightly towards the British. "That is not, of course, an indication that we lack confidence in our British colleagues. It is our conception of this being a global, not a national matter."

The insularity jibe had been as subtle as his father's thrust, decided Pike, looking at the discomforted British. Handshakes last night, arm's length today, he thought.

The American Treasury Secretary moved at the praise of the man trying to unseat him. "Are we not moving with too many assumptions?" he said. "Isn't there a risk of humiliation with Moscow rejecting an IMF approach?"

The IMF managing director didn't reply immediately, allowing a silence to heighten the rebuff: Pike wondered if the slight, but clearly perceptible head-shaking was going too far. "As I tried to make clear in my opening remarks, it will be an *invitation,"* he said, measuring his words. "If there is a rejection, then it will be to the IMF, not an individual government: an argument again, I would consider, for giving the Fund the responsibility. And let us not overlook the fact of our being in a dominant position. We're the lenders; they're the debtors. The ultimate move is ours in declaring default."

Bell flushed at the other American's patronizing attitude. "Default is an empty threat," he said, too quickly. "We all know the Western banking system couldn't withstand what that would mean."

"Could the Eastern bloc?" demanded Pike's father. "It's a poker game, I agree. But we've always got the last call."

"At the beginning of this morning's conference, the managing director of the IMF commented that there was little need for protracted discussion because we were all far too well-acquainted with the problems," said Luigi Gambino, the Italian spokesman. "I agree. I'd like to propose, therefore, a vote from the member countries represented here today on what I consider a commendable suggestion that the IMF should directly approach the Soviet Union. I recommend, also, that the Interim Committee give serious and immediate consideration to the establishment of a central monitoring system."

The debate did continue, however, for a further hour, with little substance and no fresh or contrary proposals, individual delegations merely wanting to be seen to contribute their views. The vote was taken first on referring the proposal for a centralized fund for consideration by the Interim Committee, then upon standby finance for Britain, France and Germany. Both were unanimous. So was the decision to make the IMF responsible for the contact with Russia; Pike saw the British were the last to record their agreement.

The ending of the conference was as disorganized as it had been the previous day, made more difficult this time by individual bankers crowding around his father to offer congratulations. Pike was conscious of the Treasury Secretary and Harry Ambersom being jostled away, on the outside of the circle.

He didn't see Jane approach. She was just suddenly in front of him, red with anger.

"Bastard!" she said, her voice controlled against being overheard. "You absolute bastard. You used everything I told you last night . . . turned everything to your own advantage. . . ." Her control faltered in her rage, so that the words were blocked, but again she managed to sputter, "Bastard. . . ."

"I want you to marry me," Pike cut her off.

"Oh."

The drug rehabilitation center was the most exclusive in New York State approved by the courts—a solid, brick-built mansion secluded in an estate of hills and trees. Janet was allocated a suite on the second floor with a living room, separate bedroom and a bathroom. The matron who showed her to it allowed her time to unpack and then returned to take her to the first interview. The doctor was a small, rumpled man who wore tweeds and played with a pipe he never attempted to light. Janet thought it odd he felt the need for his name—Harris—to be displayed on a plaque on his desk. She wondered what the initials D. S. stood for.

"I hope you're going to be comfortable here," he said.

"Do I have a choice?"

Harris looked down at the pipe. "I suppose so," he said. "You could always go back to the courts and ask them to place you somewhere else."

"Which would probably be the psychiatric wing of a prison."

"Probably."

"What do I have to do?" asked Janet.

"Learn to stop wanting heroin."

"I'm not an addict!"

"I'm glad to hear it," said the doctor. "That should make it easy." He put the pipe on his desk. "Were you shooting up every day?"

"No," she said at once.

"Sure?"

"Of course I'm sure!"

"So you won't want any methadone?" asked Harris.

"Is one better than the other?"

"Methadone is addictive; but it helps."

"No," said Janet. "I don't want any methadone."

He picked the pipe up again. "There'll be a full medical examination, of course; that's routine."

"What about a psychiatric examination?"

"If we feel it's necessary; it'll just be general observation for a week or two."

"Under surveillance!"

He smiled at her. "That makes it sound worse than it is. There's one thing I want you to promise me."

"What?"

"If you feel the need, tell someone. Don't do anything silly like trying to leave the hospital and make your way back to New York, to score there. If you do, that'll be a breach of the court order. And you won't be able to stay here. We try to work from the basis of trust, right from the start."

Janet looked at the windows. "I wondered where the bars were."

''This isn't a mental hospital,'' he said. ''Is there anything you'd like to know?''

''Yes,'' she said. ''Why do you keep playing with that damned pipe?''

Harris smiled again. ''I'm trying to give up smoking. It isn't easy''

28

Pike wanted to collect Jane from the Jefferson, but she refused, arriving instead with her luggage at the Mayflower. Pike had checked out and was waiting for her. They packed the car at once, but it was still late by the time they set off for the country.

"The traffic is always heavy on a Friday," he said. "It'll take some time."

"I'm glad," she said. "I want to talk."

"You haven't said yes yet."

"I know."

"Are you going to?"

Instead of answering, she said, "You stole the ideas."

"That's not true," he said. "Establishing a central monitor was obvious; it's presumptuous to imagine that only your people would have thought of it."

"Why didn't you say anything?"

"Because we didn't decide it ourselves until just before the conference began this morning. The main discussion was about making direct contact with the Soviet Union."

She was sitting sideways in the passenger seat, looking directly at him. "Is that the truth?"

"Of course it is!" he said. "What sort of question is that!"

"They've started an enquiry, into a leak."

"Is that why you wouldn't let me collect you?"

She nodded.

"It didn't come from you," he insisted.

"There's no way I can prove that, is there? Or that they'll believe me?"

"Have you been asked?"

"Sir Herbert called a meeting, back at the hotel," she said. "We were all asked."

"What did you say?"

She didn't answer at once. "Nothing," she said.

"That isn't a lie; it didn't come from you."

"Feels like a lie."

Pike turned over the Memorial Bridge, towards Rosslyn. "It'll blow over."

She shook her head. "Paul said he was determined to run it down." She hesitated and said, "He was waiting for me when I got back to the hotel last night."

"What for?"

"Said he wanted to be sure I got back safely."

"Does he know you were with me?"

"Of course not; there would have hardly been the need for an enquiry if he'd known that, would there?"

"What was said about your not returning with the main party?"

"Paul wanted to know where I was going."

"What did you say?"

"Just that I was staying with friends."

Pike got on the Beltway, settling in the center lane. The direct approach *had* been his idea. And he'd discussed a central monitor with his father before talking about it with Jane. "He's being petty," Pike insisted. "It was logical for everything to be handled by the IMF."

"His feeling is that the Fund misinterpreted it before."

"Arrogant bastard!" exploded Pike. "Who are among

the most exposed? British clearing banks, that's who. If he was so sure of himself, why's it been allowed to develop to the point it has? He could have stopped it months ago, before a warning would have created any problems."

"He was in the minority," reminded Jane. "He tried."

"So the Bank of England misinterpreted it, too, if a misinterpretation has been made at all?"

"I suppose so," she said.

"Shouldn't we be talking about something else more important?"

"You confused me," she said. "I was going to say this morning that I never wanted to see you again."

"You've come away with me for the weekend!"

"I told you that you confused me."

"It's a pretty simple question."

"I don't think so."

"Don't you love me?"

Jane had turned from looking directly across the car at him, looking now through the windshield at the lights of the commuter traffic kaleidoscoped around them. "You've never said you loved me," she said. "Not the actual word."

"I didn't think I had to."

"And you call Paul Burnham arrogant!"

"I love you," he said.

They reached the slip-road before she spoke. "I think I love you, too," she said.

"That still isn't a reply."

"Yes," she said. "Yes, I'll marry you."

"So, to hell with Paul Burnham," said Pike.

There was the inevitable house party and they were among the last to arrive. His mother was in her dressing room, so Pike took Jane there and introduced her and then made the announcement. His mother kissed Jane and then summoned her husband, and the four of them stood awkwardly in the room, no one sure what to say.

"Don't be offended," said Mrs. Pike. "But I'm surprised."

"I'm not offended," said Jane. "I'm surprised, too."

29

To get away from the house party, they went riding, Pike enjoying the role of guide. He took her along the floor of the valley and then up through the trees to the rise beyond, eventually to the plateau from which there was the best view of the house and the countryside beyond.

"That way is Maryland," he said, pointing. "That way is West Virginia, and to the south is North Carolina, which sounds a bit illogical but isn't."

"Do you think your parents approve?"

Pike didn't answer at once. "Like my mother said, I think they're surprised. Give them time."

"We're both going to need that."

"Why?"

Jane shrugged, letting her horse graze. "There's so much to think about. Where are we going to live, for instance? Are you going to be in Europe? Or here, in America?"

"I don't know," admitted Pike. "Europe, for a while, I guess, and eventually, here." Although he was concealing it better, Pike was as uncertain as Jane what their marriage would involve; he still wasn't completely sure what had prompted him to blurt out the proposal at all, without more consideration. He was glad he had; if he hadn't, he knew he would have lost her. Maybe back to Burnham.

"I suppose it'll mean leaving the Bank."

"Will you mind?"

She didn't reply at once. "It meant a lot to me, proving I was able enough to do it."

"There's no need to quit, not immediately." He moved the horses on, riding parallel to the ridge.

"When *will* we get married?" she asked. "And where?"

"Whenever you want, there's no need to wait, is there?"

"What about the Russian thing? Aren't you going to be involved in that?"

"I suppose so," said Pike. "I haven't spoken to my father about it yet."

"Maybe we should wait until that's sorted out."

"It could take months." He saw another group from the house making their way along the valley floor, too far away for him to identify who they were.

"I don't want to wait months," said Jane at once. "Just a little while."

"I haven't bought you a ring yet."

"I'll have to go back tomorrow," said Jane. "I only told them I was going to spend the weekend here."

"We'll buy one in London, then."

"When?"

"As soon as I can get back."

"This is going to be a pretty funny courtship, isn't it?"

He looked at her and realized she was joking. "I can come for weekends if I'm kept here."

"Trying to impress me again?"

"If I can," he admitted.

"There's only Ann and Harry on my side," said Jane. "I suppose we should get married here, where your parents are."

"They'd probably like that."

Jane gestured towards the faraway mansion. "Is it always like this?" she said. "Big gatherings?"

"My father seems to enjoy them. Don't you?"

"It's a long time since I attended one. My parents used to give them quite often in India, but nothing like this. And I was young, home from England on holidays."

"You didn't say whether you liked them."

"I was wondering about being a hostess," she said. "I don't want to fail you."

He frowned at the unexpected lack of confidence. "That's a strange thing to say."

It had been, and she wished she hadn't said it because it hadn't been how she wanted to begin. "Maybe I'm still getting over the shock," she said. That was wrong, too; that was avoiding it. She was riding behind him, hidden from his look and was glad. "What happened?" she said at last. "The first time."

He reined back, level with her, not initially understanding. Then he realized and said, "With Janet?"

She nodded, wishing he'd remained in front.

"I told you," he said. "It was one of those understood things, between families. No one really considered whether we wanted to. . . ." He let the sentence trail. Was it fair, to replay the recorded message? "And I guess neither of us tried very hard."

"What's that mean?"

"We played around; did silly things. We were both young."

"You make it sound like a game."

"I guess that was how we considered it."

"How will you consider us?"

He leaned across, for her animal's bridle, stopping them both. "Not a game," he said. "I promise you, not a game."

"What about playing around?"

"I'll try very hard," he said.

She swallowed. "Thank you," she said. "That was honest, at least."

"That's what I'll try to be," said Pike, at that moment meaning it.

"And I'll try not to fail you."

His father chose that night to make the official announcement, and there was champagne and toasts and the ritual of congratulations. Quite late in the evening, his mother obediently drew Jane aside, so Pike was expecting the summons when it came from his father. The older man was alone in the study, back to the fire.

"Would have welcomed some warning about this," he said. "Welcomed it quite a lot."

"It was a sudden decision," said Pike. How sudden only he was beginning to realize fully.

"How long have you known her?"

"We met at the last IMF meeting here," said Pike. "It developed when I got to Europe."

"Nice girl," said his father. "Your mother and I like her."

"I'm glad."

"Let's hope it works out better than last time."

"It will," said Pike. It was poetry-reciting time again, he thought. He decided against telling the man of the conversation with Ambersom.

"Fixed a date yet?"

"Not yet."

"Good," said the IMF director. "I want the other thing sorted out first. There's been a full disclosure to the President, obviously. Jordan doesn't want a weak stand on this. He wants the Russians confronted, even to the point of default if necessary."

"*Actual* default?"

"I think he's prepared to go right down to the wire."

"That could be a dangerous game."

"The stakes are high enough."

"It might take time," said Pike, remembering his conversation with Jane that afternoon.

"Whatever it takes, it takes," said his father vehemently. "I ended up ahead, but I've got to stay that way."

The ease with which his father could switch from public to personal considerations was dazzling, thought Pike. Realizing his father's attention upon him, Pike said, "You'll want me involved?"

The question seemed to surprise the man. "Of course. Who else?"

This was going beyond any role he'd performed until now, Pike realized—way beyond. "It should be somebody else," he said. "An established official—a diplomat, even."

"The approach isn't as high as that," disclosed his father. "We've gone through the Soviet embassy and asked for unofficial talks."

"But you've just said the President is involved."

"Of course he's involved. But not publicly."

"Any indication that the Soviets will respond?"

"Not yet," said his father.

"Absolutely unofficial?" repeated Pike.

"Absolutely," confirmed his father.

So that if they go wrong, there would be no public problems, either for Jordan or his father, Pike recognized. Would his father sacrifice him, if the necessity arose? Unquestionably. "I understand," he said.

"You *do* understand, don't you?" pressed his father.

"Completely," said Pike. He was sure Jane would understand, too, if the need arose to explain.

30

Pike missed the turning and got lost, finally stopping for directions and having to retrace his route for almost ten miles. It made him late arriving at the center. As he walked across the graveled forecourt, he saw Janet looking at him from a ground floor room. He waved and she half-waved back. She was walking towards him when he entered the room, which was full of people sitting in separate groups.

"Hi," he said.

"Hello."

He leaned forward, kissing her lightly on the cheek. She stood stiffly, as if she were surprised by the gesture. He looked around, seeking somewhere to sit, aware people were looking at them.

"It's communal," she said unnecessarily. "Let's not stay."

"Where, then?"

"We can walk in the grounds."

Outside again, he waited for her to lead. She set off to the left, away from the road. He saw other couples wandering aimlessly, as they were. He hesitated, unsure, and then took her arm. She looked down at his touch and smiled.

"It's good of you to come," she said.

"Sorry it wasn't sooner; there's been a lot on."

"Thought you were in Europe, anyway."

"Got back some time ago."

"Here for the trial?"

He shook his head.

"Made the papers," she said. "Big disgrace." She paused, then said, "Poor Daddy. Mummy, too."

"How are you?" he asked, finally.

"Fine."

Pike didn't think she looked it. Her hair appeared freshly washed but was pulled back tightly from her face, without any style. There wasn't a tan anymore and she looked gaunt. She hadn't bothered with make-up and there was no polish on her nails, which he saw were bitten. She'd never bitten her nails when they were together; she'd always been particularly careful about her hands.

"What's it like?"

She shrugged, disinterested. "O.K., I suppose. They try."

"To do what?"

"Make up their minds whether I'm an addict or not."

"Are you?"

"I haven't needed methadone."

She spoke like a child offering for approval some school work of which she was proud. "That's good," he said.

"They're very big on case histories," she said. "Long sessions going back as far as the mother's womb. I told them we used to line together when we were married. Hope you don't mind."

"No, I don't mind," said Pike. It was a hospital, he thought; doctors' records were confidential.

"I wondered if they might have contacted you. Wanted to tell you earlier."

"No," he said. "No one's contacted me."

"I'm glad," said Janet. "I didn't want to cause any embarrassment."

They reached the wooded part of the grounds. There was a seat where the copse began, and he said, ''Want to sit down?''

There was another disinterested movement of her shoulders. She sat and stretched her legs fully out in front, gazing down at her feet. ''Another three fucking months!'' she said with sudden vehemence.

''It could have been prison.''

''It feels like it is.''

''What do you do?''

''Sleep. And eat. And watch television. There's group therapy, morning and afternoon and in the evening, Wednesdays and Fridays. We all sit around and admit secrets and tell each other we don't really need to do the things we do. Only we all know we do.''

''You're pretty high on self-pity,'' said Pike. He felt sorry for her.

''Psychiatric opinion I don't need; I get it all the time.''

''What are you going to do, when you get discharged?''

''Go back to the gallery. Daddy owns it, after all. I guess people will come to look at me rather than the paintings, until the novelty wears off. Daddy's already put in someone he says will be my personal assistant. What it really means is that I'll have a babysitter, to make sure I don't start shooting again.''

''Why did you?''

''It was fun; I enjoyed it.''

And she was going to do it again, decided Pike. Did the authorities here suspect that? They were experts, so they should. Perhaps he should mention it to her father. But he didn't *know*. He could cause a hell of a lot of problems for her and everyone else, running off at the mouth on nothing more than an impression. Which he might have done already, with something else. ''I'm getting married again,'' he announced.

She turned to him with a frown, the first indication of interest since they'd met. ''Who?''

"An English girl. Her name's Jane; we've been together since I've been in Europe."

"Oh," she said, looking away. After a gap she said, "When?"

"There isn't a date yet."

"Congratulations," said Janet. "That was a bit late, wasn't it? I'm sorry."

"Thank you," he said.

"Another open marriage, like ours was?"

"No, not this time."

She shivered and said, "I'm cold; mind if we start walking again?"

"Of course not," he said, standing with her.

"It was a pretty lousy experiment, wasn't it?" she said. She moved off parallel to the tree line, still going away from the house.

"Lousy," he agreed.

"Your idea or mine?"

"I seem to remember it was a kind of joint decision."

She looked up quizzically at him and said, "That's not quite the way I have it. But it doesn't matter now."

"Does anything matter to you, Janet!" he said, suddenly angry at the continuous apathy.

"Not really," she said. "Why did you come to see me?"

"I would have thought that was obvious."

"Nothing was ever obvious with you, Tom!"

"I heard what happened and that you were here. So I decided to come and visit." And because I felt some guilt.

"Not many have. Just my parents, really."

"Then I'm glad I did." They reached the boundary fence, and he said, "Shouldn't we be heading back?"

She sniggered at the tone of his voice. "Don't worry; I'm not going to make a break."

"Have you wanted to?"

"Every day."

"Admitted it in your therapy sessions."

"You've got to be joking!"

"I don't think any of this is very amusing."

"Wow!" she said. "Spoken just like a proper, pompous banker. Don't worry, darling. I'll think of it every day. But I won't do it."

They started moving back towards the house. "What about when you get out?" he said. There was a desperation about her that frightened him.

"What about it?"

"You're going to start scoring again, aren't you? No matter what sort of watch your father tries to impose, you're going to try." Pike was sure he was right, and if he were, then he should try to do something about it. Challenge her, at least.

"I didn't think I was your worry any longer."

"Don't be stupid, Janet!"

"Welcome to the club," she said. "That's what I'm told by the doctors and by the psychiatrists and by my mother and by my father—don't be stupid, Janet."

"Well?" His voice was cold.

"Well what?"

"Haven't there been enough mistakes? Shouldn't they stop?"

She turned directly in front of him, forcing him to halt. "There was only one mistake, my darling—only one that really mattered. The mistake I made trying to get you to love me."

Pike stared down at her, not knowing what to say.

"There's a cliché they keep using, during the therapy sessions," Janet continued. "They keep warning against the danger of history repeating itself."

"Nervous?" demanded Malik.

"Yes," admitted Lydia. "It's very close now."

The Soviet Finance Minister picked up the message that had come from the Washington embassy and which they had debated before the Politburo subcommittee an hour earlier. "I wish you didn't have to go alone."

"That's the way it was always intended to be."

"I still wish it were different."

She didn't, Lydia realized. She'd spent months in the city and felt constrained by Moscow—constrained, too, by the relationship with Malik. It was going to be good to get away again. "I'll suggest Switzerland," she said. "It's got the proper sort of neutrality."

"Neutrality is for wars," said Malik. "They don't know they're engaged in one yet."

The Moscow agreement to a meeting coincided with Czechoslovakia's request to reschedule $60,000,000 of interest and $1,000,000,000 of capital debt to a six—not three—year period.

31

The Russian suggestion of Zurich as the meeting place meant Pike was able to break his journey in London. They shopped for a ring the day after he arrived, and Jane chose an antique with diamonds clustered around a single emerald. They drove to Cambridge in the evening, for a celebration Ann had arranged. Harry proposed a self-conscious toast and arrangements were made for the whole family to come to Washington for the wedding. They left early the following morning, to make Pike's connection to Switzerland.

"I'm so happy," said Jane. As always when they drove, her hand was on his thigh.

"So am I."

"How long do you expect to be in Switzerland?"

Pike shrugged. "As long as it takes; I'm leaving the schedule loose."

"There was a meeting of the unit at the Bank last week, after we heard from the Fund that the Russians had agreed," said Jane. "You've got a hell of a lot of responsibility, haven't you?"

The same attitude as everyone else, he thought. "I suppose so."

"Worried about it?"

He looked fleetingly across the car at her. "A little," he said, because it was the proper attitude to show. After all the last minute planning and preparation conferences in Washington, there had been the personal meeting with his father at which he'd got the lecture about responsibility. He'd detected his father's belated uncertainty, too: Pike knew England and Germany had openly objected to his being the delegate, when they were informed. "Burnham opposed me, you know," he said.

"The *Bank* opposed you," qualified Jane. "And they had an argument: Lydia Kirov has a government position. I know it's supposed to be unofficial, but in Washington we didn't anticipate it would be someone of her ranking."

"So you think it should have been an executive director, like everyone else?"

"*I* don't. But I can see other people's point of view. I'm so very *proud* of you; I'd loved to have told Harry and Ann what you're doing!"

At their last meeting his father had said he could choose what he wanted, wherever he wanted it, providing he succeeded. But Pike didn't see his as a negotiating role. He was a conduit, to relay information back to the necessary officials. So any action would be theirs, not his. But if people wanted to invest him in their minds with more authority and importance than he had, that was all right with him.

"Paul met her during a rescheduling meeting months ago," said Jane. "Said she's very pretty but doesn't say a lot. That was before her promotion, of course."

"The Fund had a file on her in their intelligence unit," said Pike. "Seems quite a career woman."

She moved her hand warningly on to his arm. "Be careful, won't you, darling."

"Of course I will."

They got to London by lunch time and she fixed sandwiches, which was all either of them wanted, in her apartment.

"We should be able to make plans after Switzerland, shouldn't we? . . . about the wedding, I mean."

"I'd hope so," said Pike. "I won't really know that until after the meetings."

She looked around the flat. "I suppose if you stay in Europe, we'll live in Paris?"

"Would you mind that?"

"I'd love it," she said. "Shall I put this place on the market?"

Pike shook his head. "Why not wait until after Switzerland?"

It was an uneventful flight and Pike arrived in Zurich early in the evening. The hotel had been the Russian choice as well, and Pike decided it was a good one. The Baur au Lac bordered the lake and his suite had a view of the snow-topped mountains beyond.

Pike carried all the briefing papers from Washington and studied them until quite late into the night, eating in his room so there would be no interruption. He was showered and ready when the call came. Her suite, he realized, was on the same floor as his.

A pursuer of woman, he always thought of conquest in every encounter, irrespective of either how casual or how formal a meeting was. Attuned as he was, he sometimes recognized a matching sensuality, coming out to meet his, dispensing the need for the ritual formalities of courtship or seduction. The recognition came immediately when Lydia Kirov opened the door to his knock—for her as well as himself, he guessed, because she faltered slightly in the doorway.

"I'm Tom Pike."

"Come in."

The meetings of the review unit had settled into a routine, with scheduled gatherings on Thursdays, and so Jane was surprised to get the summons from Burnham. He was standing with his back to her, gazing out over the City, when she entered, and he remained standing when he turned into the room.

"The Court suspected a leak of our position in Washington," he said. "The governor asked me to make an enquiry."

"I remember." Jane frowned. "I thought that was all over."

"I left this meeting until last."

"I see," said Jane.

"Everyone else has managed to give a very satisfactory account."

"Except me?"

"Where had you been that night?"

"I told you: out with a friend."

"I've got to know who."

Jane knew she was flushed. "Tom Pike," she said.

"You *stupid* little fool!"

"He didn't steal anything," she said defensively.

"Don't be ridiculous!" he said.

"He didn't steal the proposals," she insisted.

"I'll have to make a report," said Burnham. "There'll probably be an appearance before the Court."

"That won't be necessary." Jane decided it was anger bringing the tears to her eyes, making her vision blur.

"What do you mean?"

"I'm resigning from the Bank."

"Do you realize what you've done? What you've thrown away!"

"He's asked me to marry him," she announced.

There was a long silence between them. Finally, Burnham said, "I'll try to prevent it coming up before the full Court; there won't be any purpose now."

"Thank you."

"Christ, how I wanted it to be somebody other than you!" he exclaimed, suddenly angry.

There was no point in repeating the denial yet again, Jane thought. She said, "I'd have resigned anyway."

"I'm sorry."

"I'd have liked your best wishes," she said.

"I would have liked to have given them," he said.

32

The atmosphere lay between them like mist stretched in a valley between two opposing hills, a tangible yet amorphous thing. Hesitantly, he offered his hand, and with matching hesitation she responded; it was the briefest of contacts. Pike said, "On behalf of my Fund, I want to thank you for the opportunity of this meeting."

"The feeling within my ministry was that there could be a useful exchange," said Lydia, smiling very slightly at his strained formality. She was nervous, a feeling unusual for her, irritated by a reaction which had come before she could control it—before she realized it was happening, even. It was a ridiculous and unnecessary intrusion.

She became aware of their standing awkwardly in the center of the room and gestured sideways. Her suite matched his, with the view of the lake and the same hunchback mountains. Couches were set in front of an artificial fireplace and on either side of a low, long table. Coffee, with two cups, was set out. Pike went to one couch and Lydia to the other, actually creating the dividing valley. She sat demurely, skirt hem properly to her knees, perfect legs tightly parallel and bent to one side.

"I think we should establish some terms of reference,"

he said, still stiff. Pike was apprehensive of the woman—and considered the feeling an intrusion, too. Maybe even a danger. Didn't the Soviets use sexual entrapment? The reflection annoyed him, or its melodrama did. Sexual entrapment to achieve what? And hardly with a government official.

"Are there to be any?" Lydia felt out through the fog for the firm ground of negotiation. She'd be safe there. Just concentrate upon the negotiation he would expect.

Pike saw the immediate effort to put him into the position of the supplicant. "We're going to need a framework, don't you think?"

"The communication we received from Washington talked of the need for contact," she said. This was a preliminary, a warm-up before the actual tournament.

"Which your ministry considered could lead to a useful exchange," he reminded her. She spoke English with hardly any intonation; her voice was deep.

"An unofficial exchange," she said, knowing he would consider it a concession.

"That's an essential understanding," said Pike, glad the qualification came from her.

"I can assure you that it is the understanding from my side." She was relaxing, finally. And trying, objectively, to consider what had happened when she confronted the man. It had never been as strong as this. And in the last months there had been Malik, meeting the hitherto suppressed sexual needs, needs of which she had always been embarrassed. Ashamed, too. So what *had* happened here? Nothing, she decided positively: something to remain hidden and secret, like the other things of which she was uncomfortable.

"And from mine, also," said Pike. "A useful but unofficial exchange of views." The fact sheets and photographs hadn't prepared him for Lydia Kirov—not for the person. The person, Pike decided, was one of the most sensually attractive women he'd ever encountered. Another time, another place, another situation, he thought wistfully: definitely not this one.

"We seem to have got our framework," said the woman, confident enough now actually to show some lightness.

"It was a ministerial ranking which made us wonder at the level at which the Soviet Union was regarding the meeting," persisted Pike. It had been difficult enough for him to get here; he wasn't going to leave without answers to any questions which might arise at subsequent meetings in Washington, London or anywhere else. He was damned sure people like Burnham would have a lot of questions.

She smiled and Pike thought how perfect her teeth were, like everything else about her; he'd have to persuade Jane to get that tooth fixed. He was surprised she hadn't bothered. He put Jane from his mind—another unnecessary intrusion.

"It *is* unofficial," she insisted. "Which means no aides or support secretariat. I have the language, which is essential. And I have a complete knowledge of the financial situation of the Soviet Union and the other Socialist Republics, which was a requirement set out in the approach from your Fund. I was really the *only* person who could have been delegated."

That was an unarguable explanation if one were required, decided Pike. "I understand."

"We were, however, surprised to receive that approach," said Lydia; it was time to speed up the play.

But not too surprised to respond as quickly as you did, thought Pike; the concern made him the one in the superior position whatever debating tricks she attempted. He said, "We set out the discussion points in that approach. You're also aware of the membership of the Fund and, from what you've just explained, aware also of the mutual financial commitment between the membership and the Socialist Republics."

Lydia decided he'd been clever to use commitment rather than dependence; it showed he had prepared himself. "A departure from the past," she said.

A mistake! realized Pike. "No," he said. "Not a departure from the past. The Eastern bloc have for a long time been Western borrowers."

"I badly expressed myself," said the woman, in apparent apology. "I was thinking of the *degree* of commitment."

"So is the Fund," said Pike, moving easily with the flow of the conversation. "The degree of commitment is substantial—far more substantial than ever before."

"To the benefit of lender and borrower alike."

Pike hadn't expected her to retreat into cliché, but, then, her space of maneuver was limited.

However unofficial and lacking in status the meeting might be, Pike felt he was negotiating from strength, not weakness. He was aware of the attitude of the administration and how far the President was prepared to go. "The priority is maintaining that mutual benefit."

"I agree."

The quickness of her reply, practically a glib acquiescence, threw Pike off-balance. He'd prepared himself for maneuver, and compromise, not this immediate acceptance. Fearing that he may have misinterpreted—or that she may have misunderstood—Pike said, "What *exactly* is it that you agree?"

He was quite good, thought Lydia: properly confident, but cautious, too, careful with the words, refusing to hurry. Would he be gentle, coaxing, or rough, taking . . .? She halted the slide of her thoughts, slamming the secret door. *Fool!* She said, "The need for an orderly, regulated monetary system."

Pike was confident that he had kept from her the excitement that churned through him. She'd been careful, making it appear a personal opinion, but he knew he was looking beyond Lydia Kirov into ministry and government thinking. An orderly, regulated monetary system, she'd said. Which is what he'd said, in all the analyses. Here, from an unquestionable source, was the confirmation that he was right in discerning the proper responsibility from

Moscow. So Burnham and all the other doubters could go kiss his ass!

"An orderly, regulated, *worldwide* monetary system?" he explored, determined to get it right.

"The international monetary links have crossed the ideological differences for years now," she said. "What else could it be but worldwide?"

Pike was physically aching from the concentration, as if he had been engaged in some strenuous exercise. But it was a satisfactory feeling because he knew he was winning.

"It doesn't seem we have any disagreement, in principle," he said.

"Did you expect a disagreement, then?"

"No," said Pike at once. Falling back upon her words, he said, "A useful exchange."

It was a good recovery, but he'd meant it, Lydia decided. So this session had gone on long enough; it would be a mistake to make everything look too easy. And there was the strain of proximity, too, from which she felt the need for some relief.

"I forgot the coffee," she said, indicating the untouched pot.

"I'd already had some."

"It'll be too cold now." She'd have to be careful he didn't misunderstand.

"It's lunch time anyway." She couldn't misinterpret social politeness for anything else.

"Yes."

"I believe the restaurant has a view of the lake."

"I believe it has."

"Do you have an engagement?"

"Without aides or secretariat," she reminded him. It would be good to get away from the confines of the room, into somewhere bigger and more public.

"Join me, then?"

"That would be nice." She was agreeing to bring the meeting to an end, Lydia told herself: nothing more.

"We can continue the discussion while we eat, after all," said Pike, as if it were necessary to remind her of the reason for their meeting.

"Of course." Lydia thought she'd need the distraction.

The doctor didn't attempt to disguise his approach, but Janet didn't turn to meet him, remaining instead by the gate, staring out.

"Wondered if I'd find you here," said Harris.

Janet didn't reply.

"Missed you at therapy this morning."

"That's a pain in the ass and you know it," she said savagely. "I don't want to come anymore."

"Well, it's voluntary."

"Fine. So cross me off the list."

Harris came to stand beside her, looking out into the road. "Temptation?"

"Yes," she admitted, her voice less angry.

"Wouldn't it be a shame to throw away all the time you've spent here?"

She shrugged, disinterested. "You make it sound as if I'd achieved something."

"Haven't you?"

"You're the doctor. You tell me."

"O.K., then, let's look at it, plus and minus. The pluses are that you haven't used heroin or anything else for a long time and you managed to overcome the need without a substitute, which is important because it showed you've got the will power. The minuses are that you've treated everything with contempt and despised everyone here and constantly told lies at the therapy sessions. . . ."

Janet turned, staring, at the honesty.

"And the tragedy of that is that, because I don't know what your problem is, I can't help you and I'd guess that within a month of your getting out of here you'll be looking for a connection. Maybe less than a month. You're a sad case, Janet. Very sad."

"We've tried group therapy; now it's shock therapy," she said.

"Why the hard-shell cynicism?"

"Why not?" she said, conscious of her childlike petulance.

"What's the matter?" Harris was patient.

She stood with her throat working, not responding for a long time, and he did nothing to hurry her—just stood beside her and looked out beyond the boundary. At last, so quietly that he almost missed it, she said, "He's getting married."

Harris, who knew from the case history of the dissolution of the California marriage and the student pregnancy, said, "But he's already got married."

The woman snorted a laugh. "Not *him,* for Christ's sake. It's Tom who's getting married. He told me when he came here."

"But you divorced him," probed the doctor, gently.

She shook her head. "He divorced me. When I got involved with Hank and said I wanted to get married, Tom divorced me!"

Harris, daily accustomed to illogicality, kept any expression from his face and voice. "But you were telling him that you'd fallen in love with another man. A lot of people would have said he was doing a hell of a thing, making it easy for you."

"That's what people *always* say; it's what they said then!" she shouted, clutching out for his arm. "Tom Pike, the good guy who always does the right thing! I wasn't telling him I'd fallen in love with another man. I was telling him that I wanted to quit what we were doing—living out some crazy sexual experiment like in one of those books on the *New York Times'* best-seller lists. I wanted him to say O.K., I love you, so please don't leave me. Let's cut out all this screwing on the side and be like proper people. . . ." She stopped, breathing heavily. "We were never proper people. I spent every hour of every day living out some fucking act, trying to be the sort of person I imagined he wanted."

"What made you think he might want to marry you again?" Harris asked gently.

"We got together when I came back from California. It was good, for a long time. Like before."

"Before it was an act, as you just told me," reminded Harris.

She began to cry, unchecked, and then her nose began to run and she sniffed noisily. "I guess it was again," she admitted. "That's the trouble. I don't know how to behave when I'm with him."

"There's only yourself," said the doctor. "That's all there ever is, for anyone."

"I was frightened to hell he wouldn't be interested in me if I was just myself. That's what I've always been frightened of, since we were kids."

Harris winced at the badly expressed inferiority. Her hand was still on his arm. He covered it with his own and said, "Why don't we go back to the house? It's getting late."

Obediently, she turned away from the road and began to walk with him back to the sanatorium.

"Help me," she said pleadingly.

"Of course," he said, professionally reassuring, and at the same time wondering, *how?*

33

Lydia and Pike kept using finance as a barrier to hide behind, like footed picadors running to their wooden protection at the moment of danger. Sometimes the tormentors of the bull become distracted and make mistakes, and Lydia, increasingly uncomfortable, appeared to make hers towards the end of the meal with a chance remark that pointed Pike in the right direction. With hindsight it was obvious, the logical explanation; it hadn't, however, featured in any discussion in which he had been involved and Pike had come unprepared to Switzerland, without any statistics. For that reason he didn't pursue the Russian's remark; he had an analyst's reluctance to move without the support of facts and information.

It was Lydia who suggested they should not meet during the afternoon, wanting a time physically apart from him. Pike wanted it, too. For the same reason as the woman, but equally to get the figures he needed. It was fortunate, he decided, that there was an IMF establishment in Switzerland and that they had been warned there might be the need to provide assistance. He made the initial contact by telephone, to get the compilation underway, and by the time he returned to the hotel foyer, the hired car was waiting.

Faced with a three-hundred-and-sixty-mile round trip to Geneva, Pike drove as fast as he could, bothering with the speed restrictions only through Berne and Fribourg and Lausanne. He used the speed, too, in an effort to expel the other tension. He knew he was too professional, too involved, to let it happen. Just as she was. But it was a difficulty—an intrusion, as he had already decided. Janet had that sort of sexuality; so did a personal assistant called Miriam or Marion at Chase, with whom he'd maintained a liaison for a few months after his marriage. But not very many others. If it had to be a woman, why couldn't she have been a menopausal spinster with varicose veins and chin-hair! There had been an advantage, though. If there hadn't been the discomfort, Lydia wouldn't have shown him the way.

It had been sensible to telephone ahead. When he arrived in Geneva, the assessment was already underway, print-outs spilling from the machines. Third World indebtedness to the IMF and World Bank were immediately available, already stored in their retrieval system. Western bank consortia took longer, and here, of course, there was guesswork, but it was still possible to make that guess fairly accurate.

It was with Communist loans to the uncommitted nations of Africa, Latin America and Asia that the real speculation came into the analyses, the need to hunt through numbing statistics for announcements of a major industrial project or agricultural expansion which, by cross-reference (where possible) to the committed loans from the West and then by simple subtraction, could be shown to be financed by Moscow.

Even with the use of sophisticated computers—without which the exercise would have been impossible in less than months—it was a slow, laborious job, but by late afternoon the picture Pike expected began to emerge. There seemed, in fact, a surprising number of official announcements, and under scrutiny Pike saw that some had actually named the Eastern bloc as bankers. Which was, he conceded, another oversight, like his failure to realize the short-term bunching of the Soviet loans. There was little surprise in the final figure against the Western banking structure, something a little over $500,000,000,000.

The revelation was in the figures Pike really wanted—the Russian commitment.

It came out at $250,000,000,000.

Pike drove more slowly back to Zurich, subdued by the discovery, his mind so occupied by it that he ceased thinking of the woman with whom he was going to resume the negotiations that night as anything more than a representative of a country that seemed to have overloaned, as the West had overloaned before them, to unstable, unpredictable debtors.

Pike was later returning, but he showered and changed before going once more to Lydia's suite. She was already waiting, determinedly composed.

"I'm sorry I'm not on time," he said. "I spent the afternoon considering what we've discussed so far."

Lydia wondered if he would be surprised how she'd spent part of the afternoon. It had frequently been necessary before her involvement with Malik—and afterwards. "I called your suite," she said.

"I went out." He saw she had changed, too. It was a formal dress, black, with a high collar and long sleeves. There was just a single diamond from a chain at her neck. If she'd attempted the severity on purpose, she'd failed: Pike thought she looked spectacular.

"What conclusions have you reached?" she said.

"That we haven't spoken about anything," he said, intentionally forceful.

She blinked, surprised. "I don't understand."

"We've agreed upon responsibility, which I accept is important," said the American. "But apart from that, everything has been generalities. I think we should start talking specifically."

"About what?"

Pike accepted that she was leading the conversation again, maneuvering him into the position of having always to offer an opinion, enabling her the safe option of a reaction. But he didn't mind that. His was the ultimate control. He decided to show it. "Your problems," he said.

"I thought they were mutual," she sidestepped cleverly.

Pike smiled in appreciation. "A lender lends; a debtor borrows."

"Very epigrammatic," she said, enjoying the game. It wasn't just the sexual promise. He was sharp-minded, too. Malik had tried, in the beginning, but lately. . . . Another mental slide, she realized angrily. What reason did she have for comparing the two men?

Pike decided to play as well, easily remembering the phrase, " 'Have more than thou showest; speak less than thou knowest; lend less than thou owest.' "

Lydia grimaced. "I prefer Hamlet to Lear," she said, " 'Neither a borrower nor a lender be.' "

"You didn't finish," said Pike.

She frowned, uncertain.

"The following line," said Pike. " 'For loan oft loses both itself and friend.' "

He hadn't intended speaking directly to her, nor that she would respond by looking directly at him. Their eyes held. For several moments neither spoke. Then Pike said, "I prefer comedies. Do you know the line in *As You Like It?*—'Most friendship is feigning, most loving mere folly.' "

"Stop it!" she demanded. She jerked up from the couch, but having stood, she appeared uncertain about what to do. She wandered to the view of the lake, black and unseen now in the night. Faraway lights pricked out from the hills and mountains, like resting stars.

"I'm sorry." Pike was hot with self-anger, unable to

believe himself capable of what he'd done. The silence was longer this time, doing nothing to help.

"Do you want me to go?" he said.

"We're supposed to be here for a purpose."

"We were beginning to talk about specifics."

She came back into the room, looking determinedly at him. "What specifics?"

They were running for the barrier again, Pike knew. Behind its protection, he recited the new indebtedness of the Eastern bloc countries, itemizing them one-by-one, setting each new commitment against their previously existing loans, and then he detailed the individual Russian involvement. He rarely looked at his preparatory notes, so it became an impressive economic dissertation; recovered and more secure now, Lydia allowed the admiration to show. That admiration increased when he disclosed his awareness of the loans which Moscow, in turn, had extended to the Third World.

"You've been extremely thorough," she said.

"It was necessary to be," said Pike. "There has been practically a regularity about the requests for rescheduling. . . ." Remembering Rumania, he added: "Sometimes even an arrogance."

"Rescheduling requests are not unusual in international banking," said Lydia.

"Regrettably not," agreed Pike. "They need to become so; they need to be eradicated completely."

"So should the threat of a nuclear holocaust," she said sarcastically.

"Why did you agree to this meeting?" demanded Pike, forceful again.

"I thought I made it clear in the beginning," said Lydia. "My ministry felt there could be a useful. . . ."

"Your ministry alone couldn't have made such a decison. They wouldn't have had the authority. It had to be a government decision."

"The approach came from you, not from us." Lydia's

voice was as forceful as Pike's had been. "Whose anxiety does that mirror, the Fund or a combination of its 146 member countries?"

Assembled in an equation like that, the Western concern appeared heavier than that of the East, conceded Pike. Attempting to adjust the scales, he said "Mutual concern rather than mutual interest?"

"The Soviet Union has nothing about which to be concerned."

"What about the Third World debts?"

"Perfectly normal banking."

It was like calling a poker hand with no aces visible on the table, decided Pike. But it was the most obvious gamble. He said, "If it were perfectly normal banking, there would not have been the need for Moscow to withdraw its credit facility to Argentina. Or for the rescheduling requests from Hungary and Poland and Rumania and Czechoslovakia. It was perfectly normal banking to borrow at one rate and lend at another slightly higher, giving you a spread, but it only works if your debtor meets the payments enabling you to meet your initial commitments. And now your Third World debtors aren't meeting the payments. Which means you've had to call in other loans to meet your liabilities to the West."

Lydia appeared to falter, very slightly. She said, "There are temporary setbacks in any business arrangement. You're surely not suggesting any difficulty involving the Soviet Union?"

"Seeking clarification," said Pike. She was playing a bluffing hand without any aces, he decided.

"Our gold reserves are substantial," said Lydia. "There's been a public announcement."

"Of which I'm aware. I'm also aware that you've disposed of a considerable quantity," said Pike, pressing his advantage. "There's a limit to the fiscal responsibility of continuous sales—a reserve level."

"Of which we're aware," said the woman, picking up Pike's phrase. "Before which there is another alternative."

Pike hesitated, wondering if she had an ace after all. "What?"

"Declaring them in default," Lydia said simply.

Pike stared across the intervening space at the woman, unable immediately to respond. Not just one ace, he thought. All four and another up her sleeve, to make sure. "That's an extreme measure," he said.

"Not for us," she said. "Our banking is totally centralized, without the diffusement of the West. We're not talking about a default on every debtor. Quite obviously, we would choose the country owing us the smallest amount—one easily covered by the gold reserves we've already talked about. It would only need that one, to provide an example."

So simple, thought Pike: so horrifyingly, destructively simple. He needed time to think, to assess. And to talk. To his father. Or to Volger. Even Burnham. Anyone who knew fully the Western commitment and could understand the implication of what the woman sitting just six feet away from him had just blandly announced, as if it were some irrefutable logic. But he didn't have anyone else. He'd connived and schemed and maneuvered to do it by himself, imagining safety in being merely the conduit. But it wasn't as simple as that anymore.

"The useful exchange," recalled Pike, understanding her initial remark.

"We've agreed responsibility," reminded Lydia. "We felt there was a need to reassure your Fund and the countries it represents that there was no danger."

"I appreciate the reassurance," said Pike.

"Then it's been a worthwhile meeting."

Pike discerned the concluding note in her voice and said hurriedly, "I'd like to talk further."

"It's late," said the woman.

"Tomorrow, then," said Pike, careless of the anxiety.

Lydia seemed to consider the request. "All right," she said. "Tomorrow."

Pike felt a surge of relief at having prolonged the encounter. Straying from behind the barrier, he said, "We haven't eaten."

"No," agreed Lydia.

"Shall we?"

"I'm not hungry," said the woman, trying to remain concealed.

"Neither am I."

They stayed looking at each other, each matching the other's stare. Lydia felt again the wet warmth she achieved alone that afternoon in the locked room.

"Tomorrow, then," she said.

"Yes," he said, unmoving.

"I think you should go." Being black, her dress wouldn't show any stain.

"Do you want me to?"

"This is ridiculous!" Her voice was uneven, so the outrage failed.

"Yes," he said.

"Stop just saying yes!"

He got up, came to where she was sitting and reached out for her.

"No!" said Lydia.

Pike bent, taking her arms and pulling her up from the couch and into him. For several moments she stood stiff, arms tight against her side. He had to tip her head, to kiss her, and she tried initially to resist that, too, her lips clamped together. She twisted her head to say no, but as her mouth opened, his tongue stopped the word, and then she was biting back, not stiff anymore.

"Here?"

"No."

In the bedroom they played, undressing each other with tingling slowness, neither touching the other's sex.

"*Please!*" she said.

"No."

"Yes."

"No."

"I can't wait!"

She didn't, flooding as he thrust into her and then bursting again when he did. They ate at each other, first she at him and then he at her, both climaxing again. Then they explored the secret places and for her it was the first time and she moaned with the painful pleasure of it.

When they rested, before starting again, Pike said, "This could destroy us."

"Me more than you," she said.

"Sorry?"

"No." Lydia knew now why she had become discontented with Malik.

During his term of office Nelson Jordan had moved back into the Oval Office the desk made from the oak timbers of the HMS Resolute presented to America by Queen Victoria in 1880 and originally used by Jimmy Carter. When Pike entered the room, Jordan moved away from it, to indicate that the meeting was informal, leading the IMF official to the easy chairs bordering the fireplace.

"Good to see you, Tom."

"Good to be here, Mr. President."

"You're a bourbon man, right?"

"That'll be fine, sir."

Jordan sat with his legs straight out before him, towards the dead fireplace, and Pike thought the huge man looked constrained in the chair. The President waited until the White House orderly withdrew, then said, "Appreciate your coming like this: one or two things about this money business I want to get clear in my mind."

"Of course, Mr. President," said Pike. Would there be confirmation tonight?

"So what have we got?" demanded Jordan. "Real trouble or a passing problem?"

"There are varying viewpoints," said Pike cautiously, wondering if he could draw the politician out.

"Bell says it's trouble," disclosed Jordan, "claims there's been a gross miscalculation and everything could go down the tube."

Pike stared above the fireplace to Peal's portrait of George Washington, tempering the earlier judgment. Not confirmation, he decided: comparison, instead. "That's an extreme view," he said, still cautious. "Certainly not one with which I agree."

"A passing problem, then?"

He was going to have to be extremely careful. Aware that the Treasury Secretary would have already told Jordan of the meeting, Pike said, "I wouldn't have adjusted the conference of the Interim Committee if I'd thought it was a passing problem."

"So what the hell have we got then?" repeated the President, showing Texan impatience.

Pike refused to be intimidated by it, knowing it would be the wrong attitude. He appeared to consider the question and then said, "Uncertainty. Which is where banking can cause problems where no problems exist. I redefined the Interim Committee because I thought it right for there to be an entirely secret, secure discussion among international bankers and finance ministers just to stop that uncertainty. There's nothing in any of the rescheduling requests that can't be absorbed at the moment. . . ."

"At the moment." The President seized the words.

Pike felt a twitch of annoyance at his clumsiness. "It's necessary to clarify the Soviet position," he said. "That's why I've set up this meeting in Switzerland."

"Shouldn't that have been a diplomatic approach?"

An echo of the Treasury Secretary's objection or a genuine question from the President? "I considered it right that the approach should be on behalf of a number of nations, rather than just one specific government. The liability at the moment is that of the International Monetary Fund, not that of the United States or any other country."

"Appreciate the point," said Jordan. "Weren't you surprised the Soviets agreed as they did?"

"Yes," agreed Pike honestly. "Encouraged, too. We've assessed a new financial attitude from Moscow and their response to our request seems to support that view."

"Invested a lot of responsibility in your son."

"I wouldn't have done so if I hadn't thought him capable," said Pike.

"Remember our conversation a little while ago?"

"Yes, sir," said Pike.

"Nothing fixed, for when you leave the Fund?"

"No."

"Maybe we should talk, if you get an offer?"

"Of course, Mr. President."

"Like I said before, it's important to get this thing right," said Jordan. "Important for us all."

"Believe me, Mr. President, I know just how important it is."

34

They became satiated and sore with sex, aching from exhaustion but unwilling to stop. Throughout the night each woke the other from a half-sleep to start again until, in the morning, Pike left for his own suite because they both needed time to sleep. And to think.

Pike awoke before midday, lying unmoving on his back, considering what had happened. Stupid, he decided realistically: incredibly, insanely, ridiculously stupid. More so because he could have stopped it happening and he didn't. Instead, he had allowed a totally unnecessary, potentially disastrous difficulty to intrude into a situation where, suddenly, there were already sufficient potentially disastrous difficulties. *How disastrous?* He strained for the objectivity. Me more than you, she'd said. Which was right. The earlier reflections about sexual entrapment had been as stupid as everything else. Lydia Kirov's disgrace would be more than his. So he couldn't be publicly compromised. And so to think of it in terms of disaster was an exaggeration. Another stupidity. Would she use it, in the negotiations he wanted to continue? He didn't know the answer to that. Would he? If he could, he accepted honestly. He'd use anything to prevent what she suggested.

But it would be even pressure, neither having greater advantage than the other. Me more than you, he thought again: The *fact* was that neither had the greater advantage over the other, but the *reality* was that Lydia *felt* she had more to lose. Maybe not stupid at all. Maybe, without planning it, he was more in control than he imagined himself to be.

Not once, during the consideration, did he think of Jane.

Lydia Kirov came awake startled, instantly alert and instantly aware of what she had done. Instantly aware, too, that for the first time ever she'd lost control. What else had she lost? He could not publicly use it, because he would disgrace himself as well as her. Privately, then? It was a possibility, but Lydia felt she could confront that. She remembered what they had done and touched her own soreness, a familiar place, smiling in recollection. Perhaps she hadn't lost as much as she had initially feared.

Not once, during the consideration, did she think of Malik.

They arranged that this time she should come to his suite, and when she entered, there was an immediate embarrassment, a feeling he broke by pulling Lydia to him and holding her, feeling the instant excitement at her closeness.

"Sorry?" he said.

"You already asked me that."

"I'm asking you again."

"In one way," she said, surprising him. She pushed herself away, looking up at him. She kissed him longingly.

"What way?" he said.

"You know the way!"

"It won't."

"How can you be sure?"

"Will you let it?"

"I'll try not to."

"So will I," he said.

"Promise me?"

"I promise." As if to prove it, he moved away from her and she smiled, recognizing the gesture.

"I don't know what else there is to discuss, anyway," she said.

He led her to the couches, sitting opposite as they had in her room, and said, "Your Third World difficulties."

"I've already explained how we're able to deal with those."

"You were wonderful," he said.

"You said you wouldn't let it get in the way."

"I'm not," he said. "I just wanted you to know."

"I'm sore."

"So am I."

"You promised," she said.

"Your way wouldn't work," he said, conscious at once of her face tightening at the professional challenge.

"Of course it would work!"

"Which country are you going to declare in default?"

"That decision hasn't been reached yet. I couldn't tell you in any case."

"In Africa?" he guessed confidently.

"Probably," she conceded. "That's where the problems are arising."

"Then it wouldn't work," he repeated.

"Why not?"

"There isn't an African country not in debt to the West: I'd guess more deeply in debt than they are to you. The moment you declare default, then whoever in the West is involved will do the same, trying to grab what equity they can to minimize their loss."

"The diversification is a problem of your banking system, not ours," said Lydia, completely in control of herself.

"Not anymore," said Pike, equally controlled. "We're tied now, East and West; neither can afford the financial strain of the other getting beyond control. A sovereign default anywhere—Africa, Latin America; it doesn't matter where—would have a chain effect. Banks nervous to cover one endangered loan by calling in another would directly pressure you. There'd be a panic and there'd be collapses—a lot of collapses. The Soviet Union has considerable debts bunched short-term. Capital repayments, too. There would be a concerted demand for payment. Could you meet a concerted demand?''

''We've not sought any repayment rearrangement; neither do we intend to,'' said Lydia, stiffly.

''You're calling in loans from Poland, Hungary, Rumania and Czechoslovakia,'' guessed Pike. ''To pay you, they're seeking deferment from us. You're creating the chain effect already.''

''We're not calling in loans,'' said Lydia. ''Merely insisting that they're met on time.''

''And what's happening proves my point,'' said Pike, triumphantly. ''Pressure from one side immediately creates pressure on the other.''

''We've sought repayment from our debtors, as is our right,'' persisted Lydia. ''That's sound banking principle.''

''There is an alternative,'' he said.

''What?''

''Bridging finance.''

She frowned at him. ''Where's the logic of increasing our indebtedness?''

''In maintaining the status quo,'' said the American. ''What assets, in practice, could you seize if you declare someone in Africa in default? Virtually none.''

''That wouldn't be the point,'' said Lydia with strained patience. ''The object would be one of example.''

''Which I've already explained wouldn't work.''

''The repercussive danger is certainly one which needs relaying back to Moscow,'' conceded Lydia.

''You've my assurance that it *would* happen,'' insisted Pike. He was persuading her, he decided; slowly it was coming his way.

''Would additional funding be available?''

He had no authority to offer any commitment, Pike

realized. But he'd been right in what he'd told her. It *was* the only alternative. "Yes," he said. "I believe it would."

"How much?"

"What would you be seeking?"

"That would need detailed assessment," said the woman. "If it's to be a full cushion against the short-term capital as well as interest—and cover, too, the failed payments from our own debtors—I would estimate something in the region of $250,000,000,000."

She looked expectantly at him, and Pike said, "That's a figure I could put forward to the Fund, for consideration."

"I can't make a formal request to you."

"I wouldn't propose it as such. I would put it forward as a discussion proposal, nothing more."

"And I'll make sure the difficulties of default are fully appreciated." She smiled hesitantly across at him. "There's nothing more to discuss, is there?"

"I don't want to go, not yet," he said.

"No," she agreed.

"Tomorrow will be soon enough."

"Too soon."

"It'll hurt."

"I want it to."

They ate in the room—disinterestedly, because of their impatience to make love again. It did hurt, for both of them, but not enough to take away the pleasure. They remained in bed throughout the afternoon and spent the evening consumed and cocooned with each other, with no awareness or concern about anything happening outside, just resting and loving and resting and loving. In the morning, before it was properly light, she lay cradled in the crook of his arm, her head against his chest. Pike said, "We could arrange another meeting like this if there were an approach for refinance."

"Yes," she agreed.

"I'd like that to happen."

"Not as much as me, my darling," said Lydia.

He hadn't made a mistake at all, decided Pike. The reverse, in fact. He felt very happy.

There had not been an appearance before the Court, but Jane still felt humiliated by the abruptness of her dismissal. And that's what it was, she decided, even though she'd been allowed the formality of tendering her resignation. Just an hour after submitting it, she had the official response, agreeing to her departure and adding that she was not required to work any period of notice but to be out of the building that evening.

Jane left quietly, without good-byes to her staff, which she supposed would confirm her guilt to Burnham and to whomever else he'd told. So what! she thought in near tearful belligerence. The Bank didn't matter, not anymore. And she'd never liked official leavings anyway, with awkward ceremonies and insincere speeches. Far better this way, in fact. She was quite free now, able to fit into whatever arrangements Tom might like to make. It was going to be wonderful, married to Tom. She knew it was.

By the time he telephoned from Switzerland, her concern was more at the absence of contact from him than at what had happened at the Bank. Despite which—and as reconciled to it as she now was—Jane would still have liked Tom to have shown more sympathy when she recounted the story.

"I was worried, when you didn't call," she said.

"What the hell for?"

Jane grimaced at the abrupt question. "I just thought you might have telephoned."

"You know what I've been doing!"

"Yes."

"Then you must surely know how busy I've been."

"I'm sorry," she said. "I wasn't trying to make a big thing out of it."

"My father wants to talk to me straight away," said Pike. "I'm flying home direct from Switzerland."

Alone in her Kensington apartment, Jane's face twisted again. "Oh."

"I'm sorry."

"I understand," said Jane.

"I'll call you from Washington."

"I could come out," she said hopefully.

The suggestion seemed to surprise him. "I'm going to be busy."

"There's no reason any longer for me to be in London."

"It would mean living in a hotel," he said. "I gave up the Manhattan apartment."

"I wouldn't mind that," she said. "We'd be together."

There was a pause from his end of the line. Finally, he said, "I'll fix it and then I'll call you."

"Do you want me to come out?"

"Of course I do; what sort of question was that?"

"Nothing," she said, in immediate retreat. "I'm sorry."

"I've got a plane to catch."

"Be careful," she said automatically.

"I'll call you from Washington," he said again.

"Tom."

"What?"

"I love you."

"Yes," he said impatiently. "I love you, too."

35

His father was waiting in the car at Dulles Airport, to be briefed on the drive back into Washington. The executive directors were already convened at the IMF headquarters when they arrived, and Pike went straight into the conference, rehearsed by the limousine discussion with his father. Unlike previous occasions, he spoke directly to the conference and not through his father. He talked looking towards the British delegation, disappointed that Burnham didn't appear to be included in it and therefore wouldn't see the elevation in status.

There was an eruption of questioning when he stopped, with the British chancellor leading. "There was no doubt that they are considering default?" demanded Stephen Wilder.

"Absolutely none," said Pike. "She specifically told me that was the measure they were contemplating. It's definitely Third World indebtedness."

"How sure are you that the woman understood the knock-on effect if they did that?" Bell demanded.

Pike looked towards him, inexplicably offended at hearing Lydia described as "the woman." He replied, "I'm quite sure."

"Isn't it surprising that they hadn't realized that before?" Bell wouldn't let go.

It was Pike's father who answered. "The financial responsibility . . . the awareness . . . is a new thing: We've established that over the last few months. With their centralized system, as opposed to our own, I can understand it being an aspect easily overlooked. They had no way of knowing, after all, if Western consortia were involved."

"We're involved in every African country," said Volger.

"We hadn't anticipated the extent of the Soviet move there," said Pike. "That took a specific analysis when I was in Switzerland. If we, with our supposedly more advanced banking system and expertise, hadn't considered it, why should Moscow?"

There were nods of agreement from several of the delegates around the room.

"Did they appear to consider themselves in a position of strength in Africa?" asked the Bank of England's Sir Herbert Course.

"Absolutely," assured Pike. "The attitude was clearly that they intended to bring any doubtful debtors into line, with one convincing example."

"So the possibility is that it will be a hard attitude to change," persisted the Englishman.

"She *did* understand the effect," reiterated Pike.

"But will she be able to make others understand?" took up Bell. "I argued against the informality of the meeting before and I say again that it should have been a fuller and more authoritative delegation."

Pike's father sensed that Bell was politicking and moved to confront it. "The information we've gained and the conference we're able to have here today is precisely because the contact *was* informal. We would never have made the sort of progress that we have with a delegation, any more than we would have been able to prevent some public awareness."

"I agree," said Henry Ambersom. Looking directly

towards Pike, the World Bank chairman said, "I think you are to be congratulated."

Pike flushed at the open praise. Neither the British group nor Bell joined in the muttering and head movement of agreement.

"I think we are overlooking a very practical problem," persisted Bell. "The IMF and the World Bank can cover minimal problems. But I don't consider the $250,000,000,000 minimal in any degree. We've confirmed a problem we feared might arise, a problem that *will* arise anyway if they persist in default. How do we stop it if they don't? We don't have the finance available to offer that bridge they need."

There was a moment of absolute quiet throughout the room as Bell produced the specter that haunted them all. Prepared by the report from his son, the elder Pike said, "There is a way."

The concentration was entirely upon the IMF managing director, as he intended it should be, because the proposal was going to be the one to project him right into the Treasury Secretary's seat and he wanted everyone to realize it, not necessarily now but later, in hindsight. He said, "This has, quite obviously, got to be considered as an international problem. And internationally there is an imbalance in the spread of the loans to the Soviet bloc. The preponderance of debt is concentrated throughout Europe and the Far East. In total, American institutions are only extended to $150,000,000,000. There has been detailed discussion in the past of the United States of America providing safety net finance, through the IMF. I think that facility should at last be created. . . ."

"Are you actually suggesting that the United States of America makes itself responsible for $250,000,000,000!" said Bell, overanxious to express his contempt.

"Of course not," said the older Pike, further exposing the Treasury Secretary. "I'm suggesting an increase in all the quotas, from every country. But I am proposing that the contribution of the United States is correspondingly bigger. I am suggesting that additional U.S. finance be made available, to provide whatever safety net might be necessary if there is a short-fall. And I am also proposing that an approach be made. . . ." He hesitated, looking directly at Bell, intent upon every advantage. ". . . an official approach, to Saudi Arabia. In the past the Saudi Arabians have reacted favorably to requests to advance funding. No country would be exempt from the effects of a world banking collapse—certainly not a country which has its oil priced in dollars, as Saudi Arabia has. It is a fact of which they are fully aware. I am talking in generalities, but the details could be easily equated, to calculate the percentage increase necessary, from the individual quotas from member countries, from America and from the Arabs."

It had about it exactly the sort of flair he knew appealed to the President. And there would be no reason, once it was created and the Soviets involved, why Jordan couldn't make public what had happened. The idea of the United States snatching everyone else back from the brink would appeal most of all.

"I think the proposal has much to commend it," said Henry Ambersom.

"So do I," said Volger, adding to the inferred American approval.

"Have you any conception of the total indebtedness you are considering!" demanded Bell, aware of the discussion moving away from him.

"I would be interested to hear if the American Treasury Secretary has an alternative proposal," said Ienari Tanaka, the Japanese minister, entering the discussion.

Adjusting the cliché to fit the surroundings, Pike supposed that was the sixty-four trillion dollar question.

"Yes," said Bell. "I have."

Now it was the Treasury Secretary who commanded the attention of the directors. "Surely," said Bell, "a more sensible and far less costly undertaking would be to provide standby cover to Western banks likely to be affected by the default of any African country?"

It was fortunate, thought Pike, that he had anticipated the suggestion. Prepared, his father rose from beside him and said, "No, I do not consider such an undertaking either more sensible or far less costly. The most obvious problem is that we do not know of which of the indebted African countries the Soviet Union intends making an example. If we are going to prepare a contingency for the entire continent, then the sum involved would be $195,000,000,000. I consider the difference immaterial in view of the respective debtors. The developing African countries have consistently and persistently rescheduled and declared moratoria. Certainly, by covering Western banks, we could avoid a collapse, but the element of lending is repayment. The Soviet Union has consistently repaid. Indeed, we know from the Zurich meeting that the very proposals they are considering now, coupled with a gold sale, are to meet their commitments. I consider a loan to Moscow to cover their short-term difficulties much sounder business than shoring up Africa yet again."

It was a strong rebuttal, uncontestable among the countries assembled, all of which had suffered from African debts.

"I would be prepared to suggest to my government the increase in quotas," said Pierre Larouse, from France.

"So would I," said Luigi Cambino, the Italian minister.

From around the room came indication of agreement to the idea of additional funding for the Soviet Union, and after gauging the feeling of the meeting, the IMF managing director proposed—and had unanimously adopted—the reference to committee for the details of individual contributions to be calculated. There was a further decision to have the Saudi Arabian delegation composed of members of the Interim Committee, headed by the British chancellor.

After the formal ending of the meeting there were the inevitable private groupings, several of the delegates coming forward personally to congratulate Pike. The British contingent made no approach. It was thirty minutes before Pike managed to extricate himself, making towards the exit and feeling for the first time the tiredness of the flight from Europe and the concentration of the meetings. Henry Ambersom was at the door, obviously waiting.

"You did an extremely good job," said the World Bank chairman.

"Thank you, sir," said Pike.

"It was good of you to find time to go up to see Janet."

"I said I would," reminded Pike. "How is she?"

Instead of answering, Ambersom said, "I've got a favor to ask."

"What?"

"Could you go up again? The doctor treating her is anxious to see you."

"What about?"

"He didn't say."

"I'll try," promised Pike.

Lydia Kirov's return to Moscow was practically a duplicate of Pike's to Washington.

Malik was waiting for her at Sheremetyevo airport and they drove directly to a meeting of the Politburo Committee. Lydia had prepared her briefing on the homeward flight, and she delivered it without interruption, conscious, towards the end, of something like impatience from the three men confronting her.

When she finished, Lenev said, "So default would be sufficient?"

"That's what he said."

"So let's declare it. . . ." He shuffled through papers before him. "Let's default Zambia," he said. "We've sufficient reserves."

"I think refinancing requires further consideration," said Lydia.

"If it goes wrong, it could destroy everything," said Korobov.

"No," said Lydia. "There's more to gain."

"It's an unnecessary extension," said Pushkov.

"The proposal always allowed for an approach from the West," reminded Lydia.

"We've achieved enough," said Lenev.

"I think we should wait for further contact—to see their proposals at least." Lydia was insistent. "The American commitment is still slight, compared to the rest of the world. And there's the provision for influence, in the undeveloped countries."

Her last was a telling point, which led to a continuation of the discussion for a further two hours. At the end of it Lydia felt as strained as she had with any negotiations during the preceding twelve months.

"You consider it worthwhile?" demanded Lenev finally, clearly making it Lydia's personal responsibility.

"Yes," she said, recognizing the commitment the man was demanding. So scared, she thought: every one of them.

"There should be a time limit," further qualified Korobov.

"Three months," came in Pushkov, completing the pressure.

Anything, thought Lydia. "Three months," she agreed.

She sat away from Malik in the car taking them to her apartment, and Malik said, "Is anything the matter?"

"I'm tired, that's all. They were difficult; they're stupid."

"What sort of man was he?"

"Who?" she said, knowing what he meant but pretending she didn't.

"The American."

"Very good." She was looking away, out of the car. *Very* good, she thought.

"Was it difficult?"

She looked back at him. "Yes," she said. "Extremely difficult."

In the apartment he kissed her and Lydia forced herself to respond. Why were her needs more than he could provide?

"Look!" he said.

Lydia saw he had used his own key and arranged champagne—it was French, not Russian. She should love him, not compare him.

"I've got some news," he said.

"What?"

"I told Irena," he announced.

"Oh."

"Just oh?"

"What did she say?" He must never know. She couldn't hurt him by ever letting him know.

Malik pulled the cork and poured the wine, offering her a glass. "She's agreed to a divorce—whenever we want it! Isn't that marvelous!"

"Yes," said Lydia quietly. "Marvelous."

He looked at her curiously, glass held before him. "You sure there's nothing wrong?"

"Just tiredness," she said. "I told you."

"Happy?"

She sipped, to give herself the pause. "Yes," she said, "very happy."

36

With his preference for caucus decisions, President Jordan spread the discussion on the IMF plan. There was a conference of the entire Federal Bank board of governors, which included the five Reserve Bank presidents forming the policy-making Open Market Committee, another private Oval Office discussion with Pike's father and a further one with Henry Ambersom. Nelson Jordan sought discussion papers from every member of the Cabinet, and when they met, finally, to discuss it, there was immediate support from Henry Bowen, the Secretary of State, who argued control through lending at the first meeting at which the Russian financial changes had been discussed months before. Jordan's careful preparation allowed time for people to assess attitudes. Guessing the President's, Secretary of Commerce William Johnson pressed American involvement, which left the Treasury Secretary as the only serious dissenter. It was very clear that Bell's opposition was futile, but he tried until the impatient President publicly humiliated the man by demanding a practical alternative proposal to that of the IMF. The conclusion was an agreement in principle to safety net funding being the entire responsibility of the United States and to an additional—and majority—quota contribution to the IMF's General Arrangement to Borrow facility. With the backing of the implied confidence of America, the approaches then began to the other member countries of the IMF.

Pike was allocated a staff to co-ordinate the creation of the package, to register the country-by-country response and also to monitor Africa to warn immediately if Moscow carried out its threat of default. Pike worked with his customary absorption, arriving at the Fund headquarters early and rarely leaving before ten in the evening, which was the reason he gave for postponing Jane's arrival from England.

Saudi Arabia proved difficult. Representatives of the IMF's Interim Committee, headed by Stephen Wilder, formed the delegation to Riyadh. The Saudi response was that they had already provided substantial emergency funding to the IMF and that their dollar-maintained reserves were affected by the lowering of world oil prices, restricting the liquidity available. It took a week of arguing that those dollars would be worthless anyway if there was a world financial collapse before there was any concession, and then it was only for $3,000,000,000. It left the emergency package short by $40,000,000,000. Renewed approaches were made to member countries and Japan, Germany and England agreed to increase their already enlarged quota by one per cent. There was a further special meeting of the United States Cabinet at which it was agreed the remaining short-fall of $23,000,000,000 would be covered by America raising the limit of its specially created safety net finance.

With existing loans it represented the biggest extension in the history of world banking.

Pike felt a curious deflation when he met with his father on the day the second approach was made to Moscow through the Soviet embassy in Washington. It was an attitude in marked contrast to his father's ebullience.

"We got it together!" said his father.

"There's no guarantee the Soviets will accept it."

He shook his head at his son's caution. "The alternative was default," he said. "And if they were going to declare default, they would have done it by now."

It was a reasonable assumption, Pike supposed. Which meant another personal success. There was still no lift to his feeling. "I'd like to go if they respond," he said. This time the Russians could always send another representative, he realized. Perhaps it would be better if they did. He frowned at the thought, unsure why it had occurred. It had been sex, nothing more. No, not nothing more. The best ever.

"After all the activity, it's going to be a quiet time, until they react."

"Yes," agreed Pike. There was no reason to delay Jane any longer. Maybe there'd be time to see Janet's psychiatrist, too.

"Thought about what you'd like to do?"

"Do?" said Pike, unsure of the question.

"In the future," said the older man. "It's not just me. You've made it, too, Tom. Everybody knows it. Whatever you want."

"No," said Pike. "I haven't decided yet."

The man frowned at his son's disinterest. "This isn't a city to stand back in, you know."

"No," agreed Pike. "I know."

In his own office, Pike decided that his father was right: Everything did suddenly seem quiet. He made the call to the psychiatrist and then to Jane, in England. She asked to fly out immediately and he agreed, thinking fully of her for the first time in a month. Which was, he supposed, a sobering realization. But why should it be? He'd called often enough, despite the fourteen-hour days. And with a work schedule like that, there'd been no point in her coming earlier. He'd give her enough attention, once this thing had been settled. And not fool around, like he had with Janet. He wished the psychiatrist had said on the telephone what he wanted.

There was an obvious nervousness when he met Jane at the airport. She seemed almost embarrassed when he kissed her and Pike thought it seemed much longer than a month since they had last been together. A lot had happened since then. On the way into the city, he told her about the creation of the emergency package, and she said, "It's an odd sensation but I feel very much on the outside of things now."

"I'm sorry about the job," he said.

"So am I," she said. "The circumstances, that is." She paused, then said, "I've put the flat up for sale. Is that all right?"

The question made Pike frown. "I guess so."

"That's another funny feeling."

"What?"

"Coming here, like this. I feel I've cut myself off."

"An immigrant, to the New World!"

Jane shivered, as if she were cold. "Want to know a secret?—I'm frightened."

He looked at her briefly. "What of?"

"I don't know, just frightened."

Pike had taken a suite at the Mayflower again and had arranged for flowers. Once inside, they kissed more fully than they had at the airport.

"Glad to see me?" she asked.

"Of course I am."

"It *is* going to be all right, isn't it?"

"You know it is." He found her uncertainty irritating.

"I'm going to try so very hard."

"You won't have to."

"Want to know another secret?"

"What?"

"I got very worried when you didn't suggest I come out right away."

"You know why!"

"Yes," she said hurriedly, frightened of annoying him. "And I understand. But by myself in London, I started thinking that maybe you'd changed your mind."

"Why should I do that?"

"I don't know," said Jane. "I suppose I was upset by what happened at the bank."

"That's all over now."

"Yes," she agreed. "All over."

Because he had made arrangements to go up that weekend, Pike told her about Janet, and Jane said, "Poor woman."

"Yes," he said.

"I'm glad you're going up."

"It'll only be for the day; you won't mind being by yourself?"

"No."

"You could go out to my parents' house if you wanted to."

"We'll see," she said. Then she said, "You would tell me, wouldn't you? If you stopped loving me, I mean."

He smiled at her. "Isn't this kind of a strange conversation, before we're even married?"

She shook her head positively. "I think there should be proper understandings, *before* we're married."

"Yes," said Pike patiently. "I'd tell you. Would you tell me?"

She came to him to be kissed again. "I'm never going to stop loving you," she said.

Jane decided to remain in Washington and visit the Smithsonian, and Pike flew up on the first available plane. The psychiatrist was waiting when Pike arrived at the clinic. Pike thought there was a stiffness about the other man.

"Janet's due for discharge very soon now," said Harris.

"I guess she is," said Pike.

"She'll start scoring again," predicted the doctor. "That's the feeling I got when I visited her."

Harris frowned. "Didn't you think of telling anybody?"

"You're the expert," he said. "I hadn't any right to intrude."

"I would have hardly regarded that as intrusion," said the psychiatrist.

"Would it have helped?"

"It might."

"You realized it anyway," said Pike. "Can't you prevent it?"

"I don't know."

He hadn't traveled five hundred miles to be lectured like some recalcitrant child. "You wanted to discuss something with me?" Pike said.

Harris hesitated and then said, "Janet and I have had some long sessions together—talked about a lot of things. She says California was attention-getting. Trying to shock you into some reaction. She says you made it into an experimental marriage—experimental with drugs and with sex—and that she went along with it not because she wanted to but because she didn't want to lose you."

"What the hell are you talking about?" Could this man hurt him, Pike wondered, with the stories Janet told him?

Ignoring the question, the psychiatrist went on, "She says that when she came back East, after the California marriage broke up, she thought there was a chance of your getting back together again."

"That's bull; it's all bull."

"It's important, that I know," said Harris. "It's very common for someone going through the sort of difficulties that Janet has to blame someone else rather than themselves. She sure as hell won't stay here as a voluntary patient after her sentence is up. So, in the time available, I've got to know the truth if I'm going to stand any sort of chance at all."

For several moments Pike stared down at the floor. Then he looked up and said, "Janet Ambersom is a promiscuous woman, in every way; she always has been. She cheated on our marriage, and she's fooled around with drugs for years—grass, at college. Coke, too, I think, although I don't know for certain. If it would help, I could make the divorce papers available to you. Everything is set out there."

"So she's lying, when she says you led and she followed?"

"This isn't very pleasant," said Pike.

"It's not meant to be pleasant," said the psychiatrist. "It's meant to save someone."

"Yes," said Pike. "She's lying."

The American suggestion for a second meeting lay between them on the table directly in front of Yakov Lenev, and Lydia felt an excitement from just looking at it.

"From your discussions in Zurich last time, to declare Zambia in default would achieve what we want?" said the Politburo committee chairman.

"Yes," agreed Lydia. Her proposals had been discussed and examined too exhaustively for her to make any other reply. Why did the fool need reassurance?

"So, is there any purpose in our responding to this invitation?"

"I think so, as I have already stated," she said. She spoke looking at the small strip of paper, wanting to be with him again.

Ivan Pushkov, sitting to the left of the chairman, said, "From the Zurich meeting we know their concern; we know we've succeeded. Why endanger everything by going further?"

"I do not consider there would be any danger," said Lydia. She was careless of Malik's obvious curiosity.

"Throughout everything Comrade Kirov has never been wrong," reminded the Finance Minister.

Taking the point, Lenev said, "In your judgment, is there sufficient value in agreeing to further contact?"

"Yes," said Lydia. "Every value."

37

The first flights from Moscow landed in Zurich earlier than those from Washington, so Lydia was already in the suite, tensed, when he arrived. Pike didn't enter the room at once, remaining instead in the corridor, looking in at her.

"They could have sent somebody else," he said.

"I thought about that, too."

"Christ, I'm glad they didn't."

"Don't just stand there."

"We're supposed to talk," Pike said.

"Later."

The first time was too quick; both were overanxious. The next time they relaxed into unhurried play. "The other way," she insisted, "no one else does that." And he did. They established a rhythm, one leading, the other following, changing each time.

"You're amazing," she said.

"So are you."

"Do you think I'm a nymphomaniac?"

"No," he said, surprised at the question.

"I worry about it."

"Why?"

"Because it wouldn't work with anyone else."

"I don't think you are."

"Would you believe I hadn't made love less than a year ago?"

"No," he said.

"It's true."

"What's wrong with being a nymphomaniac?"

"Just stay there inside me; don't move until I say so."

"Like that?"

"Yes," she said. "Being a nymphomaniac would also mean I didn't have control: I don't like not having control. No! Don't move yet."

"Who's in control now?"

"I am," she said.

"Do you know what satyriasis is?"

"I haven't heard the word."

"The male equivalent of nymphomania."

"Are you?"

"What do you think?"

"Why do you think I want you?"

"Can I move now?"

"Slowly."

He did, but almost at once he began to laugh, falling over her and losing pace, and she pulled at him in annoyance. "Do you realize what a lot of people believe we're doing?"

She started to laugh with him. "If they knew!"

He kissed her and said, "If they knew, they'd be jealous."

"You stopped moving."

"Sorry," he said, starting again.

"I'm supposed to be getting married," she said.

"So am I."

"Do you love her?"

"I'm not sure," he said. "Do you love him?"

"I'm not sure," she said. "Oh, that's good; that's very good."

"How long can you stay this time?"

"About the same as last time," he said. "I'd like it to be longer."

"Couldn't it be?"

"I don't think so; there's a limit to madness."

"Is that what this is—madness?"

"You know it is."

"Marvelous madness."

She began to quicken, leading, and he followed, arriving with her.

"Marvelous madness," she said, panting. "I think you've got it."

"Got what?" he said.

"Satyriasis. I think it's wonderful."

"Nymphomanic."

"Satyr."

It was the same pattern as before, loving and resting, loving and resting. In the evening they got up, finally, and ordered food in the room.

"We're supposed to be talking," he reminded her.

"We've talked."

"About other things," he said. "Your people didn't declare a default."

"There was never a time limit to their doing it."

"You mean they still might." He felt a flare of alarm.

"There's still a strong argument being put for doing so."

This discussion was necessary, she supposed, but she wished it weren't.

"Didn't you explain what that would mean?"

"Of course I did," said Lydia. "The reaction was

that the West could stand it. They've withstood things before."

"No," said Pike urgently. "Not a sovereign default—not for a very long time. And then conditions were different. Now the commitments are too interlocked."

"There was agreement at least for this meeting," she said, extending the hope. It was ludicrous to imagine the chance of another.

'There's finance available," said the American. "I can tell you that officially."

"Rescheduling is expensive," complained Lydia. "Averaged on last year's interest rates, it could cost us an additional $400,000,000."

"That's a generalization," he argued.

"Still an approximate figure."

"The rates would be advantageous, believe me."

"It would still only be postponing the problem, not curing it," said Lydia. She had to do it. Would he remember precisely, later?

"They *are* repaying," said Pike. "I know that hasn't been the case in the past and I know that there seems to be a problem for you at the moment, but over the past six months our banks have been paid by the Third World."

"And we haven't," said Lydia. "Isn't there an expression for it in the West—robbing Peter to pay Paul?"

"They owed Paul first," he said.

"And you think that indicates the system is working?"

"Doesn't it?"

"What if it's a temporary attitude, to establish confidence before the application for further loans?"

"There's no indication that it is."

"There wouldn't be, at this stage, would there?"

"I'm not sure I follow your argument," said Pike.

"Do you think Western bankers have shown proper caution?"

The American hesitated. "No," he admitted. "I don't think they have."

"Neither do we," said Lydia. "Money has been handed out as if it came from a bottomless pit, so every developing country has been borrowing without any thought of repayment. . . ." Now she paused, smiling. "And we made the same mistake," she admitted. "Only we don't intend getting caught in a spiral from which we can't disengage ourselves."

The bedroom was beyond the closed door and what had happened in it was put aside now, Pike realized. She'd come briefed to argue a position. Which meant they *were* prepared to consider an alternative to default. So what were the conditions towards which she was moving? "We've talked about what would happen if you disengaged," he said.

"To us both," she said.

Poker time again. "So what's the answer?"

"The sort of control that's been lacking in the past," she said. "Not a reversal of Peter and Paul in a few months time, with the West advancing money for our debts to be repaid."

It was an easy undertaking to give, Pike decided. "I think I can offer you the assurance on that," he said.

Lydia shook her head. "It's not me that needs the assurance," she said. "It's the people who still consider a default worth the risk."

"What then?" said Pike.

"A public declaration that it's not going to happen. And not just from your Fund. From the World Bank and from Western governments."

How politically difficult would that be? wondered Pike. "I'll put the view forward," he promised. It was nothing more than sound financial sense, after all.

"It's important," she stressed.

"I understand that." He added, "My people will be looking for assurance, too."

"It can only be a personal opinion, of course."

"Of course."

"I said there are people who consider default worth the risk," she reminded him. "They fully realize now just how severe that risk is."

"That's not much of a reassurance."

"That's all I can give."

"Any declaration would be meaningless if you defaulted anyway."

She smiled at the pressure. "Yes," she agreed, "it would be, wouldn't it?"

"So one action needs to precede the other."

" 'He has almost charmed me from my profession, by persuading me to it,' " she said, playing their game.

Momentarily Pike didn't understand, and then he remembered the contest of the previous encounters. He supposed it was Shakespeare because it had been before, but couldn't remember the quotation.

Needing to match her in everything, because it was his nature, he said, " 'Suit the action to the word, the word to the action.' "

"*Hamlet,*" she identified again, waiting.

"I don't know," he confessed.

"*Timon of Athens,*" she said, smiling sadly. "We couldn't be together, could we?"

"What do you mean?" asked Pike uncertainly.

"It's too important for both of us: to win."

"I don't think of it like that."

"That's a lie," she said. "I've thought you've been honest up to now, but that was a lie. Please don't."

"Succeeding is important," he admitted.

"To me, too," she said, an admission of her own. Then she said, "Had you thought about it, our being together?"

"No," he said, the earlier uncertainty returning.

"Thank you for not lying this time."

"Have you?"

"Yes."

"How?"

"There isn't a way," she said. "It's a fantasy. What's happened between us is a fantasy."

Thank God, thought Pike, she hadn't considered anything as preposterous like defection. But why should she have? Neither regarded what had occurred as love. "There's probably a fitting quotation," he said.

"Probably," she agreed. "I can't be bothered thinking of it."

"Official business over?" he said.

"I haven't got anything more to say."

"It might have worked, our being together." He thought she might want him to say it and there was no danger in the remark.

She shook her head positively. "We'd have ended up hating each other," she said.

"I can't imagine that."

"I wouldn't like you to hate me," she said.

The parting was easier than Pike expected. She seemed to conclude the episode with the finality with which she might have closed a book or snapped shut her official-looking briefcase. Only at the actual moment of leaving did she revert, coming forward to him and staying with her head against his chest, for a final moment of contact. He held her there, lips against her hair.

"It didn't happen," she said, her voice muffled.

"Yes, it did."

"I prefer it as a fantasy."

He brought her face up, to kiss her. "Good-bye," he said.

''Good-bye.''
''Hope your marriage is happy.''
''And yours.''
''This is unreal,'' he said.
''That's what I keep telling you.''
''Neither won this time.''
''I didn't want to win,'' she said. ''Not this time.''

38

It took two weeks for the Russians to make their initial application—and for Pike to realize that he had succeeded, absolutely. He experienced a feeling of completeness that he had never known before, a sensation of standing above everything and looking down, able to see things and know things that no one else did.

It was the best high he'd ever had.

His father insisted they celebrate, with Jane. There was champagne and his mother got slightly drunk and the date was arranged for the wedding, which was an excuse for more toasts. The decision gave Jane something with which to occupy herself. They moved out of the Mayflower into a rented house in Georgetown, a detached, three-story clapboard in a secluded street running parallel with Constitution Avenue—which meant decorators to oversee and furnishings to arrange. She had to plan, too, for the arrival of her sister's family from England. Pike's mother became involved as well, coming daily into the city to discuss invitation lists and wedding lists and visiting dressmakers and then, when they agreed to the reception being in Fauquier County, consulting about caterers.

His father had warned him to expect it, so the invitation

to the White House did not come as a surprise to Pike. The two men drove there together and entered through the East Gate, the entrance Pike remembered from his visit with the Federal Reserve delegation months before. He hadn't imagined marrying Jane then, he reflected, following the Secret Service guide along the picture-hung galleries. Or imagined so many other things, either. He thought frequently about Lydia, even seeking her name in the financial intelligence material coming through the Fund. There hadn't been any mention of her since Zurich. Would she be married by now? She hadn't said when it was going to be, but it was possible it had already happened. She'd make a demanding wife, thought Pike, stirring at the recollection. He'd enjoy meeting her again, if ever it were possible.

Nelson Jordan sat them beneath the Washington portrait but remained standing before the fireplace, between them. To Pike, he said, "I thought it was time personally to congratulate you upon all you've done."

"Thank you, Mr. President," said Pike.

"Not unusual for governments to use independent intermediaries, but I can't remember anything which ultimately became as important as this working out so well."

"I'm glad it did so," said Pike. How much no one would ever realize, he thought.

"A lot's developed beyond what you know," disclosed the President. "Had some discreet enquiries made by Bowen, in State, through the Soviet embassy here; didn't want to cause any upset, at a delicate stage like this. Seems they don't mind this refinancing being publicly known, after considering the points we made. I'm going to make it an address to the nation and use it to issue the public warning to the developing countries."

It would make a consummate piece of electioneering, decided Pike: Jordan would have his second term practically sewn up before the first primary. Everyone had won.

To Pike's father, Jordan said, "How about you, Tom?"

"Zambia made an approach in the last month; Zaire,

too. We refused both, without further indication of good intent. Stipulated a year in each case. The official warning will follow your broadcast. A separate one from the World Bank, too. There's a statement scheduled from the Bank for International Settlements in two weeks.''

''It's going to be a bit more difficult with Latin America,'' said Jordan. ''That's our hemisphere; don't want too much antagonism too near to home.'

''The Fund has established the best possible scrutiny arrangements, because of what's happened in the past,'' said the IMF director. ''We can keep the lid on anything there.''

The President nodded, allowing a pause in the conversation. Then he said to the older man, ''Like to have a conversation with you in private during the next day or two. Think it's time we discussed the future.''

''At your convenience, Mr. President,'' said the elder Pike.

Jordan turned to Pike. ''What about your future?''

It was an unexpected question, one for which he hadn't made any preparation. ''I haven't thought about it, sir,'' replied Pike.

''Know Richard Sheldon?''

''The Virginia senator?''

The President nodded. ''He's not running again next term. On his doctor's advice. Nobody knows that yet, of course. Good seat for a young man with talent. I think I could guarantee a lot of party support. Few people in the Senate with the sort of experience you've got; imagine you could create quite an impression there. I've always thought the Senate a good starting place for other things, haven't you?''

''Yes, sir, I suppose it is,'' said Pike inadequately. The confusion was going now, replaced by excitement.

''Why don't you think about it?''

''I will, sir,'' said Pike. There wouldn't be the need, he thought.

His father twisted to Pike in the back of the limousine taking them from the White House, his face flushed with excitement. "Do you realize what he meant?"

"I think so," said Pike. It wouldn't be right to overreact.

The other man gestured through the rear window, to the retreating mansion. "He was offering you the way to get *there!*"

"Yes," said Pike. He'd beaten his father, he realized. It was the best feeling of all.

"For God's sake, man!" exploded the man, unable to understand his son's subdued reaction. "Don't you want it?"

"I think I do," said Pike. "I think I want it very much indeed."

The White House leaks were carefully placed, so there was a lot of speculation leading up to the Prsident's announcement, which got prime-time television coverage in a live broadcast from the White House. They watched it from their newly decorated home, Jane with her feet tucked beneath her on the couch, head against Pike's shoulder.

Jordan gave a superb performance. He used graphs and charts to compare the financial difficulties of the past to the situation which existed now and, in the middle section of his speech, issued the Soviet-required warning that to ensure the maintenance of stable finance that now existed, developing countries could no longer expect automatic extensions and delays on current loans from American institutions, nor automatic advance of new funding. When he disclosed publicly for the first time the American support for the international monetary package to safeguard the Russian loans, he produced fresh graphs to prove the reliability of that indebtedness. For more than three decades, continued Jordan, East and West had sought a peaceful path to coexistence. He was proud to have discovered and pursued it. He looked forward not only to an unparalleled future of global financial security but to an unparalleled future of friendship. Jordan concluded as cleverly as he had begun, turning from the international to the domestic and stressing with fresh visual illustrations the effect of the stability he offered upon United States home markets and production.

"No more welfare lines, no more job lines," the President finished. "From this moment, prosperity."

Neither of them spoke for several minutes. Then Jane said, "You did that; you made it all possible."

"Yes," said Pike.

"Could you *really* get to the White House?"

"After time in the Senate," he said.

"I'm so proud of you," she said. "Everything is going to be incredibly exciting."

"Yes," said Pike. "I guess it is."

Within a month every international and Western financial institution repeated the United States President's warning to the uncommitted nations.

Because of their official positions, after the ceremony in the Hall of Marriages there was a reception in one of the small Kremlin chambers. Lenov and Korobov and Pushkov attended, with four other members of the Politburo and their wives. There was champagne and beluga and vodka, and Lydia became embarrassed at the speeches, because Malik's name was frequently omitted from the praise. It was late when they returned to Lydia's apartment and her head hurt from the wine she had drunk. She felt achingly miserable.

"I'm going to like it here," said Malik, turning in the middle of the room. It had seemed logical for him to move in and leave his own apartment for Irena. He'd drunk too much and he was disarranged, shirt undone and suit crumpled.

"I'm glad," she said.

"Have you ever been to Sochi?"

"No."

"You'll like it there," he promised. "It's practically tropical. And the dacha is one of the best; shows how important we're considered."

What was there going to be to do, now that her part in it was all over? she wondered. "It was flattering that so many people should come to the reception."

"I've just told you the reason," he said. He opened more champagne, but she shook her head against the offer; so he drank alone. "Are you sure $200,000,000,000 is sufficient?"

"More than sufficient," she said. "It makes our total debt $825,000,000,000, in addition to what else exists!" Empty, she thought; she felt absolutely empty.

"The President's speech did more to bring the developing countries to us than anything we've tried in the past five years," said the Finance Minister. "Africa is practically queueing at the door. You're brilliant."

"That was the effect it was calculated to have," reminded Lydia. The man was inclined to pomposity, she realized, belatedly.

"I'd like to be the one to let them know," said Malik.

Lydia realized she was taking a risk, doing what she intended. But she didn't care. She had the absolute power now. Empty, she thought again.

Epilogue

The ceremony was in the arbor room and an awning was erected over the flowered avenue to the open-sided marquees in which the reception was held.

For security reasons there was no advanced announcement, but the President's attendance was correctly interpreted as outright public support for Pike's declared candidacy for the Senate by the three hundred guests. Everyone of any importance or influence in Washington was there, which was why the gesture was politically important. The Ambersoms had been invited but declined, which was politically important, too.

Jane moved glassy-eyed through everything, and Pike realized that even his parents were impressed. He had the feeling of looking down upon everything again.

There was no way, of course, that Lydia Kirov could have known the coincidence; nor would she have intended it. The toasts had finished and so had the reading of the telegrams when Carlton approached, which was fortunate because the best man had moved away and it was Pike who received from the butler the message transmitted through the Soviet embassy from Moscow.

It was Jane who saw him standing, transfixed, gazing down at the paper.

"Darling!" she said. "What is it?"

"She had to do it by a quotation," he said distantly. "That was the game."

She got near enough to look over his shoulder. " 'If I owe a million dollars, then I am lost. But if I owe fifty billions, the bankers are lost.' "

Jane stared up at her new husband. "I know it," she said. "It's by the Brazilian economist, Celso Ming. What does it mean?"

"Wrong," he said, his voice breaking with disbelief. "It means I got everything wrong. We all did."